BLOWBACK

Kah Wilde

BLOWBACK

As the only female member of the Hellfire Riders, I've fought for everything I have. But now I'm going to lose it all…

One stupid bet made years ago is going to ruin me. I'd forgotten all about it — but the Riders' warlord hasn't. Now the club's most dangerous member is determined to collect his winnings: a night in my bed.

But it's not me that Jack Hayden wants. He's been trying to get rid of me since I patched in. He thinks I'm weak. He thinks I'm vulnerable. The only possible reason he's following through on this bet is to try and tear me down in front of our brothers. So I won't let him get to me, no matter how much pleasure he gives. I'll never crave his touch…

LOOKING FOR CONTENT WARNINGS? FLIP TO THE END!

To avoid putting spoilers up front where readers might accidentally see them, I've listed the content warnings on the very last page. If you are browsing through a "Look Inside" feature and can't flip to the end, please feel free to visit my website and look for the content warnings link in the menu.
www.katiwilde.com

BLOWBACK

THE HELLFIRE RIDERS

KATI WILDE

BLOWBACK

ISBN-13: 978-0989461184

Printed by arrangement with the author.
For copyright inquiries, please contact:
Mick's Awesome Book Stuff
Melissa Khan, Owner
mick@micksawesomebookstuff.com

Cover design by Kati Wilde
Motorcycle grunge vector silhouette by lapencia
Fire by Sergey Nivens
Licensed through Adobe Stock

kati@katiwilde.com
www.katiwilde.com

The Dead Lands
Fantasy Romance

THE MIDWINTER MAIL-ORDER BRIDE

THE MIDNIGHT BRIDE

PRETTY BRIDE

THE MIDSUMMER BRIDE
(COMING SOON)

Wolfkin & Berserkers
Shapeshifter Romance

BEAUTY IN SPRING

HIGH MOON

TEACHER'S PET WOLF

SHERIFF'S BAD BEAR
(COMING SOON)

Other Romances by Kati

GOING NOWHERE FAST[1]

SECRET SANTA

THE KING'S HORRIBLE BRIDE

ALL HE WANTS FOR CHRISTMAS

THE WEDDING NIGHT

EVIL TWIN[2]

---

[1] Includes cameos by the Hellfire Riders
[2] Set in the same world as the Dead Lands

CONTENTS

...

FOREWORD

You might have noticed a slight structural change as you read Saxon & Jenny's novellas—the first novella is in Jenny's point-of-view only, then I bring in Saxon's narration in the later stories. The same is true of Jack & Lily's novellas (though in every book following theirs, dual POVs are the norm).

The reason for it is simple: not having the hero's POV adds a bit of uncertainty and angst regarding his motivations and feelings, especially if the heroine doubts how much he cares for her. Taking away the hero's POV means that the reader might be uncertain, too (and part of the fun as a reader is picking up those cues that tell you how crazy he is about her, even if the heroine misses them.)

So I used that technique in the first novella, but couldn't see any reason to continue concealing the hero's feelings from the reader after that, and at that point the "awwwww" feeling kicks in, because he really does care about her! We knew it all along!

Dual POVs are sometimes a curse and a blessing. I remember back in the day, when I was a baby romance reader, almost all romances were written from the heroine's POV only. And when I came across a book that unexpectedly included the hero's POV—usually only for a short scene or two, not the dual narration that has become so common—it was such a rush! And when alternating narration became even more common, it was this romance reader's dream come true.

...but only sometimes. Having the hero's thoughts and feelings out in the open sometimes undermines the emotional tension, because even if he hasn't admitted it to the heroine, *we* know how he feels. On the other hand, there are books where having his POV is such a blessing, because we know how he feels...and so when obstacles show up and insist on parting them—or when he screws up and she leaves him—oh, the pain is just delicious.

So these novellas gave me a chance to write the best of both POV worlds, and that isn't an opportunity that comes along often! I hope you enjoy it just as much.

Happy reading!

—Kati

A NOTE ABOUT READING ORDER

The Hellfire Riders series was originally conceived as a series of novellas for readers who want heat, emotion, and a happy ending, but who don't have the time to read a full-length book. Jack & Lily's primary romance is featured in three novellas: *Betting It All*, *Risking It All*, and *Burning It All*. The first three novellas were originally collected together in *The Hellfire Riders: Jack & Lily*, and the bonus content (which leads into the next book) was available in the print edition *Giving It All* — which unfortunately put it out of order in the series. So now it's in the proper order, and you can either read it as a teaser for Gunner's book, or simply to get a look at some of the characters ten years before the series begins.

BETTING IT ALL

ONE

"Almost there, Lily." Gunner raises the punching mitts on level with his too-pretty face. "Left jab."

Muscles screaming, I snap my fist at the padded target. *Thud!*

"Left cross and finish with a right."

Pain rips from my elbow to my shoulder on the left swing. Gritting my teeth, I follow through. *Thud.* The right. *Thud!*

My chest is heaving and my eyes are watering as I pull back my fist. The workout's over but I bounce in place, waiting for him to say we're done.

"You went soft on the left." Frowning, Gunner glances at the livid streak above my elbow. "You okay?"

Aside from wanting to cry because it feels like someone knifed my arm? But I wasn't knifed. I was shot. Only a flesh wound, though—practically nothing. And it's healed enough that my skin isn't tearing open or bleeding anymore, so it pisses me off that the pain still flares up. "Just fine. Want me to go again?"

"Nah. We're good."

Good. I tear open the Velcro straps around the wrists of my sparring gloves and grab a hand towel to wipe down my face. I'm ready to hit the showers, but if I do before I cool off I'll just keep sweating. Gunner tosses me a bottle of water and we both look toward the ring, where Spiral and Beaver are throwing down. Though it's only practice, they're going at each other like it's not—preparing for the fights coming up at the next biker rally. Most of the brothers have gathered around, watching.

Most of them. Stone Wall's over by the weight room with Knucklehead, who's measuring the door frame. This used to be our clubhouse, but after the Hellfire Riders moved out to the Erickson ranch and merged with the Steel Titans, it became the club's gym-away-from-home, instead. Pretty soon, though, it won't just be the Riders here. Stone, Gunner, Blowback, and our prez own the actual property and they'll be opening gym membership to the public as soon as the renovations are finished.

Smart. Though not as populous as Bend, Pine Valley's

growing. A lot of young professionals are moving into town, preferring to commute the thirty miles to the bigger city rather than live in it. A gym will pull in good business.

And if I'd been born with a dick, it would have been mine.

My dad used to own this property. He founded the Hellfire Riders and served as president for decades. I grew up running around the clubhouse and helping the brothers fix their bikes, but he never let me wear a kutte under his watch. It didn't matter that I loved to ride, loved to fight. I had tits so the best I could hope for was spreading my legs under a Rider and becoming an old lady. My dad wanted that for me.

I wanted more. So I fought for more—and I got it. But not from him.

When my dad died in a wreck five years ago, Saxon Gray was voted in as the Hellfire Riders' new prez. I came home from Afghanistan, and Widowmaker—one of the Riders' old timers—sponsored my bid for a kutte. The first day I showed up wearing a prospect's patch, there was an uproar among the brothers, but the club's Constitution says that anyone who served in the armed forces can't be rejected without good reason.

So I got in. It wasn't easy, but I got my colors. I owe Saxon everything for that. And I don't hold it against him and the others for buying this property after my dad bit the grill of that semi truck. They were looking out for the club, making sure the place didn't pass into someone else's hands—and it was my mom who sold it to them.

On days when I'm honest, it hurts that she wouldn't sell to me. I asked her to more than once. But she said my dad wouldn't have wanted me to own the clubhouse.

That's my mom. Always taking my dad's side. Even after he's dead.

Chugging the water, I join Widowmaker beside the ring. It's a Tuesday night and he's got a wife, kids, and grandkids to keep him busy, so usually he doesn't hang out with the brothers except on weekends. But lately, he's been coming in to help coach the guys who are fighting. He's never fought MMA-style like they'll be doing at the rally, but he's been boxing for most of his life. His advice is well worth listening to.

Not just in the ring, either. He's the one who first taught me about engines. He's the one who showed me how to throw a punch. He's the one who told me about the armed forces clause in the club's Constitution and said I should take advantage of it. In some ways, he's been more of a father to me than my dad ever was. I used to wish that Widowmaker *was* my dad—and considering the way my father used to share my mom with other members of the club, it could have been possible.

But there's no mistaking where my genes came from. I've got my dad's pale blond hair and gray eyes. I've got his height, too. My mom's just a little thing, but I stand about a millimeter shy of six feet—and I've got two inches on Widowmaker, easy.

Now he bellows *"Move your fucking feet!"* and Beaver picks it up a little, but I can already see that he won't last much longer. He's tiring, slowing down, whereas Spiral's got a gleam in his eyes that says he's just getting started.

Widowmaker glances at me, then over at Gunner. "You fighting tonight?"

The other man shakes his head. "Just working the bags, then heading out to the Barracks. You coming, Zoomie?"

To the strip joint the Riders recently took from the Eighty-Eight Henchmen MC. We've expanded our territory; to keep it, we've got to maintain a strong presence there. Usually I'd be up for drinks and tucking a few bucks into the dancers' g-strings, but I can't tonight. "I'm taking my bird up early tomorrow."

Flying a survey crew into the Diamond Peak wilderness area. My helicopter doesn't need a runway, so I can touch down anywhere I've got enough clearance. Around here, that makes me the go-to girl whenever someone needs to be in the middle of nowhere but doesn't want to hike there.

"Damn." Gunner heaves a dramatic sigh. "I guess it'll just be me and this tight-mouthed motherfucker, then."

Tight-mouthed—? *Shit.* I hadn't realized that Blowback had come up on the other side of him. The Riders' warlord moves like a goddamn mouse.

But Blowback could never be mistaken for a mouse. Quiet, but never timid or small. If anything scares him, I can't imagine what it is. I'm on eye-level with a lot of members in this club and look down at some; there's not many who make me look up, but Jack Hayden is one.

And he's *dense*. Not stupid—not by any measure—but packed solid with muscle covered by black jeans and a long-sleeved black T-shirt, even though the air-conditioning's off during renovations and it's sweltering in here. Combined with short dark hair and the shadow of a beard on his jaw, he's just dark and solid, like a black hole, and whenever he's around my attention always gravitates toward him.

I can never simply look away. I have to take in everything first, from boots to face. I want to know how he's standing—like a soldier at rest, feet shoulder-width apart. I need to see where his hands are—arms crossed over his massive chest, fingertips resting lightly on the opposite biceps. I have to know where he's looking—up into the ring, his profile as unyielding as a Roman centurion's, his gaze assessing every punch, every kick.

It doesn't make any damn sense that it's Jack who draws my eyes like this. Gunner's so pretty it hurts. If he walked into any New York modeling agency, they'd sign him on the spot. Gunner's features have been sculpted; Jack's were shaped with an axe that hacked away everything that might have softened his appearance. Heavy slashing eyebrows darken every expression. His nose is bold, his jaw strong, his mouth firm. He's not pretty. He's not even handsome.

Somehow he's still fucking gorgeous—and so fucking

male. Like that axe was wielded by the God of Testosterone and the blade sharpened on a stone dick.

My spine stiffens when he glances over and his gaze catches mine. If anyone notices my reaction, they probably assume the wrong reason for it. With his flat dark eyes and I-don't-give-a-fuck stare, Jack makes a lot of the brothers uneasy. As they should be. Every Rider is good at throwing down. And a lot of them are in friendly competition with each other—in the weight room, in the ring—so they're always improving. Jack could wipe the floor with any of them. Spiral's up there feeling pretty damn good about himself but Jack could have him crying for mercy in seconds.

Yet he'll never step between the ropes. These guys fight for fun or money or pride; when Jack fights, he's aiming to hurt. He's aiming to break bones and see blood—and he's taken out some of the Riders' enemies as easily as a tank rolling over a bug.

None of that scares me. I've seen the damage he can do, but I've seen his control, too. He's not a cocked gun waiting to go off or a bomb ready to blow; he's the patient assassin who knows exactly how to use every lethal weapon in his possession. He's also a Hellfire Rider, so he won't use them against the other club members.

But a man doesn't always need to use his fists to break someone. My back's up because being around him is just an exercise in waiting—waiting for him to tear me down. Never directly. It's always subtle. Yet it's a knife in my gut every time.

And Jack Hayden's been stabbing me for years.

It didn't start out that way. We started out okay. At least, I thought we did.

Unlike many of the Hellfire Riders, Jack isn't someone I've known all my life. He patched in while I was deployed—so I only met him after my dad died. Back then, he was the Riders' vice president instead of the club's warlord, but his eyes were just as flat and cold, he was just as quiet, and I didn't need a big flashing sign to tell me that he was pretty fucked up. Damaged, like he'd seen and done things that nobody should see or do. Here's the kicker, though: right away, I liked him. Because my dad was dead without me ever getting a chance to prove myself to him, I'd just returned from Afghanistan, and a part of me was pretty fucked up, too. So something in me connected with something I saw in him.

I was also a prospect, and I wasn't going to screw up my chance to become a full member of the club—especially since the question of whether I should be allowed in had started a full-out war between some of the brothers. So I kept my head down and my mouth shut, spending most of my time in the clubhouse garage, helping to fix up and maintain the bikes. More often than not, Jack was there, too.

Those days, seeing him never got my back up. We worked together easily. Any other time, I'd have asked whether he wanted to play together, too. Big, dangerous, and with engine grease on his hands? Hitting that would be like hitting the jackpot. But I never asked because I was in no position to follow through. Fucking a patchholder while I was a prospect? I could have just written OLD LADY across my forehead instead.

It turns out, that's all Jack thought I was good for, anyway.

I learned that on what would have otherwise been the best day of my life—the day the club voted to patch me in. A day that started out so rough, as I stood there and listened to a few of the brothers give their trumped up, shitty reasons I shouldn't be allowed to join. Most of the reasons boiled down to: She's got girl parts instead of boy parts.

Then Jack spoke up. Until that second, I thought he supported my bid for a kutte. Quietly, as is his way. But still supported me.

Doubt came out of his mouth instead. "Pussy or dick, I don't give a fuck. What matters is if she's strong enough to have our backs—if she can fight. I haven't seen anything that says she can."

That was the first knife in my gut. I hadn't seen it coming, so his doubt stabbed right in and hurt so fucking bad. But I wasn't a stranger to being cut down. My dad had been doing it all my life. So I did the same damn thing I've always done.

I showed him.

Jack only laughed when I challenged him then and

there, but a few of the patchholders who were eager to get rid of me picked up the gauntlet. They laughed at first, too. They stopped laughing when I beat their asses down.

That day I left the clubhouse with two broken fingers, a kutte with a Riders' patch on the back, and a hell of a lot more respect than I walked in with. And I left with an ache in my gut that still hasn't gone away.

Jack's doubts haven't gone away, either. I can't count how many times he's subtly undermined me so that I have to step up and prove him wrong. Normally I wouldn't care—some of these guys aren't even subtle. Coming in, I knew I'd have to work twice as hard as any of the brothers to keep my place here. It's crap but it's the way of this world. I had to do the same thing when I enlisted. And the overt sexist shit? I can just roll my eyes and shake my head, and most of the guys will do the same. But Jack's brand of doubt creeps in. So instead of working twice as hard, as I expected, I have to work double that. It's frustrating and exhausting. Sometimes I wonder if that's what he's going for—wearing me down until I say this club isn't worth the effort I put in.

I won't. Not to prove him wrong, but because this club is where I belong.

It's where Jack Hayden belongs, too. I can't argue with that. A better warlord isn't going to come along. So I'll keep on dealing with this endless ache and hope that, one day, he'll grow tired of stabbing me.

I just wish he'd stabbed me the first day. If he had,

I'd never have liked him. I'd never have cared whether he doubted—so it never would have hurt.

And I wouldn't be so damn tense now.

Spine rigid, I force my gaze away from his, back toward Spiral and Beaver. I can still feel him watching me. He's always watching me. Looking for weaknesses, probably.

Up in the ring, Spiral's closing out the round. Beaver doesn't have much left in him. He's moving around the canvas like he's wading through tar.

"One thing's for damn sure," I say under my breath to Gunner. "I'm not putting money on Beaver at the rally."

His pretty grin flashes but he doesn't respond. By the flick of his gaze past my head, I realize someone's coming up behind me.

"Hey, Zoomie." Valentine slings his heavy arm around my shoulders. A real friendly gesture. I'm not friends with him. He's one of the assholes I beat down the day I got my patch. Protesting that a cunt shouldn't ever wear a kutte, he turned in his colors and joined the Steel Titans.

I know the prez didn't want to reinstate the three Titans who abandoned the Hellfire Riders when I came in, but when we merged with the other club he decided to give them a second chance, with the understanding that my being a Rider isn't in question. So far, everyone's been amiable—trying hard not to stir up any shit.

So I grit my teeth and keep it amiable. "Hey."

"Who would you say's got it?" He nods toward Beaver

and Spiral.

Only a stupid fuck couldn't see who's got this one in the bag, so obviously he's angling for something else. I'm pretty sure I know what it is. Duke is another Titan who left the Riders when I came in, but he's mellowed out in the past five years. Even apologized to me for being a dick—and told me Valentine hasn't ever gotten over having his ass handed to him. I haven't given Valentine much thought at all, but apparently he's spent a lot of extra time training in the ring. He's definitely a lot bigger than he used to be, carrying around an additional fifty pounds of muscle.

"Spiral has it," I say. "What's going on, Val?"

"No one's up after these two." His mouth is fixed in an easy smile but his eyes bore into mine. "Wanna go for a rematch?"

Knew it. I shrug. "I guess. Not tonight, though."

"No? You're already warmed up. Unless the sergeant here wore you out."

There's a sly intonation tacked onto that. Fuck and fuck. I get so tired of this shit. "I wore him out, actually," I say and am grateful when Gunner laughs and nods. He's irritated, too, but he knows better than to step in. Unless shit turns ugly, he'll let me handle this. "But I'm just about to head home. I've got an early flight."

His blond brows shoot up. "Since when has that stopped you from being out most of the night, drinking and licking pussy? You won't even get home late. By ten at the outside, yeah?"

Jesus. The pussy licking always comes up somehow. As if they don't lick it, too.

I think it bothers assholes like Valentine because they know I lick it better—and because when I want dick, I don't ride theirs.

This time, my shrug is hard enough to dislodge his arm. "How about this reason: Maybe I don't feel like it?"

"Why?" His eyes narrow. "Afraid you'll lose? Or afraid the first time was pure luck?"

Hardly. "I just don't like watching a man cry."

I say it with a big smile. Everything's staying friendly. Just a few Riders messing around, joshing each other.

Even if I want to pound his fucking head in.

He snorts like my response is funny, but I just hit a real sore spot on his inflated ego. His smile is a baring of teeth. "Then let's get in the ring and see who's crying—"

"Stand down, Valentine."

Jack. The ache in my gut instantly sharpens, the knife slipping in. My gaze shoots to his face. His dark eyes have Valentine locked dead in his sights. I pray he'll stop there, but he just keeps going and his voice is never amiable. Instead each word fires like a round from an assault weapon.

"Her arm is fucked and she's been at it with Gunner for an hour. You've been parked on your ass. You want a rematch, wait until she's fresh and uninjured. Make it equal."

A thick knot twists in my throat. God damn him. I

didn't want to fight tonight. I'm so fucking tired and my arm is screaming and I really don't give a shit about Valentine's ego. But now I don't have a choice. And just like always, Jack's making me work harder than I should have to.

Because it'll never be equal. And now that Jack's brought my injury into it, the next time someone's asking whether I can hold my own, they'll bring this incident up, but they'll make it sound like I backed down. They'll say that if I've got a scratch, I won't be good for anything, that I'll take an easy out. No one would say a damn thing if I were one of the brothers and passed on a fight until a bullet wound healed. But if *I* use an injury as a reason to skip a fight, without a doubt, someone's going to say I can't be relied on to watch a brother's back, because all it'll take is my period to put me out of commission.

Screw that. And screw Jack fucking Hayden, too.

I stare at him so he can't mistake exactly what I think of him. He just stares right back, his gaze flat. Like he doesn't give a damn.

Swallowing the hurt and anger, I look to Valentine. "Fuck my arm," I tell him. "Let's do this."

TWO

If I were nice, I might feel bad for Valentine. But I'm not nice. So instead I silently wrap my hands and enjoy the way some of the brothers suppress their grins when Valentine glances their way. He's already in the ring, warming up, and looking cocky as hell.

He shouldn't be so confident, but that error isn't really his fault. The two clubs only recently merged so we've only been working out together for a few weeks. In that time, I've been taking it easy in the gym. It might have appeared like Gunner was pushing me hard, then leaving me behind to get a real workout with Stone or Jack, doing the kind of hardcore sparring that makes everyone else in the gym stop and watch. But if I hadn't been shot, I'd be sparring with them, too.

The guys who came over from the Titans wouldn't know that. And because we're all a bunch of assholes, no one's rushing to tell Valentine that he's in over his head. They've seen me fight. Valentine hasn't seen me do anything but hit a mitt—but I've seen him up in the ring several times now. I know exactly what he can do.

Gunner checks my protective headgear. In a real fight, we wouldn't be wearing anything but gloves, but we're keeping this amiable. Satisfied, he slaps me upside my padded head. "Make it quick."

I intend to. I strip off the loose tank I was wearing over my sports bra. My gym shorts cling to my ass and upper thighs like a second skin. My braid is tucked up under my headgear. Fuck if I'm going to give Valentine anything to grab. As I climb up to the ring, Widowmaker pounds his big fist against the canvas, calling for attention.

"This is a rematch," he says. "So same rules as five years ago. If your back hits the mat, you're out. Match over. No crotch shots, no eye gouges, no hits to the spine. All right?"

"All right," Val says quickly. Eager to get this going.

I nod when Widowmaker looks to me. He's giving me the same repressive stare that he used to give when I mouthed off to my dad. It's his way of telling me not to go overboard. To keep it friendly. This isn't just Valentine versus me. Humiliating one of the former Titans isn't going to be good for anybody. I nod again to tell him I got his message, then glance over at Jack fucking Hayden, who hasn't said a word since I agreed to fight. Instead he just glowers at me.

Bastard. But though I know exactly what he is, there's still that damn ache in my gut. And it's stupid for me to be looking at him when I should be focusing on Valentine.

So I focus. Val and I are about the same height but he outweighs me by seventy pounds. Big, heavy—a little slow. That's why I'll win.

Widowmaker taught me to throw a punch; he also taught me that a punch would never be enough. It's physics, pure and simple. Force equals mass times acceleration— and I don't have the mass. I'm fast and strong, but my body runs lean. I don't pack on muscle like some of these guys do, so I'll never hit as hard as some do. Instead I have to be quick and smart and use my opponent's mass against him, because if I went toe-to-toe against Valentine in a boxing match, trading punches back and forth, I'd be toast.

But this isn't a straight-up boxing match. Pretty much anything goes.

I know how Val will probably go. When he spars, one combination gets more play than any others. He'll start with a left jab and a right uppercut, then he'll pivot on a spinning hook kick followed by a roundhouse kick. Tossing him onto his back during the hook kick would be easy-peasy. I'll let him get a few more swings in first, though.

His blue eyes are narrowed as we bump fists in the center of the ring. "You can back out now, if you like—being injured and all."

Fuck off, I think, but reply, "You can back out, if you like—being outclassed and all."

Valentine snorts out a short laugh and I dance back, grinning. He can't say he wasn't warned.

Despite not wanting to fight, despite the ragged pain in my arm, I'm feeling pretty good. My fists are up and I'm watching his eyes. He's improved in the past five years, when he thought fighting meant swinging as hard as he could, but he still telegraphs each punch.

And there it is, a left jab. I avoid it easily and expect the uppercut but his gaze flicks to my left arm before he whips his right fist around. A haymaker. He's going for my bullet wound.

Not just aiming to win this fight but aiming to *hurt* me.

My amusement bleeds out like it's been gutted. The stupid fucker. He's giving me all that momentum to play with.

I snap hold of his swinging wrist. Pivoting, I shove my hip into his stomach, lifting his weight off his feet. His arm is still swinging and I keep all the mass behind it moving.

His back slams into the mat. He looks up at me, stunned and blinking.

My blood's pounding in my ears. Laughter explodes

from some of the brothers watching. Crap. Widowmaker's going to be pissed. *Keep it amiable.* Even though this asshole tried to hurt me. It's damn hard but I offer him my hand.

"Sorry, brother. Maybe next time—"

Valentine comes up swinging. Shit. Jerking my hand up, I dance out of the way. The brothers' laughter drops into uneasy silence.

I don't take my eyes off Valentine. His face is as red as a blood blister. Was that swing just an angry reflex or was he really going at me? Holding my hands out, I say, "Val—"

Roaring, he charges. I've got a split second to decide—dodge or take him down. Jack's already at the ropes. Gunner's right behind him. Widowmaker's shouting something, probably for me to get out of the way.

To let the guys handle it. Screw that.

I shift my weight onto my back foot and Jack slams into me, shoving me out of Valentine's path. I try to counter but my balance is fucked. My feet tangle. Steely hands pin my arms and whip me around, facing Val again, but Gunner's between us. I can't see anything but his back.

Anger roughens Jack's deep voice. "Stand down, Lily."

Like hell. I try to rip out of his grip but my arms will tear off before his fingers let go. "I have him, goddammit!"

"Your match is over. This is Gunner's job." Jack yanks me back against his chest, his muscled arms locking around me in an iron cage. "So stand the fuck down."

Frustration rises like a scream but I bite it down.

Gunner's job. He's right. As the Riders' sergeant at arms, it's Gunner's duty to keep order between the club's members.

And Valentine's standing down, too. Through the roaring in my ears I hear Gunner ask Val what the fuck he was thinking, but I don't care to hear the answer. I know what it is. A girl beat him and he lost his goddamn head.

"Let me go," I say, and my voice is mostly even. Only a little rage shakes through it.

After a short hesitation, Jack's grip loosens. I pull away without glancing back at him, without glancing back at Gunner or Valentine. Ripping off my gloves, I head for Widowmaker. The old man's mouth is tight, his eyes hard. My chest feels like a leaden block is wedged behind my ribs.

"Sorry," I tell him softly.

He nods, still looking up at the ring, and I realize he's not pissed at *me*. "He went straight for your arm."

"Yeah."

"You had a clean win. So hit the showers and get the hell out of here." The words are rough but I hear the affection beneath them. "We'll deal with this shit at the meeting tomorrow."

Not the club's monthly meeting, but the executive board. Great.

My stomach's in a knot as I grab my bag and head into the rear of the building. My injured arm is on fire. My adrenaline's still surging, the anger still burning. I'm going to be in the shower a long freaking time before I cool off. At least I won't have to deal with anyone until I do.

When this was the clubhouse, they had bunks back here, communal showers, and a few private rooms for anyone who needed a place to crash for the night. Mostly the private rooms were used for fucking, but I use them to change. I would visit the communal showers—I don't care if the brothers see me naked—but some of them act all shy because they can't stop their dicks from getting hard when I'm bending over or soaping up, and watching them scurry around with their hands over their crotch is a sad, sorry sight.

But mostly it's because Widowmaker once walked into the showers while I was naked and that was just too freaking weird.

I don't realize Jack's following me until I try to slam the door of the private room and the wood hits his palm with a dull *thunk*. My gaze shoots to his face. His jaw is locked and his eyes are flat. Pissed.

But unlike Widowmaker, Jack's pissed at me. If he wasn't, he'd still be outside, glaring at Valentine.

I toss my bag onto the narrow bed. "Say whatever the hell you want to say and get out."

Softly he closes the door. Apparently whatever he has to say is going to take a while. Shit. Well, he can talk. I'm going to take a damn shower. Turning my back to him, I strip off my bra.

His voice is dangerously quiet. "What the hell were

you thinking, Lily?"

My jaw clenches. I screwed up by losing my temper and taking Val down so fast. I know I screwed up. But I already apologized to Widowmaker, who's one of two men in this club I owe anything to. If our prez wants answers and a sorry from me, I'll give it to him. But I'm not going to answer to Jack fucking Hayden. Instead I drag the elastic band out of my hair and start pulling my fingers through my braid.

The silence only lasts a second before he's going at me again. "Val had blood in his eyes before you stepped into that ring. His balls were on the line. He'd have done anything to win, and if he hadn't gone for your arm, he'd have gone for your knees or your head. It was going to turn ugly no matter what you did. So why the hell didn't you take the out I gave you?"

"Are you kidding me? An *out*?" Disbelief sharpens each word as I face him. "After you stuck your nose in, I didn't have any other choice but to fight him."

His eyebrows shoot together, his expression darkening. "Bullshit. I told him to wait."

Oh, for fuck's sake. Like he doesn't know exactly how that left me with zero options. Too disgusted to reply, I shake my head and grab my towel.

The room is small and he crosses it fast. His strong fingers snag my wrist and spin me to face him. My neck's so tense that my muscles feel like they might snap and suddenly I'm aware of my bare tits, my heaving chest, my tightening nipples, but his flat gaze never veers from my eyes.

"Bullshit," he snarls again. "So explain that fucking answer. How is it no choice?"

"Gee, Jack—what do you think? Maybe it's just like every other time you 'have my back'." My air quotes around *have my back* suck because he's got my hand trapped between us but the sarcasm gets through. His eyes narrow like he's about to call bullshit on that, too, but I don't give him the chance. "And instead you give an opening to every brother who wants to take a shot at me. This time, it's, *'Ooooh, poor fragile Lily can't fight if she has a boo-boo.'* Fuck that, fuck you, and now get the fuck out."

I yank my wrist away and he lets me go. Anger blinds me as I step into the shower. It's a concrete box with a frosted glass door that conceals me from shin to shoulder. I flip the towel over the top of the door and realize I'm still in my shorts. Swearing, I rip them down my legs with my panties and toss them outside.

The water starts out freezing but I stick my head under the spray anyway, closing my eyes. Damn him. Jack fucking Hayden. I slam the heel of my palm against the concrete wall. I wish it were his goddamn face. Fuck him. Just fuck him.

Fuck him.

I grit my teeth. No, no, no. My brain's not going down that road today. I've imagined sex with him before and I'll probably imagine it again, because I like rough, I like big and gorgeous, and he's always right *there*. Always pissing me off. And I think of how sweet it would be to have all that power between my legs and to make the bastard beg for more.

Because I'm not nice. And I'd love to see big, dangerous, Jack fucking Hayden fall apart at the touch of my hands, my mouth.

But he wouldn't. The world would end before he fell apart. And me? Jesus, I'm trying not to fall apart right now.

I brace my hands against the concrete wall beneath the showerhead. The water's finally hot, beating down on my bowed head and shoulders. My hair hangs in a thick blond curtain on either side of my face, pale even when it's wet. I can't see anything but my tits and my feet—toenails painted a cherry red—and the stainless steel drain.

Did Jack leave? I don't want to turn my head and look. I haven't heard the door close behind him. That doesn't mean anything, though. The bastard's so quiet he could probably slip into this shower without me noticing.

And damn it. Damn it. I didn't mean to think of that. Didn't mean to think of him slipping in. Because he's angry and I'm angry and the only possible outcome would be my back slamming against the wall with my legs around his waist and his cock shoving deep inside me. Then I'd bite his shoulder and he'd pin my hands and ride me hard, so hard, until I came with my teeth clamping down on thick muscle and my pussy squeezing his dick.

God. Now every nerve in my body screams for that

shower door to open. My skin's tight with anticipation and need. I know what this really is, though. Five minutes ago I was pumped up, ready to roll over Valentine's ass. Then Jack comes in with his *I was giving you an out* bullshit. All the rage is churning around inside me and congealing into sexual frustration.

I don't want him. Because in an hour I'm not going to be hot when I think of him; I'm going to be hurting again. How many times has he slipped that knife into my gut, trying to cut me down? If I took him to bed, I'd be sharpening the blade for him. Fucking a brother—any brother—could tear apart everything I've earned in the club. With just a few words I could be reduced to a pussy and a pair of tits.

But I know myself. If Jack *did* step into this shower right now, I'd screw the shit out of him.

My fingers curl against the wall, the concrete scraping my knuckles. I don't turn my head. Maybe he's still here; maybe he's not. It doesn't really matter.

Nothing matters but holding it together now. To walk out of here cold and hard, as if I don't have a single fuck to give. Some days, that's easier than others. I'm not cold by nature. I'm too much like my dad, who only lived to fuck and fight and ride.

My dad was also a raging egotistical asshole. I'm not nice, but I don't want to cross that line. I never want to be that much like him. The Riders already have their share of egotistical assholes in the ranks. Add one more, now that

Valentine is back.

Valentine. Holy shit, his face. Stunned and staring up at me, as if his thick brain couldn't process that I'd flipped him like a dirty mattress.

I grin at the wall for an endless minute. Remembering his shock is never going to get old. But I will if I stay in here much longer—and my arm is hurting like a motherfucker. All I want right now is my bed and a Vicodin. Not in that order.

Steam fills the small room when I shut off the spray. Jack *is* still here, standing with his back against the wall adjacent to the shower door. His gaze pierces straight through me as soon as I look up.

My heart stutters against my ribs but my movements remain smooth as I squeeze the water out of my hair and reach for my towel. Maybe he's been watching this entire time. I don't know. I study him over the frosted glass while I dry off. He's not pissed anymore. Instead he's regarding me steadily, dark brown eyes unreadable.

"You must not have heard the 'get the fuck out' part," I say easily. I'm not looking for a fight now.

"I heard." There's no apology in his deep voice. "I wasn't done."

"Not done telling me that I shouldn't have gone up against Valentine? Or is it something else? Because I'll listen to one."

"It's other business," he says but doesn't go on. Instead he falls quiet when I tuck the towel between my breasts and exit the shower. I can feel his gaze follow me to the bed, where I dig through my bag and grab the prescription bottle.

Normally I wouldn't take a painkiller in front of him but it's not like this injury is a secret. It's hard to hide anything from him, anyway—Jack sees everything. He's likely seen that I'm hurting. I probably give it away every time I move.

I shake out a pill and swallow it dry. "What business can't wait until the meeting tomorrow?"

"It's not club business."

"So it's personal?" I fish clean underwear out of my bag and try to think of a single personal thing between us. There's nothing. Just the club. I hardly know anything else about him, except that he was in the military once. I don't even know which branch, though considering the way he fights and how ruthlessly he deals with the club's enemies, I'd bet my ass he was special forces. Now he owns an auto repair shop in town, but I've never taken a bike or vehicle to him. I repair my own. "Is that why you need to bring it up while I'm naked—are we overdue for a hate fuck or something?"

Jesus, he's quiet. So quiet. I barely realize he's coming for me before he's here, a solid wall of muscle catching my hips and spinning me to face him, then crowding my body back against the wall so fast I can't ram my knee up.

Tension pulls the skin tight over his cheekbones. Everything inside me stills as his right hand grips the back of my neck. I've seen him snap a man's spine like this but I'm not afraid he'll hurt me. Instead of fear chilling my skin, heat rages through me again.

This is how I knew it would happen—up against a wall. He's hard against me. So hard and big. The thick ridge of his cock digs into my stomach and a dangerous edge sharpens his cold stare.

He doesn't look away from my eyes. Not a single glance at my lips or at the towel slipping away from my breasts. A shiver rips over my skin when his fingers slide up the outside of my thigh beneath the edge of the terry cloth.

"Are you offering me a hate fuck, Lily?"

I don't recognize his voice—it's so low, almost hoarse. And he's not lifting me up and slamming into me. He's waiting for my answer.

Damn him. I don't want to say no. I want him inside me, big and deep. I want to *own* him when he comes, I want to yank at his hair and make him see me when he does, so that he knows that he's not fucking me but that I'm fucking *him*.

But I can't say yes. Not when he'll use it to tear me down. I bare my teeth in a smile, instead. "I would, Jack, but you're already doing it wrong."

His expression doesn't change. His gaze doesn't waver. So I don't get any warning before his left hand slips between my thighs. Oh, Jesus fuck. I'm drenched. My body shudders as his long fingers slick through my aroused flesh, and he doesn't need to say a word. My pussy is saying it for him. Obviously he's not doing everything wrong.

"So what?" I throw at him. "I get hot when I get pissed. Where you're going...wrong..."—*he's rubbing my clit, oh shit oh shit*—"is that when you're hate-fucking someone... unh."

His two longest fingers thrust deep and I can't stop my breathless grunt. My inner muscles greedily clench around him. My knees almost collapse. I clutch at his arms, my hands twisting in his cotton sleeves. Oh, my God. He feels so good inside me, thick and rough.

And I haven't even felt his cock yet.

He releases my neck. Bracing his right hand against the wall behind my head, he leans in closer, his steady gaze still on my face. I have to bite back a moan when his thumb slides up to circle my clitoris. "When you're hate-fucking someone...?"

"When you're hate-fucking someone—" *You don't ride his hand. You don't. Even if you're already so damn close. Jesus God.* Gritting my teeth, I finish, "You have to actually *hate* them."

But Jack doesn't hate me. Hate takes effort, it means caring about something enough to hate it, and I don't think he actually gives a shit about me. His dick's hard but I don't know if he's getting off on being with me or just getting off because he's got me up against the wall. There's almost nothing in his dark eyes, though his fingers are buried in my wet pussy. He's just watching me, gauging every reaction.

And that *almost nothing* in his eyes suddenly seems even emptier, as if my reply wiped away every vestigial emotion.

"Then you'll hate me enough for both of us," he says gruffly and his fingers resume a maddeningly shallow thrust, his thumb teasing my clit. "So are you offering?"

I want to. So damn much. But not like this—with me offering, telling him to take me. Because fucking him will be stupid enough. I'm not going to let anyone twist it around to say I was begging for it.

My grip tightens on his tense forearms. His tendons are like steel beneath my fingers. "Ask me for it."

His expression doesn't alter but his hand stills. So Jack fucking Hayden doesn't like being the one to beg for it, either.

Ice races through me when he grips the back of my neck again. "I don't have to ask," he says softly. "Because I've already won it."

Sick dull pain twists in my gut. *Won it?* There's only one fight between us, only one thing that he could consider a victory—finally ruining me. Undermining me so completely that I have to leave the club. Is that what he came in here to do?

My throat feels raw as I ask, "What did you win?"

"Get the fuck out," he abruptly growls—not at me.

Someone's at the door. Shit, someone's at the door and Jack's fingers are in my cunt and my towel's hanging open. He doesn't let me move and I realize his big body is blocking mine from sight. At least there's that. Whatever he's won, he's not humiliating me with it.

Yet.

"Okay, man, but listen a sec first." The nervous reply belongs to Hashtag, one of the Riders' prospects. Shit shit *shit*. Hashtag is a smart kid but he talks a lot. In a rush he says, "Stone said you have to come because another club just rode into the lot."

Even with his fingers inside me, Jack is instantly all business. "What club?"

"The Devil's Hangmen."

Who? My gaze locks with Jack's. A frown darkens his face and he's searching my eyes, as if looking for a sign of recognition. I don't think he's heard of them, either.

I shake my head and Jack nods. "We'll be there," he says and pulls away from me as soon as the door snaps shut. "We'll finish this afterward, Lily."

Like hell we will. But I only grit my teeth and drag my panties on. He doesn't glance back as he leaves—and as he walks out the door, he doesn't wipe off his fingers but slides them into his mouth to quickly suck them clean.

Enjoy it, Jack fucking Hayden. Because that's the last time you'll be tasting me.

And no matter what he thinks, he hasn't won *anything*.

THREE

The Devil's Hangmen. I haul on my jeans and shove my feet into my boots, trying desperately to recall whether we've dealt with them before. We meet up with a lot of other clubs at bike rallies. If we know they'll be traveling through this area, sometimes the Riders invite other MCs to our house before we take a run together.

But we prepare for those meet ups. Our prez and veep would be here to greet the club. We'd make sure our chrome was shining, the liquor was flowing, and our kuttes were looking sharp. We sure as hell wouldn't be in our gym clothes.

Another club showing up unannounced at our house is the equivalent of knocking on our bathroom door while our pants are down. And not just knocking, but *knowing* they're knocking at a bad time. Which means they either ran into trouble on the road and are desperate for friendly faces to help them out—or they're trying to catch us off guard, disrespecting our colors and trampling over our territory.

If it's the latter, there'll soon be some serious shit going down.

The gym's empty. Everyone's out in the lot. My kutte hangs on its peg by the door. Jack wasn't wearing his a few minutes ago, but his peg's bare. Most of the other brothers' vests are still hanging, because they'd look like idiots in some '60s biker musical wearing their kuttes over their shorts and sweats.

This property used to be an old car dealership before the Riders took it over. Back then, this was on the outskirts of town but Pine Valley has spread out. Now we're facing a strip of small shops, with a frozen yogurt joint and a laundromat sitting on either side of our fenced lot. The street's become crowded and public, which are two of the reasons the club recently moved out to the Erickson ranch.

Since the Devil's Hangmen have come here instead of there, their intel is old. Not too old, but our prez would have verified his info before showing up at another club's house.

Or rather, Jack would have verified it for him. As the

prez's right hand, he makes sure there aren't any fuck ups.

He'll be the one to make sure there aren't any fuck ups now. Most likely nothing will go down here in town. But if it does, we're outnumbered. The Devil's Hangmen came in with two dozen bikers. The streetlights give me a good look at them in the dark. Though they've shut off their engines, they're all still sitting on their hogs in a loose formation that instantly tells me who the prez is. He's taken point; Jack's talking to him. Every Rider who's wearing a kutte is standing with Jack—Widowmaker, Stone, and Knucklehead. Gunner's standing back with the others who are in their workout clothes. I pause for a second at his side. At first glance everything in front of us appears amiable, but judging by the tension in Gunner's stance, I'm guessing it's really only as amiable as Valentine and I are.

"Heard of them?" I ask under my breath.

His reply is just as low. "Out of Nevada."

Nevada, yet when one of the Hangmen turns to glance at the street behind him, I see he's sporting a bright new *OREGON* rocker beneath his back patch. So they're not riding through; they're establishing a chapter in-state. "Are they bad news?"

His chin dips in a slight nod. Great. I keep my eyes sharp as I stroll forward to join Jack and the others. Instantly almost every Hangman is looking my way. Some start to grin like I'm a welcome fuck-wagon. There's a lot of younger guys, maybe twenty to twenty-five years old.

Probably hoping to make their mark in the new chapter and move up the ranks. They're going to be following orders so I focus on the Hangmen with more miles under their belts. They're the ones who are frowning, as if they're trying to figure me out and disliking every conclusion they're drawing.

I've seen those looks before. Nine times out of ten they decide I'm club pussy who didn't know enough to stay in my place and not to wear my man's kutte, because the alternative conclusion—that a woman has been patched in—is too much for the tiny little brains housed in their dicks to take in.

The officers all have shiny new patches. The enforcer is a big dude with a long brown beard and thick biceps ringed with tribal ink. Pure muscle, but I'd put my money on the blond guy beside him. He's not an officer but he's been around a while. The patches on his kutte tell me his road name is Creek, that he's spent time in prison, and that he's killed four men. His eyes tell me more. His gaze only flicks my way to take my measure before he starts watching Jack again.

Smart. Keep your attention on the guy who's most likely to fuck you up.

The veep's not as smart, staring at me before wagging his tongue in my direction. I dub the veep Dickhole, because his road name, Sherlock, obviously doesn't fit him as well. He's young, too. Too young to have earned the position. So I'd bet my ass that he's actually Dickhole, Jr.—

the son of some higher-up in the Nevada chapter.

The prez was probably one of those higher-ups. Maybe the vice president or enforcer. Someone who could be trusted to establish the new chapter and keep the young brothers in line.

One look and I have no doubt they picked the right guy. *Croc,* his name patch reads. Rough-edged features, weathered skin, his dark hair and short beard showing slivers of gray. Mature but not slowing down. Tattoos sleeve arms thick with muscle. He sits low on his chopper, body at ease. Appearing friendly, but he's scoping everything out, as if weighing weaknesses and strengths.

Though he's still talking to Jack, his expression freezes when he scopes me coming toward them. His gaze shoots to my kutte before returning to my face. I know what he's debating—not just whether a woman has been patched in but whether anyone with a face like mine has a brain in her skull. I've got a mirror and I've got no illusions about my appearance. I turn heads. Partly because I'm tall and partly because I've got my dad's sharp features and high cheekbones combined with my mom's lush mouth. Guys like it, girls like it—hell, even I like it. I'd screw myself in a hot second.

Considering the number of toys I keep in a drawer at home, I guess I already have.

Whereas Dickhole doesn't think past my lips, though, the Hangmen's prez does. His gaze slides head-to-toe, assessing—not how fuckable I am, but taking in my height, the lean strength of my legs and arms, and resting on the livid scar above my elbow.

He comes to the right conclusion but he's not any less of a dickhole than his veep. I catch the tail end of his response to Jack when I stop next to Knucklehead.

"—you ask your prez to call me and we'll arrange a meet up." His gaze shoots to me again before returning to Jack. His brows raise a little and his voice drops into the bro zone, like the Riders' warlord is suddenly his best friend. "Is that shit serious, man? You put your colors on a pair of tits?"

Jack's already wearing his don't-fuck-with-me face— it's basically the only face he has—but his stare goes from hard steel to dead cold. "Zoomie earned her place."

And that's why I can't hate-fuck him properly, either. He pisses me off and his doubt hurts, but I don't *hate* him. I can't. Because he might tear me down but at this second he's behind me, one hundred fucking percent.

Not all of the brothers are. Beside me, Knucklehead's gone scarlet and he brings his elbows in a little as if to put distance between us.

Croc doesn't miss that reaction but he doesn't push. Instead he holds up his hands. No harm, no foul. "All right, man."

He's chuckling when he says it. As if taking Croc's amusement as his cue, Dickhole pipes up, grinning. "We can guess how she earned it."

The other Hangmen find that hilarious. Me, I've

heard it a million times, so it's nothing. Jack isn't the only one with a don't-give-a-fuck stare; mine has gotten plenty of use.

My lack of response dampens their laughter. Croc quiets them all and reaches for his starter. Getting ready to leave. "Only joking, of course. I'm sure your prez knows what he's doing. So you ask him to contact me and—"

"I'll tell him you showed up at our house," Jack interrupts. "But if you want a meet up, you request one. The club e-mail is on our website."

For a long second, it's as silent as a church on Friday night. A muscle jumps in Croc's cheek and he stares at Jack like he's weighing whether to put a bullet in his head. Finally he nods. "Will do."

His engine roars to life. My fists clench as he pulls out, riding in a circle around our little group before heading toward the exit. Anger boils in my blood. He might as well have just spit on our boots and now his brothers are doing the same. The others start up and follow his path, exhaust blowing into our faces and tongues wagging—

What the fuck was that?

Creek rode by and his eyes caught Jack's. Not just the same old 'I'm trying to look like a badass to intimidate you' glance, but a 'I recognize you, too' glance. Jack's gaze stays on him for a long second.

We're all quiet until the last Hangman rides through the gate. Then Knucklehead mutters, "You couldn't have stayed in the goddamn shower?" before stalking off.

Asshole. Those fuckers were disrespecting us before I came out. But his comment still puts my throat in a knot, and I'm just as pissed at myself for letting Knucklehead affect me as I am at Croc and his buddies. I don't care when someone from another club shits on me. But when my own brothers add to it?

Yeah. Sometimes that gets to me.

I don't expect us to hold hands and sing Kumbaya. I expect the trash talking and the fighting and the back-stabbing, just like there is in any family. I never liked my dad much and I don't like some of these guys, either. But you don't side with another club against one of your own. You just don't.

Not everyone did, though. So I stand with Jack and Widowmaker as Gunner closes in. Stone is texting, his scarred face washed pale by the light from his phone. Probably sending a message to our prez.

"This is going to be real fucking ugly," Widowmaker says quietly.

"Uglier than the Eighty-Eight?" I wonder. After they killed one of our brothers, we spilled a lot of blood taking those skinheads out, and we walked away all right—but not before our prez took a shotgun blast and I took a bullet.

"Or uglier than Stone?" Gunner asks, nodding toward the enforcer. "Because that would scare me more."

Stone flips him a middle finger before looking up from his phone. His gaze narrows on Jack. "You had no idea they were coming?"

Jaw tight, he shakes his head. We all stare at him for a long second as that sinks in. Jack didn't know they were coming. He *always* knows when clubs are moving through the state. And moving *into* the state? He'd never have missed that.

"So what does that mean?" I ask him. "They flew under your radar? They *knew* to fly under your radar?"

Yet didn't know that we'd moved out to the ranch? Probably not.

"It means they moved fast and quiet after we took out the Eighty-Eight. They're grabbing that territory. And probably the supply routes the Eighty-Eight were running." He glances at his phone when it lights up. "Gunner, Stone—the boss wants us at his place. Widow-maker, you let the board know their asses better be in their seats tomorrow."

At the executive board meeting. Apparently that's when I'll hear more, too. I haven't been summoned so I'm not heading anywhere but home.

"I'm going to snag my clothes." Gunner raises his fist and bumps mine. "See ya, Zoomie."

"Yeah." My stomach drops as I look back toward the building. I've got to grab my bag, too—which means walking right past Knucklehead, who's jawing with Valentine and a few other brothers. I don't miss the resentful looks a few of them are casting my way. They probably didn't hear what Croc or Dickhole said but Knucklehead is making sure to fill them in.

Well, screw them. I lift my chin and head that way, then spot Hashtag standing off to the side, frowning. I veer toward the prospect and get in close, our eyes on level. His shoulders go back like he's facing a drill sergeant.

"Hey," I say quietly. "We're going to vote whether to patch you in pretty soon, right? Maybe a month or two?"

He nods, his gaze suddenly wary. "That's right."

"One vote against you and you're out," I tell him. "And you know what I admire in a brother? The ability to keep his mouth shut about things he sees in private rooms. A loose tongue is a reason to turn down a bid for a kutte, because if we can't trust a man to keep quiet about something trivial, we can't trust him to keep quiet about the shit that will bring us down. Don't you agree?"

His eyes hold mine, steady. A good kid. A smart kid. So of course he has the right answer. "I do."

"Right on." I see his relief and have to laugh. "Hang in there, soldier. The worst is almost over."

"I will. Thanks. Hey, Zoomie," he says as I start to go. When I pause, he tells me under his breath, "Nice take-down earlier."

Against Valentine. I grin and thump his shoulder in thanks as I head past. I'm expecting to take some crap as I pass Knucklehead and the others but no one says a word. I'm feeling triumphant about that until I realize Jack's on my ass.

Oh, shit. *We'll finish this afterward, Lily.* It's afterward but I don't really want to know what Jack thinks he's won, because I'm feeling pretty generous toward him right now and I don't want that ache in my gut to return. "Aren't you supposed to be heading out to the boss's place?"

"I will." He comes up beside me, matching my pace. "We're not done."

We will be if I can throw him off. "How do you know Creek?"

He doesn't seem thrown. "The Bamboo Bowl. It's been two years."

What? I stop and stare at him in disbelief. The Bamboo Bowl is a vegetarian restaurant down on Oak Street. Word is that Jack eats lunch and dinner there every single day—and considering how often I've seen his bike parked outside the place, I assume the rumors are true. But he's saying he remembers Creek coming in two years ago?

"So you saw him ordering a tofu burger way back when, and that's why he looked at you as if he knows you? I didn't realize vegetarians had such deep spiritual connections. Did you hum together over hummus or something?"

That amuses him. His lips twitch. And the sight doesn't make my gut ache. Warmth spreads through me instead. He's so damn big and gorgeous. But I'm still wary, because he braces his feet and crosses his arms over his chest. I know that stance. He's determined, immovable.

So I'm in deep shit.

His flat gaze holds mine. "You said the place wouldn't last in a red-meat town like Pine Valley. You bet that within two years, a burger joint would be standing there, instead."

What? That does sound like something I'd say, but… *Oh, holy fuck.*

I remember. We were at the Wolf Den. At the pool table. Gunner, Stone, Jack, and me—all of us talking shit. Well, Jack wasn't saying much. But we'd been talking about that new restaurant opening up. Jack had quietly mentioned that it was a good business investment in a growing town like Pine Valley and I'd replied with almost the exact words he just used to remind me. A red-meat town. A place like that wouldn't last. But that wasn't all I'd said. I'd gotten up into his face and told him, *If that place is still in business two years from now, I'll let you tie me up and have your way with me all night.*

I can't believe he's serious. "You're going to hold me to that?"

His chin dips in a slow nod. His eyes are dark and empty, just watching me.

My chest is tight as fuck. "I was drunk off my ass."

"But you're not now."

Is he saying I have a choice? That I could back out of the bet?

Because I can't. Just like I couldn't back out of the fight with Valentine after Jack shoved my injury into it. If I go back on my word and the brothers find out, then my word is shit. Then *I'm* shit.

Jack has to know that. He's got me backed against a

wall. And not in the hot-as-fuck rough and sexy way I've imagined; not the way he had me against the wall before. Instead my guts are spilling out over the floor.

Not that I'd ever let him see it. "Okay," I tell him, adding a careless shrug. "Whatever. I'll let you know when I have a night free."

He catches my wrist as I turn away. Immediately my fist clenches, though I know I can't beat him—I just want to pound him, to hurt him as much as he just hurt me. But it wouldn't matter. I'd only be exposing all of my anger and pain, and a few punches would mean nothing to him. To really hurt him, he'd have to give a fuck.

Obviously he doesn't.

"Creek and I served together until about eight years ago," he tells me and I stare blindly ahead, not looking back at him. "When he got out, he headed to Quantico. To the academy."

The FBI academy? I pull in a sharp breath. Shock snaps my gaze back to his. "You think he's undercover?"

"I'll find out," he says but I'm certain he's already sure, that something about Creek already gave it away. He wouldn't have said anything otherwise. "Hold it to yourself for now."

I nod. His thumb slides over the sensitive skin of my inner wrist. Involuntarily I shiver, then anger hits again and I yank my hand back.

"Just so you know," I warn him. "You should have screwed me in the shower. Because doing it like this? I'm going to make sure it's the worst fuck of your life."

Something sharp and bleak moves through the emptiness of his eyes. "I've already had the worst. Now I'll just take whatever I get."

"You're also gonna get the Asshole of the Year award. You'll take that, too?"

He actually grins. "If you give it."

"Well, I *was* going to hand it to Valentine. But, hey. You've earned it." I give him a double thumbs-up and start backing away. "Don't forget to bring the lube. I'm sure I'll need a full tube."

His grin vanishes, his expression suddenly dark and intense. "I'll make sure you're wet enough. Then you'll come for me. Repeatedly."

Want to bet? I almost say. But I'm not setting up round two. "I'll make it the *Delusional* Asshole of the Year award."

"I'll take that, too. As long as I get a night in your bed with it."

He's going to get that. And what am I going to get? I don't know. I can't see his end game.

But I think I can manage the *hate* part of a good old hate fuck now.

FOUR

My night with Jack will have to be a fight. Not with feet and fists, but when we're in bed, I need to beat him at his own game. I just have to make sure I'm beating him at the *right* game.

So what does he want to win? Not just sex with me. He could have asked for that a long time ago.

The question twists through my head most of the night but my brain's too cluttered to think straight. I keep feeling the heat of his skin and the rough pleasure of his fingers inside me. I keep hearing him tell Croc I earned my place. I keep seeing the emptiness in his eyes when he said that he doesn't need to ask because he's already won.

He hasn't. He won't.

I'm up before my alarm goes off. On the road, I open the throttle. The engine roars in the pre-dawn light. Nothing cleans me out like miles of asphalt and the wind in my face. If I could, I'd keep going all day. But the sky calls—and flying a helicopter is almost as good as riding the road. There's no time to brood or sit around with my thumb up my ass, so by the time the afternoon rolls around and I'm back on the ground, my head's back where it should be.

This uncertainty and doubt isn't me. As soon as I decide to do something, I'm all in.

I *am* going to spend the night with him. I *am* going to win.

I'm also suddenly looking forward to following through on this bet—and *really* looking forward to denying Jack fucking Hayden any kind of victory. Somehow, he must be looking to tear me down. It's what he's done for five years, so I've got no reason to think he'll do anything differently now.

So how do I beat him? First I'll make sure there's no question whether I'm keeping my word. Easy enough to take care of that in the board meeting.

And what else did he tell me? That I'll come. Repeatedly.

Normally I'd be cheering if a guy wanted to make me come all night. But if that's what Jack wants, then he must have a reason for wanting it. So I'll deny him that, too. I'll probably get wet—God knows I can't help that—but getting off? Pfft. If I'm not focusing and working for it, an orgasm is as likely as catching a unicorn. I'll just close my eyes and think of repairing my bird's engine.

I'll be the lousiest lay he ever had. It'll be great.

EXCEPT FOR WHEN SPECIAL GATHERINGS are called, the club meets once a month. The executive board used to meet every two weeks, but ever since the Riders and the Titans merged, the prez has been holding the meetings every week—keeping his thumb on the club's pulse and making sure everything stays amiable. The club's officers all sit on the board, along with a few non-officers appointed by our prez. Together they manage any conflicts cropping up outside the club and between the brothers. If rules are broken, the executive board acts as a court—with the understanding that the prez's word outweighs every other patchholder's.

I didn't sit on the board until the Titans joined us. Saxon appointed me along with two new patchholders— Bull, the Titans' enforcer, and Duke, who wasn't one of the Titans' officers but was once a Rider. He turned in his colors when I was patched in. Duke and I get along all right now, but I assume his appointment to the board is also why the prez brought me in. He's making sure the Titans are represented, but he's also quietly telling anyone who questions his decision to patch me in to fuck off.

I'd rather have earned my spot on the board, but I'll take it like this because *keeping* my spot has to be earned. Saxon will toss me out if I'm not pulling my weight—or if I become one of the conflicts they always have to manage.

Today I am. Or rather, Valentine is. But since Jack asked me what the hell I was thinking, fighting Val after he'd given me a bullshit "out," I know some of the blame will come down on my head. It pisses me off but I'll deal with whatever comes.

It might be worse than I expect, though. Widowmaker's already giving me the eye as I come in—a warning not to mouth off. So I zip it and sit.

In the old clubhouse, the board met in the Crib—a loft reserved for the officers' use, which included a crowded conference room. We've got a lot more space out here at the ranch clubhouse, and the building's former life as an overpriced lodge where tourists forked out hefty amounts of cash to ride a horse for a weekend has left a classier mark on the place than the car dealership left on the club- house in town.

The conference room is like something out of an old boys' smoking lounge on the east coast, with leather club chairs surrounding a carved oak table, dark paneling on the walls and thick rugs over gleaming wooden floors. Big windows look out over tall pines and a rocky creek bed— dry now that it's late summer, but I bet it's like a postcard in the winter and spring.

Typically the executive board meetings are more

casual than the club meetings. At club meetings, nobody eats or drinks unless the prez calls for a break—and even then, anything stronger than water is rarely passed around. I don't know how the board meetings went at the old club-house, but here frosty pints of ale are always waiting for us, and our new veep's old lady lays out a hell of a spread. Today it looks like she fired up the grill. Some of the guys are at the sideboard, loading up their plates with thick burgers and all the fixings.

My stomach rumbles but I sit tight. Valentine's here, too, though he's not on the board, and his glowering mug kills my appetite.

Shit. I knew I'd see Knucklehead, because he's the club's road captain and always at these meetings. But I hoped the prez would discuss Valentine's behavior without him here—there were enough witnesses that he doesn't need Val to tell the board how it went down. Instead Saxon must have called him in.

Now the prez takes his seat at the head of the table. He's a big, mean-looking fucker and there isn't anything I wouldn't do for him—partly because he's the one who opened the club's doors for me, and partly because he would never ask us to do something he wouldn't do himself.

Red Erickson claims the seat beside him. The former Titans president, he wears the Riders' colors now, and I have a hard time knowing how to feel around him.

Growing up, my dad used Red Erickson as an example of everything a biker shouldn't be. He called Red disloyal and yellow. Years passed and I figured out my dad was an egotistical prick. I also found out that the bad blood between the Titans and Riders fell squarely at my dad's feet. But that early image of Red stuck, and every time I looked at him, I saw something that shouldn't be respected.

Until recently. We've fought together against the Eighty-Eight. I know he isn't yellow; I know he's fair and smart.

I also know he's a better dad than mine ever was, and when I look at him now, I don't see something to hate, and I don't see the Titans' prez—I see his daughter's face. Jenny and I have been hanging out since she hooked up with Saxon. But each time I see her lately, she seems a little more tired and heartbroken, because cancer is eating away at Red's chest and he's got maybe a month or two left. Saxon's helping her hold on but it won't be easy when Red takes that final ride. Hell, I despised my dad and his death still knocked my heart onto its ass. So all I can think when I see him is how much my friend is going to be hurting.

The two presidents sitting is a signal to the others and they start settling into their places. A pint thunks down in front of me. My pulse trips as Jack takes the chair to my right, his own beer in hand. I didn't even see him come in.

I reach for the glass and shoot him a grin. "A full tube of lube. Right?"

He regards me with that flat stare for a long second. His voice is too low to be overheard when he replies, "Only if I fuck your pretty little ass."

"Do you plan to?" God, I hope so. Chances of an orgasm would be zero. "Because I'm not a fan of anal."

"You will be when I've finished."

I snort into my beer. "Because you're so good at it? Or because you're so bad, every time previous will seem like sweet angels were pounding my ass, giving me a newfound appreciation?"

The corners of his mouth quirk in amusement. I wish he wouldn't do that. I immediately picture myself licking those wide, firm lips, then we both shut our yaps when Widowmaker reads the first item on the agenda.

As club secretary, Widowmaker sends everyone an email listing each item of business we'll be discussing, but the list is hilariously brief. Each item is given a vague one- or two-word description, so half the time we don't know what the actual topic is until we get here. There's the treasurer's report—listed as "Money"—and it always goes first. The next item is "Ride." I assume that's regarding plans for the Labor Day weekend ride, and "Hashtag" is most likely about setting the date to patch in the prospect. The fourth item is "Altercation." That's probably Valentine and me. The last piece of business will be "Hangmen."

I'm right about the ride; I'm wrong about Hashtag.

"Next up," Widowmaker says before looking to Stone. "This is yours."

Because Stone is the prospect's sponsor and responsible for him. The enforcer gives a heavy sigh and spreads his hands. "He's been shadowing one of the La Pine girls."

Oh, crap. The girls aren't from La Pine—that was just where we took the women we found chained up in the Eighty-Eight's compound when we burned down their meth kitchen and clubhouse. We busted our asses making sure we couldn't be connected to anything that went down there but we didn't expect to stumble across women being sold as sex slaves. We couldn't leave them. We couldn't let them identify us. So we blindfolded them and dropped them off at a church in the next county over.

But some of the women weren't able to walk out on their own. I remember the girl who'd been clinging to Hashtag, sobbing in relief. She couldn't have been older than twenty. Hashtag's noble little heart probably didn't stand a chance. "It's the one he carried out, isn't it?"

Stone nods. "Turns out she's local—she lives up in Bend. I didn't see the harm at first. I told him to keep his distance but that he could make sure she was all right. But if she connects him with—"

"End it," Saxon breaks in. "Do it without losing him."

"That's why I'm bringing it here. I can forbid it but I think he'll walk. So other suggestions are welcome."

"Throw pussy at him," Spiral says. Like me, he's one of the non-officers on the board, and that's typically his solution for everything: more fucking.

Stone is already shaking his head. "Not going to work with him."

"Double his load." Gunner speaks up but his pretty

eyes are fixed on his plate. "Keep him too busy to think about her. Eventually it'll pass."

Yeah, that has worked real well for him. He's been mooning over Stone's sister for years. "He's a smart kid, Stone," I butt in over some of the other suggestions being tossed at him. "So tell him why he has to keep his distance. Tell him he'll be putting a target on the club, because even if she doesn't figure out who he is, anyone keeping an eye on her will notice him eventually."

"The feds will be looking," Jack says quietly. "They're still trying to figure out who took down the Eighty-Eight and where the assault rifles we used came from. So they'll keep swinging back to the women, hoping to shake out information."

Maybe they're already looking if Creek is undercover. But Jack doesn't mention that so I don't either. Instead I say, "Pointing out the threat to the club is just half of it, though. Hashtag doesn't know her, so part of the reason he keeps going back must be because she makes him feel like a hero. He saved her; now he's protecting her. So you remind him she doesn't need protecting now, make him feel like a hero for backing away and looking out for the club, and accept that you're going to break the kid's heart."

"*Then* you throw pussy at him," Spiral adds.

"All right." Stone groans and rubs his hands over his face. "Shit. I'm never having kids. It's too much fucking pressure."

"You don't know pressure until you try raising girls,"

Widowmaker says dryly. "Next item is regarding the altercation in the ring between two patchholders, Valentine and Zoomie. Boss?"

The prez glances at Val before looking to me. Oh shit shit *shit*. I know that look in his eyes. He isn't called the Wolf for nothing. That stare means the boss is out for blood and someone's colors are going to run. I drop my hands to my lap to hide the sudden tremor in my fingers.

Don't let it be my colors. Please don't let it be mine. But it might be. Merging these clubs means the Hellfire Riders are stronger than we ever have been before. Fucking it up would threaten everything—especially with the Devil's Hangmen at our door—and I didn't keep it amiable.

The prez isn't going to let that pass like it's nothing.

"Tell me your piece, Zoomie," he says.

My heart's thumping so hard I can feel the blood throbbing in my head. "I screwed up," I say. "I knew it wouldn't stay friendly if I took him out too fast, because his ego was wrapped up in the rematch. But I lost my temper and threw him down."

I hear Valentine scoff from the other end of the table but I don't look away from the prez.

"Cool. Fucking. Head." Each word drops like a brick and is joined by the thump of his knuckles against the table. "Get pissed all you like, I don't give a damn. But you hold it in."

"I will, boss."

He nods and leans back, eyeing me thoughtfully. "Five hundred dollars."

A few of the guys around the table suck in a breath. Fines don't ever run that high. I've seen patchholders pound each other bloody and only get tapped for one-fifty. The prez isn't just drawing blood—he's gouging deep.

But I'll scrape it up. Relief's hitting me so hard I'd be happy to scrape up diamonds. I'd rather bleed money than have him take my patch. "Yes, boss."

"Gunner's going to pay half of it because he didn't keep you out of that fucking ring." His gaze moves across the table, zeroing in on the sergeant at arms. "These other brothers probably thought it'd be real funny to see him try taking Zoomie down. Maybe you did, too. But joking's not your job. Keeping the peace is."

Gunner winces but nods. "Yes, sir."

The prez's gaze finally moves to Valentine but he only says, "Red?"

Handing it over to the Titans' former prez. Maybe because Val will be less defensive, maybe just Saxon's way of keeping the peace.

Red asks, "So what's your piece, Val?"

A seething one. I heard Val scoff as I was telling my part but I hadn't looked his way. He's sitting with his fists clenched and his face red.

"It's bullshit!" He spits it out like he's been holding it in. "Just bullshit."

"What is?" Red's tone is easy. His eyes are like chips of

green ice. "That we're here asking you about it or you don't think Zoomie's fine was steep enough?"

"Bullshit that they're saying getting into the ring with me was a joke."

"Did she win your match?"

Val turns even redder. "She got lucky."

"Did you take a swing at her?"

"Maybe. Shit. Should I apologize for that?" His furious gaze shoots to me. "Sorry. I shouldn't have tried to hit a girl. Especially not one the Riders treat like their fragile little doll."

Silence drops. The only sound is Val's ragged breathing as a dozen pissed-off Riders surrounding the table bite their tongues. Even Knucklehead's looking irritated at him. I don't have the guts to glance back at the prez. When Saxon's angry, it's best not to draw his attention, and he's probably enraged after having that disrespect tossed at him.

Calmly Red says, "Apology is a start. And instead of taking a swing, you should have asked her to teach you the move that took you down."

Valentine's head snaps back like he's been slapped. He stares at his former prez. "You know what? Fuck this. Fuck *all* of this."

His chair scrapes back and he shoots to his feet. Immediately Gunner, Bull, and Jack are up—just watching. Waiting. Not a word comes from either prez as Valentine tears out of his kutte and throws the leather to the floor.

"The fucking joke? Is this club." His eyes land on Red. "She must have spent the last five years sucking their dicks to get them all on her side like this. I don't know when she started sucking yours, too."

"Get out," Saxon says quietly. "While you can still walk out."

"I'm going." He looks to Knucklehead. "You coming, too?"

The asshole has the grace to appear disgusted that Valentine would even ask him. "Fuck off, man."

Valentine glances at Bull. The other Titan shakes his head. Val throws up his hands and slams through the door.

There's only quiet as Jack and the others sit again. Then Stone exhales a long breath and says, "Hold up your hand if Zoomie has sucked your dick."

I flip him the bird but Spiral's already running with it. "Does fantasizing count?"

"Nope. Oh, look. No hands."

"Shit." Face dejected, Bull sinks deep into his chair. "I only stayed because I thought there was dick-sucking going around."

My huff of amusement joins the brothers' laughter. God. I don't know Bull well but I sure as hell love him for that. Instantly the tension eases around the room.

Saxon raps the table and the laughter quiets. "Blowback, see that he's left."

Quiet as fuck, Jack's gone an instant later. A shiver rolls over my skin. Valentine better pray Jack doesn't find him still here.

"All right. But, boss—" Knucklehead's voice pulls my gaze to him. He's looking half-apologetic, half-determined. "I'm not siding with Val. I know Zoomie can kick ass. She's earned her spot. But he had a point about her making us a joke."

Big hands clasped, Saxon leans in and puts his elbows on the table, his stare burning the distance between his seat and Knucklehead's. "You step real careful now."

Swallowing hard, Knucklehead nods. "When the Hangmen rolled in last night, it started out all right. Then she comes out wearing her kutte, looking like Blowback just fucked her in the back rooms, and any respect they had for us was gone."

My throat is tight. "They didn't have respect to begin. If they had, they'd never have showed up like they did."

"Maybe. But they weren't laughing at first, were they? They weren't until they saw you and asked how you earned your colors." He looks back to Saxon. "They made a joke out of us. Ask any of the brothers who were standing with us. Stone, Widowmaker—even Blowback when he gets back. That's exactly how it went down."

The prez doesn't even look at them. "I know how it went down. They mentioned her tits because they think having tits means we're weaker. And you don't want to be slapped with shit like that again. You don't want tits making you into a joke."

"I don't."

"So you can't handle ten minutes of dealing with the same shit Zoomie deals with every single day? Thing is, I've never heard a single complaint about it coming from her. Not in five years. But you're going to whine to me about a few minutes?"

"No, boss." Knucklehead's face has become a frozen mask. "I can handle it."

"Then handle it." The prez's gaze slips past my head. "He gone?"

"He is." Jack takes his seat again. I can feel his eyes on me but I'm still trying to process what just went down between Saxon and Knucklehead, and I'm not sure I can take whatever I see in Jack's expression. He must have heard the end of it. I don't know if he heard the part where he was fucking me in the back rooms, though. I know Hashtag didn't say anything. So had our encounter been that obvious? Maybe Jack wanted all the brothers to know.

If so… Well, screw it. I'm already all in. "To be clear, I wasn't fucking Blowback in the back room. I was banging his fingers, but I haven't had his dick in me yet."

Pin drop silence.

Good, because I'm not done. "*Yet,*" I repeat, "because I lost a bet. So he gets to tie me up and screw me all night. Probably tonight, since I have tomorrow off. Does that work for you, Jack?"

He's absolutely still, watching me with eyes dark and flat. His voice is gruff. "Tonight's good."

"Great," I say before turning back to the others.

Everyone's staring at me and most of their faces resemble a scream queen's wide-eyed horror, like there's a killer at my back but fear's petrified their tongues, so they can't get a warning out. "Anyway, that answer about whether I've fucked another Rider is going to change. Next time, Jack can raise his hand. I'm sure it'll be the worst sex I've ever had, but a bet's a bet, and there's no real reason to back out."

"Uhhh…" Stone says, like he's about to offer a reason, then his gaze flicks to Jack's face and his mouth snaps shut.

So that's that. I look to the prez. He's frowning at both Jack and me, but he only says, "Next item?"

"Ah." His face scarlet, Widowmaker clears his throat a few times. "The Devil's Hangmen."

The prez nods. "Blowback?"

Jack didn't recognize them last night but he's apparently made up for that in the past day. "They're out of Nevada. Las Vegas area. Their mother chapter's been riding for twenty years. They've got seventy members, plus forty in a chapter down in New Mexico, and now twenty five here. They've put out that they'll provide security for hire but word is their annual take is ten to fifteen million, so chances are they're running guns, meth, or girls. Maybe all three. They're small-time for Vegas, but they've got connections—and they're aiming to grow."

He looks to Gunner, who picks it up. "I've got a buddy who rides with the Bedlam Butchers in New Mexico. About five years ago, the Devil's Hangmen set up that chapter down there. Right away they start throwing their weight around, grabbing territory and putting all the surrounding clubs under their thumb. My guy in the Butchers says his club didn't have a run-in because the Hangmen were on the other side of the state and because the new chapter had some kind of business arrangement with the Eighty-Eight. So the Hangmen and the Eighty-Eight weren't stepping on each other's toes."

"Then what's this move about?" Spiral asks. "Because if they're coming up and taking over the Eighty-Eight's territory—instead of letting the Eighty-Eight send up men from other chapters—I'd say that's stomping on their damn feet. Are they going to take each other out?"

Jack shakes his head. "Don't know yet. But it's more likely someone else is calling that shot. A mutual business connection."

Who would have so much sway with the Eighty-Eight that they'd just sit on their hands when they were told to? "So the skinheads got toasted," I say, "and instead of letting their mother chapter send more men here, some asshole with money tells the Devil's Hangmen to take over. So you must be talking cartel kind of money."

"He is. Which means this is a big move for them," the prez says. "One they won't dare fuck up."

"Not unless they want to be skinned alive—or whatever else the hell their business associates think up," Stone adds.

"Jesus." With a grimace, Spiral pushes away his plate

as if the burger suddenly doesn't look so appealing. "I, for one, am damn glad of the Riders' policy of not getting mixed up in that kind of shit. I just want to fuck and ride."

He bumps fists with Knucklehead beside him, and a general rumble of agreement comes from some of the others. It all falls quiet when the prez says, "We're not going to have a choice. We won't get into the business but we're going to be mixed up in this shit real quick."

"They came in the same way they did in New Mexico," Jack tells us. "Only two dozen men. That means they'll be looking for strength from the local MCs. They'll try riding over us first—and do the same to the Blue Coyotes—and they'll be recruiting the strongest men to fill their ranks. They might dangle cash or use other methods of persuasion."

"You're talking threats," Stone says flatly.

"To property, family. And they'll try to make an example of someone first, so we'll know the threats aren't bullshit." Jack's cold gaze sweeps the length of the table. "I expect that example will be me."

"*You?*" My heart slams against my ribs. "Why?"

"I took inspiration from you." He looks at me, his firm mouth taking on the slight curve that makes me want to crawl all over him. "He wanted the boss to call on him like a lap dog. So I flipped him. It pissed him off. Now I expect him to come back swinging."

A few of the guys snort with laughter. I ignore them, searching Jack's face. His lips suggest amusement but his dead-eyed stare is all business. So he meant to infuriate Croc by telling him to use the club's e-mail. He meant to put a target on himself. "You ought to be fined for pulling shit like that. Five hundred bucks is the going rate."

Now he grins. "Not when it's my job to pull shit like that."

I can't argue that. And there's no one who can handle himself better if Croc does send someone after him.

I still don't like it.

My disapproval doesn't bother Jack at all. Expression even, he regards me steadily as I glower at him, neither of us looking away while the prez says, "The rest of us, our primary job is watching each other's backs and holding on to our territory. You hear of anyone receiving a threat—or if they're acting like something's off—you come to me. The Barracks strip joint is closest to the Eighty-Eight's old territory so we'll keep our strongest presence there, and I'll reach out to the Coyotes. All right?"

With my gaze tangled up in Jack's, we both add our "Yes, boss" to the chorus going around.

"Then unless there's anything else, we're done. Blowback, with me."

"I'll be right there," Jack says before leaning in, his voice deep and low. "What time you heading home?"

Home. Where he's going to fuck me. All night.

Everything inside me winds up hot and tight, but I keep my answer cool and easy. "I'll be there by nine."

"Then so will I."

A second later he's up, joining the prez and heading out of the conference room, and I'm resisting the urge to grab my beer and gulp it down. Nine o'clock. Two hours.

Two hours until Jack Hayden is inside me.

"Hey, Zoomie." Stone drops into the chair Jack just vacated. I must look a little dazed because he says, "You all right?"

"Yeah." Of course I'm fine. Just on my way home, where I'll let Jack fucking Hayden fill me up with his big thick cock— Oh, shit, that sounds so freaking hot.

God damn it. I shouldn't be wet already. *Worst lay ever.* That's the goal.

"She's lying." Gunner joins us, sitting back on the edge of the table. "We just got hit with the biggest fine the boss ever laid on anyone, and that's *after* it's split in half. She's reeling."

"Only with relief." I force my head out of bed with Jack and reach for my beer. "I thought it might be worse."

"Worse?" His eyebrows shoot up. "You mean taking your colors?"

"Yeah."

Stone chuckles like I'm joking. "Not you. The prez likes you too much to yank your patch."

That sticks right in my throat. "What does that mean—he likes me so I won't ever get thumped? I'm his fragile little doll so he has to protect me?"

"Shit. *Fragile little doll?* I can't believe you let that asshole get to you." The enforcer bumps the leg of my chair with his boot, but I get the feeling he'd rather kick my head and knock some sense into me. "The prez *respects* you. Can't say he felt the same for Val. Am I right?"

He looks up at Gunner, who nods. "Hell, yeah. The only one who goes out of his way to protect you is Blowback."

Right. I choke on a laugh. They laugh, too, but theirs sound different from mine. More like "that poor, sad bastard" laughs than "wasn't that a good joke?" laughs.

I stare at them in disbelief. "You guys are serious."

Stone gets a gleam in his eyes as he leans in. Oh, shit. I know that look. He's found a way to poke at me so he intends to have fun doing it—and that means Gunner will be joining in. Clowns, both of them.

"You don't think so?" He glances at the scar on my arm. "Seems I remember when you got that little graze, the next second Blowback's charging in like a white knight to pull you out of the line of fire."

I was ready to joke right back, but recalling how that went down still pisses me off. "Are you freaking kidding me? He was coming to pull me out because he thought I fucked it up. That I compromised my position. He obviously didn't think I could finish the job."

Stone's eyes narrow, like he's considering that. After a second he shakes his head. "I don't buy it. He always has your back."

"Oh, like yesterday? Gunner knew enough to stay out of it. I wasn't getting into that ring until Jack mentioned my injury. He gave me no choice but to prove I could throw down while I'm hurt."

He cocks his head and pulls back a little. "Okay. I can see that."

But Gunner's grinning. "I only kept quiet because I knew if I spoke up, everyone would start thinking I've got it as bad as Blowback."

"Oh, for God's sake," I mutter and take a long drink to fortify myself. Apparently the clowns aren't ready to stop juggling their balls yet.

"It's all depends on the scope you're looking through, gorgeous. You see Blowback trapping you. Everyone else sees it as him having your back. Hell, even the day you were patched in. Everyone was squabbling until he says the only thing that matters is if you can fight. You remember?"

I'm not fucking likely to forget. "He also said he didn't think I could."

Gunner's grin only widens. "He knew you could. The first board meeting after Widowmaker sponsored you, Blowback asked him how long you'd been fighting. That was after he watched you for about a day. So Widowmaker told us he oversaw your training himself. At the patch meeting, I figure Blowback decided the only way to shut the assholes up was for you to show them."

So much bullshit. Of course Stone wades back into it. "And I figure what happened then is the same thing that always happens now: He just can't deal whenever someone starts throwing crap at you for more than a few seconds.

He tries to hold it in, but then he snaps, and jumps in to defend you without thinking it through.”

“Oh, that’s real funny.” Jack doesn’t do *anything* without thinking it through. “You guys are so full of shit.”

“Nah.” Stone chuckles, looking pleased with himself. “But you can believe that if you like.”

“What I believe is that you’re a pair of pussies.” I set my beer aside and stand.

Still grinning, Gunner comes up off the edge of the table. “Look at you, using pussy as a demeaning term even though it pisses you off whenever you’re dismissed for possessing one.”

“You mean she’s insulting us?” Stone pouts like his feelings are hurt. “I just figure she’s always talking down to our meathead level.”

“And perpetuating its derogatory usage.”

“Aw,” I say and give Gunner’s chiseled jaw a condescending little pat. “It’s real cute when all that book learning comes out. But big tough bikers don’t like a Mr. Smartypants. So you just sit quiet and look pretty for Mama Lily, all right?”

Laughing, Gunner nods. “Yes, ma’am.”

“And take it as a compliment, dickhole. That’s what I do. When someone says you’re a pussy, you say ‘thank you.’”

“Thank you, Zoomie,” they chorus.

Damn straight.

Outside, the sun’s dropping behind the mountains and casting long shadows. I expect the ride to clear me out but I don't even get onto the main road before Jack crowds into my head again. Jack and every bullshit thing Stone and Gunner said.

He always has your back. Yeah, sure. That's why I've had a knife in my gut for five years. That's why I've carried around an ache that won't go away.

That's why my chest is tight now, like a giant fist is squeezing my ribs. Because some stupid part of me wishes it was true.

But I know it's not. Gunner said it all depends on the scope you're looking through—and both he and Stone are decent guys, so they're looking through a decent-guy lens. Jack isn't a decent guy. A decent guy wouldn't force someone to follow through on a bet like this. Instead he could have asked, "Hey, Lily, want to fuck?" and I'd have said yes.

God damn it all. Despite everything, I'd have said yes in a heartbeat—and Jack is the only Hellfire Rider who'd have ever gotten that answer from me.

He'd just needed to ask.

And this bet? Sure as hell isn't about having my back. Jack's got some other purpose.

But no matter what that purpose is, I'm going to burn his intentions to the ground.

FIVE

I've got two hours, so I ride. The highway first, but Jack's still in my head and I can't get him out. I turn off toward the Newberry caldera and speed toward the peak, but it's not long before I have to slow. Pavement gives way to rough gravel. The sun's setting, and rounding the hairpin turns in the growing darkness demands my full attention. No more Jack.

Not until I'm heading back.

As I roll into Pine Valley, my chest is tight and my gut knotted, but the tension isn't an ache now. I don't know what it is. My emotions won't settle. The stupidest crap runs through my head—like wishing that I hadn't taken the ride, that I'd gone home and picked up the laundry scattered around every room. Like regretting that I hadn't made my bed or taken care of the dirty dishes piled in the sink. I'm not a slob, but I'm messy, and Jack's a hardass about keeping the clubhouse's garage uncluttered. His auto shop is an OCD dream. Everything's in order and has a specific place. I haven't been to his apartment but I've heard it's exactly the same. My house will probably flip his clean freak switch.

But that's what I want. That's what I want, damn it. He thinks he's got everything under control. I just want to tear that control apart, to rattle him. If anything, I should have ridden home early so I could throw more shit on the floor.

It's full dark as I turn onto my street. Automatically my gaze runs down the block to my driveway, where my headlight beam catches the gleam of polished chrome.

A heavy thump beats through my chest. My fingers tighten on the handlebar grips.

He's here. Straddling his bike with his boots planted on the concrete, all in shadow except for the faint glow from the streetlight and the sweep of my high beam. I'm not late. It's only just nine. He must have been waiting a while, though—at least a quarter hour. The security lights above the garage door would have turned on when he rolled into the driveway, and since he's waiting in the dark, that means the fifteen-minute timer has already shut off again. But he's sitting easy, like the waiting is nothing. Like he'd wait a lot longer for me to come.

For a second my throat is an aching lump. God, I wish he hadn't done it this way. I wish he hadn't used a bet. Because just seeing him, knowing what's going to happen, my body feels like it's being dragged toward his, taut with awareness. The leather of my kutte lies heavy against my breasts, the soft cotton of my shirt rough against my hardening nipples. Suddenly this entire ride with the bike rumbling between my legs just seems like a precursor to having Jack between them.

If he'd just *asked*, we could have set my bed on fire. Instead it's going to be a fight—one that I'm going to win.

And it's time to go all in.

I hit the remote for my garage door and the security lights pop on. From the outside, my split-level looks like a smaller version of the Brady Bunch's house but it's been completely updated inside. Despite having put a ton of work into the interior, the previous owners wanted to unload the property as fast as possible after the bottom fell out of the market, so I got lucky and snapped it up a few months after I returned from Afghanistan.

As I pull in, Jack rises from his bike and slings a pair of saddlebags over his shoulder. Not a change of clothes. Though he's won a full night with me and his auto shop opens early, his apartment is right above his garage. He doesn't need to bring anything for tomorrow.

Judging by the bulge in one of the leather packs,

though, he's definitely brought something. Maybe a whole damn gallon of lube.

I pause in the driveway, my engine idling, partially blinded by the brightness of the security lights. "Want to push her into the garage?"

If Croc's gunning for him, leaving his bike outside overnight would be like painting a target on my place. Jack's already painted that target on his own chest. I don't like it but he's probably got some kind of plan working. Best not to have it turned sideways by this bet.

"I'll roll her in." His deep reply is barely audible over the noise of my engine. "You'll keep sharp after?"

Watching out for the Hangmen. "Always."

"You call me if you get a buzz on the back of your neck. I'll take care of it."

If I get a feeling someone's hanging around the area or is a little too interested in my place. I can't stop Stone and Gunner's words from popping back into my head, but Jack's offer to take care of any trouble isn't for me. It's just what he does for the club. He'd tell any patchholder to call him. My chest tightens up anyway, so I simply nod and ease my ride forward, slipping into my spot in the garage. Even with my dad's old truck taking up the second bay, there's plenty of room for Jack's bike.

God, and she's a sweet ride. He's got two Harleys he switches between. One is a blacked-out Iron 883, which serves as his workhorse. But this is his baby, a 1959 Sportster. She doesn't have the most powerful engine and she's not tricked out; she's just solid and runs like a wet dream. That's where the real beauty lies—in the care Jack has taken restoring and maintaining her.

And thinking of his big hands working her over? I'd be lying if I said that wasn't a huge turn-on. It always has been.

Which is why I shouldn't be checking out his ride right now. My breath feels short as I tear my gaze away, up to his face, and my lungs stop working altogether.

Between the dark night and the blinding lights, I didn't get a good look at him outside. He's as tense as I am, his gaze locked on my face. I can't read anything in the flatness of his dark eyes but something's changed. He's a weapon, but usually I only see the broad side of the blade, the dull gleam of the gun.

Now he's the razored edge. Now he's the bullet.

But it's not fear that trips my heart into double-time, sending my pulse thundering. It's anticipation. He'll be fucking me soon. And, God—I want him to. I want to feel his cock thrusting deep inside me. I want to be tied and taken hard.

This isn't how I'm going to beat him, though.

Dragging in a steadying breath, I drop my helmet on the workbench and head for the door connecting the garage to the house. I know Jack's behind me, though I can't hear his steps. The door opens to my basement and a short flight of stairs takes me up to the main foyer. I shrug out of my kutte, taking care to hang the leather on the coat rack beside the front door. My vest is the only thing I remember to put away every single time. I never just throw it somewhere—unlike my running shorts, which have been decorating the back of my red sofa since yesterday morning.

Jack hands me his kutte. The leather's warm from the heat of his body. I don't let myself breathe in the scent as I hang it beside mine.

I glance at the shoulder holster he's wearing. "Your weapon, too?"

"I'll keep it in the bedroom with us." His gaze slips down and he watches me toe off my boots. The road grit collected at the hem of my jeans spills onto the tile. "You went for a ride?"

"I did." And I'm covered in a thin layer of dust. "You want me to shower before you fuck me? Or do you want to join me in the shower and we can get started there?"

I should have been ready. But he's so quick. Before I've even realized he's moved, Jack's already caught me up against his hard body and is pushing his long fingers into my hair.

"We'll start here," he says gruffly and his mouth captures mine.

Kissing. I didn't imagine this. I've only imagined fucking so I'm not prepared for the thrust of his tongue or the surge of heat through my veins. God. I taste the dust on my lips and the mint of his mouth, as if after the board meeting he went home and got ready for me. He smells like soap and the hair at his nape is slightly damp, his jaw shaved smooth.

His big hands grip my ass. Easily he lifts me, wedging his thick erection between my legs. My inner muscles clench on a sharp pulse of need. A hungry moan builds in my throat and my fingers tighten in his—

Oh fuck oh fuck. My hands are in his hair and I'm kissing him back as if I'm starving for this.

Desperately I tear my mouth from his. "Wait!"

Jack immediately stills, his dark eyes searching mine. He's not handsome. He's not. So why the hell can't I ever look away? Especially now, when arousal paints ruddy flags on his angular cheekbones. When his firm lips are wet from our kiss.

I just want to make them wetter. Instead I repeat, "Wait," while forcing myself not to grind against his rigid length. "There are rules."

"What rules?"

"The terms of the bet were that you get to tie me up and have your way with me. So the first rule is that unless I'm tied up, you don't touch me."

Though I'm not bound, though he's touching me now, he doesn't let me down. "All right."

"Rule Two: We never talk about this night again. *Ever.* Not to each other, not to any other Riders. As far as I'm concerned, as soon as you head out the door in the morning, none of this ever happened. I'm going to forget all about it."

I expect him to shoot back the same arrogant crap he gave me before when he told me that I'd come repeatedly or that he'd make me a fan of anal fucking. Something like *You'll never forget* followed by his gorgeous grin.

Instead his face is like stone and his voice like gravel. "I never expected you'd want anything different."

The way his answer twists me up inside pisses me off. "I also reserve the right to bite anything that comes near my mouth," I tell him. "So if you think you're going to make me choke on your dick, think again. No more kissing, either."

His dark gaze drops to my lips as if he's about to test that rule. "Anything else?"

"Yeah. If I'm ever drunk and make a stupid bet like this again, you let it go."

He meets my eyes again. "I can't do that. I'll take whatever I get."

"That's pretty fucked up."

"Yes," he replies evenly, as if I'd said one plus one equals two. "Any more rules?"

Only the most important one. "You wear a rubber every single time. You brought a couple?"

"More than a couple." He sets me down and backs off a step. "Take off your shirt."

Just like that, huh? Well, what the hell. I'm all in, anyway.

I strip my T-shirt off and toss it down the stairs, where it'll land somewhere in the vicinity of the washing machine. Wearing only my jeans, I stand before him. My breasts are on the small side, two pert little handfuls, but my nipples are big and tight. They're sexy as hell when I'm as aroused as I am now, stiff and rosy and just begging for someone to suck on them.

Begging for Jack to suck on them, but he's not even looking at me.

From one of his saddlebags, he pulls a long strip of condoms and a small bottle of lube and tucks them into his back pocket. A roll of dark cloth follows, then he slips a coil of cotton rope over his arm. Next come a pair of leather cuffs.

Holy shit. I'm not sure whether I want to know what else he has in there.

He closes the pack and slides it over his shoulder again. "Give me your hands," he says roughly, and my pulse races as he wraps a wide leather cuff around each of my wrists. The rip of Velcro is loud in the quiet foyer when he unfastens my left cuff. "You can open them with your teeth if you want to."

I nod and he smooths the leather cuff closed again. A small metal loop attaches to each. Jack winds the soft cotton rope through both loops and pulls my wrists together before finishing it off with a mooring hitch knot—I can easily pull that free with my teeth, too.

He tugs on the long trailing end of the rope. "Now you're tied."

So I am. If he thinks he's going to lead me around

on a leash, though, we're going to have a new fucking rule. "Yes, but—"

But nothing. The rope drops from his grip and his big hands catch my waist. He drags me forward. His hot mouth latches onto my breast, and when he sucks hard on my sensitive nipple I can't stop the sound that erupts from me, a combination of a grunt and a whimper and sheer pleasure. I clench my jaw too late—and oh, my God, his face, cheeks hollowed and eyes closed, as if he's savoring this first taste, savoring my involuntary response.

Then his teeth scrape my nipple on a sharp tug and my legs almost give out, but it's Jack who's sinking to his knees, his mouth moving down my stomach, over to the curve of my waist. A shiver races through me when he licks my hipbone, then nips the taut stretch of skin above the waist of my jeans.

His long fingers pull at my belt and unbutton my jeans. My body stills, everything inside me suddenly focusing on his hands as he drags the denim down my legs. His tongue slides over my hip again before he begins making his way down, his strong fingers digging into my ass to hold me in place. I'm not even naked. I'm wearing my panties, a pair of black cotton boyshorts, but I tremble as his lips near the junction of my thighs.

His mouth reaches my pussy and he inhales. "You smell so good." His voice is a hungry growl. "And you're soaked."

My heart thundering, I swallow hard and make my

mouth form a few words. "I was riding. The vibration always gets to me."

Bullshit. I need more stimulation than that.

I need more, like his warm breath whispering over my skin. Like the gentle nudge against my clit when his tongue flicks the drenched cotton. Like his groan when he tastes me. His fingers tighten on my ass as if he's going to haul me closer and eat my pussy right here.

Instead he slides his arm down behind my knees and picks me up. Holy shit. Caught off balance, my lower legs still trapped by my jeans, I loop my bound arms around his neck—and he's carrying me against his chest. *Carrying me.* As if I'm six feet of nothing, through the living room and into the kitchen, where he drops his saddlebags onto the small breakfast table. They land with a heavy thunk amid piles of mail and magazines.

Still reeling—*holy fuck he's carrying me*—I ask, "What the hell do you have in there?"

"Dinner, since neither of us ate at the meeting. Or fuel for later, if you ate when you went riding."

"I didn't."

"Good." He continues on through the dining room, where I finally manage to kick my jeans down over my ankles. They land somewhere on the short flight of stairs leading to the bedrooms in the upper level. "There's also more lube."

I can't stop my grin when I see the amused curve of his lips. God, even if he screws my ass, I really am going to enjoy this.

Enjoy winning, I mean. Not *this*. Not the carrying or the licking or anything else.

And definitely not enjoying the way he lays me in the middle of my bed, gently, like he's some chivalrous hero and I'm some virginal damsel. Tension suddenly rides over me again, holding my body in a taut grip. At least the romantic image is shattered when he takes hold of the long rope and lashes it to the headboard, drawing my hands up over my head.

Gruffly he says, "There's enough slack that you can still open the cuffs with your teeth."

I nod, my body stiff. Time for the fucking to begin. "I'm lucky I don't have a padded headboard. You'd have to tie me somewhere that isn't as comfortable and it'd be harder for me to fall asleep while you're poking your dick into me."

"Not luck." He pulls off his boots, setting them neatly beside the bed. "I reconnoitered."

My mouth drops open. I stare at him as he places his shoulder harness on the nightstand, searching his face for the smile that says he's joking. He's not. "You scoped out my place? You *broke in* and scoped out my place?"

"Yes."

Jesus. "That's so fucked up."

Still fully dressed, he eases down on my left side, stretching out the length of his hard body against mine. "Yes."

Yes. So easily. As if he already knows it's fucked up. Just as he knew making me follow through on this bet was fucked up, too.

The bet. "When did you break in?"

"About six months ago."

I tug on the ropes to draw his gaze up to the cuffs. "You've been planning *this* for six months?"

"This, for two years." His thumb slides across my open lips and down over my jaw before I remember to bite him. He pauses and his gaze returns to mine. "No. I've been thinking of this for five years. The bet just made it possible."

Five years. Since we met. I hate both the warmth and the ache that follow his admission. "Fuck all that. No matter how long you've planned, I'm still going to win."

"I know, Lily." His fingertips trace the upper slope of my right breast. "You're the only one here who *can* win."

"What?"

"I lose either way." Leaning over me, he bends his dark head, warm lips following his callused fingers. His mouth is gentle but each word is harsh. "I take you this way, using this bet, I never have you again. I don't use this bet, I never have you at all. No matter what happens tonight, tomorrow I lose—but at least this way I have you once."

Something hot and tight swells in my chest. "You could have asked."

"You don't fuck other Riders because you don't want anyone looking at you like a brother's old lady. You'd have risked that?"

I can't see his face and I'm glad he doesn't look up at me, because he'd see something I don't want to give away. I *would* take that risk. I've earned my place. I've earned respect. I might survive being with another Rider now. If it was someone I trusted. If it was someone worth the shit being with him would bring down on my head.

But saying that I'd have slept with Jack would risk admitting too much, so I only shake my head.

He can't see my response but must have felt the movement. His eyes are dark and empty when he looks up. "Not just Riders, either. No local men. Women here, men in Portland."

My body goes rigid. He's right, I never sample the local dick. But I don't talk about my trips to Portland, about trolling a hotel bar hoping I'll find a partner worth having for a night. About wearing my red dress and heels because that combo catches exactly what I want and because my kutte usually scares them off.

I hate that Jack knows anything about it.

How does he know it? But I don't ask. Instead I see the dark cloth he pulls from his pocket and shake my head. "No blindfold."

He hesitates. Actually hesitates, like he's considering it anyway.

"No fucking way," I snarl. "The bet was you tie me up. You don't get to blind me."

Jaw clenched, he watches me for another second. I don't know what he's debating but it must be something important—Jack fucking Hayden *never* hesitates. Finally he nods and rolls over to place the blindfold on the night-stand.

Jesus. What the hell? He accepted every other rule so easily. No touching without being tied. No kissing. But he hesitates over a blindfold?

What doesn't he want me to see?

But there's nothing to see. He rolls back against my side, his expression flat, eyes empty. Just the same old nothing as always.

Unless he doesn't want me to see him touching my skin. Unless he doesn't want me to see my nipples standing stiff as he circles the peak of my breast with his thumb, or the goosebumps that race over my flesh as he bends his head to my tits.

God. That can't be what he doesn't want me to see, because when I close my eyes and try to shut him out, I can still feel him. The roughness of his fingertips, the hot glide of his tongue, the erotic pinch of his teeth that he soothes with a lick. His hand slips down my belly as he sucks, thumb dipping into my navel, fingertips sliding beneath the waist of my boyshorts.

Desperately I grip the headboard, trying to anchor myself, to control my ragged breathing. I can't stand this tenderness. I'm not ready for it. I thought he'd just push my legs apart and start fucking. Instead he's tasting me, touching me, and I can't get my head out of this bed like I planned to. I grit my teeth as his strong hand pushes between my legs, but he doesn't rub my clit, doesn't fuck me with his fingers, just cups my pussy in his big palm.

Then his teeth roughly clamp down on my nipple and my hips shoot up off the bed, my back arching. Oh, fuck. I choke back my pleasured cry but he knows. He knows because his hand is all over my cunt and I just got so much wetter.

Quietly, he tests me. Every reaction. My response to a soft bite. A slow lick. A long suck. All over my neck and breasts and belly. It's sweet torture and through it all he doesn't say a word, doesn't crow about how aroused I am, though my pussy is a sweltering ocean against his cupped palm. He does nothing to distract me from his mouth and fingers, offers nothing to piss me off.

But I need something. Anything. At my hip, he licks the taut skin. He licked me there earlier, too, but now he's sucking hard enough to draw a bruise.

Panting, I try to get my head back in the game. "Either you've got a hip fetish or you seriously need a road map."

Oh, shit. He's not supposed to smile. But he does and I force myself not to squirm against his hand. Why isn't he fucking me yet?

"Your jeans are always right here"—his tongue traces a line parallel with the waist of my panties, just below the point he was sucking on—"and your shirts always cover this spot. Except when you mount your bike and your shirt rides up. So I'll still have this tomorrow."

Still have…what? A bruise?

What the fuck— "You're *marking* me?"

His teeth flash in a grin before he sharply nips the reddened spot. Between my legs, his thick fingers plunge deep into my pussy. My outrage dissolves into a strangled groan that I desperately try to stifle, but I can't stop the clench of my inner muscles. Sweet fucking hell. I can't think of my hip or his mark. It takes everything I have to stop myself from squeezing his wrist between my thighs and keeping him inside me.

I want to cry when he withdraws his hand, until his fingers hook over the waist of my panties. His big body slides down to the end of the bed and he drags the drenched cotton down my legs, painting a wet trail along my inner thighs. His hands grip the underside of my knees as he comes up over me again. Mercilessly he pushes my legs wide, exposing my pussy to his ravenous gaze, the aroused flesh plumped and slippery with need. Stark hunger lines his face.

Oh, God. I can't watch this.

His head dips and I close my eyes. My body shudders as he begins tasting his way up the inside of my thigh, but I clench my jaw and focus. No orgasms. Worst lay ever. I'm just going to picture the turboshaft engine that powers my bird, then mentally pull all the components apart before putting them back together—

Jack licks my pussy and the engine flies apart. Gasping, I grip the headboard tight. His tongue runs up the seam of my cunt and flattens over my clit, rubbing hard.

Oh, my God, he's good at this. He's *so* good at this, licking and sucking on my clit, never hard enough or fast enough to make me come, never light enough or slow enough that I can concentrate on anything else.

But I *have* to concentrate. And put the engine together.

Except it's so hard when Jack groans that I taste so fucking good and digs in, his thumbs spreading the lips of my pussy. His tongue spears up into me, fucking past my slick entrance in long swirling thrusts and setting fire to the nerves in that tight, sensitive flesh. I know my body's undulating beneath him but I try to ignore my response, try to ignore the burning pleasure, ignore his mouth, his incredible mouth, and the way he eats me out like he knows just how I love it, rough and sloppy. I try to ignore that it's so perfect, that he's so hungry and I'm so wet.

And the engine isn't enough. I have to think of combat, think of flying through the night over arid mountains, knowing a missile could come any time.

With a barrage of hard, quick licks, his tongue targets my clit. His broad fingers invade my pussy and slowly begin to thrust. I picture the fiery tail of a missile streaking across the dark sky and mentally perform the counter maneuvers. I'm going to die if that missile hits my bird. I can't be distracted by Jack fucking Hayden.

My legs are shaking. Oh, fuck, I'm going to burn.

The tension's so tight I almost scream at him when he lifts his head and his fingers slip out of me. *Oh, no no no.* My eyes snap open. My legs are spread, held apart by his body as he kneels between them. He's looking down at my face, his mouth glistening with my juices and I want him to kiss me, I want to taste my pussy on his mouth. I want to bite his lips and suck on his tongue and hear him groan.

"Giving up?" The words sound raw, as if I've been screaming with pleasure instead of holding the screams in.

"No." Jack's gaze doesn't leave mine as his hands drop to his belt. "I'm going to fuck you now. Unless you tell me to go."

I barely hear anything after *fuck you now*. "Unless I what?"

"Tell me to go. I'll walk out." He pulls the belt free of the denim loops. "Just tell me to."

"Right. So you can tell everyone I backed out of our bet?"

His expression darkens. "I wouldn't tell anyone a fucking thing. No one would know about this bet now if you hadn't announced it at the meeting."

And there wouldn't be anything to know if he'd let the bet go. I'm not going to apologize for covering my ass.

But every retort dies on my tongue when Jack unzips his jeans. Oh, Jesus save me. His dick is long and thick and utterly gorgeous, heavily veined and capped by a broad flaring head. His big hand roughly strokes his shaft as if easing the ache while he waits for my answer.

My need doesn't ease; instead it grows until I can't feel anything else. I want that big cock inside me. I want

Jack fucking Hayden and I don't care if this is how I get him.

Hoarsely I tell him, "I'm not backing out."

His fingers tighten, squeezing the broad head of his dick before he releases his shaft. His breathing roughens, but neither of us speaks as he tears open a condom and smooths the latex down his thick length. Gripping the base of his cock, he moves over me, bracing his free hand beside my shoulder.

Still fully clothed.

"Wait," I say and his body immediately stills. His dark gaze jumps to meet mine. "Shirt and jeans off. Give me something other than your face to look at."

He only hesitates a moment before sitting back and tearing off his shirt—and I just made a huge fucking mistake. Oh, God. Sometimes when he's sparring, Jack will wear a sleeveless T-shirt but I've never seen him without one. I've never seen his chest but he's beautiful. Broad shoulders thick with muscle, his sculpted pectorals darkened by coarse hair that narrows into a treasure trail. His stomach is tight and ripped. Ink covers the left side of his chest and shoulder, a combination of script and illustrations. On the right side, the Hellfire Riders' emblem decorates his upper arm.

I've seen that tattoo before. But not his chest and not the scars, from bullets and knives to burns. Jesus. Is that why he hesitated? My gaze shoots to his face but as always there's nothing there.

He shoves his jeans down heavily muscled thighs. "Do you plan to close your eyes?"

Not if he wants me to. Silently I shake my head, my pulse pounding as he settles between my legs again. Bracing one rigid arm beside me, he grips his cock and I can't look away when he aims that thick length toward my cunt. My fingers tighten on the headboard. Jack's breath hisses between his teeth as he slides the broad head through my slick pussy lips and wedges his cock against my entrance.

Slowly he pushes into me. God, he's big. So big and I'm tight, my inner walls swollen with arousal. His heavy shaft sinks into me and I shut my eyes. The sight of his dick stretching and penetrating my cunt is too fucking hot, but now Jack is all I can feel, thick and sliding deeper and deeper and deeper, until he's seated firmly within the greedy clasp of my pussy.

With a groan, he reaches forward and grips the headboard. His voice is strained. "All right, Lily?"

I reply through clenched teeth. "Just get on with it."

Please, please. Get on with it.

My body shudders as he withdraws, my inner muscles clinging to his heated iron length. He pulls out, that big flaring crown catching every nerve lining the sensitive entrance of my pussy before pushing back in.

Oh, God. My back arches as I'm stretched and penetrated again and again, as I take his cock as deep as I can. I'm supposed to be thinking of something else and distracting myself from these sensations but I can't. It shouldn't be this way. When I'm with someone I'm always all in, determined to make my partner come and to find my own pleasure, but I have to work for it. I have to concentrate. Now I'm working *against* it but the way Jack fucks keeps sucking me back in. He's not just hips and cock banging away; instead his thighs are pushing mine wide and his knees are shoving into the mattress as if to make sure he gets into me as deep as he can. His strong hands are wrapped around the top of the headboard, his carved biceps bunching and pulling his upper body against mine each time he fucks into me, my tits swaying with each long, rocking thrust.

My thighs come up to grip his hips, to hold him tight, then I realize what I've done and try to let them fall open again, but Jack reaches back and catches my leg, ratcheting it up higher around his back as he slowly sinks into me.

God. *God.* Where's the hard fuck? On a shuddering breath, I open my eyes and watch his big cock fill my pussy again before lifting my gaze to his face. I need to see his empty eyes to remind me that this is nothing to him, that he feels nothing for me.

But his eyes aren't empty.

Stunned, I stare up at him. Jack freezes mid-thrust, his body poised above me, his dark gaze locked on mine. And I see, I see—

—*agony, longing, need*—

So much. Bleeding from the darkness of his eyes,

swelling inside me, and I'm suddenly so full.

My body trembles beneath his. "Jack."

I only breathe his name but the sound seems to blow every emotion away. His eyes shutter and flatten. Abruptly he grips my waist and rises onto his knees, hoisting my hips high into the air and slamming his dick into my cunt with spine-jarring thrusts, as if a hard fucking might make me forget what I've seen.

But it's too late. I've seen and it changes everything.

I'm still all in. I'm still going to win. But the game is suddenly different and so much more important.

"Jack, I need—" I can barely catch my breath as his cock pounds into me. "I need…to feel you…against me."

A groan rips from his chest and he leans forward, lowering my back to the mattress and bracing his hand against the headboard. Not close enough. The rope securing my arms has enough slack for me to loop my bound wrists around his neck, bringing his head down to mine. His brutal rhythm stutters and slows as my lips find his in an open-mouthed kiss. All at once he's fucking me like a man starving for my taste, sucking on my tongue and pistoning deep into my pussy.

Writhing, needing more, I lock my legs around his waist. "Make it hard, so hard."

"Lily," he growls my name and I cry out as he grinds against me, rocking against my clit in sharp thrusts, fucking me with his entire body, his strong fingers digging into my ass, the coarse hair on his chest abrading my nipples, and

I can't hold on, I'm going to shatter apart.

Oh, God. My fingers fist in his short hair. Moaning with each slide of his cock, gasping for each breath, I tell him, "I love the way you fuck. It's so good, Jack. It's so good, so good, so good—"

The orgasm slams into me like a fist into my stomach, curling me against him, stealing my breath. My pussy clamps down on his dick as he's shoving into me and I can't take it, it's too much sensation all at once, but his cock relentlessly fills me, my hips bucking beneath his as my body shakes through its release. As if the convulsive clench of my flesh snaps his control, Jack groans and fucks me harder, until I'm crying his name through the wave of another orgasm. Abruptly his powerful body goes rigid above me.

He comes quietly. Deep inside, I feel the heavy pulse of his release and I hold him tight, loving his weight as he settles over me. Loving the thickness of his cock still lodged in my pussy and how wet he made me. Loving the sweat on our skin and the raggedness of his breath when he buries his face against my neck.

The sweat has almost dried when he finally pulls away. Swiftly he tugs the rope free from the headboard and rips open the leather cuffs, then scoops up his jeans and heads for the bathroom, dragging off the condom. I hear the sink run and he returns, wearing his jeans and zipping his fly.

His empty gaze slides over me. "I'll make us something to eat," he says gruffly.

My heart pounding, I watch his broad back retreat through my bedroom door, then fall against my pillows and stare up at the ceiling. All this time, I thought Jack Hayden didn't give a shit about me. But now I think he does.

I think he cares more than I ever imagined.

SIX

I clean up in the bathroom, then pull on Jack's long-sleeved shirt. The hem falls to my upper thighs and covers everything important so I don't bother with underwear before heading to the kitchen.

But I take my time getting there. Each step is heavy and slow, as if weighed by the questions crowding into my head. So what if Jack cares—what does that mean? Maybe nothing. Or maybe Gunner and Stone were right and he meant to have my back all this time.

That doesn't mean I was wrong. Tossing up shields to protect me *can* tear me down. If I can't show I'm capable of defending myself the brothers would have no reason to think I can stand strong at their backs.

And maybe none of it means anything. Maybe there's no wrong, no right. But it still matters.

Jack's standing at the stove, facing away from me as I enter the kitchen. I don't wait for him to turn before asking, "Did you mean to tear me down yesterday at the ring? Or every other time you supposedly had my back?"

His spine stiffens but his reply is deep and even. "Intentions don't matter if you're hurting someone. You can't intend to shoot a man and hit a little kid, then claim what you meant to do matters more than what you did. So if you felt I was tearing you down, Lily, then I was tearing you down."

He's right. Except that the person doing the hurting doesn't get to decide if intentions matter. The person who's been hurt decides.

And if he didn't mean to, that changes everything, too. Exactly how, I don't know yet. But I want to find out.

I move toward the stove. "So you didn't realize you were tearing me down, but you didn't wonder why I was always so angry with you?"

The long muscles in his back flex when he shrugs. "A lot of people are uneasy with me. Sometimes that pisses them off. If it pisses them off long enough, they start to hate me for it."

He's so used to people hating him that he just assumed I did, too? Jesus.

"Maybe they wouldn't be uneasy if you didn't sneak into their houses."

"Maybe." He glances over at me when I join him beside the stove. "But I think they'd be uneasy, anyway."

"I'm not uneasy."

His dark gaze searches my face as if trying to figure out exactly what that means. "And you're not angry now?"

"I guess not. Even though you broke into my house, reconnoitered, and found out my stove has a grill." With thick fillets already sizzling over it. "Steaks?"

Nice cuts that had been wrapped in butcher paper, not picked up at the supermarket.

He smiles and shoots me a wry look. "I ate at that damn Bamboo Bowl every day for almost two years, hoping it would help them stay afloat. Now I want some meat."

Hell, yeah. I grin but my amusement fades as his words sink in. He ate there every day for two years…so he could win a bet that would let him spend a single night with me.

My chest tightens. Jack's smile vanishes and his jaw hardens, as if he's realizing what he's given away.

He looks to the grill again. "How do you like yours?"

Raw and dirty. "Rare and with a lot of pepper. Do you want your shirt back?"

"There's no point." He turns toward me, gripping the counter on either side of my hips. "You've already seen me naked."

He doesn't mean his skin; he's talking about what I saw in his eyes while he was fucking me. My breath catches as I look up into his eyes again. They're flat, but not empty—yet I still can't read them.

And I don't know how much to push now. Not too much. Because I think that's why he wanted the blindfold. Not to conceal his tattoos or his scars, but because he couldn't conceal what I ended up seeing in his eyes. He's probably not used to being exposed, and he's already retreated. I don't want him to go any further.

"I just thought you might get splattered." I flatten my hand against a solid pectoral. Warm skin, steely muscle, and I don't ever want to stop touching him. He's built like a freaking god. "Blistering those sexy abs would be a damn shame."

"I don't care about my abs," he says gruffly. "But that's why I zipped my jeans."

God, yes. I laugh and slide my forefinger down the middle of his chest. The illustrations and script on the left side of his body stop exactly in the center of his torso, like a canvas cut in half. "Why only one side?"

"The left side is what hurts. The other side is what feels good."

"Jesus, Jack," I whisper. That means he's covered in hurt and he's only got the Riders' emblem on the right side. And the biggest hurt, right over his heart, are the words *Mom* and *Pop* written in the mouth of a big flaming demon. Thorns twist around the demon's horns, their sharp points drawn as if they're piercing Jack's skin, inked blood dripping and spelling another name. *Jaime.*

A man's name? A woman's? "Your first girlfriend?"

"My brother."

The roughness of his voice starts an ache in my throat, so I trace the faint scar running from his right shoulder down to his collarbone. A knife wound. He's taken a bullet in his side and another blade tore through his right pectoral. A soldier's wounds, but he's seen combat in closer quarters than I ever have. Bullets, shrapnel wounds—usually the enemy is at a distance. The ones who wield knives aren't.

My gaze lifts to his. "You don't need tattoos on your good side when these scars are here. You should be proud of them."

He smiles again. God, I could get used to seeing that. "Want a drink?"

"Always. You, too? I've got—"

"I've brought some."

He grabs two short glasses off the counter—wet glasses, and I realize he had to wash them. Shit. My sink full of dishes. My face heats and a glance confirms there are clean plates in the strainer, at least.

My gaze swings back to Jack as he pulls a liquor bottle from his pack. Widow Jane. Though a little too pricey to drink often, it's my favorite bourbon.

Somehow I'm not surprised he knows that.

"Thanks." I accept the glass he pours and watch him turn the steaks. "So that bottle isn't lube after all."

"No." Though I was hoping to see his grin again, his jaw has hardened, and he glances at me before he says, "Why did you change your mind?"

"About what?"

"About tonight. You were fighting me. Then you decided not to."

Because everything changed. But I'm not any more accustomed to laying out my feelings than he is, so I simply say, "I realized I might have been operating with faulty info. And you know me—I don't do anything halfway. I'm either all in against you or all in with you." I sip the bourbon, letting it roll over my tongue, loving the burn. "That's the first thing my dad ever taught me, actually. *'Go full throttle or don't bother going.'* So that's what I did."

I know I didn't answer him, not the way he probably wanted. His gaze searches my face as if looking for a more complete response, but he doesn't ask what the faulty info was. He only says, "It's a good lesson."

"Yeah." My smile is bitter. "It's also the only one he taught me that was worth anything. What was your first?"

He doesn't even stop to think about it. "*'Take what you get and don't ask for more.'* I don't remember if I learned it at my mom's table or from my pop's fists. But they taught me the same thing."

"That's a pretty shitty lesson."

His expression is bleak. "It gets me through."

I wonder if it does. Taking another sip, I step closer as he turns to the grill again and transfers the steaks onto a plate, then covers them with foil. My hand curls up over his shoulder, gently holding him in place so he doesn't face me again too fast.

There are more demons on his back. More writing, too, most of it in Arabic or Farsi. Because of something that happened while he was in the service? If so, these illustrations don't just show what hurts him, but also what haunts him.

And the central demarcation is different. It runs down his spine, but it's not in a razor-straight line as it is in the front. Another illustration crosses over from left to right between his shoulder blades. A flower, with six curling petals—

A lily. Jack's body stiffens as my fingers trace the stem.

I can hardly breathe. "Does this hurt or feel good?"

His voice is hoarse. "Both."

"Why?"

He doesn't answer. And I've already seen him naked, but maybe this is something that would force him to dig beneath his skin. At least the roots and bulb are on the good side. The flowering petals are, too. Only the stem crosses over into the side that hurts him.

So mostly good, not painful. Just like everything within me now. But I don't understand what's happening here. He could have covered this up, just like he covered what I saw in his eyes. Instead he leaves the lily exposed. Maybe he really thinks it doesn't matter—that I've already seen what's lurking beneath, so this doesn't tell me anything new.

Except that I don't know what I've seen. Everything seems tilted, as if I'm peering through thick eyeglasses. Even the way Jack turns to look at me. Like I'm suddenly brand new to him, too.

As if he's trying to figure out a Lily who doesn't hate him. As if he can't figure out why I wouldn't.

I step back and set my glass on the counter. "I'm yours for the night. Yet you eat me out and fuck me senseless and then feed me. Why don't you have me on my knees sucking your cock?"

"The bet's about what I do to you. Not what you do to me." Despite his response, new tension seems to tighten his shoulders and his gaze drops to my lips, as if he's suddenly thinking of my mouth wrapped around his dick.

Suddenly I'm thinking of it, too. "You could ask for it."

"No."

I narrow my eyes at him. "Your parents taught you well."

Take what you get and don't ask for more.

That bleakness returns to his gaze. "Yes."

Jack didn't ask the night I fought Valentine, either. Instead he wanted to know if I was offering a hate fuck… so that he could take what he was given.

"What if I offer?"

Gaze dangerously focused, he pushes away from the counter. "Are you?"

"The steaks have to rest, right?"

"Yes." His eyes gleam a little as he stops in front of me.

God, I love having his big body so close. "How long? They're pretty thick."

"Five more minutes."

"So what do you think?" I hook my forefinger through his belt loop and tug him even closer. "Can I make you come again in five minutes?"

"No."

His answer throws me. I blink up at him. "Did you just say no?"

Strong hands catch my arms. "I just remembered that you refused to come against my mouth." He tugs the too-long sleeves down over my hands and knots the ends together. Tying me. "So I'm going to eat my dessert early."

Oh, God, yes. But I keep it cool as he backs me toward the breakfast table. "And you think you can make me come in five minutes?"

"Don't much care how fast." He hefts me up onto the small table and takes a seat between my legs. "The longer it takes the wetter your pussy gets and the better— You're not wearing any fucking panties under my shirt."

Grinning, I set my bare feet on his shoulders. "Nope."

"Christ." He leans in and my heels slide down his back, my knees hooking over his wide shoulders. His voice deepens. "Don't you fight me now, Lily."

I won't. This is the one thing I'm not going to fight. My breath shudders when his warm breath whispers over my pussy. "God. Just go hard at my clit. And— *Oh, fuck, yes.*"

He goes hard. So hard. And just right, his fingers sinking into me, his tongue merciless, and all of it loud and wet and rough, and I don't know if it's one minute or ten before I'm coming with Jack sucking on my clit and my hips jerking uncontrollably, my voice hoarse from crying his name. My pussy's still clenching when he flips me onto my stomach, scattering magazines across the table. He rips open a condom and impales my cunt with a single deep thrust. I cry out, my fingers curling inside the knotted sleeves, then he lifts my knee up onto the table, holding me open and slamming into me again, deeper, harder. His big hands pin my hips and he fucks me relentlessly, skin slapping skin and all of it louder and wetter and rougher, and so good. I can't catch my breath. His hand shoves between my legs and he pinches my clit and I didn't think I could come again but now every hard surge into my pussy brings me closer and closer, until I'm chanting his name with every stroke of his cock, need twisting to a frantic pitch.

His teeth clamp down on my shoulder and I break, my body rigid, crying out in agonized release. Grunting, Jack fucks hard into my pussy again before his body stiffens. His thick shaft pumps convulsively inside me.

"God." I lay sweating, with my cheek flat against the table, my pussy stuffed with his cock and my arousal sliding wetly down my inner thighs. "So good."

Those few breathless words are all I have left. Jack chuckles and presses his lips to my shoulder, his chest heaving against my back, then he groans and pulls out.

And I have more left, after all. I pivot back and fall to my knees, my hands trapped within my sleeves. Jack stills, his long fingers curled around his shaft, stripping off the condom. His cock is still rigid.

"Take off the rubber," I tell him hoarsely.

He drags it off and I swiftly lick the cum dripping from the broad crown before swallowing as much of his length as I can. His body curls in like I've sucker punched him, the chiseled muscles of his abdomen tensing, his fingers sliding into my hair as if to pull me away. But he doesn't, and I suck hard, knowing that it's too much, that he just came and he's too sensitive, that each stroke of my tongue will be as much agony as pleasure. Still he takes what I give him. I'd like to give him more.

But I ease back, and grin when Jack collapses into the chair behind him. I rise and straddle his lap, then kiss his smiling mouth.

I could definitely get used to this.

THE STEAKS ARE AMAZING. WE'RE quiet as we eat but the silence isn't full of tension, just hungry appreciation for a damn fine cut of meat. But even though my mouth's all in, my stomach isn't big enough to eat the whole thing, and I slide my plate over to Jack for him to finish if he wants it.

I start picking at my salad. "Have you had a chance to

contact Creek yet?"

"No. I'm hoping he's pushing Croc to let him be the one who comes after me."

"He probably won't come alone. He's not the enforcer."

"I'll work it out."

"And find out why he's here without exposing him?"

Jack nods and stabs my steak, dropping it onto his plate.

I reach for the bourbon and splash more into my glass. "You saw the patches he's wearing? If he's spent time in prison, if he's killed for the club, he's gone under pretty deep. That takes years. So he must be after something big. There's nothing that big around here."

"It's best if it stays that way."

Amen to that. My gaze slides down his heavy shoulder, watching the flex of his biceps as he cuts the steak. The club's emblem inks his skin, wings of flame and wheels of steel. The one good thing.

"How'd you end up with the Riders?" I know Saxon sponsored him about eight years ago—back when my dad was still the prez. "Did you know Saxon in the service?"

Jack shakes his head. "He shared a cell with my brother."

While doing time for manslaughter. "What was your brother in for?"

"Selling prescription meds." He pauses briefly, his gaze on the knife cutting through his steak. "He wouldn't have made it in prison. So I asked Saxon to look out for him."

He asked Saxon? No. Jack doesn't ask. I roll the bourbon over my tongue and study him. "So what you really said was that you'd kill him if anything happened to your brother."

Jack glances up at me, amusement lighting his eyes. "I did."

"And that made you best buds?" Close enough that Saxon appointed Jack as his vice president five years ago. During the recent merger with the Titans, Saxon appointed a new veep from that club, and made Jack a warlord, instead—which makes him Saxon's right hand man. He answers only to the prez. "Your brother must have gotten through all right."

"He got out alive." His shrug suggests *all right* is relative. "After I left the service, I came by Pine Valley to thank Saxon for looking out for Jaime. He told me to stay and ride with the club. I did."

"So you knew my dad."

"I did."

For a second I wonder what Jack thought of him, but I don't really want to know. My dad could be a charming motherfucker and Jack might have liked him. I poke at a piece of lettuce. "How'd you know about Portland?"

He sets his knife down and sits back. "The boss heard you rode up every couple of months. We knew you didn't have any family up there and he worried someone was holding something over your head. So he sent me up after you."

My throat is tight as hell. "You saw me in that red dress?"

"Looking like a supermodel? Yeah, I did."

Fuck. "If I'd wanted any Rider to see me that way I'd have walked into the clubhouse wearing it."

"I figured that." His voice is low. "Is that dress for you or for them?"

"For them. It makes it easy. A lot easier than wearing a kutte." But I'm still picky. I'm more likely to turn down invitations than not. "Did I get lucky when you saw me?"

"No. What I saw was how many you sent away." His dark gaze seems to glitter with a dangerous light. "I thought about sitting next to you."

Where he might buy me a drink. Where I might decide to take him up to my room. "Why didn't you?"

"Because even when you're not wearing a kutte, you're still a Rider. And I'm still one, too."

"And you thought I might send you away?"

"Yes."

Every breath I draw seems to ache deep in my chest. God. How many hookups have I had? Girls mostly in town. Trolling for guys out of town. And it never got to me—until now, when I think of how everything would be different if he'd just sat down. Or if I'd seen him at the hotel, because I know myself. I'd have reeled him in, taken him up to my bed.

And I'd never have stopped taking him. I don't know how I'll stop now.

The pressure in my chest erupts on a bitter laugh. "Well, I guess that is one good thing—this bet saved me a trip and hotel bill. At least until next time I need some dick."

Jack leans in, his eyes like heated stone. "Do you need more now?"

My heart thuds. "Yes."

"Good." He takes my hand and sweeps up the Widow Jane in the other. "Because my dick needs to fuck your ass."

I grin and let him haul me toward the bedroom. "Still not my favorite hole."

"That's why I've got this." He sloshes the bourbon around in the bottle. "If the lube doesn't work I'll just start pouring liquor into you. You'll end up liking it one way or another."

I snort out a laugh. "It might take a lot of liquor."

"Whatever works. Get on the bed so I can tie you up again."

Still wearing his jeans, he tosses the lube and strip of condoms to the mattress beside me, then he cuffs my wrists and fastens them to the headboard. "Got any toys? I bought a few but didn't know what you like."

So he didn't reconnoiter my stash? "In the big dresser. The top drawer."

I watch his face as he looks through. Nothing in there seems to surprise him and finally he pulls out a smooth G-spot vibrator with a clit stimulator.

He glances back at me. "You like it?"

"Love it. But, I just realized I forgot to take off your shirt before you tied me." And with my arms stretched over my head and my hands bound, it's not coming off the normal way.

"I didn't forget. I like seeing you in it."

He returns to the bed and pushes the hem of the shirt up over my tits, bunching the material at my neck. His big hands slide up the sides of my ribcage before swooping in to pinch my taut nipples. Fuck. My back arches, and I moan when his hot mouth replaces his fingers, the ache of arousal already building in my pussy again.

His lips taste my neck, my jaw. His voice is like gravel when he says, "Are you going to bite me if I kiss you?"

We broke that rule a while ago. But I'm never that easy. "I won't draw blood."

And that must be good enough because his mouth devours mine, tasting of bourbon and pepper and the sweetness of this need. His cheeks are flushed when he pulls back, his cock a thick ridge behind denim. Gripping a pillow, he wedges it under my hips, then grabs another when the height doesn't satisfy him. Finally he kneels between my splayed legs, watching my face as he eases the slim vibrator inside my slick pussy. The stimulator covers my clit.

On low speed. Immediately frustrated, I roll my hips. "That's not going to do it. Turn it up."

Ignoring my demand, he leans forward between my legs and catches my left nipple in his teeth before sucking hard. His hand slides down to my cunt, his fingers lightly teasing the lips of my pussy before gripping the base of the vibe and slowly, slowly pumping it in and out, maddeningly shallow thrusts.

Oh, God. He's going to fucking kill me. The toy isn't big enough or deep enough and it's not vibrating fast enough to do anything but drive me insane.

"Fuck." Groaning, I try to lift my hips, to get more sensation, but he pins me down.

"More, Lily?"

"Yes." I grit it through clenched teeth, because he's squirting lube onto his fingers and I know the more he's going to give. "You bastard."

He grins and his hand slides farther back. God help me. It *is* more. Just one long finger, and although it doesn't feel bad I still don't like it much, either. But the slow thrust into my tight channel seems to enhance all the rest—and yet it's still not enough, my body clenching and squirming but I can't get to the height I need.

"Jack! God. Do it!"

No longer smiling, his face taut with hunger, he sheathes his cock. "You want me to fuck your ass?"

"Or turn up the fucking vibrator."

That's apparently not his choice. Fisting his shaft, he begins pushing into me. I expect him to pull the vibe from my pussy but he leaves it in, the stimulator teasing my clit as his cock slowly fills my ass. My fingers twist in the ropes. Jesus. I groan and lift my hips, trying to ease the pressure. The vibe isn't thick but now I feel it, my inner walls seeming to tighten the deeper Jack goes. He's big and it hurts, and I still don't like it, but it's so much *more* and that feels so fucking good.

With a grunt, Jack tips me up higher. He thrusts fully into me, his pelvis hitting the base of the vibrator and pushing it deeper into my pussy, harder against my clit. I cry out and he slowly withdraws, but I wrap my legs around him and try to force him back, to fill me up again. He shoves into me, hitting the vibe, oh God, like that, and he's evil, fucking evil, because somehow he's got me begging him to fuck my ass. Then he turns up the vibe to high and I'm suddenly screaming for more, and he gives it, fucking me hard until the buzz against my clit blows me apart.

Jack groans long and low as I come, bracing his hands beside my shoulders and gentling his thrusts. I lay shuddering as he finishes and falls forward over me, sweat dripping down his taut back.

"You bastard," I pant, tightening my legs around him. "You dirty fucking bastard."

He grins, looking down at me, brushing away the long hairs clinging to my sweaty face. "Want that liquor now?"

"Screw you," I say but my laugh ruins it. Never would I have guessed Jack fucking Hayden is fun in bed. Intense? Yes. Sexy and gorgeous? Oh, yes. But not fun.

Yet here I am, laughing and enjoying every second with him—and loving that he seems to like it all as sloppy and as rough as I do.

Jack reaches up and tugs the rope free but doesn't release my cuffs. He pulls his shirt over my head. Sliding his arms beneath me, he lifts my weight easily and carries me into the bathroom, where he trashes the condom and tosses the vibe into the sink. I turn on the shower and he slides under the hot spray with me, pulling me back against his chest. God, this is nice. After so much great bourbon and spectacular sex, I'm languid and warm and feeling good all over.

Jack's hand strokes down my wet hair. "How long does the water last?"

"Forever. I have a tankless water heater."

"Then we'll take forever," he says and grabs the cake of soap. He lathers my back, then tenderly slides his sudsy fingers between my ass cheeks, washing away the lube. "All right back here?"

"Mmm-hmm." Lazily, I turn my back to the spray and lay my head against his shoulder. "And I'm not saying you made me a fan. But it did feel like sweet angels were pounding my ass at the end there."

Though his broad chest I feel the rumble of his laugh. His fingertips gently skim from my shoulder to my elbow. "Is your arm hurting?"

"Not too bad."

"So it is." His arm tightens around me. "Want to take a break before round two?"

"Sounds good," I mumble against his neck. "Fair

warning, though. I'm going for a knockout."

"No need." His hand tangles in my hair and he holds me closer. "I went down in round one."

I guess we both did.

Back in my bed, Jack holds me against his side, my head pillowed on his shoulder. I'm still boneless and sleepy and utterly happy. I've had some wild nights but I can't remember being this well fucked, this satisfied. In the dim light, I listen to his even breathing, feel his heart beating slowly beneath my palm. A demon's inked mouth devours his parents beneath my hand. His brother's name bleeds beneath my fingertips.

We've been quiet for a while, but I know he's not asleep. "Where's your brother now?"

"Tulsa."

"Is that where you're from?"

"No. Up near Seattle."

A long way from Oklahoma. "Do you ever see him?"

"I see him. He doesn't see me."

Unless his brother is blind there's only one way that makes sense. "So you don't visit. But you check in, make sure he's doing all right."

"I do."

Just like he made sure his brother was okay in prison, too. "Is the distance your choice or his?"

"His. I killed our father when I was fourteen and he was ten. He hasn't forgiven me for it." During my stunned silence following that announcement, he adds, "My mother never did, either."

Heart pounding, I come up onto my elbow. His eyes are flat, but I know better now than to think they're empty. I just can't see what's behind them.

Fucking hell. This might be *why* I can't see what's behind them. And didn't he say that he learned his first lesson from his father's fists? "Why did you kill him?"

"He started in on Jaime. I tried to stop him and that pissed him off. But when he dragged me into the kitchen and got me over the table, I got my hands on a knife—and I didn't take what he gave me that time."

Jesus. What was it he said to me the other day? I told him I was going to be the worst fuck ever and Jack said he'd already had the worst. "You say he started in on Jaime. You don't just mean beating."

"No."

My throat and stomach hurt like I'm going to cry, but Jack's relaying it all like it's somebody else's past. "What happened to you after? Were you arrested?"

"No charges were brought. But my mother wouldn't take me back. So they put me in a place."

No charges. That probably meant the evidence of abuse was so severe that the cops didn't even think to. That it was self-defense or justified. Fourteen. With his father's blood on his hands after being sexually abused by the man for God knows how long. Then rejected by his family. No way that didn't cut something out of him. "How the hell did you get into the service? I thought you were fucked up after you came out but obviously you must have been before you went in."

A short laugh shakes through him. "I was. I failed the psych evals, but in just the right way. I was perfect for other operations."

"In what branch?"

"Not any. I just did what needed to be done to protect the country."

I can hear what he isn't saying. That he was recruited to carry out operations where he had to work alone. Maybe operations where the government didn't really want to claim involvement, so if any of his missions went south they'd have washed their hands of him. "And you had the right mindset for it."

To work alone. To kill without hesitation. And not to expect anyone to have his back.

He says gruffly, "It's the same mindset that will force a woman to follow through on a bet, just so I can get my dick into her for a night."

Yet he still gave me a choice. I won't ever forget that. "You are *incredibly* fucked up."

His mouth curves with wry amusement. "No argument here."

I bend to kiss that sexy smile before laying my head on his shoulder. "It's all right. I like you this way."

And love the way he holds me closer.

"So that's how you met Creek? He did the same covert

shit you did?"

"Yes."

I frown up at him. "Then Creek has that mindset, too. He'll do what needs to be done to protect something. So how far will he go to protect his mission? You could expose him. He might not be coming to talk to you but to take you out, make sure you never talk."

"No."

"How can you be sure?"

He's quiet for a second, as if he hasn't had to put his answer into words before. "It would be disrespectful."

"But he's been under for a while. You can't know if he's changed."

"People don't change."

I'm pretty sure arguing that point won't change his mind. "Just be careful." I rise over him, straddling his stomach. His rough fingers slide up over my thighs. "Ready for round two?"

His hands shoot up, catching my jaw and hauling my mouth down to his.

I take that as a "Yes."

SEVEN

The sexy rumble of a Harley's engine and the rattle of my garage door wake me. Faint gray light peeks through the bedroom window. Dawn.

Jack is gone.

No, Jack is *going.* My heart clenches and I scramble out of the bed, but I'm too late—the sound of his engine tells me that he's already out of the driveway. I rush to the window and catch a glimpse as he rides down the street. My fingers curl against the cool glass when he rounds the corner, out of sight.

Fuck.

Disappointment sinks through me. I knew he would leave early for work, but I intended to see him off, find out when he plans to come over again. I could text and ask but everything still feels tilted, as if I'm seeing him through a new scope, and it's already hard enough to read him. I don't need the additional distance of a text message—and I don't want it to feel like a hookup.

I want asking him to come over to feel like it means something.

With a sigh, I climb back into bed, and every ache from round two and round three seems to settle in with a vengeance. Groaning, I pop a painkiller, pull the sheet up over my head, and hug Jack's pillow to my chest. It's a poor substitute for the man.

But that's all right. I'll have him again.

I'M ELBOWS DEEP IN DISHWATER when I see Jenny Erickson pull up in her truck. I meet her at the door, dripping onto the tile because I couldn't find a single freaking hand towel.

I give up and use my shirt, instead. I look her over. Shorts and sandals, a flowery little top, her dark hair up. She's always cute as hell, but she usually just wears jeans and a tee when she's working. "Were we meeting for lunch?"

"No." Her pale green gaze runs all over my face. Her forehead is creased with concern. "Saxon suggested that maybe I should check in on you while I'm in town."

"Check in on me? Why?"

She follows me back to the kitchen. "He didn't say why. But I heard from Anna that you got slapped with a huge fine."

Anna Wall—the bartender at the Wolf Den. The brothers probably have no idea how much she knows about club business.

But apparently no one has mentioned my bet yet. Maybe they're afraid to, considering that it involves Jack.

I don't care if Jenny knows about it, though. "I lost a bet with Blowback. So last night, he tied me up and screwed me."

Her pretty mouth drops open. Her gaze does another head-to-toe before she scans the room, as if looking for the damage. She won't find any. Every sign Jack was here has been scrubbed or taken away. It was already like that when I finally got up. The vibrator washed and back in the drawer, our plates in the kitchen cleaned, the rope and the cuffs missing. Even the trash had been emptied, the butcher paper and the used condoms gone.

Her astonished gaze returns to mine. "And you're all right?"

I have to laugh. "I'm fine."

"Well, okay. I was going to meet up with Anna and grab something to eat. Do you want to join us?"

"I do. Let me just rinse this shit."

Of course she helps. That's Jenny. I'd just wait for the other person to finish doing their own crap but she jumps right in. "So you *are* all right?"

I give her the side-eye. "Why are you so surprised?"

"Because there aren't little pieces of you buried out in the forest."

Realization hits me. Jack makes a lot of people uneasy. Sometimes I forget exactly how uneasy.

"Like he's a serial killer?" I laugh so hard I almost fall into the sink. "Oh, God. He's fucked up, yeah. But a different kind of fucked up."

The kind of fucked up that will tear someone apart, sure. But only if they threaten something he's trying to protect.

Her eyes narrow on me, like she's realizing there's more I haven't said. Like how freaking good it was.

It's crazy sometimes how quickly she reads me. I haven't even known her that long— No, scratch that. I've known her all my life. Of course I knew about Red Erickson's spoiled little princess. But I didn't *know* her.

Now I do. And she's not spoiled. Sure, she has a big house and money, but she also works her ass off. She's nice, too, like I'll never be.

She's also the only person I've had sex with that is still a friend. And it wasn't even full on, one-on-one sex. She was with Saxon; I just helped them out by licking her pussy.

There's no other friend whose taste I know. Everyone else I've been with, they're all hookups. They didn't mean anything to me before I fucked them, and they never stick around after they get to know me. But I don't stick around, either. I don't even know if I know *how*. Sometimes I think the only reason Jenny's still around has nothing to do with me and everything to do with how nice she is.

Shit. *Shit*. Jack wasn't a friend. Not really. I was too angry at him for so long. Last night changed everything, though, and I think we could be damn good friends. The sex is amazing but I'm pretty sure we'd get along great during the down time, too. But maybe I'll be no good at being with him. Or maybe he won't want to stick around, either.

And that worry is suddenly tearing at me. God. Before he left, I wanted him back again. For another night. For another week.

But the truth is…I want him a hell of a lot longer than that.

"Lily." Jenny's looking at me with concern again. "You're all right?"

"Yeah." I shoot her a wide grin, shut off the water, then run up to my bedroom to change.

As soon as I'm alone, I make myself shake off the worry. Because I know Jack's secret. He cares more than he shows—and he cares about me.

So it'll be okay.

Unless I'm wrong.

At the Barracks, I've been nursing a beer for almost an hour. Jack is here, but he's sitting with the prez and Thorne, our new veep, along with two Blue Coyotes. I know better than to interrupt them. But I'm already rethinking my plan to ask him over. Because he's facing me, he can see me, but there's nothing in his dark gaze when he glances my way.

Maybe it's just business, though. So I wait, watching a few dancers work the pole before heading over to the pool tables, where I lose a twenty when I sink the eight ball, then another twenty when I go again.

Shit. My game is completely off. It's cheaper to stuff dollars into the dancers' g-strings. I head to the bar and ignore some of the looks I'm getting. A few of the brothers who are on the executive board keep giving me the same once-over that Jenny did. Like they're surprised I'm still standing.

Of course I am. A pussy can take a pounding. It's only balls that can't.

The Blue Coyotes are gone so I head back to the table I'm sharing with Gunner and Stone. Now it'll be real easy. Jack just has to get up, come over. He doesn't even have to sit down.

But there's still nothing when he looks at me. And I can't go to him in here. I can't. He has to know it. Stupid Zoomie, she got fucked and now she's clinging, because she thinks sex with a man who won the use of her pussy in a bet meant something.

Jesus.

I last another half hour, then sit in the parking lot like a pathetic dickhole, thinking that maybe Jack believed he couldn't go to me in there, either. But he'd have seen me leave. He can follow me and there's no one out here to see us.

After fifteen minutes I know he's not coming, and I ride home.

I get drunk on a bottle of whiskey while staring at my phone, debating whether to text him, then finally crawl into bed and hug his pillow to my chest. Just that morning, I did the same thing, certain I'd have him back here with me. Certain he gave a shit.

Instead I fall asleep alone.

EIGHT

That shitty night turns into the shittiest week on record. A wildfire breaks out in the Deschutes forest over the weekend and I'm immediately called in to drop a helitack team at the front line. When I fly back it's to pull their bodies out. I worked with a few of those guys for years. I've attended barbecues with their families, met their wives and kids. Then the wind shifts and the fire spreads and I spend the next few days flying through smoke and fighting to keep hot drafts and wind shears from bringing my bird down.

By the time the executive board meeting rolls around,

I'm one solid, tired ache. I've got nothing left.

Except more hurt. Jack looks at me as I come in, his eyes empty. The ache deepens to tearing pain when he looks away like I'm nothing.

I don't know what lens I should be looking through now. If I still had my old one, I'd believe this was what he'd meant to do. Tear me down. Strip away the defenses I'd built up against him so he could rip out my heart.

Because of course my heart went all in, too. Even though I didn't mean for it to.

And I don't know what to do now. I've got two choices: Go ask him if he wants another night, which is the stupid choice. Or I can just let it ride. Put it behind me.

That would be smartest. I changed my game with him because I thought I saw something. But it was probably just what I wanted to see after Stone and Gunner were clowning around with me. I went into that night looking for a reason to believe he cared.

I don't believe it anymore.

The meeting's short. Only two items are on the agenda—"Money" and "Hangmen"—and there's not much new to say about either topic. I don't hang around after, and Gunner catches up to me on the way out of the conference room.

"Hey, Zoomie. You heading out to the Barracks with the rest of us?"

"Yeah." Though there's nothing I feel less like doing. "But I'm leaving early."

"Don't you have tomorrow off?"

"I've got funerals to attend."

"Shit. I heard what went down. That's just rough."

My throat is a fucking lump. "Yeah, well. Shut up about it."

And that's why I like Gunner so much. He's a damn clown but he can see when someone's holding on by a thread. He doesn't take offense but simply shuts up and walks with me.

I'm in the lot outside the clubhouse before I realize Jack's right behind us. His fucking quiet feet. And he's still with me as Gunner veers off toward his bike. Jack's blacked-out workhorse is right next to mine.

Jack's long stride pulls him up even with me. His voice is low and deep. "You had friends on that team. You all right?"

"You don't get to fucking ask me that."

Not after I sat in another parking lot last week desperate for him to say a word to me. He doesn't get to pretend to care now.

He doesn't get to say *anything* to me. And he doesn't, just stands beside his ride and watches as I swing my leg over my bike's saddle. This his gaze drops to my hip and his jaw clenches.

Because of the bruise. The goddamn mark he left on me. It's almost gone. Pretty soon it'll be nothing.

But it still hurts. "Did you mean to teach me the same lesson your parents taught you?"

His dark gaze snaps up to mine. "What lesson?"

"Take what you get, Lily," I tell him. "Don't ask for more."

The skin stretched taut across his cheekbones pales. "No."

"Well, you taught it to me anyway—" I break off as he starts for me. "Don't fucking touch me."

But he does, cradling my jaw in his big hands. His eyes aren't empty now but I don't trust anything I see. "Lily," he says hoarsely. "What were you going to ask?"

Like I'd ever tell him now. "Did you lose? You said you'd lose whether you had me or didn't. So did you lose?"

His gaze is suddenly desolate. "Everything."

"You were right about that, then. But you were wrong about me. I didn't win. Instead I just got hurt. Which shouldn't surprise me. You hurt me for five fucking years before that. I don't know why I thought anything had changed. Now let me go."

He does, watching me, his expression bleak as I start up my bike. I barely hear the low gravel of his voice over the engine.

"I didn't want to hurt you, Lily."

"Well, your intentions mean shit, don't they? So what *do* you want, Jack? You want me? You want more?"

Face tortured, he closes his eyes. "Another night. Just one. If you're offering."

"I'm not. So you better ask me for it," I tell him, then pop my ride into gear and make my engine roar.

* * *

I'm ABOUT TO POUND BACK a shot of tequila when I realize Jack might be too fucked up to ask.

What did he say about killing his dad? *I didn't take what he gave me.* And he lost so much. Losing his dad couldn't have been so bad, but his mother and brother turned their backs on him. Because he broke that rule.

And now? Everyone he protects doesn't want to have anything to do with him. His family, first. Then the army said he was too fucked up to join but someone decided to make use of him, though they'd never claim him as one of theirs. Even some of the Riders. There's a couple of brothers who are comfortable with him but the others would rather keep their distance. And Jack's so used to it that for five years he assumed I was doing the same.

So even if he wants to ask, God knows if he *can*. At least not yet. Not until he believes that he won't lose me— or that I won't push him away.

Shit. So that changes the game. Again.

I lower the shot glass and slide it over to Stone. "I'm heading out!" I shout to him over the music.

He nods and Gunner bumps my fist. "We'll hold down the fort."

Surrounded by liquor and strippers. Such a rough job.

On the board meeting nights, Jack often shows for a few hours, but he's not here. That usually means he's working late.

I ride back to town, slowing through the dark streets. He's left his bike out in front of his auto shop—so he's here. I roll in and run up the exterior stairs to his apartment. The windows are dark. I'm about to knock when I hear his voice come from below.

"Lily?"

He's at the bottom of the stairs, looking big and dangerous and so damn gorgeous. His shop door is open behind him. Faint yellow light spills through. The rest of the garage is dark so he must have been back in his office.

"Jack fucking Hayden," I say and start slowly down the stairs. "Why the hell didn't you call me last week? You just fucked and ran."

He studies me for a long second before his stance shifts, bracing his feet and crossing his arms over his broad chest. So he sees that I'm coming for a fight.

Not with fists. But it will probably always be a little bit of a fight between us.

"It was your rule," he says quietly. "I don't talk to you about it. You forget it ever happened."

"A *rule*? That's a bullshit reason. We broke every single rule after I made it. You didn't tie my hands in round two. And we kissed a hell of a lot."

His eyes gleam. "But we used a rubber each time."

So the rule about protection was important enough not to break? Yeah. That fits him. And maybe it fits this, too.

I stop two stairs above him. "Are you protecting me

by staying away?"

"I'm just doing what needs to be done." His voice roughens. "You don't want to risk your place in the club by fucking a patchholder."

My heart twists. I did tell him that. Then never told him I'd risk it with him.

I take the next step and my blood freezes as a red dot appears on the side of his auto shop just beyond his head. A laser sight. The dot disappears— No, fuck, fuck, it's on Jack's shoulder.

"Down!"

I leap for him, slamming into his chest and knocking him back. A *pfink!* sounds as a bullet hits the side of his shop and we're scrambling into the garage, low, low, swinging the door closed. Jack hits a switch on the wall and we're plunged into darkness.

"Are you hit?" He's crouching with me, his voice hoarse, his hands all over me. "Are you hit?"

"No." Heart pounding, I catch his hands. "I'm all right."

My eyes are adjusting to the darkness, to the faint light in the small windows. Jack draws his gun from his shoulder harness, checks the rounds. His gaze is on the door and his face starkly lined by shadows. "Don't you *ever* jump in front of a bullet for me."

Stung, I clench my jaw. "I have your back."

"Then have my back. Don't be my shield." He glances at me and knocks his knuckles against his chest. "It's just fucking meat. So you don't get hurt for me. All right?"

No. But I keep quiet because we're both listening. Nobody's closing in on the shop yet.

Quietly he says, "I'm going to see how many there are. You stay low and get into the office. There's a vest and a .45 in the bottom drawer of the filing cabinet. Wait for me there."

I nod, legs tense as I shift in that direction. "All right."

"Shoot any fucker who comes into that office who isn't a Rider."

"I will."

"Christ, Lily." He suddenly pulls me in, his warm mouth against my temple, his left hand tangled in my hair. "You're so fucking steady. I'll have you at my back any time. But *not* as my shield."

My throat's tight. "All right."

Then he's gone, so quiet, disappearing into the shadows of the garage. The shop's big, with five bays in the main garage. A truck's hoisted in the nearest one. Keeping low, I make my way past it, back to the office. The door's open and flanked by two big windows that allow Jack to see into the garage from his desk.

The filing cabinet drawer slides open smoothly. My heart's thundering as I pull on the vest and find the pistol, a Glock 37. Ten rounds, nothing in the chamber. I head back to the front of the office, crouching beneath the window.

A creak from outside. The shop door opening. I'm far in the back, they won't see me take a quick peek through the window.

Two shadows move through the garage. I crouch again, waiting. A shot will give away my location and I don't know what kind of firepower they have, whether they can just shoot through the wall. They have some fancy toys—a laser sight and silencer—and they might have more. So I'll sit it out until I don't have any other choice.

I almost jolt out of position as something clangs nearby. A wrench or some other tool falling to the concrete. My pulse races, but it's good, it's good. I have a location to focus on now, I can hear the footsteps.

A shadow appears at the office window, blocking the faint light from outside. Quietly he moves toward the door—but not quietly enough. I know that's not Jack. Steadying my aim on the office's entrance, I slide off the safety.

A body thuds to the floor, falling halfway through the door.

Big guy. Tribal tattoos. The enforcer for the Devil's Hangmen. I stare at him over the barrel of my gun. His eyes are open and staring. Neck broken.

Jack slips through the door. Silently, he motions me closer. "Stay right behind," he says quietly. "Creek is with him."

"Anyone else?"

"No. But keep your eyes open."

I nod and blink as Jack hits a switch on the office wall. Lights flood the main garage. Stepping over the enforcer's body, I stay at Jack's back, our weapons up and ready.

Creek's in the third bay, body shielded behind a black Explorer, his pistol leveled at us. Silencer. Laser sight. The enforcer's weapon didn't have one. His gaze flicks to me before returning to Jack.

"You know your choices," Jack says. "You've got just one, and that's only because you were sloppy outside."

With the laser sight, I realize. So Creek let me see it—and probably deliberately missed.

The other man waits a beat before slowly lowering his gun. Jack doesn't lower his, so I don't either. That doesn't seem to bother Creek. He comes out from behind the Explorer. "Tank?"

"Dead in my office. Why are you in with them?" When Creek's gaze shifts to me, Jack tells him, "I trust her more than I trust you. She won't say a word."

Creek looks back to Jack, his eyes narrowing. "Your club took out the Eighty-Eight. The higher ups on both sides are assuming it was someone else. It was too fucking clean to be an MC. But the Riders have you."

Jack doesn't confirm or deny. "Are you looking at the Riders?"

"Not at you. Not at the Hangmen."

"You're going after one of their connections."

This time it's Creek who doesn't confirm or deny, but Jack must be right. The Hangmen are too small. Creek must be going after a bigger target and using the Hangmen as an in.

"Is it the girls?" Jack asks and I realize he means the La Pine girls. The ones we pulled out of the Eighty-Eight's compound.

The other man's gaze sharpens. "There's more, but that's part of it. Do you know where they were headed?"

"No."

Creek's jaw tightens. "If you hear—"

"I'll share. You tell your prez to back off."

"Croc won't." He glances in the direction of Jack's office. "Especially now."

Jack shakes his head. "You came here looking for me. I was already gone. He wrecked his ride on the way back."

"That'll only hold Croc off a short time."

"We'll be ready." Easing back, Jack holsters his gun. "You get his feet."

I DRIVE THE TRUCK. THE body's in the back. Jack takes the enforcer's bike. There's only one place to go: Lucifer's Break. It's a long curve that narrows beneath a concrete overpass. My dad tried passing a car on that curve and ran into a truck instead. But even before then, every biker heard warnings about that stretch of road. There's always gravel on the asphalt and if you hit that curve going too fast, a bike's tires will slide out from under.

Even knowing the plan, I'm still not ready when I see Jack take the curve—and goes straight, instead. He bails out of his seat at the last second, hitting the asphalt and rolling. The enforcer's bike smashes into the concrete wall.

Jesus. I'm out of the truck as fast as I can but Jack is already up, pulling off his helmet. The shoulder of his jacket is shredded. Creek rides up behind me, engine rumbling.

"Let's be quick," he says and hands me Tank's helmet. "You slam this against the concrete wall. We'll get him laid out."

So easy. And only possible because Jack snapped the enforcer's neck instead of shooting him. But then, he probably figured all this out ahead of time. He knew Creek might not be coming alone.

All the assholes who keep their distance are right about one thing: Jack *is* scary. But what they don't get is that the only reason to be afraid is if you come after him—or the Riders.

I finish with the helmet. Creek takes it and crouches, strapping it onto the man's head.

"You'll handle this from here?" Jack asks him.

"Yeah."

We head back to the truck and he pulls off his ruined jacket. Neither of us is wearing a kutte. We left them back at his garage. No need to fuck this up by having someone say they saw a pair of Riders out here around the time Tank ran into a wall.

I drive. The light from Jack's phone throws harsh shadows over his face as he texts. Probably sending a message to Saxon.

"Want me to drop you off at the ranch?" I ask. He

won't send details over the phone, so that means he'll need a face-to-face with the prez.

"At my place. I'll take my bike out there." He glances at his phone as a reply comes in and he pushes it into his pocket. "Why'd you come?"

To his apartment tonight. My knuckles are white on the steering wheel. I watch the road, not glancing his way. "To make another bet."

His voice suddenly roughens. "What bet?"

"I made reservations at the Hilton in Bend for Sunday night. I'm going to be at the bar. I bet you won't sit next to me."

"If I win?"

"Thirty nights with me." It's a bet I don't want to win. And if Jack wins, he doesn't have to ask—and neither do I.

Not this time.

He's quiet. I know he's watching me but I don't glance over as we roll through town and pull into the lot of his shop. He opens one of the bay doors and I pull in.

When I get out, I toss him the keys and gesture to the bed of the truck, where the body had been. "You're going to take care of the back before you go or do you need me to?"

"I'll clean it up," he says.

And he's so quick, coming for me, pushing me back against the garage wall, his fingers at my belt. God. Need bites into me, sharp and painful. I grip his shirt and tear it over his head. Fuck, his chest. Greedily my hands slide over hard muscle, warm skin.

He shoves my jeans down. I'm already wet. So wet. I groan when his fingers slide into me, my hands clutching at his shoulders. His mouth finds mine and he lifts me, shoving my back higher against the wall. His thick cock pushes deep in a single hard stroke.

I cry out, my body stiffening at the sudden invasion, but it's good. So good. And it's a fight, like I knew it would be. My fists clench in his hair and I hold his dark gaze and just fucking dare him to look away, to shutter his eyes, to hide again, but he can't, he doesn't, and he's mine as he fucks me and fucks me and fucks me. He's mine as I come, crying his name against his lips and my back against the wall. He's mine, my pussy holding him deep as his fingers dig into my hips and he shudders against me.

I hold him tight as we catch our breath, his face buried in my neck, my legs wrapped around him. Quietly I say, "You should come over to my place after you're done at the ranch."

Sudden tension transforms his muscles to steel. Gruffly he says, "Are you asking?"

"No. Just saying."

His chest expands on a ragged breath before he nods, his rough jaw scratching my neck. "I'll be late."

I don't care. "If I'm asleep, you can just break in again."

It's almost dawn before I feel him against me. I begin to turn, but his arms wrap around me and pull my back against his chest. In my ear is a low, "Just sleep, Lily."

I snuggle closer, loving every inch of his warm skin and hard muscle against me. "Okay."

"I have to leave early." His hand slides through my hair. "I'll be gone for a few days."

"Where?"

"Vegas. I want to get an eye on how the Hangmen operate, see who's calling the shots in the mother chapter. I want to know what to expect. I'll be back by Sunday."

"I bet you won't."

His lips press to the back of my neck. "Nothing could stop me. I'll have my thirty nights."

He'll have a lot more than that. By the time the month is over, he'll need me as much as I need him. He'll ask for more.

I'm betting my heart on it.

NINE

The hotel bar is busy. It's summer, so some fami-lies sit in the dining area, but this late it's mostly just business travelers and couples left. This time of night, sitting alone, I'd usually have had about five or six offers by now. There haven't been any here. I've seen a few men glance at my face and it seemed like they were going to make a move, then their gazes fell to my kutte and they hesitated. If they took a step closer, I gave them a look that scared them away.

I know Jack's here when the guy checking me out is scared away before I even bother with the look. I don't glance over until I feel him slide into the barstool next to me. He sets his helmet on the bar. His saddlebags are over his shoulder.

My heart is in my throat.

He orders a beer and I look him over. His knuckles are raw. There's a cut on his cheekbone and his lower lip is split. So he's been fighting. But I know Jack. His opponent wouldn't have touched him if Jack hadn't allowed it. So he went down to Vegas, got info, but getting that info meant pretending he was someone else. Maybe stroking some asshole's ego by taking a beating.

Losing, but still winning. That might be our theme this weekend.

He takes a swig of his drink, looking straight ahead. "No red dress?"

"Did you want the red dress?"

"Not here. I like you like this. It's who you are."

"Yeah, it is." A girl in a kutte and with her heart about to pound through her chest. "I might catch some shit from the brothers for this."

His shoulders tense. "No."

"Yes. But when I do, just have my back. *Don't* come to my defense. Don't be my shield. All right?"

He struggles with it. But finally he nods.

Good. I slide off my barstool, taking my drink with me. "Room 319."

His helmet in hand, he follows me to the elevator. My hands shake as I pull the keycard from my back pocket and unlock the door. I don't get more than a step inside before he sweeps me up against his chest.

I cling to him, my arms tightening around his neck. He carries me across the room and lays me on the bed before coming down over me, settling between my thighs. His cock is hard and thick; his big hands are gentle as he cups my face.

Finally, his gaze meets mine. His dark eyes are flat, but not empty. Heat burns within.

"I win," he says softly and his mouth captures my lips in a searing kiss.

So I win, too.

RISKING
IT ALL

ONE

LILY

"You look like shit, Lily," Jenny says when I slide into the booth across from her.

"Good freaking morning to you, too." I don't say she's looking a little tired herself. Her dad's sick. Dying. Jenny's got a good reason to lie awake half the night. She just did a better job of concealing the damage than I did.

So did Anna, who's yawning even as she crowds in beside Jenny. She was slinging drinks at the Wolf Den until closing—then after her shift was over, she had to drive me home because I was too wasted to ride. Thirty minutes ago, I woke up sprawled on the floor of my living room with Anna pounding on my front door and shouting something about brunch at Willy's Pancake House, and how we'd be total assholes if we didn't meet Jenny and help get her mind off her dad for a while. I was still trying to slit my eyes open when I folded myself into her Prius.

That's me. The tough biker who gets her wheels taken away because she can't hold her whiskey.

Except that's bullshit. I can hold my whiskey. I can hold a lot of whiskey.

I just drink more than a lot when my heart's hurting. And that? Is a crappy thing to discover about myself at this stage of the game. All these years, I've gotten along so well. Whenever I got drunk it was for fun. No moping, no crying. I thought my heart was pretty damn impervious. But, nope. Apparently all it takes to lay my heart to waste is one big, dangerous, completely fucked up warlord.

But I'm not going to think about Jack Hayden right now. I'm going to have a good day, damn it.

I grab the laminated brunch menu and read through it, even though the options at Willy's haven't changed in years and I order the same thing whenever I'm here. Though maybe this time I'll order more. When I woke up, with my mouth tasting like dead rat and my stomach still deciding whether I was going to live or die, I never wanted to eat again. Now I'm desperate to shove something down my throat and everything looks good.

Over the top of the menu, I eye Anna and Jenny. They're both tiny. No way are they going to finish whatever they order. Which means I can steal anything left over. "What are you guys having?"

"French toast," Jenny says, her dark head bowed as she fishes through her purse. She comes up with a single dose packet of ibuprofen and gives me a look. "Need this?"

Wow. I must *really* look like shit. "I'm covered. Anna showed up with a bottle of water and Advil."

Anna doesn't glance up from the menu. "Because I'm the hangover fairy."

She has the face for it—all cheekbones and pointed chin. If her hair was short and blond instead of brunette and long, she'd be Tinkerbell. "Do you flit around on sparkly wings?"

"No. I just hand out pills. And sometimes I shit glitter."

"Only sometimes?" Jenny frowns at her. "I do all the time."

"Me, too," I say. "Jesus, Anna. You gotta step up your game."

"God. It's easy for both of you to say. You're club princesses. You were born with glitter powers."

"Aw." I lean forward and pat her hand. "You can be a princess, too. You just have to *believe*."

"Okay. I'll believe." She takes a deep breath and closes her eyes like she's making a wish. "Now I'll order the blueberry pancakes and see what happens."

"Just don't share the results," Jenny says.

"Oh, I'm going to share the results with both of you bitches. A special-delivery photo straight to your phones."

She probably would, too. Once Anna gets something into her head she usually follows it through. But we're saved when the waitress shows up before any plan can solidify.

I ask for the big platter combo and wait for them to finish their orders before saying, "This is on me, by the way."

Of course Jenny protests. "You don't have to—"

"I do," I interrupt. "Anna saved my drunk ass last night and this morning, and I'm still borrowing your bike. So let me pay you back."

Though the cost of a breakfast doesn't come close to settling the debt I'm accumulating with them. I don't even have to ask for anything; they just help me out when I need it, though we haven't been friends that long. We've known each other forever, growing up in the same town and with only a year separating me from them, but we just started hanging out in the past few months. Yet they're already covering my ass. And I don't do much for them. Not really. So if I have to toss a few dollars on the table to keep myself from becoming the dead weight in this friendship, that's the least I can do.

They exchange a glance I can't read but which seems to speak volumes—two long-time BFFs having a conversation without saying a word. Probably a rehash of a real conversation about me that they've had before. It ends with Jenny sighing and nodding.

"Okay," she says. "I won't argue—though you know my bike was just sitting in the garage for years, so you riding her means she's actually useful to someone. If anything, I should be paying you for taking care of her."

As if I'd ever let her do that. "That sounds like arguing."

"I'm not—" Abruptly she closes her mouth, clears her throat. "So…any word on your new ride?"

"The insurance just came through." A fat six-figure check. But the money isn't nearly as pretty as my custom ride was before a skinhead worked it over with a sledge-hammer.

The waitress swings by with the coffee carafe and Anna adds about a thousand sugars to her mug. "You gonna go with Wheels Up again?"

Jenny's brows shoot high. "Isn't the wait list about two years long?"

"That's just for a car. The wait's even longer for a custom chopper, unless you're a Death Lord. But when I told Judge how the Eighty-Eight busted up the bike he made me before, he said he'd try to move me up. I don't know, though…" I shrug and stir half-and-half into my coffee until it's a pale caramel. "I'm thinking maybe I'll just buy a standard workhorse, then find some vintage ride to restore."

"And pocket the rest?"

"Yeah. Put it into savings, maybe invest some of it."

"Sounds like a good plan to me," Jenny says and I

know she's not just being nice about it. She's never just nice when she's talking money.

I don't really care about the money, though. Sure, it's great to have such a big cushion. But my job as a helicopter pilot and part-time mechanic at the airfield pays for everything I need and I love flying, so the insurance money is all extra.

It was extra five years ago, too, when the original money came to me out of my dad's life insurance. I'd hoped to buy the Hellfire Riders' clubhouse with the cash but my mom wouldn't sell to me, because my dad wouldn't have approved. He sure as hell wouldn't have approved of my wearing the Riders' colors, either. According to him, women were good for four things: fucking, cooking, cleaning, and raising brats. And for a woman to become a full member of the Hellfire Riders? Not while he drew breath.

And no matter what I did, he never changed his mind. I can rebuild an engine with my eyes closed, I can fight, I can ride—but I could never be good enough because I could never be the son he wanted. So I didn't become a Rider until after he drew that last breath.

I'd be lying if I said that using his life insurance to buy the sweetest bike any Rider ever straddled wasn't a big "Fuck you" to my dear departed dad. It wasn't *just* that, of course—Jesus, she really was a sweet ride and I loved her—but a "Fuck you" was definitely part of it.

Five years on…I just don't care anymore. He's dead.

I'll never be anything to him except the daughter who didn't know her place and who should have become a Rider's old lady. Instead, I've earned my place as a patch-holder. Now I'd rather restore or build my ride than have one made for me. It won't be the sweetest ride ever seen, but I think it'll *feel* sweeter.

Even if Jack isn't around to work on it with me.

And shit. *Shit.* I'm not thinking of Jack fucking Hayden today. I'm not. But my chest is as tight as hell and every sip of coffee hurts going down. Luckily the waitress arrives with our plates so I don't need to talk for a few seconds, but that luck doesn't hold when two Riders show up right behind her.

That's the problem with small towns like Pine Valley. You can never really get away from people. There's not a lot of choices if you're looking for a restaurant where you can sit down for breakfast on a Saturday morning, so even if you hope to just hang out with your girls, someone you know is inevitably going to crash the next booth.

At least it's just Picasso and Spiral. They can both be assholes, but I can be, too. So we get along most of the time.

"Hey, Zoomie." Spiral—as in *downward*—stops beside my seat. He's wearing the same T-shirt and jeans he was in last night. He's looking as hungover as I feel, too. The only difference? He looks well-fucked and loose, as if he just crawled out of someone's bed. I don't. "You hear about Valentine?"

"No."

I don't really want to hear, either. A little over a month ago, Valentine turned in his colors after I beat him in the ring, because he couldn't handle being tossed onto his ass by a girl. After that blow to his ego, he figured that I must have fucked and sucked my way into the club, and told the executive board as much. So as far as I'm concerned, Val is the equivalent of dog shit. I've scraped him off my boot; I'm not going back for another sniff.

"Zoomie." Picasso joins us, nodding at me before looking to Anna and Jenny. "Ladies. You doing all right?"

As the son of an original Rider, Picasso and I go way back, though he was known as Scout for most of that time. Then about ten years ago, while he was sleeping off a bender in the county jail, a tweaker jumped him and rearranged his face. Now his features seem like puzzle pieces that don't quite fit together, so some joker in the club started calling him Picasso. Of course the name stuck.

"We're doing great," Jenny says with a pretty smile. "What's this about Valentine?"

Spiral's expression looks easy but his eyes are iced over when he zeroes in on me again. "He joined the Devil's Hangmen."

Holy shit. Okay, I *do* want to know that. The Hangmen just moved into the state—and the first night they showed up, they practically spit into our faces. Within a week, the Hangmen's prez sent their enforcer to kill Jack, trying to deliver the message that we all need to fall in line.

Jack killed the enforcer, instead, then arranged for his death to look like an accident. That's probably why a war between the clubs hasn't started yet. But we've been waiting; it's just a matter of time before the Hangmen try to push into our territory. That's the way the Hangmen roll. They come into a region, try to take it over by recruiting the strongest patchholders from local clubs, and by making everyone else too afraid to challenge them.

So how did the Hangmen get Valentine? Did he go them? Or did they lean on him until he joined up?

Val is stupid enough I can believe he went to them. And he's cowardly enough I can believe he caved after the first threat.

I just can't believe the Hangmen would want the Riders' leavings. But maybe they aren't too picky about who wears their colors. "How'd you hear?"

"From Maurice." Picasso names another Rider before sliding a pointed glance at Jenny and Anna. *Can't tell you any more while they're listening,* that look says. *It's club business.*

I barely stop myself from rolling my eyes. These guys have no idea. Whenever Anna's working the bar at the Wolf Den, she hears more about club business than most of its members. By the end of the night, she'll probably know more about how our prez intends to take care of Valentine than Spiral and Picasso do.

"Anyway. We're gonna get some grub." Spiral bumps his fist again mine. "We'll see you at the Barracks tonight, yeah? You cut out early last night."

"And Blowback showed up about a half hour after you left," Picasso adds, and he's watching me close as he asks, "So are you two not hooking up anymore?"

All at once my stomach tangles up in a painful, rotted knot. Around midnight—about the time I assumed Jack wasn't going to show—I left the strip joint. But I didn't want to be alone, so I stopped at the Wolf Den and got smashed.

At the Barracks, Jack must have heard I'd been and gone. He could have tracked me down easily. He just didn't bother.

Now I'm too ripped up to answer. Anna saves me, her eyes going wide as she focuses in on Picasso. "Oooh, you want to chat about boys?" She pats the seat. "You slide right in, and we'll paint your nails and do your hair and talk about which Rider is the best kisser."

"Saxon is." Jenny sighs the prez's name like he's Prince Charming instead of a big, mean motherfucker. "His kisses are *so* dreamy."

"Yeah, well." Clearly recognizing the danger, Spiral backs away, his hands going up in surrender. "I'd like to prove my candidacy for the top spot, but the prez would kill me if I gave you a kiss to compare his with, so…" He cocks his fingers into a pair of guns and shoots me. "See you tonight, Zoomie."

"Tonight," I echo as they head off toward their own booth. I reach for my coffee, wishing it were whiskey.

Aware of Jenny and Anna trying to look everywhere but at me, I power through the ache. "For the record, I'm the club's best kisser."

Anna grins, but after a second, concern creases her expression. "So Blowback never showed up?"

God. I really don't want to talk about this. But of course I already did. I spilled my guts all over her counter last night because when I'm drunk enough, I start running my mouth.

And I know better. Jesus, running my mouth is why I'm in this situation. I was drunk and made a stupid bet—then lost that bet—which landed me in bed with the Hellfire Riders' warlord, where he tied me up and fucked my brains out. It was supposed to be one time only. But I ended up wanting more.

I got more, too. I made another bet and Jack won thirty more nights.

Today is day thirty-one, and Jack didn't spend last night with me. He stayed at the Barracks, instead, even though there were plenty of Riders to hold down the fort if the Devil's Hangmen tried crowding into our territory.

It wasn't the first time, either. If Jack missed a couple of nights, okay. No big deal. We've both got shit to do and it's not like we're married. But in the past two weeks, he skipped six nights, even though in the first half of our month together he showed up every evening—and sometimes that meant arriving at two in the morning, after he finished up work at his auto shop or handled some club business. And I didn't expect him to stay with me every night. But I thought he'd at least show up for the last one.

I thought he'd at least tell me he wanted more time.

"He just lost interest, I guess," I say with a shrug.

That casual reply doesn't fool either Anna or Jenny. They don't push, though. Instead they start chatting about some British cop series they're binge-watching on Netflix, which basically sounds like *Scully vs the Serial Killer*, and I keep telling myself not to think about Jack but it's like telling myself not to scratch an itch—I only become more desperate to dig my fingernails into my skin, even though I know I'll just make it worse. I think about the scent of his skin when he comes to me straight from his garage, the odor of oil and exhaust that you have to scrub to get off. I think of the hot taste of his mouth, the urgent thrust of his cock, the way he fucks me like he'll never get enough. I think of his arms wrapped around me when we sleep, and I can't fucking believe he didn't call or text or show up last night. I can't believe he'd let this end so damn easily.

But maybe a part of me knew he would. Because I'm hurt, but I'm not surprised. No one who's taken a roll in the sheets with me has ever stuck around. Sure, they want a fuck. That's all they want, though—and it's all I wanted from them, too. Spending two straight weeks with Jack is some kind of record for me. So I should have expected his interest would peter out before the month was up.

I wish mine had.

"Lily," Jenny says quietly, her gaze locked on someone

behind me, and for a bright, terrible moment I think it must be Jack.

The rush of pain and anticipation falls flat when I see my mom, instead. Of course. Because my crappy luck just keeps getting crappier.

She looks as fantastic as always, sleek and tanned and polished like armor. It *is* armor, built up over years of living with my dad. The former first lady of the Hellfire Riders, she's got an image to maintain, and maintain it she does. As if she can still feel my dad pinching the skin at her tiny waist and hear him saying, "Putting on a few pounds, aren't ya, Meggie?" Or maybe it's her own voice saying it now. I don't know. My mom and me, we don't talk much.

After my dad died, I thought we might start talking more. I thought things might change between us. They never did.

But she's great. Everyone says so. She volunteers for pretty much every charity in Pine Valley, gets along with all of the MC's old ladies, is funny and sweet and says all the right things. So a long time ago I started thinking of her as a prism—like a clear crystal that you can shine white light through and see the rainbow of colors that make it up. Everyone else gets to see the colors with a lovely glow. I get the *disappointed* and *bitter* end of the spectrum.

I see it now when her gaze lands on me. For a moment, her face stiffens into a smiling mask. That's not happiness curving her lips, but I'm never sure whether it's embarrassment or anger—because here I am, six feet and a hundred fifty pounds of evidence that her world isn't as perfect as she'd like everyone to think it is. She's got a girl who became a Rider instead of a Rider's old lady.

"Mom." I get up and hug her, because if I don't she'll give me a hurt look and say *What, no hug for your mama?'*—even though she doesn't really want one. But I can't deal with that manipulative shit right now.

The top of her head only comes up to my shoulder. I know she hates that. When we're this close, her giant daughter looks even more giant by comparison. She's rigid against me. Probably smelling the long night on my clothes.

Probably wishing she'd chosen another restaurant.

My poor parents. They really got a bum deal when I was born. My dad wanted a son to follow in his footsteps and got me, instead. My mother wanted a daughter to follow in her footsteps and got me, instead.

So they each got half of what they wanted…but neither is the type to ever settle for half. Just like me, when they want something, they're either all in or all out. Eventually they both decided *all out* was preferable.

Unfortunately, a kid doesn't just go away. No matter how much they'd have liked me to. On my dad's part, he just stopped giving a fuck and let my mom deal with me. That was her responsibility, after all. The woman takes care of the brat.

Of course, she didn't resent *him* for essentially making

her go it alone. Nope. He wasn't wrong; I was.

I still am. At least her resentment toward me has faded. Probably because she doesn't have to take care of me anymore—and because I finally did go away for a while, serving as a helicopter pilot in Afghanistan.

I didn't receive a single call from my parents while I was deployed. Didn't get a single letter or e-mail. At the beginning, I picked up the phone a few times, sent a few messages. After a while I just didn't bother.

I don't bother much now, either.

She awkwardly pats my arm. "It's good to see you, Lily."

Yeah, I can tell. My duty done, I slide back into my seat and grab my coffee. My mom aims a warm smile at both Jenny and Anna as she greets them. That warmth is real enough, especially toward Jenny. She likes the prez's woman. Who doesn't, right? Jenny's so freaking nice. But with my mom, there's another layer to it. Jenny is Saxon's, which makes her the Riders' first lady—a role my mom used to claim. There's no jealousy there, though. No queen whose position was usurped. Instead, Jenny's exactly what my mom wishes I would be. Smart, sweet, petite.

I'll never be sweet or petite. My mom's convinced I'm not all that smart, either. If I were smart, I'd have taken her advice five years ago when I came back from Afghanistan. My dad was dead and Saxon Gray had just been voted in as president of the Hellfire Riders. Her suggestion? Get into his bed as fast as I could. Secure my spot at his side.

I didn't. And I prefer the spot I have now—at his back, whenever he needs it.

Jenny's sandaled foot presses against my shin. She's smiling at my mom as she asks, "Will you join us, Megan?"

I stiffen and her toe pokes me harder, as if she's trying to say, *Trust me, Lily.* Or maybe just, *Shut it, Lily.*

It's probably a good thing, too, because without that poke I'd have shut that shit down. But there's no need. My mom gestures behind us. "I'd love to, but I'm meeting up with Crystal and Barb. I see you're almost finished, anyway." Her gaze lands on my empty plate—on my empty *plates*—and her eyebrows arch. "This was all yours, Lily?"

Here we go. I jab my fork into Jenny's leftover French toast and drop it onto my plate, then casually cut off a bite. "Yes."

"Just don't let it catch up to you." The lightness of her voice suggests she's teasing, but she's not. "Though I suppose softening you up a little wouldn't hurt."

Because God forbid that a woman has steel in her muscles and not just her spine, right? "What's that Daddy used to say?" I shove the triangle of syrupy toast into my mouth and act like I'm trying to remember. But I don't have to try. I remember clearly. "Oh, yeah. *'Soft has no place in the club.'*"

Oh, there's the resentment, bright and clear in her eyes. "He said *you* don't have a place in the club, either. But that's progress, I guess. Women get to pretend they're men."

I don't want to be a man. Who the fuck wants to be a man? I love being a woman. And I think progress is women getting to be who they are, not shoved into a box that someone else built.

But I just shrug and keep on chewing, because we've had this argument a million times. She's not going to change her mind now. Nothing I say will ever make her give a shit about me, and I'll never be the daughter she wants, because I refuse to crawl into that box.

Her gaze drops to my chest, and for a second I think she's going to make a crack about the *Mother of Dragons* written on my tee. Maybe something about needing a man before I can have kids, or how my tits aren't big enough to feed a baby, or that me giving birth to a dragon sounds about right. Instead she looks over to Jenny again, with that warm and lovely light back in her eyes.

"How is Red doing, Jenny? If you think he's well enough, I thought I might pay him a visit."

Jenny's voice goes tight and she nods. "He'd like that."

"Then I'll give him a call. Oh, and there's Crystal waving me over. It was lovely seeing you all."

"You, too," Jenny says, and as soon as my mom's gone she looks to me with a grimace. "Sorry."

"For what?" I push my plate away, stuffed so full I can barely swallow the last bite of French toast. "You didn't ask her to show up."

"Yeah, but…" Jenny doesn't finish, and both she and Anna are quiet and awkward for a minute. Maybe because they've both got parents who love the hell out of them. Or loved, I guess. Jenny's mom is dead. But every time Jenny or Red mentions her, it's clear they were some kind of fairytale family. And Anna's mom, Jesus. She's the high school counselor and talked me down more than a few times when I was a teenager. Anna and she still get along great, even though her mom's whole purpose is to bring out the best in people, and to help them reach goals, and Anna's been puttering around the Wolf Den for years. But it's like that doesn't matter. She loves Anna, anyway.

Yet it couldn't be more obvious that my mom would like to trade me in for a softer, nicer version—someone who doesn't fly helicopters or fix engines or wear a kutte that says I'm a patchholder instead of property.

The waitress swings by with the check and my stomach tightens. Okay, so brunch was nice. But I've got a whole day stretching ahead of me and a lot of thinking I *don't* want to do.

"What are your plans for the day?" My gaze skims the bill without really seeing it. "You working, Jenny?"

She nods. "I have to open up the storefront at noon."

"My shift starts at the same time," Anna says and glances at her watch. "That's pretty soon, actually. So I guess we're heading the same way, Lily."

Because my bike is still sitting in the Den's parking lot. Straddling a Harley is always something I can look forward to. So I'll just ride—then take this day one mile at a time.

                                    * * *

THE FIRST MILE TAKES ME back to my place, a split-level
in one of Pine Valley's older neighborhoods. I brought my
helmet when I caught a ride to Willy's with Anna, but I
don't wear my kutte while I'm in a cage. And although I
don't need much gear for a day trip, it's best to grab my
emergency kit before heading out.

A shower wouldn't hurt, either.

Just inside my front door, I strip off my slept-in
clothes and toss the bundle down into the basement. They
land at the bottom of the stairs, where I figure they can
wait until I get around to doing laundry. It's a habit that
I'm pretty sure drives Jack crazy, but he hasn't said—

No. Not going to think of him.

Jesus, but it's difficult. Only three days ago, I got
home from the airfield to find him waiting for me in the
driveway, just like he waited the first night of our bet.
Easily straddling his bike, boots solidly planted, his dark
gaze like the edge of a blade. Less than two minutes later
he had me sprawled on these stairs, his strong hands gripping my hips and his thick cock slamming deep. God, he
fucked me hard. So hard, with pleasure splintering through
my senses with every rough stroke, the inner muscles of
my cunt clutching his iron length until my entire body
was shaking with the need to come. As soon as I did, he
carried me up to the bed and devoured my pussy until I
shattered against his tongue.

Each night he came over it was like that. Crashing together, our hands and mouths all over each other. Fucking again and again. When we were spent, we'd grab something to eat, or take a ride, or kill a few hours at the Barracks or in the clubhouse garage. Then we'd ride home and fuck all over again before falling asleep in my bed.

Now there's nowhere in this house I can escape him. And it was only a month.

Except it didn't take a month for Jack's presence to be imprinted on every room he was in. It took one night. One night, and I was seeing him at my table, his dark hair tousled by my fingers. I was seeing him in my bed, his features as hard as sculpted stone even in sleep. But even when I close my eyes to shut him out, he's here. I slide beneath the shower spray and feel him against me, his muscles like steel, his bronzed skin slick with soap.

I never thought it would end this way. The way we go at each other, I expected an explosion, a fight. Not this slow, quiet end.

I hoped it wouldn't end at all. When I made the thirty-day bet, I thought he just needed time. Everyone has issues, but Jack could medal in the Shitty Childhood Olympics. Beaten and raped by his dad until he was fourteen, the abuse stopped only because he killed his father after the fucker moved on to his younger brother. But his brother never forgave Jack. Neither did his mom. He'd protected them; they'd rejected him. A few years down the line he tried to join the armed forces, failed the psych evals, and was recruited for covert ops, instead—because he was good at working solo, he could kill without blinking an eye, and he never expected anyone to have his back.

So is he fucked up? Beyond a doubt. And I knew it when I made that second bet. He's got demons riding his back and he's no good at asking for what he wants. Instead he waits for an opportunity and takes it.

These thirty nights left me wide open for the taking. Hell, he could have moved in and I'd have let him. But although I can feel him here, see him here…he's not here. Not just physically absent—he's left nothing of himself behind. When I brush my teeth, there's no toothbrush next to mine. When I put on my clothes, I don't find any of his stray socks in my laundry. Not a trace of him remains. Like he was never here.

Like he never meant to stay.

I've got a choice now. I can try again. I can make another bet. I can make it so easy for him.

But I don't really see the point. This is the story of my life. I have to fight tooth and claw for everything I want. But no one I've been with has wanted me for more than a fuck. They sure as hell never wanted me enough to fight for me.

Jack let me go so easily. Do I really think thirty more nights will make a difference? Because I believed they would last time. I thought for sure he cared enough to hold on. I risked my heart on that belief.

I risked my heart and I lost.

My chest feels like someone is drilling a hole past my ribs as I pull on my boots, then sit on the stairs and stare at my phone. Last night, I wrote and erased a million messages to him. My throat is a solid ache as I write one more.

Our bet was for a month. That ended last night. So I guess we're done?

My thumb hovers over 'send.' That question mark. Why am I *asking* him whether we're done? Jesus. By not showing up last night, he already said we are.

That question mark just drags this out.

Before I can think it over, I replace the mark with a period, then hit 'send.' And I wait. I don't even know what I'm waiting for.

Yes, I do. I'm hoping for a response. I'm hoping Jack says he lost track of the days—that he intended to ask for more. No reply comes. That doesn't mean he won't answer. If he's on the road, he probably won't check his phone right away. If he's at the clubhouse, the message won't hit his phone until he leaves the property. Reception is shit out at the ranch.

I know all that. Yet every passing minute drills a deeper hole into my chest and it hurts so fucking bad. Only two things might numb it: a bottle of whiskey, or the wind in my face.

I already drank all my whiskey. So I head for my bike and ride.

TWO

JACK

"The way I see it, we've got three options," the prez says. "We let Valentine be, we remind him it's best to keep his mouth shut, or we put a bullet in his head."

As the Riders' warlord, I'd carry out two of those options, using my fists or my gun. They probably won't be needed. I can see the prez is leaning toward the first option. But he's leaving the question open for discussion.

It'll be a short discussion. A meeting like this doesn't include most of the brothers. There's just the VP, the enforcer, and me in the prez's office today—the two men who'll decide Valentine's fate, and the two men who'll make the boss's orders happen.

Thorne knows Valentine best. One of the old-timers, he's got steel in his hair and a leather kutte worn thin over the years. He was the VP for the Steel Titans before the Riders folded that club into our own. Valentine came with them.

"He never could keep his mouth shut," Thorne says now. "He'll flap his gums to any Hangman who'll listen."

"And it'll all be hot air," Stone Wall adds from his seat next to Thorne's. "That boy likes to exaggerate the size of his dick. Anything he says will only be about making us look like shit so that he looks better."

"Do we care if he's talking shit?" the prez asks.

Stone shakes his head. As enforcer, his role isn't much different from mine. We both only answer to the prez. Stone makes sure that people outside the club do whatever we've asked them to do. If someone sees Stone coming, they've got one chance to fall in line. If someone sees me coming, it's already too late. I take care of the shit that goes unasked, making certain everything runs smoothly—and if it doesn't, I clean up the mess.

Valentine is a mess, but only a small one. He had it in for Lily. She took him down. So he turned in his colors, throwing shit at us all on his way out, but making sure most of the disrespect landed on her. I can still her face as she silently absorbed every insult, her spine rigid and rage flushing her skin.

Killing isn't something I like or dislike; it's just something I do. But I'd enjoy putting a bullet between his baby blues.

"Talking shit does us a favor," Stone says. "If he makes us sound weak, they'll underestimate our strength. That'll give us the early advantage."

"He'll just puff himself up," Thorne agrees. "I can't see that anything he'll say is a threat to us. He'll talk about the brothers, their ranks, but it's not anything the Hangmen couldn't have learned from anyone with eyes."

From behind his desk, the prez turns his gaze on me, waiting. I make sure things run smoothly. That means I do the risk assessment.

That means my word weighs more heavily than any other.

"He doesn't know anything worth telling," I say. "He wasn't on-site when we took down the Eighty-Eight. Maybe he'll tell them the Riders took out Reichmann and his crew, but they'll figure it's more of his bullshit because he won't have any details to share. The feds believe a cartel was behind it. The Eighty-Eight's mother chapter is convinced the DEA burned them down. No one's thinking we did."

"Will they start looking at us if he says so?"

"He'll only bring pain on himself if he does. Not from us." The Riders would shut him up if it came to that. But we wouldn't get the chance. "Because that would mean he was with us when we took out the Eighty-Eight, and their California chapters still have strong business ties to the Hangmen. The Hangmen would hand Valentine over so that they can find out more. Then they might start looking at us. But he'd be dead before they do."

And I'd head out to clean up a much bigger mess—first by spilling a river of blood, then by mopping it up. Our assault on the Eighty-Eight's compound will never come back on the Riders, not as long as I'm alive.

The prez's eyes narrow. "So maybe that's all the reminder he needs. If he opens his mouth about the Eighty-Eight, it won't be us stringing him up. It'll be his new friends."

"I'll see that he gets the message." And when the prez keeps eyeing me, I tell him, "I'll deliver it gently."

He smiles a bit before looking to the others. No arguments from them.

So the decision's been made. Business done, Stone gives a heavy sigh like he's disappointed. "I guess it's best. It might start some shit if we whack their new boy."

"Shit's going to start anyway," I say.

Thorne nods his agreement before looking to the prez. "Why hasn't it yet? We've been expecting it for the past month."

"They haven't been as successful recruiting local muscle as they were in other chapters." The prez moved quickly when the Hangmen came into the region, reaching out to other MCs and offering our support and protection.

He nods to me. "Blowback figures they've also had their hands full taking over the Eighty-Eight's operations."

"But now they've had time to get a handle on it," I add. Running meth, girls, and anything else their business partners tell them to run. "So they'll be making their move soon."

Stone shakes his head. "You think Valentine has any idea how lucky he is?"

"No," the prez says.

Because the little shit didn't just insult Lily on his way out, though that would have been enough to earn Valentine a lesson in respect. He all but pissed on the Riders' colors. If the Hangmen hadn't rolled into the Eighty-Eight's place at the same time Val walked, he'd have been schooled several times over by now. But although the prez would probably like to pound his fist through Valentine's face himself, he's not important enough to warrant the effort.

The meeting's over, but I stay put as Thorne and Stone head out of the office. There's business that even the VP and enforcer haven't been looped into.

The prez rocks back in his chair. "You hear anything from Creek?"

One of the Devil's Hangmen, and an undercover FBI agent. A man without family ties or friends, he wouldn't have expected to be recognized—or to run into me, an operative he served with years ago. But I'm not interested in exposing him. He's here to discover who's providing the

Devil's Hangmen with their merchandise, to map their supply line, and eventually take the network out. As long as he doesn't touch the Riders, I'm willing to exchange info with him.

"Nothing worth repeating," I tell the prez now. Aside from Lily, he's the only Rider aware of Creek's background.

He nods, but by the way his expression tightens I see he's already thinking about something that doesn't have anything to do with Creek. "The Hangmen will be looking to make us fall in line. Do I need to worry about Jenny?"

His woman. Hurting her wouldn't make him fall in line. It'd destroy him—but not before he flayed every Hangman to the bone.

"Their prez won't come after you. Not through her. Croc is looking to cut your legs out from under you so he can step on you later. That means taking your strength." The Riders' officers and the strongest patchholders. "But put Hashtag and Scarecrow on Jenny, anyway."

All at once he's rigid. "Why?"

"Because you'll worry anyway when this shit starts going down, and you'll worry less if you know they're looking over her."

He eases back a bit. "I'd tell you to fuck off, but you're right."

That doesn't warrant a response. It's my job to know what the prez needs. He needs Jenny. So I'll do whatever necessary to make sure he always has her.

Now he pushes up out of his seat, goes to the window

overlooking the pines behind the clubhouse. "First the Eighty-Eight. Now the Hangmen. I bet that nomad's life started looking good again these past few months."

Because of the shit that's been coming our way? Escaping trouble was never why I considered taking a nomad's patch all those years ago—still wearing the Riders' colors, but roaming rather than living in one place. No, I considered leaving Pine Valley because the club was the only reason I had to stay. I'll be a Rider until I die but it's not enough. A man's got to belong somewhere and I didn't feel I belonged here.

But over the course of a few months, it all changed. The owner of the garage where I was working offered to sell it to me. Shortly after that, Lucifer died, Saxon was voted in as the Riders' prez, and he appointed me as his VP.

Then Lily Burns came home from Afghanistan and fought her way into the club. Fucking Lily Burns, with engine oil beneath her fingernails and steel behind her gray eyes. With her husky laugh and her endless legs. With the fire inside her that keeps blazing no matter how many motherfuckers have tried stamping it out.

I had plenty of reasons to stay after that. Taking care of this shit is just the price of belonging, so it's one I'll gladly pay.

Besides, I don't mind trouble. It gives me more to do. "Croc will come after the others. Probably not the old-timers, but he might try to pull them in because it'll be a kick in the balls to see them wearing the Hangmen colors. If he does, he'll target their kids, their old ladies. But I expect he'll threaten the younger brothers first, especially anyone with standing in the club. The only one he won't touch is Lily. Croc's not going to recruit a woman."

The prez's eyebrows shoot together. "Will Croc come after you?"

"Maybe." Or try again to have me killed. He would if he knew I snapped his enforcer's neck.

"Then he might go after Zoomie," the prez says, then narrows his eyes when I frown at him. "You said they target old ladies."

"Lily doesn't belong to me." She'll never belong to anyone—a fact that I'm all too fucking aware of. She's invited me to share her bed for a short time. That doesn't make her mine.

"You think that matters? They look at you, at her, and they'll have a way to come at you. You don't see that?"

No. I only see Lily.

But fuck if he isn't probably right. Weighing risks means calculating them. I take most threats at face value and don't always add in the shithead factor. When assholes like Croc see Lily, they only see pussy—and that pussy belongs to anyone who's sticking their dick into it. What she really is doesn't matter.

All at once my chest is tight as hell. All this time, I figured she was safe. "I'll look after her."

The prez snorts out a laugh. "You think you need to?"

I won't be able to stop myself. But I keep my mouth

shut on that point.

He reads me, anyway. He's wearing a grin as he stands. "You're fucked, my brother."

I know it. But I was long before this.

I SHOULDN'T HAVE MADE LILY follow through on that first bet. Shouldn't have tied her up and fucked her. It was another situation I took at face value: She would never screw another Rider. She would never back out of a bet. And she hated me. That all added up to my one chance to have her—and when she hated me afterward, nothing would change.

But I didn't include the Lily factor. She fights until the end. It doesn't matter if she's been kicked to the ground. She'll just get on her feet and try again.

And all these years, she didn't hate me. Instead I learned every time I defended her, she thought I was cutting her down. For five years, I hurt her. What I thought was hate was just Lily fighting back.

So I got what I wanted. I won the bet. I tied her up, tasted every inch of her, and pumped her full of my cock.

Then I had to let her go. Riding away in the morning was like ripping a knife through my own gut. Knowing how bad I'd fucked up. Knowing that if I'd just asked, she'd have taken me into her bed without any goddamn bet between us. Knowing she'd never give me another chance.

All that won't compare to what's coming. I figure the only reason she made the second bet was because of what she was crying against my mouth as her pussy clenched around my cock the first night. *I love the way you fuck.*

As if there's any other way to fuck a woman like Lily—as if every time was the first, the last. The only.

Soon it *will* be the last. I burned through the time so quick the first two weeks. Every night, having her. Under me, over me. Every way I could get her. I just couldn't fucking stay away—until I realized how few days I had remaining. Until I realized how I wasn't giving her any room to breathe. Treating her like she was mine, though nothing could push her away faster.

Now I only have six nights left. Just six. And when I'm down to one…I'm fucked. Riding away the first night was hard. This time it'll kill me.

So I won't be going. That'll be when the real fight between Lily and me begins.

Until then, I've been hoarding the remaining nights like a miser counting out each penny in his pocket. Tonight's another penny to spend, and if I do, only five will be left. But it's early afternoon. Lily's got today off. If she's home, I can make this one night stretch to include part of the day. I'll taste her again. Her hot mouth, her smooth skin, and the sweet juicy heaven between her thighs. And when she's wet enough, after she comes against my tongue, I'll bury my cock deep inside her tight cunt and stay as long as I can.

My dick's hard by the time I reach the end of the club-house driveway. I pause at the stop and check my phone.

A message from Lily. Anticipation is hot and hard. Then each word of her message hits me like a bullet, filling my gut with lead.

Our bet was for a month. That ended last night. So I guess we're done.

Done.

I read the word a dozen times before backing up to *a month*. That wasn't the bet. She gave me thirty nights. I've been counting every single one. Apparently she's been counting differently.

And I wondered if she'd want more time when our bet was over. Now I have my answer.

We're done.

Slowly I put my phone away. My cock's so fucking stiff that the tug of denim as I push the device into my pocket kicks off a throbbing ache. I'm hotter and harder now than before I got her message. She thinks this is over? Fuck no. This fight's just begun. And my gloves are coming off.

Because I'm *never* going to be done.

THREE

LILY

It's full dark when I get back to town. I blow straight through, heading for the county line. Pretty much everywhere in this part of the state can be called 'the middle of nowhere,' but the Barracks sits out on the edge of nowhere. That's the way everyone who visits the strip joint likes it. Fewer eyes prying. Fewer deputies driving by.

Jack's black workhorse is already sitting in the parking lot. Fuck. My gut tightens up again. I haven't checked my messages in the past hundred miles, but as of ten o'clock, he hadn't replied.

I find an open spot at the far end of the lot. Buckcherry's *Crazy Bitch* spills through the Barrack's open front doors. The lighting outside is crap and the bright glare of my phone's screen blinds me for a second. A message from Anna—a picture of glitter in a toilet. Still no reply from Jack. Maybe I should have expected it. After our first night, I didn't hear anything from him either. He just froze me out.

I don't know if I can bear looking into his eyes and seeing nothing again.

But it's not like I have a choice. I pocket my phone and start for the door. With every step, I lock all the hurt down. The only response Jack fucking Hayden is going to get from me is *"I don't give a shit."*

A solid shadow peels away from the side of the building. "Lily."

My heart slams into my ribs. Jack. Tall and gorgeous and waiting for me. And I do give a shit, because I sure as hell don't deserve to be treated like it. No matter how monstrous his dad was. No matter how screwed up he is.

"Fuck off," I say and keep on walking, but his reply stops me in my tracks.

"I've got six nights left."

Gravel grinds beneath my boots as I round on him. "How do you figure that? Because I've got a hotel receipt where we spent night number one and it has the date right on it. Our bet began one month ago, plus one day.

So it's over."

Jack moves in closer. The back of my neck tenses but I don't give an inch. Jesus, he's big. It's one of those facts my mind accepts without even thinking about it, like 'water is wet'—Jack Hayden is built like a tank—but every once in a while the full meaning of it comes home. Usually when he's carrying me to bed and I actually feel small against him. Or when his body is braced over mine, fucking me, all those thick muscles flexing as he grinds deep, and he's all I see.

He's all I see now. At my height, there's not many men I have to look up to, but he's one. In the dark, his face is all shadows and angles, but I've memorized every feature. The roughly hewn planes, the high-set cheekbones, his wide and firm mouth. The slashing eyebrows over eyes that see right through you, brown irises so deep they're almost black.

"It's not over." Voice rough, he crowds in. "You didn't say a month. You said thirty nights."

Disbelieving, I stare at him. I *did* say thirty nights. But who the hell takes a statement like that so literally?

Jack fucking Hayden, that's who. I should have expected it. He always takes people exactly at their word. But that still doesn't explain why the hell he was missing so many nights. "Were you saving the days up?"

His dark gaze drops to my lips. "Yes."

Instead of just asking for more? So maybe he still can't. Maybe he's still got all that fucked-up shit in his head holding him back.

The warmth of that thought cools when I remember how there's no toothbrush. No trace of his presence at my place at all. No sign that this has ever been anything other than a hookup for him.

"So was that the plan?" Each word is as strained as my throat. "You scratched an itch hard the first two weeks. But now, hey—you've been well scratched. So you can just bank the days and wait until you're horny again, because you know I won't back out of our bet. I'll be available whenever you want. The easiest hookup anyone ever had, outside of a morgue."

"A morgue, Lily?" The corners of his wide mouth flick up in a smile. "Even I'm not that fucked up."

Oh, shit. I don't mean to laugh. But it huffs out of me on a sharp breath, and he's so damn quick. His big hands capture my face, his long fingers slipping into my hair. He catches my parted lips with his, and holds me still as he tastes, as he takes.

God, the way he kisses. It's like the way he fucks. Not just with his mouth or his cock but as if he's putting every-thing behind it. I don't have a defense against that. I don't have a defense against *him*. A single touch is like running a live wire through my system. So when he licks into my mouth, sucks on my tongue, the shock of pleasure lights up every nerve. My nipples harden to aching points, my inner muscles clenching.

My breath shudders over lips moistened by our kiss

when he eases back, his dark eyes locked on mine, his hands still holding me tight. The deep gravel of his voice shivers over my sensitized skin.

"I want the rest of the time due to me, Lily."

Sharp pain pierces my chest. Not *more* time. Just the rest of it.

Six more nights.

But I can do that. No big deal, right? I'm the queen of hooking up. This won't be any different.

On a deep breath, I nod. "Whatever. I said thirty nights, so you'll get thirty nights."

Jack's fingers tighten, as if my breezy response wasn't agreement. "Good."

"But no fucking around this time. Six *consecutive* nights. Not just whenever you feel like getting some pussy. Each night counts whether you show or not."

"I'll show." The iron in his tone leaves no room for doubt. "Starting tonight."

Tonight. God, I want that. But I want it too much, and after getting so little sleep last night and riding all day, I'm too damn tired to deal with all this emotional shit. I've got to lock it down first.

"Starting tomorrow," I tell him. "It shouldn't be too hard for you to wait. You weren't interested last night, or the past few nights, so one more day won't make much of a difference."

His eyes narrow. "Not interested?"

He's just echoing my words, but it sounds like a threat.

Like he's about to prove something to me.

But his thumb only glides over my bottom lip as he softly says, "I'll always be interested."

Oh, that's a laugh. My entire life proves what a joke it is. I scoff and finally pull away. I've sparred with him enough times to know I'm only able to go because he lets me go.

His deep voice follows me to the Barracks' entrance. "I'm not done, Lily."

Not yet. But he will be. And a month ago, I risked everything by believing otherwise.

I won't take that risk again.

JACK

THE STRIP JOINT SMELLS LIKE piss and sweat and beer. A disco ball and laser lights flash color across the stage. Some of the brothers are watching the dancers but most don't give a shit about seeing yet another pair of tits. Most of the club pussy will shake theirs for free, and the working girls aren't the only ones warming the brothers' laps. They're just the ones who don't have a cock in them when they do.

Lily heads straight for the bar, her anger like a steel rod across her shoulders. She's got two modes when she's out with the brothers. Either she's having a good time or she's pissed. Usually she's having a good time. But if she's pissed, there's not anyone who doesn't know it.

What they don't know—and what took me too fucking long to figure out—is that her anger is a cover. Not always, but sometimes. It's how she protects herself. Never showing vulnerability. Never showing weakness. Never giving anyone reason to say she should be an old lady instead of a patchholder.

It's why she never fucked any Rider before the night of our first bet. It's why she never even flirted with or teased one. It's why she didn't invite any local men into her bed. She'd have too much shit thrown at her.

It's why I believed I'd never have one night with her, let alone thirty. Why I waited two years to win the bet that allowed me in.

I didn't see that her mind was changing, or that she started believing her place in the club was solid enough she could finally fuck anyone she wanted. Instead I saw that her place should have been solid enough from the day she patched in. I saw that she's stronger, quicker, meaner than some of the brothers. More loyal, too.

I never saw the hurt.

In the past month, I've gotten better at looking. Although I'm seeing anger now, it's not sitting right. She was pissed from the moment she saw me outside. She *arrived* pissed. But Lily doesn't hang on to her temper very long. She hangs on to her hurt.

And she believes I'm not interested in fucking her anymore.

Not interested. In fucking Lily Burns.

She's either making shit up or she brained herself while riding today, because I've never heard her say anything so goddamn stupid.

But she's not stupid. So if she's not just throwing shit out and hoping it'll stick, then she truly believes I don't want her.

One thing for damn sure—she's never going to make that mistake again. By the time these six nights are over, she'll know exactly how much I want her. She'll know I never intend to let her go.

She's standing between two stools, waiting for the bartender when I come up on her left side. The glance she spares me is dark and gray, like polished flint. Her light blond hair hangs down her back in a thick braid that I love to wrap around my fist when I'm pulling her close. Her helmet matted and flattened the rest. Road dust outlines the shape of the sunglasses she wore earlier in the day, leaving paler circles around her eyes. Her full lips are windburned, and thin into a tight line when she glances at me again and sees that I'm still looking.

Of course I'm still looking. She's fucking stunning.

She turns away again when the bartender slides two bottles across the counter.

"Water and a Bud for the lady."

"Thanks, Pete."

The old man looks to me. "What'll it be?"

"Whatever you have within reach." I watch Lily screw

off the bottle cap and chug the water. She's still chugging when Pete digs his fingers into a nearby bowl and flips a lemon wedge in my direction before leaving us alone again. "Long ride?"

Still drinking, she raises her middle finger to my face.

The message is clear, but I wait anyway. I like to hear her say it.

But she goes one better than a *Fuck off*. Wiping her mouth, she tells me, "You don't get to say a fucking word to me until tomorrow night."

"All right." I lean in so close I can smell the dust in her hair. She doesn't back away. She never backs away. "But tomorrow I'll say that I don't know what I love more—sucking on your nipples or your juicy clit—but I love the way you squirm and moan when I do. I'll say that I love the way your tits look when they're dripping with my cum. I'll say that I love how your cunt clenches around my cock, and how you beg me to fuck you deep and hard. I'll say how much I love eating your pussy after you've come with me inside you, when you're so soft and warm and wet. And I'll tell you that I'll never lose interest in any of it."

I have her until the end—breath caught, lips parted, eyes locked on mine, and something like hope sparking through the flint gray. Then her gaze shutters and she shakes her head.

"Back the fuck off, Jack," she says.

For now, I will. But I don't even move a step before a drunken bray of laughter comes from her right.

"Oh, *shit.* You in the doghouse, Blowback?" Burnout half stands, half slumps against the bar, his eyes running over Lily's rigid posture, sizing up the tension between us. "What'd'ya do? Leave the toilet seat up? The ladies are so pissy about that kind of thing."

Her jaw locks. This is exactly the shit she was trying to avoid when she wasn't fucking anyone local. We're all Riders, but when she's taking dick they treat her as something different, as if that difference matters more than the colors she's wearing. Sometimes she gives back twice as hard. This time she's biting her tongue.

It used to be, I'd tell him to shut his fucking mouth. And that's how I gutted her for five years—by shielding her instead of having her back. By making her work harder to prove herself, to prove she didn't need a man defending her. So this past month I've kept my mouth closed when the shit is thrown, watching how she handles herself. Figuring out where I went wrong.

And where I went wrong was thinking it was about her. It's not. It's about the assholes shitting on her. Burnout thinks he's real funny. The truth is, he's got a rock for a brain.

But the brother's not so stupid that he doesn't recognize the danger when I zero in on him. Though he looped me into his joke, he's usually too uneasy to say more than a few words in my direction.

There's good reason a lot of the brothers are uneasy around me. I lean in, try to look friendly. Lily told me once that I only have two expressions: *I don't give a shit* and *Don't fuck with me.* Judging by the way Burnout pulls back, my friendly face looks just like the *Don't fuck with me* one.

His eyes dart back and forth, as if he's looking for an escape, but as soon as I start talking his gaze snaps back to mine, as if watching to make sure I don't come closer. "The first time the boss sent me out on business, it meant getting past two fuckers guarding the house where they'd stashed the shit they'd stolen from us. If they make a noise, wake up the rest of their crew, I'm fucked, so I pull a knife from my boot and hit the first one in the throat. When the other fucker looks to see why his buddy's choking, I rip out his tongue before stuffing it back in his mouth."

Burnout's not laughing anymore. And although I don't move, he draws back a little more, his lips flapping shut and sucking in over his teeth, like an old man testing the seat of his dentures.

I can't smell his fear over the booze, but I know it's there, as sour and yellow as the lemon on the bar. "I do all that without breaking a fucking sweat, then stop for a steak on my way home and eat it bloody. Yet when shit's going down between Zoomie and me, you assume that *she's* the one with the problem?"

"No, man." Face pasty, he swallows hard. "I'm thinking you're probably the one who fucked something up."

"That'd be good thinking." I raise my fist. He flinches before quickly tapping my knuckles with his.

I glance at Lily. She's staring at me. There's not a hint

of unease on her face. No anger now, either. Just a slight frown, like she isn't sure what to make of what I just laid on Burnout.

She'll work it out. I tip my head toward the tables. "You sitting with Gunner and Stone?"

A short nod, then she grabs her beer and heads in that direction. I scoop up my lemon before following. She takes a swig from her bottle and gives me a sidelong glance.

"Was any of that true?"

Only some. "Who rips out a tongue when snapping a neck will do the job?"

The sight of her grin is like a firm hand around my dick. Needing her, needing to do something with my mouth other than telling her again how much I love her pussy, I sink my teeth into the lemon wedge and suck out the juice. She gives me another sideways look, this one bemused. "Did you give up drinking?"

I can't imagine that day coming. "I asked for something within reach. If he'd used his left hand I'd have gotten his shotgun."

She grins again. "Pete just doesn't give a shit."

And doesn't take any. "No."

"He'll probably charge you five bucks for that lemon."

"Then it's fortunate that I don't give a shit, either."

"And that's what I like—" She abruptly stops, smile fading, her gaze shooting away from my face.

Because that's what she likes about me. A few days ago she'd have finished that sentence.

Not angry now. But she's still hurting. Or just wondering when I'll hurt her again, so she's not lowering her defenses.

Tomorrow I'll start tearing them down. But right now the headlights I'm seeing through the Barracks' open front doors tell me I've got business coming in. Maybe for the best. Knowing she's hurt, knowing she's wary, my chest is tight as hell and ripping out a few tongues sounds pretty fucking good.

Lily's step slows as she spots the bikes outside. Her gaze flattens and her arms tense. Instantly ready for a fight, and never afraid to throw down.

Just one more reason I'll never lose interest.

"Go to the boss," I tell her and she nods. "Tell him there's six Hangmen, including Croc and his veep. Creek's with them. So is Valentine. Tumble's their new enforcer. He'll likely stay at the door with Hunter."

Who's just muscle, not a ranking brother. I don't expect them to flex the muscle. This'll just be the message.

But I've got one of my own to deliver.

LILY

THE MUSIC GOES QUIET JUST as I finish relaying the heads-up to the prez. The strippers stop gyrating and look to the grubby little DJ booth, probably assuming the crappy sound system finally gave out. But they know the score, so when they see Hashtag there, it's clear the prospect has been told to cut the noise, and the dancers head through the curtain at the back of the stage. The brothers go quiet, too, but they take their cue from the prez and their asses stay in their seats. At the bar, Pete stands within reach of his shotgun and braces his big hands on the counter. He scowls out over us all, but it's just more of his growly bullshit. The Riders can be rowdy, but we treat the girls and the place with respect. If shit gets broken, we'll pay for it. Pete knows he won't get that from every MC. He practically kissed the prez when the Riders ran the Eighty-Eight out of this place.

I'm already standing by Saxon as the Hangmen come in, so I just straighten away from his ear and step to the side.

Croc walks ahead of the other Hangmen. Mid-forties, tough and weathered, he's a stone cold bastard. Jack never says much about the work he does for the club but when the Hangmen rolled into the area, he took a trip down to Vegas to look at their mother chapter. To see what sort of MC they came from.

And he found that the Hangmen call each other brothers, but it's all business, not family. You do your job and prove yourself useful, or you find yourself with a bullet in your skull.

I prefer the kind of ship that Saxon's running. Our prez is a mean motherfucker, but if one of the brothers falls, he'll see that the club helps pick him up.

Right now, the prez is just sitting easy, watching Croc come. Not even bothering to size the other man up, the way Croc is looking at him. Maybe Croc has heard that the last time Saxon met another MC's prez at the Barracks, the other man limped away missing three of his fingers.

There's always a party going down at this strip joint.

And Jack's missing it. A quick scan of the floor tells me he's taken off. Maybe heading outside to make sure there aren't another two dozen Hangmen waiting down the road a bit.

As Jack predicted, Tumble and Hunter take the door, blocking the exit. A classic intimidation tactic. Stone taught it to me when we shook down a meth dealer last summer. You put either your biggest men or your most heavily armed men by the exit. The people inside feel like they can't get out, can't expect help—so they feel trapped, controlled. Then it doesn't matter how many men you send in, because by controlling the door, you give the impression of controlling the whole room.

It's all a mental thing. But all this shit is mental right now. As Valentine passes Gunner's table, the sergeant at arms calls out, "Hey, Valentine! You back to get your ass kicked by Zoomie again?"

Usually I hate the "you must be a wimp if a *girl* kicked your ass" crap but it's damn effective against dickholes like Valentine. Though he looked cocky as hell walking in, now the little shit's face reddens. He turns to the side and throws his arms wide, as if inviting Gunner to take him on, but before he can open his mouth Creek claps him on the shoulder and keeps him moving forward.

Croc and his veep seem to ignore the drama behind them. The veep is young, probably too young for the position, but Jack says his dad's got big connections in Vegas. He's a petulant fuck who goes by Sherlock. That just makes me hate him more. I'm pretty sure the only time the Hangmen's veep pulled out a magnifying glass was to fry bugs with it, and that he probably couldn't detect shit at the end of his nose.

Another dickhole. I bet he and Valentine have become good friends.

Croc glances at me standing by the prez's side. Saxon's got a little smile that says, *This is all real fucking amusing,* so I'm wearing the same smile. I let my gaze slide from Croc's head to the toes of his boots.

I've only seen him on his bike. Turns out, I'm just a bit taller. He's heavy with muscle and outweighs me by half my body weight, but he notices the height difference at the same time.

Widening my smile, I give him a saucy wink.

Jaw clenching, Croc glances away from me and looks pointedly to the other chairs at Saxon's table. Obviously waiting for the prez to order the Riders sitting around the table to clear out, so that he can sit. Not gonna happen. The old-timers are sitting at Saxon's table tonight. The prez would offer his own seat before asking them to give up theirs—especially to some asshole who is showing him disrespect by coming to the Barracks without an invite.

But assholes like Croc don't see it as disrespecting our club. Instead they figure we're so far below them that they're the ones being disrespected when we don't immediately bend over and spread our cheeks.

And Croc's pissed. But it's cold, so the anger only shows in the tightness of his jaw, the gleam in his eyes.

Saxon enjoys every second. He lets the silence drag out, takes a drink like he's got nothing better to do. Finally he sets down his beer and glances over at me. "You hear a word out of him yet, Zoomie?"

"No, boss," I say. "I guess he's just here to waste your time."

"Do I have time to waste?"

"Not tonight, boss. You're real busy watching the dancers shake their tits."

"That's right." His steady gaze is on Croc's face, but he's not smiling with amusement now. Instead he's wearing the look that gave him his name. The Wolf. "So he'd best stop waiting for an invitation and tell me what the fuck he wants."

If Croc's raging inside, he's got the anger under control. Instead he appears as easy as Saxon did before. Either damn confident or just good at pretending he is.

His voice is deep, with a smoker's rasp. "Valentine here tells us this property used to be the Eighty-Eight's."

The prez nods. "Used to."

"And what was once the Eighty-Eight's is ours now.

So you see where I'm going."

"I see. And now I ought to see your asses heading back out the door, because your boy Valentine got it wrong. This here's the county line." Saxon draws his finger across the table. "This side's all the Eighty-Eight's territory—yours now. And on this side is the Riders' territory, with the Barracks right here. So it's real simple. You stay on your side. We'll stay on ours."

"Real simple," Croc says, but it isn't agreement. "We can make sure it stays that way."

The prez takes another drink, studying him over the length of the bottle. "Since you're here now, I guess you're not real good at staying on your side."

"No."

"So what do you propose?"

There's genuine curiosity in Saxon's voice. I know he doesn't have any intention of giving up the Barracks. Just wondering how Croc will move forward.

Croc doesn't pussyfoot. "We'll give the Riders a week to clear out."

The prez's eyebrows shoot up. "You call that a proposal?"

"It's one you should take." The other man's gaze hardens. "We're proposing to keep relations amiable. Neither one of us wants to lose any men."

Because Croc wants the Riders' members to bolster his ranks. But I'm guessing he'll sacrifice some on both sides if necessary.

The prez knows it, too. There's steel in his voice as

he says, "I think you'd best turn tail out the door before I forget to be amiable now. You've fucked up, coming here."

"I don't think so." When Croc smiles, it's easy to imagine how he got his name. There's no humor. It's just a steel trap. "Next week, you'll be offering me a seat. Then you'll be offering to suck my dick."

Holy fuck. The way every Rider just pulled in a breath I don't know how there isn't a windstorm raging through the joint. But although half of the brothers are out of their seats, although my own fists are clenched and I'm ready to take the fucker out, Saxon just grins and holds up his hand.

"Just let him walk out," he says. "We can be amiable, too."

No one wants to. But they sit, and when Croc turns to go, I want to smash the smugness off his face. Like he's thinking that Saxon just backed down.

But the prez didn't. Did he? He wouldn't.

So why the fuck is he letting Croc walk away?

I realize exactly what's happened at the same time Croc's smooth stride hitches through a single step.

The two Hangmen at the doors are gone. Not waiting outside. Not knocked out on the floor. Just fucking gone.

And Saxon's making their prez walk through those doors, knowing Croc can't say shit. Knowing there's nothing he can do that won't make him look weak. Two men gone and he can't ask what the hell we did to them, because whatever happened, it happened right under his nose, and he didn't see or hear a damn thing. None of his men saw or heard a damn thing.

Jesus Christ. How could they? I was *facing* that direction and didn't notice a damn thing, either.

But now I know where Jack went.

FOUR

JACK

Killing's easy. It's what comes after that's a pain in the ass—making sure the kill doesn't come back on you. Years ago, before I was ever sent on a single mission, that lesson was drilled into me. *Clean up after yourself. If the kill comes back on you, it'll come back on the country. Protect the flag. Protect the president. Don't leave any trace.*

What I do for the Riders is the same. The colors just aren't red, white, and blue anymore.

I roll by Lily's place when I drive back into town. The

sky's already pink. She'll be getting up and heading out for a run soon. Five miles on a Sunday, plus at least an hour of sparring in the gym this afternoon. I've joined her on a few of those runs in the past few weeks, and for the past few years, I've scheduled my workouts to match hers. I'd wait for her to wake up now, run alongside her, but I'm on fumes and covered in the dirt of a night's work. I have to wash away the trace first, so it can't come back on her. My dick can wait until tonight.

Except my cock's not on fumes. Just the thought of sliding into the silky heat between her thighs leaves me aching and stiff on the drive home. In the shower, I don't even soap away all the trace before fisting my dick. Just a few hard strokes, remembering Lily's taste, remembering her full lips wrapped around my shaft, and I fucking blow, milky strands of cum mixing with the dirt swirling down the drain.

I chase it with a gallon of bleach and hit the sheets.

I've only been up about ten minutes when I hear a handful of bikes in the lot below. Most of the Riders run Harleys, and if they don't have the bike then they've got the engine. None of them straddle the new Thunder Stroke V-Twin, which is what I'm hearing now.

But I've heard it before.

Croc. Val's with him. So is Creek.

Creek's a potential threat. Val's an annoying shit. Croc's just interesting. Last month he sent his enforcer to put a bullet in my head. Now I suspect he's coming to make an offer. That's a hell of a turnaround.

Most likely, he's feeling the pinch of losing two enforcers and a piece of muscle. Maybe he'll end up ordering his men to kill me again. But he can't afford to do that without trying to recruit me first.

My kutte fits easy over my shoulders, my weapon snug in its harness. Wearing both is just habit; I'm not worried that any shit's about to go down. My auto shop is just off the corner of the busiest intersection in town, and my apartment sits above the auto shop. Even now, families are driving by in their minivans, most of them heading to the church a little farther down the block. Others have parked on the street and are making their way along the sidewalks in their Sunday best. Pretty soon they won't be able to find any spaces and they'll start filling up the east end of my lot. So even with the shithead factor added in, there's no chance Croc's going to kill me in the next thirty minutes.

He's looking at my ride, instead. "Beautiful. You restore her yourself?"

I did. And he's buttering me up. Maybe he thinks a little flattery will sway me—but then, he doesn't know I'm aware he sent Tank after me last month, or that I killed three of his men.

Bottom line: He doesn't know who the fuck he's talking to. I'd never walk let my prez walk into a similar situation. If I don't know exactly what type of person he'll be dealing with then I go alone.

Behind him, Valentine's got his chest puffed up. The important new brother with all the info on the local MC.

He doesn't know shit. Fortunately the one Hangman who might be able to tell Croc what I am can't reveal it without exposing himself.

Creek's just watching us. He knows exactly what happened to the two Hangmen last night, but he won't say a word. Probably he's been downplaying his own talents for years, or else he would have already been in the enforcer's position. Otherwise I can't figure why Croc hasn't appointed him there yet. Lack of trust, maybe. Or maybe Creek pissed off someone in the mother chapter and Croc's playing his cards carefully.

He's playing these carefully, too. When I don't answer, he takes a long look around the property. "It's a nice setup you got here. Valentine tells me you pull in a hefty amount of business."

"Valentine says a lot," I tell him. "But I've never heard him say anything worth listening to."

Croc enjoys that. Valentine doesn't. I don't give a fuck what either of them feel.

When he's done chuckling, Croc starts getting around to it. "Maybe you should have listened. He has good things to say about you. He says that you're a resourceful man. That you get your prez anything he needs. Namely, information."

"Like I said, nothing worth listening to."

"What I have to say is. Because I could use a man like you."

Fair enough. "And if you were my prez, I'd find you one. But since you aren't, I'll just tell you good luck searching."

His faint smile tightens. "I figure I've found him— and that you'll come around to my way of thinking once we talk about the benefits to you. Because a man with an established business could be useful. There's things you can do no one would question."

Like cycling cash through my books. Like taking in cargo and letting it sit in my garage. Like changing VINs and repainting vehicles.

"I got all the business I want to handle," I tell him.

"I'd see you get a hefty cut."

If I gave a crap about money I wouldn't be puttering around engines every day. "I'm still not hearing anything worth listening to."

Behind him, Valentine starts blowing some hot air. *Fucking asshole. Watch your mouth.* Some more, but I stop listening to it. It's all shit that he wouldn't have the balls to say if we were alone.

After a second, Croc turns and gives Val a look, shutting him up. I've seen that before. Croc lets his boys shoot their mouths off so he can appear calm, even. But those boys are just saying what he wants to say.

Last time, they were all saying Lily fucked her way into the club.

His gaze falls to my name patch. "Blowback," he reads.

"That's what they call it when something you do blows back on you, isn't it? Like pissing into the wind."

Considering I'm what comes after someone if they've pissed on the club, it's close enough. But I don't need a lesson in my own name. And I don't know which face I'm wearing, *Don't fuck with me* or *I don't give a shit*, but they both seem like answer enough.

Croc only wants one answer, though, and it's not the one I'm giving. "Now, I think that makes you the perfect example to show everyone what 'blowback' really means. So that everyone can see the consequences of what saying 'No' might be. Consequences like… Well, let's see. If your business isn't useful to me, then it's not useful at all. So maybe seeing that will persuade you. Or maybe my boys will have a conversation with the dyke you've been fucking, and that'll bring you around."

"There's no rivers around here," I say and in my head I'm ripping out his fucking tongue. "But I know of a dike on the Klamath. I never fucked it, though. I've just buried a few body parts there."

"No, you dipshit," Valentine breaks in. "He means—"

"He knows what it means." Creek's watching me warily. Because he knows what it means, too. Croc threatened Lily. So the Devil's Hangmen are going to need a new prez pretty soon. "He's joking."

"Good. I like a man with a sense of humor." Croc claps my shoulder and before heading back to his bike. He straddles his ride and says, "I'll be seeing you at the

Barracks next weekend. So why don't you think about it until then."

I'm thinking about it.

I'm thinking he needs to learn exactly what 'blowback' means.

And I'm thinking that, bet or no bet, it'll be a miracle if Lily ever lets me touch her again.

So I'd better get one last night in.

LILY

ON MY WAY.

Jack's message buzzes through my phone just before ten. Sharp relief replaces the tension I was pretending not to feel while staring at the TV.

Then the relief fades and I'm staring at my TV again with a dull ache climbing through my chest. *On my way.* He doesn't say how far away he is, but with all the shit Croc stirred up today, I'm guessing he was probably out at the ranch meeting with the prez and the message came through as he hit the road. Twenty minutes away, then. Late, but I'm surprised he's coming at all.

Not because he missed the last few days. After last night, I knew he'd come. I expected him earlier, actually— maybe showing up before I headed to the gym or while I was there.

It was while sparring with Gunner that I heard how

busy the Hangmen have been, trying to make friends with at least a half dozen Riders. Telling them no harm will come to their houses or families if they just stand down on Saturday night, and to let the others do the fighting. A little later I got notice from the Riders' secretary that the prez was calling every patchholder in for a meeting at the clubhouse tomorrow night. So I assumed Jack was still working, visiting all the club members, seeing if they've had any visits from the Hangmen and arranging extra protection for their families.

Now he's on his way.

But it's nothing. Just a hookup.

I keep telling myself that. I told myself that the first night, too. Told myself he only wanted to fuck me so he could tear me down, and I was determined to make him regret that he'd trapped me into following through on a stupid, drunken bet.

But tonight is nothing like that first night. My feelings were so mixed up then—wanting him, pissed at him, hurt that he'd forced his way into my bed when he could have just asked and I'd have let him in.

That hurt was nothing compared to the thick pain rising in me now. I keep trying to ignore it, to push it down, but it's filling all the empty spaces that ripped open when our last night passed and he didn't show.

I can't ignore this pain though. So I'll just fuck it away. I've done it before. Jesus, half the time, that's what hookups are *for*.

So that's what this will be. That's all it will be.

I just need to take control. Easy enough. In the living room, I strip off my shirt and toss it on the floor. My bra drops in the kitchen. My jeans on the stairs leading to my room.

Leaving a trail for him to follow.

My front door is locked, but that never stopped Jack. After he knocks once, he waits about a minute before breaking in. I don't mind. I just wish he wasn't so damn quiet, because even though I knew he was coming, all of a sudden he's there, big and dangerous and filling up the entrance to my bedroom. Desire makes his eyes burn like hot coals as he takes in the sight of me waiting in the middle of the room, wearing nothing but a scrap of black lace.

His voice is rough. "Christ, Lily. You're so—"

"No." I stop him before he can get another word out. "You don't get to talk tonight, either. We're just going to fuck."

Of course he doesn't listen. Of course he has to make it a fight. So he opens his mouth and I'm on him. A kiss shuts him up but Jack fucking Hayden is never easily beaten. He groans as I lick past his teeth, take a hot taste of his tongue, then his fingers tangle in my loose hair, yanking my head back, and he's biting my throat, the little nips beneath my jaw that drive me crazy.

God, yes. Just like this. Hard and rough, with my panties already drenched and the iron rod of his cock digging into my stomach. There's no pain now. Not while I'm touching him. There's only need.

With urgent fingers, I grip his T-shirt and drag it over his head. I knock his hands away when he reaches for his belt. When my hands take their place, slowly drawing the leather through the buckle, his body stills and his gaze locks on my face.

Jesus, he's such a beautiful man. I could look at him forever. When I'm with women, I don't have a type, unless that type is 'everyone.' But with guys, I definitely prefer big and rugged and a little bit deadly.

Jack punches all of my happy buttons. God, he punches them so hard. Hard enough that I'm almost dizzy with it sometimes.

Dizzy with it now, I rise onto my toes. He knows what I want, his strong fingers gripping my ass, hauling me against his solid chest. His mouth crashes down on mine. He devours me like a man starving, until I have to pull back, gasping for breath.

My skin burns from the scrape of his whiskered jaw. More than a day's growth, as if he didn't have a chance to shave this morning. Maybe he didn't even have time to sleep. Not after taking care of the two men who'd vanished from the Barrack's entrance last night.

Jack isn't just a *little bit* deadly. And holy fuck, that makes my body sing.

Everything does. Still holding me against him, he's quiet, just watching me as I trail my fingers along the breadth of his shoulders. His torso is stacked with muscle, his arms roped with steely strength. Ink covers the left side of his chest, a hellish illustration with demons swallowing the names of his mother and father. His brother's name bleeds. All the shit that hurts him is on his left side and there's hardly an inch not covered colored in. Only the Riders' logo and part of a lily decorate the right side. The only things that feel good.

I'd tattoo his chest on my right side. I'd tattoo the feel of his warm skin and hard muscle beneath my palms. I'd tattoo the pounding of his heart, the stiffness of his cock, the heat of his mouth. I'd tattoo the whisker burn on my chin, knowing my inner thighs will soon have the same burn, because Jack is always hungry and rough and won't leave any of my pussy untasted and unfucked.

But I'm always hungry, too.

The rasp of his zipper is loud in the silence, parting the denim straining over his erection. Slowly I slide my hand in and grip his meaty shaft. A vicious shudder rips through his big body before he goes absolutely still.

Jack always goes rigid when I touch him. When I take him into my mouth. As if he's afraid any movement will make me disappear.

I'm not going anywhere but the bed. With my hand wrapped around his cock, I pull him in that direction—leading Jack by his dick, his jeans open and his belt hanging loosely around his hips.

His grin is wide and swift. "Lily—"

"No talking." I give his cock a warning squeeze. "Only fucking."

His response is a deep groan and a heavy pulse through his shaft. This is nothing like the first night, either. That was all about learning what he likes, but I've had a month to discover how his body responds to mine. I've learned that he loves to ride on the edge of pain. Not with teeth or fingernails or floggers, though he's loved all that, too, but with arousal so keen it's almost too painful to come—and too painful not to.

Backing across the mattress on my knees, I pull him onto the bed. God, that becomes a fight, too. When I push him onto his back and head for his cock, he grips my hips and tries to swing me around to straddle his face. Panting, I roll out of his grip, knowing that his mouth on my cunt will tear my control away.

This is only a hookup, and I always make sure my partners have a damn good time. So he just needs to lie back and let me make him come.

But Jack never just lies back. I kneel at his side and his big hand slides around the back of my thigh, waiting, waiting as I swallow his cock as deep as I can. A strangled noise rips from this chest. His hips jolt upward, his dick shoving into my throat, making me choke, but I love it, love his taste and his earthy smell and the tremble through his body as I draw back, my fist stroking behind the slick path of my lips. I love his cock, so thick and long and sensitive.

His body curls in as I take him again, his stomach flexing, each ridge of muscle standing in sharp relief. I flatten my palm over those ridges, feeling his bronzed skin quiver beneath my hand.

So fucking sexy.

And I just want to drive him wild. I want him to lose control, to grab my hair, to fuck my throat. Hungrily I suck, my tongue swirling. His big body shakes, his groans the tormented sounds of a dying man, but he doesn't jerk against me again, doesn't ram his dick past my lips.

He's not losing control. He's taking it.

Fighting me again.

His curled fingers slowly glide up the inside of my thigh. My skin prickles, goosebumps radiating outward from that light touch. I'm hyperaware of every millimeter his fingertips travel, though I try to push the sensation away, try to lose it in the salty taste of him against my tongue, the flavor of the precum that I lick from the tip of his dick.

Oh, but he's teasing me, fingers digging into my flesh when I begin to pull away. His thumb traces the crease of my inner thigh, following the edge of my underwear. I shudder, my helpless moan muffled by the length of his cock.

His hand abruptly wraps around my lower thigh and he drags my left knee closer, forcing my legs apart. His fingers slide up again and tug aside the soaked crotch of my panties.

God. But if he thinks I'm going to stop, he's so fucking wrong. Not even when he groans, slicking his fingers through my drenched inner lips. Not even when he circles my clit. Involuntarily my hips buck, seeking a rougher touch. Everything's so slippery, so wet, there's almost no friction.

Until he pushes two broad fingers into me.

With his cock lodged at the back of my throat, I whimper, a desperate note of pure pleasure. I love feeling Jack inside me. His fingers, his cock, his tongue. And when he begins to pump his hand, thrusting his fingers deep, all I want is for him to feel this same need. Moaning, I suck wildly, needing his response, needing his cum, needing to know that I'm not alone in all this. Needing Jack to love it as much.

But it's too good, coming on me too fast. I cry out and shudder when his fingers slide out of my pussy to tease my clit before plunging into me again. God help me. I'm shaking, losing it.

On a gasping breath, I raise my head. I feel his fingers tighten, trying to catch me as I lurch forward, but my skin and his hand are slippery and he doesn't get a good grip.

Swiftly I wriggle out of my panties. Condoms lay on the nightstand. I grab one and throw my leg over his hips, facing away from him in a good old cowgirl. In control again.

I sheathe his cock and sink down.

Not far. Just a few inches, my breath catching and

my back arching as the fat head of his cock breaches my entrance. Oh, Jesus, that's *so* good. Slick and hot, the flanged head is the thickest part of his long, deliciously thick cock, stretching my pussy to the limit. Moaning, I rise up again, sensitive tissues hugging that broad, flared crown before releasing him.

From behind me, rough hands take my hips in a hard grip, his fingers digging into my flesh.

"*Fuck*, Lily."

The curse is ragged, a half laugh, half moan. Jack knows exactly what I'm doing. He's done this to me before—pinning my legs wide and slowly fucking into me, shallow, so shallow, pumping that thick flared ridge past the entrance to my pussy again and again, each thrust like striking a match to every aroused nerve crowding my delicate flesh, until I was begging, screaming, burning.

But I wasn't the only one who burned. I saw the effort it took for Jack to maintain that shallow tease. I felt him shake, tasted his sweat, heard his tortured groans escaping through clenched teeth.

I intend to hear them again.

His fingers tighten as his cock fills the entrance to my pussy. He's so strong, he could force me all the way down, but his powerful hands offer no resistance when my thighs flex and he slips out of my cunt's tight grip.

His body shudders. "God, that's beautiful. Tilt your ass up."

So that he can see my pussy better. I lean forward,

bracing my hands on his denim-covered thighs, then slowly take his cock again and again. I can't see him, but I can hear him, his breathing harsh and stopping on every downstroke as if he's praying that this will be the one where I take him all. Praying it will be. Praying it won't. Because it feels good, so good, and I'm shaking all over again. Not even touching my clit. Just from the drag of his flared head across my aroused flesh.

"All of it." Voice hoarse with need, Jack suddenly pleads for more, his body arching beneath me. "Christ and fuck, Lily, take all of it."

Not yet. God, not yet. Each shallow thrust is torment, is heaven, and I didn't mean to be caught up in this, too, but I can't stop it, panting as I ride that thick cockhead, the muscles of my thighs on fire. I should have known. I saw what it did to him before, saw the blowback, and how it's impossible for us to torture each other without torturing ourselves. Impossible to give him pleasure without taking my own.

And I'm not fighting him now. Instead I'm fighting this need, trying not to come and losing, losing. The orgasm starts deep, clenching my inner muscles, crushing the air from my chest before blasting outward on a scream. Overwhelmed, still fighting, I try to outrun it but Jack pushes deep inside me, abruptly jacking upright and holding me against his chest, my pussy clamping down on the full length of his cock. I writhe in his lap and can't stop my "No…oh, no" when his fingers slide between my legs to gently flick my clit, and my entire body convulses from the burst of agonizing pleasure.

This isn't in control.

No more, I try to say but I can only stutter out a sobbing breath, then he's tipping me forward, pushing me over onto my knees but now we're at the edge of the bed and there's nowhere to brace my hands.

Rough fingers tangle in my hair and Jack pulls me upright again, his cock deep inside me, his mouth against my ear.

"I told you, Lily." His deep voice seems carved from stone. *"I'm not done."*

Oh, God. He begins to fuck me and I can't get away, can't reach for anything. I was wrong, so wrong. The orgasm wasn't the blowback.

This is.

Because we've done all of this before. We've fought before. He's held me immobile like this before, his cock a relentless piston, skin slapping skin. But the emotion filling me is new, and huge, and terrifying, yet when I try to scramble away from it, Jack hauls me back, grinding deep, and I can't catch my breath. Shivers of pleasure intensify to quakes, and I try to lose myself in this need, but I can't escape what's chasing me down.

I love him.

No no *no.* I've never done that before. I don't want it now but it's here, squeezing at my chest like it's trying to come out in words. I fight them but they're too big, so when Jack angles his head over my shoulder and claims my mouth I throw myself into that ravenous kiss, my lips clinging to his, stopping the words before they slip out. Stopping everything, until there's nothing but his big hand fisted in my hair, the carnal thrust of his cock, the slippery slide of his fingers over my clit. Nothing but the orgasm bearing down on me and Jack fucking me, fucking me, fucking me.

My back arches when it hits, his name a strangled cry from my lips. Groaning, Jack strokes my clit harder, makes me pay for the torture by wringing another orgasm from my clenching flesh, ecstasy crashing against need until I slump back against him, trembling.

And he's still not done.

Slowly he swivels toward the center of the bed, where he lays me on my stomach and slides deep. I moan softly, my pussy swollen with arousal, my inner muscles clasping him tight. Gently he fucks me, one knee braced beside my thigh and the other pushing my opposite leg wide, his whole body moving against mine.

I can't stop shaking. He's taking all of me. His fingers slick over my clit, gathering my juices before dipping between the cleft of my ass. I cry out as his thumb pushes inside that tight passage, a protest that dies as the sensation flares through my sensitive flesh, making everything tighter, hotter.

"Come with me," he says hoarsely, and I know I will, he's not giving me a choice, and already I'm pushing up onto my hands and shoving back against his hand and his cock, trying to take him deeper, deeper. Frantically I grind my hips, my head hanging down, my hair a sweaty tangle swinging around my face with each wild thrust. I come all at once, my pussy clenching painfully hard, once, twice, and it's all I have left but it's enough. Jack groans and seems to stagger, his weight falling onto my back, his body stiffening and his cock pulsing against my inner walls.

Chest heaving, he lays heavily against me. I bury my face in the comforter and try to breathe, try to remember what life was like before this. I don't think it was ever this good.

I don't think it hurt so much.

His mouth presses against my shoulder, tasting my sweaty skin. "I won't ever be done, Lily."

Maybe not. I don't know if that matters now.

Jack kisses my shoulder again, perhaps waiting for a reply, but I'm afraid that if I open my mouth I'll just start crying or saying that I love him. I don't know which would be worse. After a long second, he gently eases away from me, heading for the bathroom to discard the condom and wash his hands. In the past, I'd wait for him right here, and slip into his arms when he returned to bed.

This time I can't.

I make it into the kitchen before the tears come and then I don't know what to do. There's nowhere to go. Just to the sink, where I can't bear the sight of my swollen lips reflected in the darkened window. I'm well-fucked. Why isn't it enough?

And why the hell didn't I see this coming? I knew I was risking my heart. I knew it. But I had no idea what that really meant and I shouldn't have been so stupid.

Maybe some people love in nice ways, all warm and giving. I'm not one of them. I'm not nice. I'm selfish and greedy and a thousand more nights won't be enough. But if Jack's just hooking up then every night is going to hurt more. And that has to be all he's doing. I can count the number of people who have loved me on three fingers. Widowmaker, who was more like my father than my father was. Jenny and Anna—though honestly, calling our friendship 'love' is probably a stretch. We haven't been friends that long. I'm just counting Jenny and Anna because I love them and I need that love to go both ways, even if it really doesn't.

I need it to go both ways with Jack. But I know the odds.

I'm the girl to fuck. I'm not the one to love. And the ones who fuck me aren't the ones who love me.

Jack fucks me like crazy. He says he'll never be done. I can't blame him. The sex is amazing. No one in their right mind would give it up.

I'm not in my right mind. I'm just a stupid dick-hole who fell in love with a man who erases every trace of himself from my life each time he leaves. Tomorrow I won't find anything of him here. Not even the used condom. He'll just be gone until our next hookup.

But he's taking little pieces of me with him every time—and he's not giving me anything to fill the holes he's leaving behind.

"Lily?" Behind me, Jack's voice is tense. "You all right?"

My back stiffens. I didn't hear him. He's so quiet, I never hear him. But if there was ever a time I would have liked to be prepared, it's standing naked in a kitchen with tears sliding down my cheeks.

I see him in the faint reflection. So beautiful, his short hair sticking up and his chest bare. All those demons. Maybe I should do the same. Put all the shit that hurts on my left side. My mom, my dad. But they'd be small. This is the moment that would be inked across every other inch.

My fingers grip the edge of the counter painfully tight. Holding myself up, just in case I can't get through this.

Hoarsely I tell him, "I'm pulling out of our bet."

He was already standing quietly, watching me, but as I speak his entire body seems to still.

"You're doing what?"

The gravel in his voice scrapes right over my heart. "This is our last night. Just now, in my bedroom—that was our last time."

I see him move and my neck tenses, but he's only looking right and left, like a man waking from a dream and who doesn't know where he is. "Why?"

God, what can I tell him? *I love you and I need more than this? Hooking up for five nights will shred my fucking heart?*

Because this was never just a hookup. Even I can't turn it into one. I tried.

Hot tears slip over my lashes as I close my eyes. "I just can't anymore."

And I shouldn't have looked away. Because he's so quiet, and so fast, and I'm not prepared when he swings me around and crowds in, his hands sliding up and fisting in my hair like he's just going to take—

Jack freezes against me, his face ashen. "You're crying?"

Throat a burning knot, I can't reply. Bleak torment flattens his dark gaze.

"Did I hurt you again?"

Not like he thinks. This wasn't his fault. It was mine.

I shake my head and whisper, "Just go."

His throat works before he nods. His fingers slide forward, cupping my face, sweeping his thumbs across my wet cheeks. "I'll give you space. But we're not done."

Because he'll want the five nights still owed him. A painful breath shudders through my chest. "I told you I'm backing out—"

"Not the bet." His head lowers, his firm mouth tasting my trembling lips. "You and me. Not done."

"We are," I say but it's like shooting at a steel wall. Nothing gets through.

Jack kisses me again. Then he goes, and tears out another piece. The biggest piece. Leaving me so empty, I can't even cry.

    And there's not a fucking drop to drink in this whole damn place.

FIVE

JACK

ABOUT A YEAR AFTER I KILLED MY FATHER, THE SHRINK at the children's home sat me down. My eye was throbbing, as I was sporting a hell of a shiner. My lip had been split the day before and I could taste the blood every time I ran my tongue over the swelling. I don't remember who laid into me that time. A lot of the boys did. I was already bigger than most of them, but I didn't fight back. I figured I was just getting what was coming to me—and a busted lip felt a hell of a lot better than the rotted shit in my chest.

Not that I ever thought of it like that. Not until the shrink sat me down and told me I was using one pain to deal with another—and that I needed to find a different way to deal before I destroyed myself. His solution was for me to focus on one task at a time. Sometimes that task was just getting from one class to the next. And if someone tried to stop me from completing my task, maybe by jumping me in the showers, I needed to shove that obstacle out of the way and keep on going. I just had to be careful about how hard I shoved.

That shrink's way of dealing helped. Helped until I found other ways to deal.

I haven't needed to deal at all in a while. There's hurt inked all over my skin, but putting it there helped me put it away. I don't hate myself or brood over the past. I don't fucking cry over my shitty childhood. It made me who I am—a fucked up bastard who kills too easily and who takes what he gets. Either I started out wired wrong or something in me broke along the way, I don't know. Don't much care, either.

But now the rotted shit is back in my chest, and I'm dealing in that old way: focusing on a task. The first was gathering up my things and heading out Lily's door. It was the hardest walk I ever took—and her front porch was as far as I got before starting my second task. While Lily's hurting and vulnerable, I'll keep her safe through the night.

Tomorrow I'll deal with the knowledge that she

might be hurting because I shoved too hard. I fucked up our very first night, making her follow through on the bet. Knowing that, I made her follow through again. Six more nights. I thought she was all in, dragging me to bed by my cock.

Then she ended up crying.

Crying. I rub my chest, trying to massage away the pain, but the rotted ache is just growing. Because Lily was crying and she pulled out of a bet.

Backing down.

She doesn't do that. She doesn't fucking *do* that. She gets up on her feet and fights harder. So whatever it was that hit her must have hit hard. So hard she hurts too much to get up again.

I didn't know anything could do that.

My cell buzzes and lights up. Message from Stone. Nothing unexpected. I reply and set the phone on the wooden rail surrounding Lily's porch. More calls will soon be coming in.

Maybe they started coming in to her, too. I hear her feet on the stairs, then Lily comes through her front door— and stops short, seeing me. Pain twists harder in my chest. Her eyes are red, her face pale. She's in a T-shirt and jeans, but no kutte, and the keys to her truck are in her hand.

"Jack?" Leaving the door open, she comes at me. "What the fuck are you doing?"

She's looking and sounding pissed now. But most likely still hurting.

That's how she deals.

"Watching your place," I tell her. "Croc wants me to join the Hangmen. Said he might use you to persuade me."

Full lips parting, she stares at me, then looks out down the street as if searching for the enemy in the dark. "You think he will?"

"Maybe." The Hangmen carry through on their threats. Mostly so that anyone else who might think about turning the Hangmen down will change their minds.

My phone buzzes again. The prez this time, or I'd have ignored the text. I reply and when I set it aside, she's frowning at me.

"Why didn't you give me a heads-up earlier?"

Because I keep fucking up. "I planned to in the morning. I figured if you knew how they were looking at you as if you were my property, you wouldn't let me touch you again."

That makes her draw in a sharp breath, like she's taken a blow. She averts her face, looking down the street again. It's late, and quiet. The only sounds are the crickets and the distant wail of a fire truck siren.

After a second, she says, "I don't give a fuck what the Hangmen think."

I know. "It isn't just the Hangmen."

She swings back around to look at me as my phone lights. Gunner. I ignore it.

"It's everyone," I tell her. "Even the Riders. I'm fucking you so they think you belong to me."

Her lips twist in a bitter smile. "That misconception's easy enough to fix. All they have to do is to come here and look around."

"At what?"

"Exactly," she says like it hurts, and before I can ask what the fuck she means by that, my cell buzzes again and she snarls, "Who the hell is blowing up your phone?"

Stone again. "The brothers. My garage is burning down."

"Your garage…" She blinks like she's sure she didn't hear that right. "What?"

"Croc wanted the business, too. Then said he'll use me as an example of the consequences of saying no."

"Jack." All at once she moves in close, gripping the edges of my kutte and giving me a little shake. "Are you all right? What the hell are you still doing here?"

What's the point of being there? "Watching it burn won't change that it's burning. And I don't give a shit if it does. It's all insured. Everything important's stored off site and since I knew it might be coming, this afternoon I cleared out everything else I don't want any inspectors finding."

She gapes at me. "You knew he'd do this?"

"Croc as much as said he would."

"Then why the hell weren't you there to kick their asses if they showed up? I can handle myself here."

"I know you can." I rub my chest again. Jesus, this fucking ache. "But I'd have missed a night with you. And

I only have…*had*…six left."

Her breath catches. She stares at me, her eyes searching mine.

"Jesus, Jack," she finally whispers. "You're so fucked up."

"Yes." But not about this. My priorities here are exactly what they should be. I glance down at her keys. "Where were you headed? I'll tag along, watch your back. Croc might be using the fire as a distraction to pull me away from you."

She looks at her keys like she forgot they were in her hand and laughs, a real laugh, low and husky. "I was going to head to the Wolf Den and get drunk off my ass. But since they burned down your place, let's kick Hangmen ass instead."

"No."

Her eyebrows shoot up. "No?"

"We'll wait until the Barracks. Saturday."

"Shit." She blows air through clenched teeth. "I guess the boss wants you to wait?"

I shake my head. "He gave me the go-ahead."

"But you're holding back? Jack, they burned down your *home*."

No. A home is where you belong. "It's just a place to sleep."

She stares at me again, the flint gray of her eyes sparking. Abruptly she turns and heads into her house, but she's only gone a second, returning with her kutte. "Let's head out to your place anyway. You don't give a shit but the other brothers will. You'll need to talk them down."

A task that'll go right along with protecting her, as long as she stays at my side tonight.

One task at a time. Tonight, tomorrow. But there's one more important than any other: persuading Lily that we're not over.

Even if it takes forever.

LILY

I BELIEVE JACK REALLY DOESN'T give a shit about his shop or his apartment, but something's whacked him hard. I've never seen him like this—but I've seen something like it before, in soldiers who were one of the few to survive a firefight or an ambush. Like there's so much hurt boiling inside they just shut down until they can deal with it.

The intersection's crowded with emergency vehicles flashing their lights. We stop behind a deputy's patrol car angled across the street. Even from this distance, the heat's like standing in front of an open oven.

A handful of Riders are already here, with more riding in. Jack goes to talk to the fire crew. I wait with the brothers and it's me they're coming to, asking how Jack's doing and what the fuck is going down and I realize that Jack was right—they *do* think I belong to him.

But he was only partly right. The brothers wouldn't

approach an old lady like this. They'd offer their sympathy, make sure she had anything she needed. Then they'd go to the brother to see how he's doing and how he wants to handle what comes next.

The way they're coming to me now…it's because they also think *he* belongs to *me*.

Maybe he does. Something knocked the shit out of him. It wasn't the news that his place was burning.

But it might have been me, telling him to go.

Maybe. It's a small hope. A stupid one.

But falling in love is pretty stupid, too, so I'm building up a good track record.

I watch Jack make his way back. The fire is behind him, his face in shadow, like he's walking out of the hell inked onto his chest. Closer, I see that some of the glassy expression has receded, and the intensity is returning to his dark eyes again. Coming back from whatever knocked him down.

He bumps fists with Gunner and Stone, who says, "We're ready to go to war for you, man."

Jack's gaze sweeps over the other Riders, all of them nodding and as eager as I am to bust some fucking heads.

"Go home." He deflates the anticipation with a few words. "Save it for Saturday."

That doesn't sit well with anyone. But before he became the club's warlord, Jack served as our veep for years, and the only man whose word carries more weight is the prez's. No one's arguing with him.

He looks to me. "You going home or to the Den?"

"The Den." Not to get drunk now but because I don't know what's coming next. But I think he's coming with me. I look to the fire again. "Will they be able to salvage anything? Any of your tools? Clothes?"

"No. But I put some things in storage."

"Then let's hit that first."

He straddles his bike. "I don't need anything tonight, Lily."

"Well, we're not busy kicking ass. So you have any other plans?"

"No." The light from the fire throws harsh shadows over his features. "They fell through."

Because he'd planned to be in bed with me. My throat tightens. He let his place burn just to have a night with me.

There's so much hope wrapped up in knowing that. And so much fear. I don't know how to deal with either. So I do what I always do.

I get on my bike and ride.

The storage facility is a twenty-four hour place up in Bend. A thirty-minute ride, with Jack at my side all the way. Long enough to turn Croc's threat over in my head a few times.

Jack's unit is as big as a two-car garage, with an overhead door wide enough to back a truck into. Jack unlocks the standard swinging door instead. I follow him though as he flips on the light. Though the space is almost packed full there's not much to see. Neatly stacked crates. A big vehicle covered by a bigger canvas tarp. Jack heads for the south corner, where garment bags hang from a rolling clothes rack. He grabs an empty duffel from a shelf.

"Croc screwed up by burning your place." Which just sounds like bluster, so I add, "Where was he getting his info about the Riders from? Val. So Croc thinks we're safe targets."

"Safe?" Jack grunts like that's the dumbest thing he ever heard. "That's because Val doesn't know shit."

"About you? No." But that's not what I meant. "I mean safe because Val will tell him you don't have any friends in the club, and there's still brothers who resent my being patched in. So Croc thinks when the other brothers are weighing his threats against their loyalty to you or me, they'll cave instead of having our backs. He's thinking our club is just like his. So he believes that he can burn your place down or that he can beat the shit out of me and no one will really care. But the brothers are ready to go to fucking war for you. They even would for me."

"*Even* would?" Frowning, he zips up the duffel. "What's that mean?"

"Just what I said. That if Croc had come after me instead of your shop, they'd have my back."

"No." He tosses the bag to the concrete floor and his dark gaze zeroes in on me. "You said 'even me.' Like they'd have less reason."

"Some of them do. C'mon, Jack. There's a lot of

brothers who are uneasy with you but not one would say you don't belong in the club. And all of them would say that I've earned my place, sure. But there's also some who'd say I still don't belong, and a beating from the Hangmen would just be what was coming to me for overstepping. 'What's she expect, putting herself out like that? Does she think it's not going to come back and knock her on her ass?' That's what they'd say. Hell, that's what my mom would say, and I know some of them think the same way. And it doesn't escape my attention that the others Croc threatened today are the brothers who had some problem with my joining the Riders. So if it *had* been me instead of your garage, well…" I shrug. "He thought they'd still look after their own asses first, come Saturday. But they won't."

Though his jaw has hardened to granite, Jack doesn't argue when I finish. Because he's a lot of things, but he's not blind. So he only says quietly, "You belong."

Fuck. That wasn't what I expected and my chest suddenly squeezes in so tight, I think I might cry again. Swallowing hard, I nod and lock that shit away. But the laugh I come up with is watery and strained, and my voice isn't nearly as even as I'd like. "As hard as I fought to get in, I fucking hope so."

My body stills as he moves in, big hand cupping my jaw. His thumb slides over my cheek, his eyes dark and bleak. Remembering those damn tears. But he doesn't bring them up. Instead he turns away, rubbing the center of his chest like there's something there that hurts him.

"You need any ammo?" he asks.

I shake my head, breath shuddering as I watch him head down a narrow aisle between stacks of crates. I bet he has a catalog of every item in each crate. He's obsessive that way. Everything in its place.

God, and he's got a lot of stuff. Almost everything's packed away, but I check out the vehicle beneath the tarp—a Humvee, armored like a tank, Jesus. A burst of color draws me to a dozen small canvases leaning against the wall like a stack of cards. Nothing fancy. Just unframed and rough—

Wait.

I know that painting. All orange and red, demons and fire. That's on Jack's back. Crouching in front of the canvases, I flip the painting forward to glance at the one behind it. Another tattoo.

This time I don't hear Jack, but his shadow falls across the wall in front of me and I know he's there. "Did you paint these yourself?"

"Yes."

"I figured your tattoo artist did."

"No."

"I should have known. They're really ugly."

A deep laugh breaks from him and he goes down on his heels beside me. "They're supposed to be."

"That's good, then. Anything I painted would be ugly, too, but it wouldn't be on purpose. Is it so you never forget—or as a reminder?"

Because he can't look in the mirror without seeing these. Although that doesn't explain the ones on his back. He'd have to make an effort to see those—including the lily that spans the good and painful sides.

"There's no chance of forgetting. But it's not a reminder. It's just me accepting that it's there. A part of me."

"Why? I mean—why start?"

"They were always sending us to see shrinks when I was in the service. This was one of the things they suggested doing to deal with shit. I tried it after I got out. Liked it enough to ink it on my skin."

So therapy of some kind. I flip past another demon. "You don't have enough good."

"I have good. I just don't know how to paint it. I don't believe in this shit—demons or Hell—but the way it looks is the way it feels. But how am I supposed to paint the way you taste, Lily? How am I supposed to paint the way you shove your feet under my leg like you're trying to warm your toes when we're on your couch watching TV?"

My throat is tight as fuck. "I don't know."

"So the only thing I can add is a lily. And that lily doesn't say anything on its own, not like fire and demons do. What's good about it has to be said aloud."

I can't breathe. Abruptly I stand and back up, hitting the Humvee. "Jack—"

"And one of those good things is that you don't back down." He's on his feet and not leaving any space to get around him. I couldn't get away anyway, trapped by the harsh lines of his mouth, the pain in his eyes. "Except you are now. Just like you did in the kitchen. And I don't know the fuck *why*."

"Jack—"

"How did I hurt you so bad? Because, Lily, I can't fucking..." Agony grinds his voice to nothing and each word is ragged when he tries again. "I can't walk away from you. So tell me why you backed down and I'll fix what it was I did."

"I didn't back down." Revealing this is like digging a knife into my chest, but I can't stand the raw anguish in his voice. I can't let him go on thinking he did this to me. "And I'm not hurt."

Not by him. Not for this. But he doesn't believe it, shaking his head like he believes I'm saying this shit just to shut him up.

"You were crying—"

"God fucking dammit, Jack. I'm not backing down!" And neither is he, goddamn Jack fucking Hayden. "I'm running scared!"

He abruptly goes still, his eyebrows drawing down and his shadowed gaze searching my face.

Slowly he says, "I didn't think you knew how to do that."

Run scared? "I didn't think so, either. It's a first for me."

And now that I've put words to it, something I'm not so proud of. Terrified because I love someone. Love should be the kind of thing I beat my chest over, not curl up into a ball.

But, Jesus—love is *really* fucking terrifying. And it's another first for me.

Jack's lips twitch a little, but the amusement doesn't touch his eyes. "Scared of me?"

"No." Christ, no. "Not like you're thinking."

"What am I thinking?"

"That I'm afraid because you kill so easy."

His dark gaze still on mine, he moves closer—slow and careful, like he thinks I might bolt if he makes a sudden move.

He's not wrong. I'm shaking all over and looking for any way out. Not because he's big and strong and deadly, but because there's no going back.

And there's nowhere to run.

This is it, then. No backing down now, though I'm a trembling mess as he gently tips my chin up.

His thumb smooths over my parted lips. "What's scaring you?"

Everything that's happening to me now. The tightness in my chest, the lump in my throat. All this hurt that comes simply because of how I feel about him, and the fear of never being the one he wants.

But damn it all. This isn't any way to live, trapped between hope and fear. The only way to live is all in, or all out.

And I'm all fucking in.

"I'm afraid I'll belong to you—"

Jack pales and starts saying, "I'd never call you my property—"but I just keep on going.

"—but you won't belong to me."

A short silence falls as my meaning sinks in. Then his fingers dive into my hair and his forehead presses against mine, our breath mingling.

Emotion roughens his voice. "I'll belong to you, Lily."

God. My throat is even tighter now. That was supposed to make this easier. Hoarsely I say, "And I'm afraid because I have no control where you're concerned. I could end it between us but you'd only have to kiss me and I'd fall right back in bed—"

Swiftly his lips capture mine, because Jack fucking Hayden is never one to let an opportunity go by. Welcoming the rough possession in his kiss, I grab his kutte and haul him closer.

I'd say he's all in, too.

JACK

IT DOESN'T MATTER HOW MANY times I have her. It'll never be enough.

I wet a cloth in her bathroom sink before returning to the bed. Skin glistening with sweat, Lily's splayed out on her stomach, her body lean and strong. The mattress dips beneath my knees.

She raises sleepy lids, makes a small, exhausted sound when she sees the wash cloth. "I'll get up in a second."

If she wants to. But her soft and tired moan says she's not in a rush to move as I gently slide the cloth between her legs. I fucked her hard when we got back to her house. Her pussy, her ass. Jesus, I love her ass—from her taut cheeks to the hot, tight heaven inside her. Usually I take her ass because it's damn fun listening to her tell me she's not going to like it, then making her scream as she comes.

But tonight I just needed to have her every way I could.

She draws in a long, deep breath as I finish wiping away the lubricant and toss the cloth onto the nightstand. Her eyes are closed, her voice heavy with sleep. "So we're going to do this, huh? You and me. No bets."

I press my lips to the dimple above her left ass cheek. Her waist is tight. Not an ounce of spare flesh and so strong. "No bets."

She smiles without opening her eyes. "It's going to be rough."

"The brothers can—"

"I don't mean the brothers. I mean you and me. It's always going to be a fight."

She's probably right. I don't care.

"I love a good fight," I say, gripping her hips. She rolls bonelessly over when I turn her onto her back, her head propped by a pillow, her breasts like small scoops of cream topped by raspberries. Her flinty eyes open as I slide down, making room for my shoulders between her thighs. My breath stirs the pale curls guarding her pussy.

Soft when I rolled her over, now her nipples stand in tight rosy peaks. Her legs move restlessly as I spread them wide.

Her hand catches in my hair, fingers tangling. "I have to be at work early."

As if that has ever made a difference to either of us. "I don't. My shop burned down."

She laughs, then groans as I dip my head to kiss her inner thigh, ignoring the pain in my scalp when her fingers tighten. I know she's sensitive, the skin between her legs abraded by a hard fuck and the roughness of my jaw. Her pussy is soft and pink and swollen.

And already wet again. "Your cunt is so damn beautiful, Lily. I love tasting it after I've fucked you, after you've come. After I was here, inside you. Right where I wanted to be for so fucking long."

"Jack," she breathes and releases my hair. Her hand finds mine, lacing our fingers together. "Do it."

I'll fucking die if I don't. I spread her wider and the second my mouth closes over her pussy, her back arches and she gives a deep-throated moan. So damn good. She tastes like the ocean, smells like a ride down the beach on a hot day. Better every time I have her, and each time I'm so much hungrier for the next taste.

But she won't fucking stay still. Without letting go of her hand, I plant my forearm across her hips, holding her down. She writhes when I suck on her juicy little clit, then I tip her up and eat out her pussy slow and gentle, taking my fill. It's still not enough. She cries out when I bombard her swollen bud with quick rough licks, her free hand sliding up to pinch her beaded nipple. Her pussy's dripping with need. Groaning, I slick my tongue up the length of her drenched slit before rising onto my knees.

My dick is a solid burning ache. She reaches for it as I go for the condoms. Jesus. If she touches me I'll blow my goddamn load. I grab her wrist and shove it over her head. Skin flushed, she laughs up at me.

Then groans when I sheathe my cock and slide into the tight clasp of her pussy. Fucking paradise. I want to stop and let this ecstasy sink in. She's so hot and wet and feels so damn good. But I can't stop. Just lace my fingers through hers, holding as tight as I can, and start up a long, slow ride, with every inch of my body worshiping every inch of hers. Her endless legs wrap me up, and when I bend my head and take her lips, I drown in the sweetness of her mouth. When she comes it's long and slow, her back bowed and her lean body rocking beneath mine. I follow her over.

I'll follow her anywhere.

Rolling onto my back, I pull her with me and tuck her against my side. Pale strands of hair stick to her sweaty face.

Softly she says, "That's my favorite kind of fight."

Mine, too. "You think it'll be that hard, you and me?"

"Not most of the time." That's all she says for a long second, her fingers idly trailing through the hair on my chest. "This past month was good. Mostly."

"Mostly?" I can't recall anything that was a fight outside of the bedroom.

"It was good. When you were here." She blows out a short breath. "When I wasn't fucking with my own head."

"Thinking I'd lost interest?"

"Yeah." Her face turns a little as she says it, like she's trying to hide whatever she's feeling.

Running scared. Just not going so far this time.

I can only imagine one thing that might scare her. "You think this will hurt your place in the club?"

"No." All at once she looks up at me, her eyebrows arched, a faint smile curving her plush lips. "And I notice you've gone from 'being Lily's shield' to 'I'm just going to scare the fuck out of anyone who throws shit at her.' Like you did with Burnout."

"It's all right?"

She nods. "It's good."

"Good." Because I don't want to hurt her again.

And because it was pretty fucking fun.

Sleepily she rubs her cheek against my chest, snuggling in. "But, you know. This is all new. And I can't promise I won't freak out again. I've never had a…a relationship. Only hookups. So I don't know how to deal with all of this stuff yet."

Shit. "I don't either. But I figured that every time you

push me out, I'll just fight my way back in."

"Good." She smiles faintly and closes her eyes. "I love you, you know."

I didn't. And it's a knockout blow, leaving me so fucking stunned I can't say another word. So I just hold her tight as she drifts to sleep and I'm still holding her when the birds start singing outside and pink streaks the sky.

Now I know what scared her so bad. Now I know what knocked her down. Because me, I'm lying here, holding more in my arms than I ever dreamed I'd have.

And the thought of losing any of it is damn terrifying.

SIX

LILY

Monday night is the special club meeting, where the prez basically tells all of us to put on our dancing shoes Saturday night—and that any Rider who doesn't have a damn good reason to show better hit the road now. I don't think anyone will miss it. Burning Jack's shop down essentially lit a fire under the whole club and we're out for blood.

But the setup isn't sitting right with Jack. All week, he pores over everything he knows about the Hangmen and makes calls to friendly clubs more familiar with the

Hangmen's larger chapters. On Thursday, he out-and-out tells me that he doesn't expect it to go down like we all think it will, because Croc's looking for patchholders to bolster his ranks. He's already down by three men, and his numbers aren't as strong as the Riders' to begin with—so tearing into each other on this kind of scale doesn't make any sense. The Hangmen will lose. But even on the slim chance the Riders get thumped, Croc only ends up with a strip joint. So Croc's challenge is most likely a bait and switch.

The question is: What the hell is the switch going to be?

Jack and I ride out to the Barracks early. Some joker's playing *Beat It* over the sound system. Probably Spiral, since he's the getting up on the stage with the dancers and moonwalking. I settle in at the bar next to Gunner while Jack and Stone meet up with the prez.

Gunner's got a beer bottle in his hand, but like the rest of us, he's not drinking much. He lifts his chin toward the stage. "You think Spiral's trying to say that we should all just bust a move with the Hangmen instead of busting their heads?"

"Maybe. Or maybe he wants a dance off. He'd be more likely to win that than a fight."

Gunner nods. "He's got good moves."

"He used to be on Pine Valley's high school cheerleading team," I say and laugh when Gunner chokes on the sip he was taking. "Just fucking with you. He really was on the cheerleading team, but he was *on* them." And because making him choke isn't mean enough, I add, "Anna Wall was a cheerleader around that time, I think."

His pretty face closes up tight but the poor guy can't help himself. He's been hung up on Stone's sister for years, but the funniest part of that is he thinks no one notices. Now his gaze shoots to Spiral again like he's wondering if Anna ever hooked up with him.

Anna hasn't. But I'm not going to tell Gunner that. Let him stew in it.

I'm not all mean, though. Pulling out my phone, I send him one of Anna's pictures.

He glances at his screen and frowns at the glittery mess. "What's this?"

"Anna's bathroom," I tell him. "I thought you might like some spank material."

Gunner looks at me like I've lost it, but I notice he doesn't delete the photo.

Poor sap. I grin and sip my beer. This is already shaping up into an entertaining night and it only gets better when Jack heads my way again. God, he's my own spank material. His dark eyes are flat and empty and he's got his *Don't fuck with me* face on tight. The long sleeved T-shirt under his kutte conceals all that glorious muscle but the fabric's hugging his skin as closely as I'd like to, so the view is still damn good.

And this past week has been freaking amazing. I made the right call by going all in with him. Now his toothbrush is right next to mine, right where it belongs. And belonging to him—belonging *with* him—feels like everything in my life just locked right into place. Even if he hasn't said he loves me.

Who needs the words? He just has to look at me.

"Scarecrow just spotted the Hangmen on the highway, heading this way," he tells us and takes the drink I slide over to him. "Thirty men."

Compared to the Riders' fifty. I shake my head. Jack was right. This doesn't make sense. The past few days we'd begun thinking Croc was going to bring in men from the chapters out-of-state. But Croc hasn't come with anyone.

"I feel like we must be sitting on a bomb," I say and Gunner nods. "Something we can't see that's going to blow up in our faces."

But Jack shakes his head. "No explosives, nothing wired. I checked."

Always so literal. But in this case, probably a good thing someone is. "Maybe it's just a mental thing. We can't figure out why he'd do this, we assume he's got something, so we'll be real fucking relieved when he makes the switch."

Dark eyes narrowing, Jack seems to roll that over in his head. "Maybe."

"What's the prez think?" Gunner asks.

"That we let them come in and see how it plays."

Saxon's sitting as his table with the old-timers again, but this time he's got a chair open. Not out of deference to Croc. He's just making his first move before the other man even comes in. What Croc does with it will determine the next step.

The music goes quiet when the Hangmen roll in. They come in with Croc at their head, walking two by two. Jesus, most of them are so fucking young. All of them probably with something to prove, probably looking to impress Croc and the Hangmen with more miles under their belts. It's so damn sad. All those little boy dreams are about to be shattered.

The prez is wearing his deadly cold smile when Croc takes the empty seat. "You seem to be down by a few men."

Croc turns and looks over his guys, then slides his gaze over the rest of us. "I think we'll do all right. What we lack in numbers, we'll make up in strength and determination."

"That right?" The prez leans back, settling in like he's about to watch some funny shit go down. "I hear you've been going around making proposals to some of my men. I suppose that means you've got a proposal for me, too."

"I do. Like I said, I want to keep this amiable. And I don't see any reason for either of us to lose any men when we can make this real simple. A chain is only as strong as its weakest link—and a club is only as strong as its weakest member. So I'll put my weakest up against yours and we'll settle this easy."

The prez's eyes gleam with amusement. "My weakest against your weakest for this strip joint?"

"You have it. And to make sure there's no cheating, I

pick out your weakest. You pick out mine."

"You're shitting me." Saxon's laugh starts deep. "Just so we're clear what you're offering: You come in here with barely over half the number of men I have at my back. You know you're going to get your asses handed to you, so you come up with this proposal that gives you at least a little chance, because otherwise your position is absolute shit. That about right?"

"We'll hold our own," Croc says. "What this will prevent is bloodshed."

Wearing that dangerous smile again, Saxon leans forward. "You afraid of a little blood?"

"I just think it's a goddamn waste." Ice cold, Croc's gaze doesn't stray from the prez's face. "So what do you say? You pick one of my men to go up against your girl."

I freeze as every eye in the place turns my way. Beside me, Jack stiffens. Gunner makes a choking sound.

"Zoomie?" The prez sounds bemused. "You want your weakest man to go up against Zoomie?"

"That's right," Croc says. "And whoever taps out first loses."

Saxon's gaze shoots to Valentine. "He tell you how she took him down?"

In less than three seconds. But apparently Valentine spun the story his way. Croc's all easy as he nods and says, "He told me he held back because it didn't feel right beating on a girl. And I've put him up against a few of my men. He held his own. But if you want to pull him in as the weakest, be my guest."

The prez sits back again. He's quiet. Actually considering it, I realize.

Holy shit. I'm confident I'll pull through, but that's a hell of a thing on my shoulders. If we lose a little territory, it won't be just this once. The Hangmen will just keep chipping away at all the rest. Saxon knows that. It's a huge fucking risk to put on one person.

But I don't think he'd be considering it at all if Croc had named any of the Riders who truly are the weakest fighters. He's only considering it because he has that much respect for me, and I watch him, my chest and throat swelled up like a hot balloon.

I guess we're doing this, though, because finally he says, "What the hell—we're in. We pick who fights her?"

There's a chorus of hoots from the Riders, most of them shouting "Val!"

Croc ignores them, looking satisfied all at once, crossing his arms over his broad chest. "You pick. And being a Vegas man, I think we should make it a little more interesting."

Oh, God *damn*. I was thinking that this one-on-one fight was the switch. But it was just the second piece of bait. Here's the switch—and a trap. Because Saxon's thrown himself behind me. He can't back out.

But although he's got to be pissed, he just says, "How interesting?"

"All the territory east of the highway."

Half our territory—including the Wolf Den, which the prez owns. Jesus fucking Christ. The warm feeling in my chest deflates to a heavy leaden lump.

"Now you're just fucking with me," Saxon says. "But all right. And if she wins, then I don't see a fucking kutte with your colors on it this side of the county line again."

Croc's eyes narrow. "No territory?"

"We like what we have. What we don't like is your filth riding through it."

"Fair enough." The other man nods. "So who are you putting her against?"

My heart's thundering as Saxon looks them over. I'm pretty sure I can hold my own and I'm ready to kick some ass, but I can't get my pulse or my nerves to settle. At least none of the brothers look worried or are questioning whether Saxon's lost his mind. Instead most of them are grinning.

"Seems to me," the prez says after a long second, "that one of my men has already lost something in this amiable little altercation we're having, and that he's been waiting to get a little of his own back. So I'll let Blowback choose."

Not just because of the fire, I know. The prez is asking because choosing Valentine is too expected, too easy. And Jack's been looking at the Hangmen as hard as he can. He'll have a better idea of who's going to be easiest to take down.

Holding his beer easy in his left hand, Jack doesn't even hesitate. "I think it's time to shut this shit down.

Putting the weakest up against the weakest doesn't mean anything. But if our weakest beats their strongest? So I want her up against their prez."

Up against Croc. Oh my fucking God. A roaring fills my ears. All the hoots and grins stop—except from Croc, who bursts out in a laugh. Because he doesn't know Jack.

And Jack doesn't fuck around when the club's on the line.

Croc seems to slowly realize it, the laugh turning into a shake of his head. "That's a fucking joke, man."

"No."

That's all Jack says. Just no. Croc looks to Saxon.

"You heard him," the prez says.

"I heard him. But I don't believe in hitting women."

"But you planned to sit here and enjoy watching someone else beat her down?" Saxon shakes his head. "You're either full of shit or you're a coward."

Jaw clenched, Croc comes up out of his chair. "You watch your fucking mouth, boy."

Still seated, Saxon just stares him down. "This was *your* proposal. These are *your* terms. Take them or we're going to have that bloodshed you were trying to avoid."

"You're going to have it anyway. Hers."

The prez shrugs and stands. Saxon's got inches and muscle on him, but to his credit, Croc doesn't back up. But then, I'm realizing he has more balls than sense. Either that, or the Vegas man thinks he's just too fucking clever for some Pine Valley yahoos.

And the prez is fucking pissed. He's hard to read so I don't know if Croc can tell, but Saxon *is* out for blood. He just intends to watch me shed it. His gaze meets mine before sliding over to Gunner.

"I think we'd best get this area cleared," he says and in the next second Gunner's up, pointing to the brothers who all snap to and start dragging tables and chairs.

Beside me, Jack says quietly, "You all right?"

"I am." Just eyeing Croc and taking his measure. He's a heavy motherfucker, solid with muscle. "What do you think?"

"He's going to be all fists unless he gets you down."

So straight up swinging. And if he connects any of those punches, it's going to feel like I've been hit by a sledgehammer.

Jack winds his fist around my braid, tugging until my face is aligned with his. His eyes are dark and intense and don't hold a single doubt. "You keep your feet moving."

"I will."

"Go for the incapacitating blows. Get him down."

The kind of moves we practice in the gym but have to hold back on. No holding back here. I can't trade punches with Croc and win. I've got to get in there and disable him. Nodding, I say, "I need your switchblade."

A knife is holstered in my boot but it's not as sharp as his. There won't be any weapons allowed when we're facing off, but this is just to make sure I don't give Croc any advantage. If he gets his hands on me, if he gets me down, I'm going to have a bad fucking time until I make it up again.

I pop the blade and grab my braid. One sharp slice at my nape and it's gone. I toss the rope of pale hair to the floor and go after the long strands still hanging around the front, hacking them away by the handful. If it was just Valentine or one of the other young Hangmen, I wouldn't bother. But there's too much on the line for me to get stomped because Croc swings me around by my hair.

While the tables were being moved, it had been noisy in the joint, wood screeching and the brothers all talking trash, but now everyone's gone quiet—as if watching me shear myself bald drives home how fucking serious this is. Maybe they hadn't realized the prez's Den is in that territory. That's the Riders' usual hangout. A couple of other places, too, that the men wouldn't be able to wear their kuttes riding into work. Even if they own the damn place.

I flip my head back up. Jack catches my chin and runs his fingers through my short, uneven hair.

His eyes burn hot. "Even more stunning than you were ten seconds ago."

Yeah, I'm pretty fucking hot. With a grin, I give him back the knife before shrugging out of my kutte. I'd rather wear my colors when I fight, but if Croc catches hold of the leather I'll be yanked around. If he takes hold of my shirt, the thin material will just rip.

"All right then." I roll my shoulders, loosen up my neck. "Let's do this."

I tap my lips and Jack cradles my face and kisses me, full on. Hard, quick. We haven't done that in front of the brothers before. But right now? I don't even give a shit.

The prez is waiting when I turn. I tell him, "I've got your back, boss."

"We've got yours," he says and bumps my fist. "And you've got this."

Of course I will. And that's not just bluster or confidence. I *have* to win. There's no other option for me. If I don't walk out of here the winner, I don't walk out. It's that simple.

My heart's thumping as I get eyes on Croc again. Fuck, he's big. Not as big as Jack or Saxon, but heavier than Gunner, my usual sparring partner.

I can't let him touch me. And I've got to get him to make himself vulnerable to a strike that'll end this.

"Zoomie." The prez raises his voice behind me, loud enough for anyone to hear. When I glance back, he's wearing that mean smile again. "Croc said there'd be some cock sucking tonight. So don't leave him with any front teeth. I fucking hate it when they scrape my dick."

And there's the noise again. Riders laughing, Hangmen talking shit about how we're going to be the ones sucking dick.

I ignore it all and give the prez a thumbs up. "You got it, boss."

Croc's waiting for me, his face red like a bomb's about to go off in his head, and gritting teeth he won't have for much longer.

Jesus, I love being a Rider.

JACK

Creek's patting down Lily, taking the knife out of her boot when the prez says quietly beside me, "Did you think this all the way through?"

I always think it through. "She'll win. If she goes down, she'll get back up again."

Lily doesn't know how to do anything else.

"That's not in fucking doubt," the prez says. "If it was, I wouldn't have laid this on her. What I'm asking is: Have you ever seen your woman get hurt?"

My back stiffens. "What?"

"Just that. You've seen her take hits. You've seen her bleed. But what if she goes down and gets *really* fucking hurt. If she's on the ground and he's kicking her face in."

Jesus fucking Christ. Everything in me goes cold. My throat is like sandpaper when I say, "She'll get up again."

"I *know* that." All at once the prez is in my face. "You know that. But you haven't *seen* it happen, so I'm asking if you're fucking prepared for it, Jack. Or if you need me to bring Gunner and Stone over to hold you back. Because if you went in, you'd rip everything out of her hands. She'd never hold her head up in this club again."

A jagged pain fills my chest. I rub at it, keep rubbing as

I watch Stone pat down Croc. The truth is, I don't fucking know. It *would* destroy her if I charged in. No matter how bad she was hurt, how hard she was down. If I went in before she tapped out, that'd be it for her.

And Lily will never tap out. Never.

I was only thinking of her and what she can do when I tossed Croc in there with her. I wasn't thinking of me.

The prez backs off a little. "I've got a woman who I love more than my own fucking life. So I'm just saying—I *know*. So do you need me to have the brothers come and hold you down? Or maybe you ought to take a walk."

I'd fucking cut off my legs before I left her. And it wouldn't do any good to hold me down. If I can't deal, if I can't stop myself from going to her, then I'd only rip through the brothers, spilling blood and cracking bones. They would barely even slow me down.

"No," I say hoarsely. "I'll hold back. Or I won't."

He nods and reaches for his beer, looking out over Lily and Croc again. "Bones heal," he says.

But the rest of her wouldn't. That's what he's telling me. I don't hold back, I take away everything she's fought for.

And I'd lose her, too.

Jesus. I rub my chest again, trying to push away this ragged fear. All this is nothing if the fight's over quick.

It won't be. I see that right away. Maybe Valentine shared just enough information to let Croc know how to approach her, or maybe the fucker can see it for himself.

But as they start in, he just circles her, keeping his fists in close. Not giving her an opening, not giving her anything to grab onto. She goes straight into the defensive, blocking his punches.

Waiting. Playing it smart. That'll be what gets her through—she's so fucking smart when she's up against an opponent. But the longer this drags on the more it'll wear them both down. Lily relies on her speed. When exhaustion sets in, the advantage almost always goes to the muscle.

She's smart enough to know that, too.

And I know what she's doing but I'm not fucking ready for it when she takes a lazy swing that gives Croc an opening. Two sharp jabs, his big fists snapping against her ribs. Her body almost folds from the impact, and I *know* those ribs cracked, fucking know it, and the blood's pounding so hard behind my eyes and I'm seeing so much red that I almost don't notice her head whip forward.

Croc staggers back, blood spurting from his nose.

A hard hand clamps over my shoulder. I almost rip it off before I realize it's the prez's. I've taken a step forward without even fucking realizing it.

His eyes meet mine. I nod and step back, my chest heaving harder than it ever has during my own fights.

"She's got this," he says.

I know she does. But I wish she wasn't so damn smart. Because she knows that every hit she gets in will come with a sacrifice, bringing Croc in close enough for her to tear him apart, a little bit at a time. Fucking with his breathing and making his eyes water by going for his nose. Slowing him down with a blow to the knee. Weakening his strongest arm by sweeping his elbow with hers. Each one is a calculated risk and soon he's broken another of her ribs and she's bleeding from her mouth.

But she's smiling. She drops to sweep his leg, and I've never seen her move so slow. It's like a goddamn invitation and Croc accepts, slamming his boot down on her ankle and when her leg folds under her—that fucking scream is *real*—he moves in for a kick to the face and she has him.

She catches him off balance, with one foot coming at her. Her expression goes stone cold. She's quick, so goddamn quick, tipping him. His back slams into the floor and she rams her elbow into his throat. His body convulses, feet kicking as he chokes.

Her bleeding mouth's in a thin line, her eyes like shards of flint. Weaving in place, she says, "You tapping out?"

Though he's choking, though he's done, Croc shakes his head.

Lily straddles his chest and goes at his face with her fists. The whole fucking place is silent. Not a single sound except the thud of flesh, the crunch of bone.

Some of that bone is probably in her hands. "Bring her out of it," I say quietly.

The prez takes a long swig, watching her. Finally he calls out, "Can he tap out? Or is he done?"

Her knuckles bleeding, Lily pauses. Her reply comes on a sharp, breathless pants. As if she can barely get air into her battered chest. "I…don't have…all his teeth…yet."

"I only wanted the ones in front." The prez looks to the Hangmen's veep, whose face is stark white. "You calling it done?"

The veep nods.

Not good enough. The prez barks "Say it!" and the boy does.

"Then you get that bleeding trash out of my joint." He glances at me. "Unless you want him?"

No. I just want Lily.

And Croc's done. I won't even need to touch him. His own club will finish him now.

Lily staggers to her feet as I head across the floor. She looks ready to fall over but I know she won't. Not while the Hangmen are still here. She simply takes the kutte I hand to her, wincing as she slips it on. Her jaw is swollen, her lips bleeding. She's not moving her fingers, just holding them carefully still. She's got the toe of her left boot on the ground but her weight's all on the right side.

And she's grinning like she just won the lottery.

"You're fucking amazing," I tell her. "How's the breathing?"

She manages a pained laugh. "Not so good."

"All right." Gingerly, I slip my fingers through her short, short hair. "We'll get you out of here soon."

And in that time, there's not a brother who doesn't

come up to her. Not a brother who doesn't see exactly what she took on herself to bring Croc down. I'm about to bust all their fucking heads for taking even a little more of her energy, but when I finally get her into my arms, helping her limp out to the Escalade that the prez rounded up, she says softly, "Do you suppose they finally think I belong?"

"You always did," I tell her and my voice is rough. I help her stretch out on the backseat, cradling her head in my lap. Gunner jumps in the driver's seat and barely waits for Stone to hop in on the passenger side before taking off. "Now just rest. We'll take care of you."

She nods, her breath just a tight rasp in her chest. Her eyes close.

Thirty minutes to the hospital. I hold her all the way.

SEVEN

LILY

Everything hurts.

I wake up in my bed. The sun's bright and peeking through a slit in the curtains. The other side of the mattress is empty but I can hear the shower running.

Jack. Naked.

The image always makes me smile but this time pain shoots through my jaw. Fuck. Groaning, I roll onto my side and wish I hadn't. Vaguely I remember the hospital, sitting through x-rays. The way I'm feeling, I'm guessing it's time for more drugs.

The water turns off. All that bare skin is wet now. He's probably rubbing a towel over every hard muscle—and here I am, laid up and unable to do a thing about it.

The one drawback to kicking Croc's ass. A big drawback. Shit.

As soon as Jack comes through the door, I rasp, "How long until we can have sex again?"

He grins. Holy hell, I hope it's not long.

"I didn't ask the doc," he says. "But even if I had a time to give you, you probably wouldn't wait that long anyway."

No, I wouldn't. "If I promise to give you a blow job on that day, will you help me up to pee?"

His hard face abruptly softens. "Any time you need, Lily. I'm here for you."

And he's careful, so careful as he lifts me. I was wrong about everything hurting. *Now* it fucking hurts. And there's a cast on my ankle. Jesus. I don't remember that happening at the hospital. I almost ask him to list the damage, then decide I really don't want to know right now.

Because Jack looks like he's in as much pain as I am, and I suspect there aren't any drugs that can help him.

Gently, I touch his face. "I know how hard it must have been."

"What?"

"Watching that fight go down." I stop him when he shakes his head, as if trying to deny it. But I know. Of all the things I thought would be rough when we got together,

I didn't think of this. But I should have. "You know why I'm not scared of you like some of the brothers are?"

"No." His voice is a rough mess that tears right at my heart.

"Because you kill easy. But you only do to protect what you care about. You think I don't know that?" I slide my aching fingers over his firm mouth. "You could have ended Croc so fast. You could have come in, torn him down. And because I was getting hurt, I bet there was nothing you wanted more than to do just that. To be my shield. Am I wrong?"

His jaw clenches for a long second. Finally he shakes his head.

"But you didn't." I lay my head on his broad shoulder. "You let me be who I am, let me do what I needed to do. I love you so much for that."

All the air leaves him on a shuddering breath. "Jesus, Lily. You fucking kill me every time you say that."

"Does it scare you?"

He stops and looks down, meeting my gaze. Once upon a time, those dark eyes were empty. Now I see everything I could want in them.

"It terrifies me," he says, then laughs. "Just fucking terrifies me."

I grin and don't care that it hurts. Then I pull him down for a kiss and don't care that hurts even more.

Jack fucking Hayden loves me. Against all odds, he fucks me *and* loves me.

And being here in his arms? Was worth every single risk.

BURNING
IT ALL

ONE

JACK

Lily texts me about an hour after I supposedly started out on a day ride with the brothers. *You kill anyone yet?*

I grin and set aside the paint-stripping coffee I bought at the bait shop. Water laps the sides of the boat. It's quiet up here on the lake. Outboard motors are prohibited so the only options for getting around are oars or paddleboat. That's partly why I'm meeting Creek here. We've both been given the same training: get in quiet, make the kill, and get out quick. But out here there's no quick getaway, and he sure as hell can't sneak up on me in the middle of two and a half square miles of water.

The day's young, I respond, though I don't expect to do any killing today.

I didn't choose this location because I thought Creek would try taking me out—although that possibility is always a factor. I chose the lake because it's October, most of the tourists are gone, and the likelihood of someone seeing us talking is pretty damn small. I'm the Hellfire Riders' warlord; he's a federal agent working undercover as a member of the Devil's Hangmen. There's no scenario where us being seen together turns out well.

Not even Knucklehead? she asks.

Not yet. Though sometimes the Riders' road captain is just asking for it. Maybe not for a bullet in the head, though. Just a bullet in the knee.

But I can't say whether Knucklehead is asking for it today and every response I send to Lily is too damn close to another lie. She thinks I'm out riding with the club. Later I'll tell her what I'm really doing—she already knows about Creek being undercover—but all at once my chest begins aching, because when shit like this comes up I start thinking about all the ways I could lose her.

I won't lose her over this lie. She understands I keep quiet about my dealings with Creek to protect the Riders. Hell, I don't even tell the club's prez when I'm setting up a meet. The more people who know about it, the more likely things will go wrong.

But I also lie to protect her, and that's where it gets complicated. Lily doesn't want any protection. She wants me at her back, not acting as her shield. But this meet is all about making sure a threat isn't coming for her. If there is, I have every fucking intention of stepping in before it reaches her.

She's already been hurt enough, risking everything to defend the Riders' territory. Last week she went up against the president of the Devil's Hangmen in a one-on-one fight that ended with Lily pounding the motherfucker's face in, but not before he did some heavy damage with his fists and his boot. I don't think I can survive seeing her hurt again.

But I *know* I won't survive if she's not breathing. So protecting her saves both of us. Even if it means living with the agony of losing her.

With stiff fingers, I rub at the ache growing in my chest, though nothing makes it go away. In the past week I've practically rubbed through my skin.

That hollow ache grows bigger every day. She loves me. Knocked me right on my ass when she told me. So if I lose that… Jesus. I just can't.

You doing all right? I know she probably is. I still need to be sure.

Peachy.

Only one word, but her frustration bleeds through my phone's screen. She's been laid up at home since the fight, her fractured ankle in a cast, her right wrist in a brace, and four of her fingers in splints. Those wouldn't have slowed her down much. Her ribs did. Three cracked, two broken, and everything bruised to fuck. Beneath the medical tape, her lean torso looks like someone splattered green and purple paint down her sides. She grits her teeth and says it's nothing, but I've been where she is now. I know that despite the painkillers, taking a breath feels like another fist slamming into her chest.

And knowing she's hurting is like a knife sawing into mine.

On the northwest shore, a kayak slides into the water. A glance through the binoculars confirms it's Creek. My phone buzzes again.

I'm about to start BSG season three.

Don't you fucking dare, I text back. Holding Lily against me while we burn through every episode of that show together has been the only upside of her being laid up. *Wait for me.*

But Starbuck is so damn hot and I'm sooooooo lonely.

Just another reason to wait until I'm there. Your fingers can't do anything but push buttons on the remote.

You cruel and dirty bastard.

That's true enough. But I know she's smiling as she sends the response.

I just hope she's not laughing, because laughing hurts her. *Watch the Avengers again. Don't forget to pause every time Thor comes onscreen.*

I feel like you're judging me. I also feel like I should invest in a Thor costume to use as soon as we can have sexy times again.

I'll wear it. Jesus, I'd dress in a tutu and a flashing clown's nose if it meant she was well enough for me to touch her without bringing more pain. Holding her should be enough, but I need to taste her, bury myself in her. Get so deep beneath her skin that she can't ever scratch me out.

The costume's for me. You can be Loki.

I grin and check Creek's location. Only a few hundred yards out. *I'm going quiet in a minute.*

Oh, good. Because it's incredibly stupid to text and ride, Jack fucking Hayden, and I've never thought you were stupid.

My stomach tightens, as if there's a razor pressed up against it. So she's already worked out that I'm not where I told her I'd be. All because she knows I wouldn't be texting if I was on my bike.

But fuck it all. If I intended to keep this meet secret from Lily, I wouldn't have responded. Texting her was careless. I knew it, but I did it anyway. Because this connection with her, this thing we've got going—it's the best thing I've ever known. I got by for a long time, just doing what needed to be done, and calling that living. But before Lily Burns, I didn't know how good living could be. Didn't know how seeing a few words on my phone could make it seem as if the sun's shining right down on me, warm and bright.

Still, there's no getting around that she caught me in

a lie. *You pissed off?*

Only because I'm stuck on my couch. Be careful.

Careful. I try to remember the last time anyone said that to me. My mother, maybe. Something like "Careful, you little shit. You'll wake your dad and we'll all pay for it."

I will, I text back. That response isn't a lie. I'll be as careful as protecting her allows me to be. I can't watch her back if I'm dead. *You rest up.*

I'll try. But I need to get out soon or I'll fucking explode.

Clubhouse tonight? A party always follows a ride. If Lily shows, this party will be for her. After the fight last week, we were off to the hospital so fast, she didn't get even half the back-slapping she deserved. The brothers would make up for that tonight. *I'll take you.*

Hard & fast, plz.

Fuck. I need to. Take her hard and fast, then deep and slow. But not tonight. Maybe not another week or two. With Lily's ribs like they are, fucking her, making her come would just hurt her worse. There's no goddamn way I'm getting off to that.

In another week or two, though… Christ. I'm going to bury my face between her legs and only come up for air so that I can slide my cock into her cunt and feel all that wet heat squeezing me tight. Then I'll have her ass, and fuck her until she's screaming as she comes, her fingernails ripping through my skin. Then, when she's sweaty and sated, I'll eat her out again, licking her pussy slow and sweet, because the way she sighs and lifts against my mouth, the way her fingers grip my hair, the way she breathes my name makes my fucking heart feel like it'll burst out of my chest. Because that feeling is agony and bliss all at once, and I can't get enough.

Losing that—losing *her*—is never going to be an option.

I'll burn the fucking world down first.

WHEN CREEK AND I SERVED together, he was called Gavin Taylor. That name probably wasn't any more real than the ones he's using now—"Luke Harris" on his driver's license, "Creek" on his kutte. He's not wearing his vest today. Neither of us wears our colors during a meet. Anyone who sees our patches might remember them.

As it is, we're both too damn memorable, physically. Too tall, too big. It's why Uncle Sam never used us for the subtle covert shit. For those operations, better to send in someone who doesn't draw attention to himself, someone who can be like a knife tucked away in a boot.

Creek and I were tanks that rolled in when knives weren't enough. We went in alone, did the job, and got the hell out. No need to lose ourselves in a crowd.

After a handful of years, I got all the way out. Creek didn't. He signed up with the feds. And for this job, he *is* the knife hidden in the boot. To anyone who looks, he's just another big motherfucker on a bike.

All the training we got is still there, though. So as he glides nearer with his kayak, he doesn't look anything like a biker. Instead he looks like an overdeveloped surfer boy up from California, with his blond hair slicked back and some kind of neon shit plastered all over his wetsuit. That's what anyone who sees him will remember. And me? I made sure the owner of the bait store got a good look at the fake scar pulling at my upper lip. That'll be what he remembers. The scar and the rest of what I'm wearing.

"Nice suspenders, bro," Creek says first thing.

"I'm partial to the hat." Tan canvas with fish hooks dangling around the rim. I picked it up years ago at a thrift shop on the coast. Junk like this always becomes useful at some point.

Creek glances at it, shakes his head. "Duuuuude. Scarface lumberjack angler just messes with my head. Having too many points of reference freaks me out."

I grin and he does, too—but we've both got our hands where the other can see them. This shit can be fun but it's also all business. I move too quick, or the wrong way, and I know he'll have a gun in my face. He knows I'll do the same.

Then the surfer dude act drops away and although we don't look alike, it's like staring into a mirror. Eyes flat, his face a grim mask that hardens with every passing year rather than wearing thin. A man who hides everything going on in his head.

Neither of us reveals anything easily. But there's one thing I can't hide, and Creek knows what it is. He knows why I'm here. So he doesn't tiptoe around.

"Your woman is in trouble," he says.

In trouble. The boat rocks gently beneath me as I let his words sink in. They don't have to go far.

Because I knew there'd be something coming back on her. The way she took out Croc? The Devil's Hangmen aren't going to let that go. If Lily were a man and thrashed their prez, they'd come after our club, not her alone, because there'd be no shame losing to a man. But she humiliated them, so now they'll want to break her. It doesn't matter Croc brought it on himself by making a wager and by assuming that because Lily had tits, she must be weak. He fucked up, but *she* will pay for his mistake. For not being what he thought she should be.

The remedy is simple, though: I kill them all. Including Creek, if staying undercover means going along with whatever the Hangmen are planning for Lily.

All that matters now is the timeline. "Will Croc come for her himself?"

"Croc's out," Creek says, and the news doesn't surprise me. I figured their prez was done as soon as Lily took him down. The Devil's Hangmen call each other 'brother,' but they'll put a bullet in each other's' heads for fucking up. "But Sherlock's eager to prove himself to the higher-ups."

Sherlock, the baby-faced little shit of a vice-president. His father is the president of the Hangmen's mother chapter in Vegas. "Trying to make daddy proud?"

"Not him. *Higher* up."

Ice splinters through my gut. He's not talking about a

motorcycle club. He's talking about the cartel paying the bills. "Why would they give a shit about Lily?"

"I don't know what Sherlock's told them. He's playing this one close to the vest. I can tell you he's been pretty goddamn pleased with himself…and that I've seen your woman, so it isn't hard to guess why."

No, it isn't hard. The Hangmen took over the Eighty-Eight's territory a little over a month ago—not long after the Riders found out the skinheads had been running girls through this area. The Hangmen are just picking up where the Eighty-Eight left off, helping a cartel move guns, meth, and girls through the pipeline.

The truth is, I don't give a fuck about the guns or the drugs. People make their own choices. The Riders come down hard on anyone trying to push shit onto local kids, but if someone wants to party on his own time? I say have at it.

But the girls, that's not their choice. And these fuckers treat them like they're trash. They aren't grabbed because of their looks or their brains or because of anything special about them; they're grabbed because they're young and vulnerable. Most of them probably lived on the street when they were taken, so no one goes looking for them. And when they've been used up, they're thrown out like garbage and replaced by another vulnerable girl.

Lily's not vulnerable. She's not as young as most of those girls, either. But motherfuckers who provide disposable sex slaves don't just cater to one kind of buyer. And

Lily? She's stunning. She's also a fighter. So some sick, rich fuck would pay a lot of money for the privilege to break her.

But these motherfuckers aren't *ever* going to touch her. "Who is Sherlock talking to? Who is paying the bills?"

With a shake of his head, Creek says, "I don't know—"

"Don't fuck with me." Each word falls dark and heavy, like a shovelful of dirt tossed into a grave.

Most men would get real uneasy when I use that tone. Creek just locks his gaze on mine. He's steady as hell, but that doesn't mean he's telling the truth. Lying is as easy as breathing to men like us. "If I knew, my job here would be done. But we can't get a fix on these assholes. We don't know where the money's going to or coming from. We don't even know where the girls end up or where the last leg of the pipeline is."

"You don't have a fucking name? A contact?"

"Croc used to talk to someone called Red Eye. I assume Sherlock's talking to the same. And now you know what I do."

Bullshit. "No, I don't."

He watches me, his posture loose, his expression giving nothing away. But I know he's waiting. Creek didn't come here just to give info. He wants an exchange.

Fair enough. "You tell me what you have. I'll reach out to other clubs, see what they've heard."

"But you don't act on that info until you've shared it with me."

Fuck that. "Then you best make sure Sherlock doesn't touch Lily, because if anyone comes after her, I will fucking *act*."

Creek nods. Probably he already knew that. It just needed to be laid out clearly between us. "These guys are ghosts online," he says. "The geeks have been tracing them back to Malaysia, Colombia, Austria—the digital trail goes cold every single damn time. But we think they're centered in-country and we know they've got people on the ground. People like Red Eye."

Because money is good whether it's transferred by hand or by a computer. But when taking on a new job, MCs will want a face-to-face.

Someone like Red Eye probably doesn't have a lot of power in the cartel. He would just be a messenger, a face to make the deals. But he'd know more about the organization behind him than the MCs do. "Why aren't you finding them?"

"They're smart. And they keep shifting shit around. We'll escort cargo and one time we'll hand it off to the Eighty-Eight. Next time, it'll be to the Desert Kings. Next time, someone else. Then they'll hand it off to another club. Never the same order. And tracing the route—backward and forward—is like untangling a fucking five-thousand-mile wad of fishing line."

"But the girls end up in a shithole somewhere."

"A distribution point. The end of the pipeline. That's what I'm looking for. That or the cage."

"What cage?" If they're moving a lot of girls, there sure as hell won't be just one.

He shakes his head. "*The* Cage. It's the one real connection I've been able to bring in. Cage fights."

"There's a lot of cage fights."

"To the death," he says. "Broadcast online. A ticket to watch starts at a million. But they make the real money on the gambling. They pick up the muscle on the underground circuit, basically put a gun to their head, tell them to fight."

Now that rings a fucking bell. A lot of clubs set up a ring during bike rallies. The fights are mostly friendly, just pounding chests and blowing off steam. But I've heard shit. That some of the patchholders who win in the ring disappear not long after. Most people put it down to some asshole sore loser from another club getting revenge—I know of a few wars between MCs that started because of that belief—or they assume the fighter took his prize money and rode off into the sunset. Bikers aren't exactly known for sticking around.

But running muscle isn't the same as running girls. "What was the connection?"

"When we were still part of the Vegas chapter, we got to watch one of the fights as a reward for the work we'd done. Or maybe it was a warning." His jaw tightens. "The prez of a club who'd pissed off Red Eye was in the cage. The prez lost."

I nod, thinking it over. The kind of questions I'll need

to ask my contacts can't be asked over the phone. I'll need a face to face. But I'm not leaving Lily here alone, and she's not up to traveling yet. Especially not if we end up in unfriendly territory. "I'll get more info. But it'll take time."

He blows out a breath that almost sounds like a laugh. "I've got six years in. A little more time doesn't matter. It's best you stick around the next week or two, anyway."

The back of my neck tenses. "Why's that?"

"We've got cargo coming. Maybe live cargo, maybe not. No firm schedule yet, and we don't know yet which club is bringing it in, because they keep that info to themselves until they're right on us."

Making sure word doesn't leak out. "And you think Lily might be added to whatever's coming."

His chin dips in a slow nod. "It'd be the time to do it. Sherlock knows better than to try holding her for long. Not with the Riders so close."

Close or far, taking Lily is a real fucking bad idea. But I see Creek's got more to say, so I wait.

"We could bring her in on this," he tells me. "She's tough as hell. She can hold her own while she's in. And we could find out where the pipeline goes."

Let Lily be taken, so that we can track her route? Then head in, guns blazing, rescuing her and the other girls, while getting our hands on the person responsible for distributing the women and collecting payments.

Yeah. Good fucking plan. Except that's never how it happens. What really happens is that they shoot Lily up with heroin or some shit, get her hooked, rape her and sell her. And even if we try to track her, that shit goes wrong too easily, too. Maybe the tracker gets found and we find it in her body later. Or they cut it out. Or we lose the fucking trail and she's gone.

I don't say a goddamn word but Creek's already backing off, holding up his hands, his gaze wary.

"Just throwing it out there," he says. "We've tried to get women inside before. Good agents. We just can't fucking…" His voice roughens and he stops, shakes his head. "These fuckers are always ahead of us."

So he thinks there's a leak in the FBI—and by putting in someone like Lily, someone unconnected, it might put his investigation ahead for once.

Good thinking. It's still not fucking happening. A plan like that, there's only one way it can go right, and a thousand ways it can go wrong. Those aren't good odds. Creek knows it, too. If he didn't, he'd have already taken this to Lily. He's only tossing it at me so I can tell him what he already knows: he needs a better plan. "You just make sure I get a heads-up when the time comes."

"I'll do what I can." With that, business is done. Preparing to leave, he dips his paddle into the water, then pauses. "I helped torch your place."

Because I crossed the Hangmen's prez, so he had his men burn down my auto shop, along with my apartment above it. "I guess you owe me one."

His gaze stays on my face for another second. Then

he nods and glides off, leaving me alone with a cold coffee and my fishing pole.

He doesn't owe me shit. I already knew he helped burn my place. And it didn't matter.

But I wouldn't tell him that. Being owed a favor is worth more to me than my garage or apartment were. They were just places to work, to sleep. A business. It didn't mean more than that, and insurance will cover the cost of building it again.

Some of the Riders would have taken it personally if the Hangmen had burned their place down. Hell, the brothers took it personally when *my* place burned down. But I can't feel anything like that, and I don't have many attachments to people or to things.

Just to the Riders. Just to Lily.

Emotionally, mentally, I'm fucked up. I know it, Lily knows it. Not all of my switches are flipped in the right direction and I don't feel some of the shit that other people feel. I know hurt well enough. My own family dealt out some deep fucking hurt, and I wear it tattooed on my skin. But I kill easy and the blood washes off without staining. No guilt, no remorse.

I've got lines I don't cross, though. A code. I don't touch anyone who's not a danger to the club. And I always go straight for the asshole who's causing the problem. No bullshit like threatening their wives or their kids or their homes.

For Lily? There's not a single line I won't cross. And

there's no ache in my chest when I think of crossing them. Only when I think of losing her.

So all these fuckers better be real careful, making sure they don't push me over that line. Because even I don't know exactly what I'm capable of. But I do know these bastards don't ever want to find out.

TWO

LILY

As soon as I hobble through the doors of the Riders' clubhouse, I realize that coming tonight was a huge fucking mistake.

Most of the brothers are here—and less than a week ago, they all watched as I beat the shit out of Croc. They all saw the damage he did in return.

Last week, those injuries were battle wounds. They were proof that I was a fucking machine. Unstoppable. Broken ribs? No big deal because I kept breathing, kept swinging. Croc stomps on my leg and snaps my ankle? Doesn't matter, I turn it around and take him down. My fingers swollen and the bones cracked? Shit, that's just what happens when you pound a motherfucker's head in. My lips busted and bleeding? Gives me more to spit in his face.

But I see the way the brothers near the door are looking at me now. I see the grimaces, hear some sharp breaths sucked in between teeth. Because the fight's over. They're not seeing *Lily Burns, Asskicker* now. They're seeing *Lily Burns, On Crutches.*

Five goddamn years, making sure they can never call me weak. Five goddamn years, proving that I can hold my own in this club. Last week, I finally cemented my place as a Rider, finally belonged.

Now I'm afraid I've ruined it all…and all because I was so damn tired of lying on my couch.

I shouldn't have come. But if I've fucked it up, it's too late now. And it's not like I can take off. With a cast on my ankle and splints on four of my fingers, I couldn't ride my bike here. Fuck, I couldn't even *drive* myself here. Instead Jack had to leave his bike behind and chauffeur my ass out to the ranch in my dad's old pickup.

Until this second, I hadn't thought twice about him driving me here. Hell, I enjoyed it. A few months ago, I'd have said nothing compares to a sweet ride on sweeter bike. But every minute I spend with Jack is just as good.

No. Every minute with him is *better.*

Except this minute. He's holding the door open for me but I can't even make myself look up at him. Not while I'm wishing I could turn tail.

The woman who fought for her place in this club never ran away. The woman Jack hooked up with doesn't back down. At this moment, there's nothing in me worth calling a Rider—and nothing that Jack would want to call his, either.

Christ. Right now I'm not *anything* he'd want to call his. I can't ride. I can't fuck. Croc clocked me in the jaw so hard I can't even open my mouth wide enough yet to suck Jack's dick. He pulled me off him when I tried to yesterday, after my split lip started bleeding again. Maybe he's wishing he could pull away completely, because this sure as hell isn't what he signed up for.

His voice low, Jack says, "You about to run scared?"

What the *fuck*? Does he think I'm a coward now?

Sharp pain shoots into rage. Instantly I want to fight. But when I snap my gaze up to his, his eyes aren't flat and empty. They're warm and teasing.

Because running scared is what I did before I told him I loved him. Somehow he saw the same thing happening now. Maybe recognized it.

Maybe he knows it's because this club means so much, because *he* means so much—and I'm so fucking afraid of losing either of them.

Warm and strong, his big palm settles against my lower back. "Trust us, Lily."

Not just him. *Us.* All the brothers.

It's hard. So fucking hard to trust that some of them won't use this weakness to tear me down. Or that seeing me like this won't change how they always look at me. I preferred the way they looked at me last week, when I was still bleeding.

But I'm not going to run, goddammit.

I'm just going to hobble through the door with my head up and not a bit of pain showing on my face. I can't hide everything, but the bruise on my jaw is mostly gone, my lips no longer swollen. My ribs are covered by the thin hoodie and kutte I'm wearing; they don't need to know about the mess going on underneath.

My spine goes rigid and my hobbling gait falters when I see Saxon Gray heading toward me, a bottle of beer in hand. Our prez is a mean son of a bitch, but he's had my back this week, making sure being laid up isn't putting my job at the airfield in jeopardy and telling me to send my medical bills to the club's treasurer. He's always had my back in one way or another. But his reaction now will set the tone for every other brother. If he treats me like I'm fragile, I'll probably just break.

He stops in front of me, and my heart pounds when he slowly looks me up and down, eyeing me over the bottle as he takes a swig of his beer. He's starting to get that pissed-off look in his eyes; I know it well. This isn't the first time he's aimed it at me.

Then he turns his head and the cold steel of his gaze

rakes over the brothers. "There's about fifty bastards who ought to be scrambling to be the first to put a drink in your hand. But it's still fucking empty."

"We thought you'd want to be first, boss!" Stone calls out.

"So I do." The prez points to a prospect, snaps his fingers, then meets my eyes again. "What'll it be, Zoomie? Bottlecap will bring it to you."

"Whiskey." My throat's so tight, I can barely even get it out. "It'll pair nicely with the Vicodin."

The prez grins. "Enjoy that shit while it lasts," he says before his expression becomes serious again. "You'll never pay for another drink at the Den."

The Wolf Den. He owns that bar, which serves as the Riders' primary hangout outside of the clubhouse—and it was part of the territory on the line when I went up against Croc.

"Thank you, boss," I say, still choked up. Beside me, Jack is suddenly laughing. Probably because he knows Saxon is going to regret that offer when he tallies up how much I drink.

Then again, maybe the prez has already prepared himself for the number. There's a slight smile playing around his mouth when he glances at Jack. "You got time, Blowback?"

The prez never asks. He just orders. But he's not deferring to Jack tonight. He's deferring to me, just in case I need Jack at my side.

I don't. I'd love to keep him there, but club business comes first. Jack didn't say much about his meeting with Creek. He just told me what we already knew—that the Hangmen will come after my ass, which means constantly watching my back. Not here at the clubhouse, though. Here, my back is covered.

"Go on," I tell him. "I'm going to park my ass by the pool table and pretend I'm wearing a crown."

"Bottlecap's yours," the boss says. "Not just tonight, not just for fetching drinks. You need anything while you're healing up, he gets it for you."

So I've got a flunky at my beck and call for the next few weeks. This night is already turning out a hell of a lot better than I expected.

Making my way over to the pool table is slow as hell. Not because of the crutches, but because the brothers are stopping me every few seconds to bump fists—or in my case, the back of my left hand—and to congratulate me for kicking Croc's ass. Bottlecap shadows me all the way, carrying my drink. Good kid. Quiet but steady, and slowly finding his place among the Riders.

Tonight that place is by me, and with the assholes I'd call my brothers even if we didn't wear the same colors: Stone, Gunner, Picasso, and Spiral. Each one more of a dick than the next, but I wouldn't trade them in.

Gunner leans on his pool cue as he looks me over. His gaze lingers up top. "So you went for the buzzcut, huh?"

I didn't have much choice. Before the fight, I hacked

away my braid with Jack's switchblade, then went after anything long enough for Croc to get his hands on, cutting some areas down to the scalp. Now my pale hair is about as long as peach fuzz, but I think it looks pretty badass. And as soon as it grows out a bit? I've worn my hair short before. It's sexy as all hell.

"Still prettier than you," I tell him and he grins, instantly making me a liar. The bastard is so damn pretty it hurts.

Shit. The truth is, everything hurts me right now, not just his pretty face. That short trek across the clubhouse felt like ten goddamn miles. When Bottlecap pulls a wide leather club chair up to the nearest table, I'm glad to finally take a breather.

Sipping my whiskey, I sink deep into the chair and set my crutches aside. Coming out here tonight *is* just what I needed. This old clubhouse used to be a lodge on a dude ranch, and although it hasn't been the Riders' home very long, this is right where I belong. Some shit loud music is pumping through the ancient sound system. It's Saturday in October, so all the widescreens are playing clips from today's college games, and half the clubhouse looks like a sports bar—but I suppose you don't see a lot of girls sucking dick in a sports bar. Beaver's sitting on one of the couches, eyes glued to the Oregon State highlights, hand resting on the blond head bobbing up and down on his lap. I haven't bothered to turn around since sitting down, but I can hear someone else jackhammering into pussy behind me, the heavy grunts and slap of flesh. Spiral's got his arm around a new woman, watching in turns the pool game and the fucking. It probably won't be long before he's got her bent over the table.

And, Jesus. Whoever it is behind me has got some stamina. They're still going at it as I finish my whiskey, and I'm halfway through my second, feeling warm and loose when Jack and the prez emerge from the boss's office. The prez is wearing a frown that says he didn't like whatever Jack had to tell him, and Jack…he's just wearing his standard *Don't fuck with me* face.

Holy shit, he is one goddamn sexy bastard. Built like a motherfucking eighteen-wheeler, long and tough and so deliciously rough, he's just one deadly, fucked-up combination of muscle and brains and hard, thick cock. In a club full of badass motherfuckers, he's the baddest. Most of the brothers will go out of their way to avoid him, as if they think Jack might casually reach out and kill them if they get too close. Not me. I know exactly who he is. And he's all mine, from his big neck-snapping hands to his dark eyes, all the way down to his shit-kicking feet.

Those dark eyes meet mine from across the clubhouse. He tilts his head, as if asking how I'm doing. I tip my glass in his direction. Doing just fine, baby.

A smile touches his firm mouth, then Jack heads to the bar with the prez, giving me a sweet view of a perfect ass encased by black jeans. Christ Almighty, I could just bite that ass. I *have* bitten it. Just sank my teeth into taut muscle—and the next second he flipped me onto my back, slammed his cock deep, then rode me hard.

I want another hard ride. My pussy's a hot, wet ache. Squeezing my thighs together doesn't help. Watching Jack makes it better and worse, all at once. Drink in hand, he leans against the bar, catches my gaze.

Oh, fuck yes. It's not just me. I don't even have to look at his crotch to see if he's hard. His face tells me. There's sex all around us, and I know what he's thinking of. Riding between my legs. Or imagining my lips wrapped around his dick.

I'll get to it as soon as I can. Because God knows I love the way he goes utterly still when I'm sucking his cock into my throat, his entire body tight as a tripwire. Hit it just right and he fucking explodes.

My smile's a tease. I know it. Maybe even a little cruel. But he loves that, too.

Then a pretty pair of tits blocks my view of Jack and a light weight lands in my lap. Oh, shit. My fucking ribs. Sasha barely weighs anything but the painful jolt of a near-naked body against mine bursts into white stars behind my eyes. I suck in a breath that just makes everything hurt more, and my smile becomes a gritting of teeth.

"Hey, Zoomie," she says, her fingers slipping over my peach-fuzz hair.

I want to shove her off my lap but I hold it together. She doesn't know my ribs are fucked and she doesn't deserve that kind of shit. We've had fun together. I've taken her to bed once or twice—though I was so drunk the second time, I'm not sure if we actually made it to the bed. I just remember a friend finding her panties the next morning, stuffed down behind the front seat of the pickup truck I was borrowing. "Hey, Sasha."

Her thumb slides across my bottom lip, gently running over the still-healing split near the corner. "I hear you're the hero of the day. And that you might be missing a softer touch…and something a little tastier than whiskey."

Ah. So one of the brothers sent her over. Maybe even thinking they were doing me a favor. Everyone knows I love pussy just as much as I love dick…and they all like the idea of me eating pussy more than they like to picture me sucking dick.

But although Sasha has a sweet pussy and a sweeter laugh, I love Jack a hell of a lot more than anything between her legs or in her head.

I brush her hand away from my face. "You know I'm with Blowback, right?"

"Yeah, I heard." Her smile's a little sad at first. Maybe because some of the partners she's had don't think that being with someone means being faithful. Attached or not, a lot of the brothers will fuck anything that opens their legs. Then she grins and pulls back, lifting up onto the table in front of me and setting her feet on the arms of my chair, giving me a look at the strip of red lace covering her cunt. She's already wet. No surprise. She's always liked performing—though before now, it's always been with the brothers. "But you can't tell me you aren't missing this, or that you don't deserve a little reward."

Her fingers dip into her panties and begin stroking her clit. That's hot as hell and bumps my simmering arousal up to burning, no lie. But I've got zero interest in joining in. Looking will do just fine.

But of course the brothers can't keep their fucking mouths shut. "Lick it!"

It takes one drunken shout and some others join in, chanting *Lick it* over and over, like they're all assholes in a fucking college fraternity. Goddammit. This is the kind of shit I always want to avoid. Not licking pussy—I've done that more than a few times where they can see me—but these stupid scenarios where backing down takes something away from me. Where backing down tears apart all the hard work I've put in.

And this could tear down more than that. I glance at Jack. By the burn in his eyes, I can tell he thinks this is just as hot as I do. I can't read anything else in his face, though. Maybe me eating out Sasha would be exactly what he wants. Maybe it would rip his guts out.

But that doesn't even matter. Because *I* don't want her pussy. And refusing it doesn't mean I'm backing down. These motherfuckers just need to step up their game.

I hold up my hand for silence, my fingers in splints, my wrist in a brace. The queen for the night.

They're damn well going to treat me like it.

JACK

THIS IS THE KIND OF SHIT I MIGHT LOSE HER OVER. Because I can see how she goes stiff, hurting when Sasha drops onto her lap. I can see she's gently giving the woman the brush-off, even though the teasing turns her on. And I can see how still her face becomes when Burnout shouts *Lick it!* and some of the others pick up the chant.

It's a challenge. To preserve her standing in the club, Lily can't back away from a challenge. For years, I hurt her that way—unintentional, but I hurt her all the same. Every time I opened my mouth, I thought I was having her back, but instead I made her work twice as hard to prove herself.

And stepping in, rescuing her now? She'd never fucking forgive me.

So I watch, my chest a big bloody ache. Not because she'll touch another woman—I know she's trapped and it doesn't mean shit—but because I can't help her without making it all worse. I've seen her lick pussy before, and it's fucking hot. But she was all in then, going full throttle. Watching her do something she doesn't really want? Nothing sexy about it.

I've got a white-knuckled grip on my glass as she raises her hand. *Just look at me, Lily. Just ask me and I'll blow this all apart.* But she doesn't glance my way. Instead she waits for the bastards to fall silent.

Her full mouth flattens into a thin line, and she shakes her head like she's disappointed in all of us. "You fuckers," she says and her gaze settles on Burnout for a second before moving on to the others. "If anyone else was sitting in my place, would you send a girl over so he could lick her pussy? Hell, no. You'd send her over to suck a dick. And you'd send someone who could suck it good. So if you want to give me a reward, you better send over someone who can do some *prime* pussy eating."

I start across the clubhouse before she finishes. Now her gaze meets mine, and she's so fucking amazing, beating all these assholes without even getting up out of her chair.

But goddamn Spiral has a death wish. The brother grins and leaves his woman standing by the pool table, heading toward Lily and saying, "If you want prime, Zoomie, you just spread those long—"

He doesn't see me coming. I'm gentle, grabbing his neck and smashing him facedown into the table, but not so hard he'll lose any teeth or blood. Shrieking, Sasha scrambles down, straight into Lily's lap again.

I lean in, my fingers tightening around the sides of Spiral's throat. "Back off."

"I'm already across the room, man," he wheezes.

Good. I let him go.

Lily's eyes gleam. Seeing me throw down Spiral fucking turned her on. And coming for her like this? I'm as hard as a goddamn rock.

Sasha clings to Lily, eyeing me warily. "You need help?"

Hell, no. But I let Lily tell her. She gives Sasha a little tap on the ass. "We both know you enjoy receiving a lot more than you enjoy giving, sweetie. Bottlecap can take care of you, though, if you want him to."

She hands Sasha off to the prospect, but I don't watch to see if they decide to hook up. My eyes are only for Lily as I sink to my knees in front of her.

Her cheeks are flushed, her lips softly parted as she watches me. Everyone's watching me. I don't give a fuck. Let them see how much I worship her. Let them see that I'd kill every one of them just for the chance to kneel at her feet.

My fingers slide up her thighs. Thanks to the cast on her ankle, she's wearing stretchy yoga pants instead of her usual jeans, and we're both damn lucky for it. I'll be able to get at her cunt without completely stripping her bottoms off.

"It's going to hurt your ribs," I say quietly, gaze holding hers. "When you come, it's going to feel like a truck dropped on you."

She slides down a little, so her ass is at the edge of the leather seat. "You better make it really good, then."

I never expected any other answer. Slowly I curl my fingers around the waistband of her pants. In her bed, I'd kiss her first, then suck on her big rosy nipples, rolling them against my tongue and teeth until she was panting and squirming. But I'm not giving the others that much of her. They've never had *this* much. Lily's licked pussy in front of us before, but not more than that. Definitely never let her ass hang out enough to have sex. She'll walk into the showers naked after a workout without blinking an eye, but doing this? She never wanted the brothers looking at her the same way they do the old ladies and club pussy. She'd seem too damn vulnerable.

But she doesn't seem vulnerable now, using her uninjured fingers to push my head down. The buzzcut makes her look a little younger, a little softer, but her eyes are the same flinty gray, always striking sparks of laughter, temper, and need.

They're fucking burning right now. I ease the pants down over her ass. Beneath she's wearing white cotton boyshorts. Some women wear fancy shit to look sexy. I've seen Lily in fancy shit, in tiny bits of silk, in lace thongs that I've ripped aside to make room for my cock, and, a couple of times when the laundry caught up with her, in some granny panties she digs out from the bottom of the drawer. It never matters—whatever she's wearing is the sexiest damn thing I've ever seen. *She* makes it look hotter than fuck. And these little shorts? The way they hug the top of her lean thighs, the way the cotton stretches over the hollows of her hipbones make me want to blow my load right here.

And the way her pussy juices are already soaking through makes my mouth water.

Gaze on her face, I slide two fingers beneath that drenched cotton and straight up into her hot pussy. A groan rips from her throat, her eyes closing, her back arching. Her inner muscles clasp me tight, her thighs tensing.

I push my thumb up to circle her clit. Her hips buck. A rasping "Fuck" breaks from her, then she's grabbing my hair as tight as she can, her breath hissing between her teeth. God, this woman. She always loves a good fight.

So do I.

Pain pulls across my scalp when she gives my hair a sharp tug. *"Lick,"* she grits out. "And make it fucking *prime."*

I pull out and lick her juices from my fingers. She responds with her low, husky laugh and another tug.

"Jack," she says. It's all she needs to.

With my hands beneath her knees, I lever her thighs up over my shoulders. Her legs and her pants are like a collar around the back of my neck, but I don't care if I'm chained here, her pussy laid out like a feast in front of me. She's perfect, from the soft cornsilk curls trimmed into a neat strip to the slick arousal coating those plump lips.

I know just how she likes it—it's the same way I like it. Sloppy. Rough. I part her swollen folds with my thumbs and dive straight in.

Teasing. Licking everywhere but her clit. She tastes so damn good, I don't care how long this takes. I can do it forever. I hear some of the brothers cheering me on but they don't even fucking exist now. Just Lily. Just the way she moans. Just the way her thighs tighten against my ears.

Just the way she gets wetter and wetter, the way her hips rock her cunt against my mouth, the way she chants my name.

The way she stiffens and cries out when I slide my tongue up through her slick folds and suck on her clit. The muscles in her legs quiver.

Fuck yeah. She's getting close. So damn close. I know it's going to hurt her but I also know that she's all in, and she's not going to shy away from the pain when she's chasing down her pleasure.

So fucking strong. So fucking beautiful. I don't have any faith in God but if I was ever going to be a believer, Lily Burns would be the reason why. She's a fucking miracle—and she's letting me taste her. This must be as close to heaven as any man will ever get.

Except her pussy's a hell of a lot sweeter than any pearly gates.

I go hard at her clit, licking, sucking. Her body bows up out of the chair and she hangs there suspended for an endless moment, then I push a finger deep inside her tight heat and she comes, the inner walls of her cunt squeezing at me, her flesh convulsing under my tongue. I groan and keep licking until her hand lands on my head and shoves me away.

My mouth wet with her juices, I look up, breathing as hard as she is. Skin flushed and sweaty, she looks down at me. And there's still no one else here. Just her.

"All right?" My voice is rough, my tongue already

missing her taste.

"I'll live." She grins and her fingers slide down the side of my jaw. "That was prime pussy eating," she adds on a breathless laugh, but I know that's not what she's really saying.

She's saying she loves me. It's still fucking terrifying. There's so much to lose. And I just want to hold her close and bury my face in her pussy again.

Lily must be thinking the same. "Let's get the hell out of here," she says softly.

LILY

I *HAVE* EARNED MY PLACE in the club. I've always said it but I still kept waiting for everything I've fought for to collapse around my head. But belonging must have finally sunk in, all the way in, because when Jack drags my pants back up over my ass and picks me up right out of the chair, I don't give a damn what the brothers might think of it.

Maybe because it still stuns me every time he does this—picking me up as if I'm not six feet tall and weigh in at more than a buck fifty. But mostly because there's no one who can tear me down now. I don't have anything left to prove.

And if any of the brothers suggests I ought to prove something? He can go fuck himself.

Jesus. A lot of them *are* fucking themselves. As Jack

carries me to the doors, I've never seen so many brothers with their hands down their pants—and of those who have a woman, he's either fucking her or watching me while she sucks his dick.

Not surprising, I guess. If I'd been watching Jack eat pussy, I'd have had my hands down my pants or shoved the nearest face between my legs, too. So we're leaving behind an orgy. Hell, we *sparked* an orgy.

The Riders always throw a damn good party.

Outside it's cold and clear, the moon shining bright through the pines surrounding the clubhouse. A pang hits my chest when I see all the bikes lined up. I love riding on nights like this. But I can't complain about a cage when Jack is sitting beside me.

He doesn't open the truck's door. Instead he sets my ass on the cold hood and stands between my legs, our faces almost on level. In the dark, with his back to the lights at the clubhouse entrance, his features are just unreadable angles and shadows.

His voice isn't unreadable. It's like a boot scraping over gravel as he says, "You all right?"

Because he knows I wouldn't have said otherwise in there. But I didn't lie. That orgasm hurt just as bad as he'd warned me it would. I was still all right.

"Yes," I tell him. "Are you?"

"Yeah," he says. But the roughness is still there.

It isn't hard to guess why. I know how I'd be feeling right now. "I wouldn't have touched her."

"I know." His strong hands slide around my waist, fingers locking together at the small of my back. "But do you want both? If you do…we'll make it work."

My heart twists. So that's it. Not worried that I want Sasha or someone else, but worried he won't be enough.

"I don't want both." I swing both ways but, with the exception of a few wild nights over the years, I only swing one way at a time. But it's not even that. It's not his dick I'm here for. I love his dick—God, do I love it. But I'm here for *him*. "We said we're going to do this thing. Whatever this is, you and me. So I'm all in. And I can't go all in with you if I'm going partway with anyone else. So I'm good."

"Good," he echoes gruffly.

Smiling, I catch the edge of his collar with my forefinger and tug him forward. "But I'm not saying it's not hot to imagine it. Or to watch. I think we can agree that women are sexy as fuck."

I feel his grin against my mouth. "We can."

Oh, yeah, we can. Especially because he's got one goddamn sexy woman in his arms right now. I catch his lower lip between my teeth, loving the heat of his mouth as I slick my tongue in to meet his.

His kiss is gentle in return. Just a soft taste.

Afraid of hurting me again. And the truth is, I don't think I could take a fucking right now. No matter how much I want him inside me, I'm feeling every hit that Croc got in. Worse now than when we first got here. But that doesn't mean Jack needs to go without.

"I want to watch you come for me," I tell him.

His big body stills. He's quiet. Not rejecting the idea, I don't think. Just weighing whether he wants to do it here.

The sound of his belt unbuckling is his answer, but he adds, "You won't be able to see."

Here, in the dark, with his body blocking the light. But it doesn't matter. "I've got a good imagination."

It's not his dick I love watching, anyway. It's him. He's jacked off for me before, in the shower, in bed, all over my tits. But as gorgeous as his cock is, the real beauty is how he loses himself when he's with me this way. How his mask peels away. I don't need to see him to enjoy all that. I just need to feel him against me.

His breathing deepens when he takes his cock in hand. With splints on my fingers, I can't help him much. But I've still got a mouth.

Leaning forward, I lick the hollow of his throat before biting gently at his skin. He smells so good, like a hot engine and the dust of the road. "You've watched me before. With women."

His breath shudders. "Yes."

"Did you like it?"

A rough laugh is his answer. The rhythmic flex of his arm quickens.

"I know you liked watching me with Jenny," I tell him. Jesus, just remembering the way Jack looked at me afterward, remembering the hard outline of his cock against his jeans still turns me on. And I fucking hated him then. "What were you thinking? Maybe you were thinking that while I was on my knees licking her pussy, you'd get up behind me."

His chest rumbles on a tortured groan. "Fuck, Lily."

I grin against his jaw. "Mmm, yeah. You'd get up behind me, push my jeans down. Then you'd slip your fingers between my legs and feel how wet I was."

The fingers of his left hand tighten on my hip. "How wet?"

Almost as wet as I am now. "Fucking drenched. You could have slid your cock right into me. So fucking deep. And I'd have had sweet pussy on my tongue and your dick filling me up."

Hot and hard, Jack's mouth latches onto my neck. He's rocking between my legs, the truck swaying as he fucks into his hand. And, Jesus. *Jesus.* I've never been this turned on just by talking about sex. I want to tear off my kutte, let him suck on my tits, find some way to ease this burning ache.

I wrap my legs around his thrusting hips. "God, do you remember? She tasted so good when she came, and I was so fucking wet when I was done. Then I looked at you, and you were giving me that dead flat stare, but I could see how hard you were. And I wanted…I wanted…"

"What?" Jack growls the question against my lips before kissing me hard, fucking my mouth with his tongue. I'm huffing like a steam engine when he pulls away. "Tell me."

"I just wanted to tear you apart. God." I lift my arms around his neck, not caring how much the movement hurts. "I just wanted to slam you down to the ground and fill myself up with your cock and fucking *make* you come. Just fuck you until you were begging me to stop."

He slams up the truck and groans. I ride the sharp jolt, hold him so close as he buries his face in my neck. His big body shudders.

Then he's kissing me again, long and slow, before he says, "I'd never want you to stop."

"A damn good thing, because I wouldn't have." No matter how he begged. He's mine now. "Also, you just jizzed all over my dad's old truck."

A laugh shakes through him. "I'll wash it."

"Don't." I pull him close again. "The asshole is probably rolling over in his grave. So I kind of like it, in a fucked up and spiteful way."

"Then I'll jack off on it every day."

God. Laughing hurts too damn much. But then Jack kisses me again, and all the hurt in the world couldn't stand against the sweetness of it.

And despite the pain, everything is perfect.

THREE

LILY

Everything is fucked.

I should have known. I've earned my place. I don't have anything left to prove. But for some of these guys, asking them to treat me like any other patchholder requires them to perform crazy mental gymnastics—and do it with brains so inflexible they can't even touch their fucking toes.

So now I'm sitting here and listening to the executive board debate whether the Riders should go in and take the Hangmen out…and if they do, whether I should be allowed to accompany them. And I'm trying to keep cool. Only a few meetings ago, the prez skinned me for losing my temper and tossing another brother onto his ass. But this shit, man. It could make even the Dalai Lama's head explode.

The meeting started out okay, too. Three things on the agenda. One was whether we should hold a vote at the next general meeting to patch in one of the prospects. One was about looking into the Cage, and trying to find out whether the fighters disappearing really did end up in some crazy death match.

Jack brought that in and set it up for the others without once mentioning Creek. Instead he laid it out simply: we need a way to take down the Hangmen without bring attention to the Riders. A few months ago, we burned down the Eighty-Eight's compound, and—thanks to Jack and his stash of smuggled weapons—the Eighty-Eight and their higher-ups think the feds did it, and the feds think a cartel took the skinheads out. If we go after the Hangmen now, there's going to be some eyes looking hard at the Riders, and maybe some retaliation coming from the Eighty-Eight's other chapters, which totals more than two thousand skinheads strong.

We're strong, but not that strong.

The Riders have friends, though. And that's who we'll be reaching out to. If we connect the Devil's Hangmen to the fuckers who are killing off patchholders from other

MCs, it won't be just us against them. No one will have reason to look at us too close.

But setting up those meets takes time and traveling money, which the board has to approve. Jack won't be the only one visiting the other clubs, either. Gunner and Stone are both regulars up in the ring during bike rallies; they've been up against some of the missing men and have solid contacts at other MCs.

The vote goes through easy. Stone and Gunner agree to make the first visit that weekend, which suits Jack fine, because I know he's still waiting to hear from Creek about whatever cargo the Hangmen will supposedly be moving soon.

Creek told him one or two weeks. It's the end of the second week now. We expected Sherlock to make a grab for me, but no one's even seen the Hangmen around.

But of course that brings us to the third item on the agenda: the Hangmen, and discussing our options if the Riders have to move against them, or if the Cage stuff doesn't pan out. And specifically, the question on the agenda is the extent of my involvement if it all goes to hell.

The scenario where the Hangmen grab me and the Riders charge in? I'm fine with that. It's the other scenario that has my peach-fuzz smoking, the one where the Hangmen push us so far that we don't have any other choice but to push back. Like the Eighty-Eight did, when they killed one of our brothers and shot our prez.

I was part of the small group of Riders who took out

the Eighty-Eight. I had my brothers' backs, using a sniper rifle to cut down any skinheads coming at them, and I took a fucking bullet in return. But now they want to sideline me?

Hell no.

If my injuries were the reason, okay. But we're talking about shit that'll happen down the road and it's been three weeks since my fight with Croc. My fingers and wrist are out of their splints and I'm back at work. Not flying yet, but maintaining the aircraft engines again. My ribs are still twinge-y, but I'm mostly good there. I can't run or fight on this cast but I'm not using crutches anymore; I can put weight on it. A few more weeks and there shouldn't be a single issue.

There *shouldn't* be. But some of these guys always come up with something. And the worst part of it is they're doing it to protect me.

Not having my back, but standing as my shield. And it's pure bullshit.

Well, most of it. Some of it's true. But that's always the goddamn problem, because they use truth to back up bullshit thinking.

Like when Knucklehead comes out with, "Look, we know assholes like this target women first. Like the Eighty-Eight did to the prez's woman. Or when they took out your ride, Zoomie. You never even looked twice at them before that, but they looked at you. Because, well, look at you."

Because I wore a kutte and rode a beautiful custom bike, and some men just hate women who step out of place. Some men want to destroy any woman who does. I knew that was the reason; I always knew it. I'm just surprised Knucklehead is that perceptive; I figured he was the one who requested the agenda item in the first place, because he could tattoo MISOGYNIST across his forehead and never see any difference when he looked into the mirror.

Then he ruins the tiny bit of goodwill he built up when he adds, "It's the same with the Hangmen. So if we move against them, they'll look for you. They'll target you. And it won't be enough to put a bullet in your head; they'll do other shit to you first. We all know it. They'll hold you down and each take a turn. And knowing that'll happen if shit goes wrong will throw all of us off. Rip our guts out."

God, I tried. But I can't keep my mouth shut after that. "So you're telling me that in a scenario where I'm gang-raped, your primary concern is how *you're* going to feel?"

He spreads his hands. "I'm just saying. They'll try to get their hands on you and hurt us with it."

"So I should just, what—sit in the clubhouse and play with my tits?" I shoot a look at the prez. "Did I not hold my own against the Eighty-Eight?"

"You did," he says simply. He hasn't been putting much into the discussion yet. Mostly just letting the other brothers talk.

Same with Jack, but that shit's complicated. He opens

his mouth to support me and it could go backward. So he just sits quietly next to me, listening and wearing his *Don't give a shit* face.

But he does. I suspect he's probably had this same argument with himself a thousand times since we hooked up. I know it killed him to watch while Croc pounded on me. Jack could have taken that bastard down so easily, but instead he let me do my job—because he knew I'd lose everything if he stepped in.

I have so many reasons to love him. But knowing how he held back despite his need to protect me, knowing how he understood and respected who I am…it meant everything to me. I'd have loved him for that alone.

Fortunately, he's not the only one in this club who knows me inside and out. I look to Gunner. "You had your ass trapped against the side of a house while I cleared a path for you. I took a bullet and cleaned up the mess. Do you think I should sit this one out?"

"No," he says. "Knucklehead's right that they'll target you. But I know you don't break easy."

"I don't think anyone's questioning whether you've got balls, Zoomie," Duke puts in, looking pained. Probably torn between both sides of the argument. He's all right, most of the time. But it's hard to forget that, five years ago, he walked away from the Riders because they let me in. He's come around about my being in the club but he's got an protective streak around women.

Which is fine, if the women like that kind of thing. I

sure as fuck don't.

Bull leans in and adds his first bit of the day. "Considering that she sleeps naked next to Blowback, I figure she's got bigger balls than anyone else in this room. Especially if you've heard his Peru story."

Shit. I haven't heard his Peru story. But whatever it is, recalling it makes half the brothers around the conference table cringe and look anywhere but at Jack. The other half laugh, as if agreeing they'd rather sleep on a bed of razors than next to Jack, and the laughter breaks the rising tension. But that's Bull. Always cracking some joke to defuse a situation. A big grizzly bear of a biker with a non-confrontational Winnie the Pooh heart.

Non-confrontational until it comes time to throw down, that is. Then his fists are like hammers. And that's fair enough. Not everyone likes a fight as much as I do.

Except I'm not really enjoying this one. My stomach's a fucking knot. Because if I get sidelined once because someone is worried about how seeing me hurt will make them feel? I'll always be sidelined.

They might as well just put the bullet in my head themselves.

"Look," I say. "I get that you don't want to see another Rider hurt. You don't want to see a *girl* hurt." I have to spit that out. "But leaving me on the bench will hurt anyone who goes up against the Hangmen more than it'll help them. That's a brother who will go in without someone to watch his back. That's a gun that doesn't have anyone to pull the trigger or lay down cover. That's two fists that could be pounding a Hangman's face in. The rest of it—the worry about what'll happen to me? It's just a mental game. Something assholes like that use to make their enemies drown in doubt. It's them beating us before we ever head in. And if someone can't do their job because I'm a woman, then *I'm* not the fucking problem."

Jack says flatly, "War often *is* a mental game. Not 'just' one. Because mental games can cause big fucking problems."

His response is a knife in my gut. Though maybe he didn't mean it to be. I can't tell. His eyes are dark and empty, his gaze steady.

He wouldn't tear me down. He wouldn't. But he would challenge me—push me to do better.

And, okay. Maybe saying that feelings don't matter is shit. They *can* be used to inflict more hurt. They *do* affect how people act.

They don't need to be the chains that hold someone else back. "All right. That's true. And the last war I was in? I flew more missions than anyone else in my unit. So I'll tell you what my superiors and the other airmen never said. '*Geez, Zoomie. This might be dangerous for you, so why don't you stay at the base this time?*' No. They told me if I went down, if I got captured, shit was going to get real fucking bad. Then they told me to hold on. To do whatever I need to survive. And they told me if all that shit happened, they'd come for me as soon as they could and mow the fuckers down. That's all I expect here. And it's what I'd do for any of you."

Silence.

I'm sure someone will come up with another argument sometime. But right now, I think they're argued out.

My heart's pounding when I look to the prez. This won't be a vote. He'll just make a decision one way or another.

Slowly he nods. "I didn't give you a patch just to watch you sit on your ass," he says and his steely gaze moves to Jack. "And I don't want this shit coming down to a shootout between us and the Hangmen. It will if they touch Zoomie. We need to keep them off her until we can connect with other clubs and hang it all on this cage fight. So if any Hangman gets to her, that's on you."

What the hell? That's not fair. And completely fucking unnecessary. Jack would always have my back.

But the prez isn't even ordering him to have my back. He's ordering him to be my shield. Protecting me *and* the Riders—so that the club can avoid the Eighty-Eight's retaliation and the fed's microscope.

It's all…exactly what Jack would want.

The billowing relief that followed the prez's decision settles into a thick, heavy weight in the middle of my gut. It grows heavier as the meeting wraps up and the brothers start filing out. Beside me, Jack's not moving, and I can't even fucking look at him.

A lot of the brothers are uneasy around him. He *is*

scary. But not for the reason most of them think; it doesn't have a damn thing to do with how many ways he can kill someone with his bare hands. No, the real scary shit is the way Jack thinks. The way he can see a goal, set everything up so it falls like dominoes, right where he wants…and doesn't leave a trace of himself behind.

Like the way we were able to take out the Eighty-Eight without any shit coming back on us. And the way Jack killed the enforcer Croc sent after him when the Hangmen first showed up—deliberately making sure Croc targeted him, then turning the enforcer's death around to look like an accident, so that it wouldn't start a war between the clubs. He's been the boss's right hand for a long time, and I knew he stopped a lot of trouble before it started, but until I hooked up with him, I didn't realize how *much* trouble he stopped and how many dominoes he arranged. Because he never left that trace.

But I see a trace now. Because the prez hides it well, but I'm pretty damn sure the boss is pissed off at him. It's in the way he's sitting, just staring at Jack, and not saying a damn word as everyone else takes off. It's in the last order he gave him, and how he laid the responsibility for my safety right on Jack's shoulders.

That was damn fucking cold. Saxon is mean, but he's not usually that cruel. Especially to a brother. So the only explanation for laying it on Jack is that he's pissed.

He's still pissed as he finally rises from his chair and heads to the door—and I figure my one chance at knowing the truth of this is about to leave with him.

"Boss," I say, and every word seems to scrape my throat raw. "Who put that last item on the agenda?"

I know he won't say. Unless a board member reveals it himself, that info is kept confidential so delicate shit can be brought to the table without blowing back onto a brother. But his gaze shoots to Jack, and his voice is like stone as he says, "Telling you would cause big fucking problems."

Big fucking problems. Just like emotional shit can cause. Just like mental games can cause.

Just like Jack said.

Yeah. I thought so.

The door closes softly behind him. I want to get up. I want to run from the hurt ripping through my gut.

I want to punch Jack's fucking face in.

"So it must have been fun watching that play out," I tell him, but I don't sound pissed. Instead my voice sounds full and thick, and wobbling right on the edge of crying. God *damn* it. "Because I know you'll never let it get to the point where the Riders are shooting it out with those fuckers, so the whole question of my being there doesn't even matter. So what was the endgame? You felt you had to strong-arm me into accepting your protection?"

"Not you," Jack says hoarsely. "Not you, Lily. Strong-arming you is what I'm trying *not* to do."

Oh, the bastard. How goddamn *dare* he sound ripped up? How goddamn dare he look at me like that, with his dark eyes as desolate as a fucking wasteland.

"Then what the hell was it about? Do you *like* seeing me on the edge of losing every fucking thing I've fought for? *Again?*"

"No. God, Lily." Despair lines his face when reaches for me and I flinch away. He freezes for a long second, his eyes emptying. His hands curl into fists and he sits back. "The boss would never pull you out."

Another knife slashes through my stomach. "So the prez fucking knew what you were playing, too?"

"No."

I don't understand. "You wanted the prez pissed at you? Were you strong-arming *Saxon*? Into doing what?"

"Putting the responsibility for your safety in my hands," he says, and although his voice is flat, he's rubbing at the center of his chest like it hurts him. "So that when I go after the Hangmen, it's not because I'm protecting you. Instead it's what the boss put on me."

I stare at him. *Not because I'm protecting you.* Except by doing this, none of the brothers would ever be able to suggest that Jack took out the Hangmen because I couldn't handle the threat on my own. No one could say Jack had to bail me out of danger.

I couldn't say it, either. I could never accuse him of standing as my shield. He would just be doing what the boss said to do.

How do I even process that? "So you didn't want me to know that you *are* protecting me."

His eyes close and he rubs at his chest, rubs while his throat works. But he doesn't say anything. Just rubs and looks like he's suffering all the levels of hell.

Good. So he feels like I do.

My breath hitches when I try to speak again. "Do you think I'm so fucking stupid that I can't see the difference between you—the Riders' warlord—taking out a threat to a patchholder, and you—the man I'm in love with—standing as my shield?"

"Lily." His face is haggard when he opens his eyes, his gaze bleak as it meets mine. "There is no fucking difference. I'm that warlord. I'm that man. And if I can protect you while I'm protecting the club, I fucking *will*."

So he does think I'm stupid. Or maybe I just *am*. Because my heart is hurting, and my head is hurting, and I still don't understand why he didn't just tell me what I was walking into.

And now I'm too close to it. Too close to him. And too full of all these goddamn emotions that cause so many big fucking problems.

Blinded by a flood of sudden, stupid tears, I nod and get to my feet. "Okay. Whatever. I'm heading home."

I hear the breath he sucks in, sharp and ragged. But he doesn't say anything. Doesn't say anything until my hand's on the door, and then the world fall apart around me.

Because he asks, "You want me to start bunking somewhere else?" but his question sounds like it's echoing from a corpse's chest, as if he's already sure of the answer and it's killing him.

Jesus, he's so fucked up.

My tears spill over and I wipe them away. "No, you asshole," I tell him. "Just give me an hour alone so I can deal with this shit. And tell me you're still all in."

"I'll never be out," he says roughly, and there's life in his voice again, but I know if I turn around I'll start bawling, and I hate these stupid fucking tears.

"Good," I say, then slam the door behind me.

I wish I could slam it on his head.

FOUR

LILY

IF MY ANKLE WASN'T IN A CAST, I'D SPEND THE NEXT FEW hours riding my bike, clearing my head, letting everything settle. Instead I drive home with the windows down.

Home is a split-level ranch I got for a steal after returning from Afghanistan. I've been sharing it with Jack the past few weeks. At first, he just stayed nights, but after his own place was torched, he's been here full time. Our lives slid together so easy. The only change I've made is hiring a housecleaning service, because I don't keep up with my mess and I don't want neat-freak Jack to try.

It's been good. So damn good. I don't ever want to lose it. I know he doesn't want to, either.

But now I realize he's been expecting to.

I feel hollowed out as I take the stairs up from the garage. The tears never developed into full-on bawling, and there's still a hot ache lodged in my chest.

I don't know what the fuck happened back at the clubhouse. I'm still trying to untangle it. But I know both Jack and I are new to this relationship shit. There's nothing behind either of us but a series of hookups. So maybe it's a miracle we got this far without a blowout.

Maybe it's a miracle we got this far at all. I mean, Jesus. Jack is completely fucked up, but he's not the only one. My dad used to be the Hellfire Riders' prez, and he'd have cut off his dick before letting me patch in. My mom is *still* telling me I should be a biker's old lady instead of a patchholder; according to her, my entire existence is an affront to my father, and even after he died, she never let me forget it. My whole damn life, every decision I've made was with an eye toward becoming a Rider. And once I got in, I spent every damn second making sure no one could come up behind me and tear me down.

I stopped watching for Jack. Because I don't *need* to. Whatever shit happened today, I know that.

It just takes a little time to remember it.

He'll give me the hour. He's always given me space when I need it. But I'm not surprised when I hear the sexy growl of his bike rolling in as the minutes pass sixty. He'll be preparing to fight—to fight *for* me. For this.

So will I.

I'm waiting for him in the living room, sitting on the arm of the sofa, when he comes up the basement stairs. So fucking big and gorgeous and dangerous—and looking like he's already been through hell, yet expecting to wade through another few levels. He stops when he sees me, his long body tense. His dark gaze sweeps me head to toe.

"You all right?" His voice is a fucking mess.

So is mine. "Yeah. I just want to know why the hell you didn't tell me what you were doing."

His jaw clenches and he shakes his head. Not refusing to answer, I know, because he makes a noise that almost sounds like a laugh. But the wry look he gives me is tortured rather than amused.

"I fucked up before and hurt you," he says gruffly. "I was trying not to fuck up again."

"By questioning whether I can stand with the brothers? Really?"

"It wasn't supposed to be a real question, because the answer was so damn obvious. I just forgot to add in the shithead factor."

The way he calculates risk. The shithead factor is the one he doesn't see because he can't think the way other people do. "Like Knucklehead?"

"And you, responding to any bullshit he says. Because I can't *see* you as someone who needs to be kept home for her own protection. So I can't imagine why you'd waste a second of your time telling him to fuck himself. But I should have. So I fucked up."

"Considering a topic of discussion was my inevitable gang-rape, I'd say that you fucked up spectacularly. Yet you still got what you wanted. Except for me knowing you're standing as my shield."

"Yes." His voice is hoarse again. He swallows hard, rubs at his chest. "I'm so fucking afraid of losing you, Lily."

And there it is. The heart of it. For both of us.

I breathe out a shaky laugh. "Good. Because that means I'm not the only one who's scared."

His jaw tightens. "Of the Hangmen?"

"No." Idiot. "Of losing you."

He frowns. "How are you going to lose me?"

"Jesus, I don't know." I spread my hands. "Maybe you'll wake up one morning and realize how you don't need me for anything."

The hand stills on his chest as he stares at me. "What kind of shit are you saying?"

"Maybe some true shit. Why'd we hook up in the first place? For the sex. But you sure as hell don't need that. The past few weeks, you didn't get anything but your own hand until a few days ago, when I could start sucking your dick again."

"You think I don't want your pussy?"

"*Want* it? Sure. Need it?" I shrug. "But maybe I'm wrong. Maybe that is what you're waiting around for."

His eyes narrow and he pushes away from the wall, heading toward me. "Now you think I'm only here for the fucking?"

"I don't know." But he's taking off his kutte and his shoulder holster, as if he's thinking of fucking me to prove he's not here for the sex. God, I hope so. I won't make it easy, though. I bare my teeth in a sharp grin. "Maybe you just need a place to stay after your own burned down."

"*Such* bullshit." He catches my face up in his hands. I'm laughing when he kisses me but the laughter's gone so fast, swept away by hunger for his taste and the inexorable will that is Jack on a mission.

I know why he's here. The same reason I am. It started as anger and sex and a stupid-ass bet, but now it's the sheer joy of feeling Jack against me, all that warm muscle and skin. I drag his shirt up and he breaks away just long enough to pull it over his head.

Another opening. I grab his belt and tug. "So this morning, when I was sucking your cock down my throat, were you going over your plan for the board meeting in your head? Maybe you were congratulating yourself for being such a big, protective hero while I swallowed your cum."

"Fucking Christ, Lily." Expression dark, he snags my wrists and drags my hands from his cock. "I don't get *pleasure* out of the shit I do. Not for the club, not killing. I do what needs to be done."

I know. He's not *that* fucked up. "Then maybe it was

when you got your mouth on my pussy and worked me up into a sloppy mess."

His fingers tighten and he yanks me closer, bringing his face down to mine. His gaze searches my features before his grip eases. His mouth softens into a smile. "Lily Burns, you're just looking for a fight."

"Damn right I am. Because it's a hell of a lot easier than dealing with the other shit."

His teeth catch my bottom lip. A shiver races over my skin, then he pulls away. Sliding his hands beneath my shirt, he begins easing it over my head. Still taking care of me, still careful not to hurt my sore ribs. "What other shit?"

"The shit you're afraid of." I flatten my palm over the names inked on his chest, surrounded by demons and flames. His dad. His mom. His brother. One a child-raping bastard dead by Jack's hand; for that, the other two never want to see him again. "Every person who ever said they loved you pushed you away, even though you were protecting them. You think maybe I will, too. You thought I would today."

He's gone utterly still. "Yes."

A single agonized word, yet it says so damn much. "I haven't had the amount of shit piled on me that you did, but I'm exactly the same. I can count up the people who've loved me on one hand. And the people who share my blood, who should have loved me? They aren't in that number."

A shudder wracks his big body and he pulls me closer.

"It's their fucking loss."

"It is. It's your family's, too. But I'm not like them, and you're not like my mom or dad. And this thing we have is more than blood. It's our future, Jack. It's our life. So I'm terrified of losing it, too."

His big hands gently cup my face. "You won't. I need you too damn much."

I give a watery smile and slide my fingers over the steel between his legs. "For this?"

"I need you just to fucking breathe, Lily," he says.

"Look at you." I laugh up at him. "The big deadly warlord, saying poetic bullshit like that."

"It's fucking true." He grips my ass and lifts me. Carrying me again, but not sweeping me up off my feet this time. Just easing down to the sofa and settling me over him. Tenderly, his hands slide up over the fading bruises on my ribs. My tits are too small to fill his palms, but they look so right nestled in his hands. "I don't need you to make me laugh, Lily, but laughing's better with you. I don't need you for sex, but it's a hell of a lot better with you. Everything's better. Coming home used to be nothing. But coming here, where I know you'll be? That's everything."

For me, too. I melt against him, linking my arms around his shoulders.

But he's not done. Clenching his fist to his chest, he says hoarsely, "And when you're not with me, or when I think of losing you, it aches so fucking bad. Like someone ripped out my lungs. Like there's no goddamn air. So, yeah, Lily. I need you to breathe."

"Jack," I whisper through a throat gone tight, then take his next breath with a kiss.

And he's right. So damn right. It's all so much better. A meeting of mouth, lips. It's just a kiss. Except with Jack. With him it's a promise wrapped up in hunger that deepens with every taste.

I can't get enough. Every touch like fire, his mouth latching onto my breast and sucking my nipple to a throbbing burn. Heat searing the fingertips that slide through damp furnace of my pussy and roughly stoke the flames, until I'm panting against him, reaching for his hot iron length.

With his big hands on my hips, he guides me as I slowly fill myself with his long, thick cock. God, and that's *so* much better.

And slower. We've never gone this slow, sitting up together, my thighs spread over his hips, my arms wrapped around his neck—and our mouths so close, breathing each other's breath. It's usually almost like a fight between us, a wild fuck, like it's our first or our last, and we're both afraid we won't have this again.

But we will. Because I'll fucking burn the world down for it. Anything tries to take him away from me, I'll destroy it. Starting with his fear and my fear. I'm going to tear them apart.

"I love you," I say and see the way the words hit him,

see all the yearning and need that ripple in its wake. I'm going to pound him with this every damn day. I grip his hair, hold him right where I want him, with his mouth against mine and his cock deep inside me. There's no hiding here. "I love you, Jack fucking Hayden."

"Lily," he rasps my name and when he kisses me I know that's not just lips, either. It's love in the silent, hot stroke of his tongue. It's love when he holds me still and pushes deeper, harder, harder, until I'm so hot and wet and my pussy's clinging to him so hard that I can't stop riding him, can't stop feeding the ache that hurts so much and feels so damn good. And even when I come, stiffening against him, my teeth digging into his shoulder and my cunt holding him tight, I still can't stop needing him, loving him.

This is still fucking. But it's also so much better.

JACK

LATER, IN BED, LILY SAYS quietly, "It's all right, you know."

It's dark. I can't see her, just feel her lying on her back next to me. She isn't sleeping on her side while her ribs are still healing, and I miss the way she curls up against me.

"What is?"

"Protecting me like this," she says.

My chest tightens up again. "Like how?"

"From shit I can't see coming." The sheets rustle as

she pushes up to sit against the pillows. "I told you not to be my shield. But I wasn't thinking of the Hangmen or anything like them when I said it. I was thinking of the shit I deal with every day. The stupid things some of the brothers say. Or what happened with Sasha a few weeks ago, and the fight with Croc. I don't want you stepping in to handle stuff I can handle on my own. But if it's bigger than what I can handle? That's different. If I'm in over my head, I won't get pissed off at you for jumping in. Or for stopping something big before it gets to me."

I come up on my elbow, finding her hand and sliding my fingers through hers. "I'll give you a heads-up if I plan to."

"If you can. I know there's club business you can't talk about."

"Sometimes." Because the fewer who know, the safer it is all around.

"Then just say you can't tell me. I won't get pissy about it." She brings the back of my hand to her lips, and I hear her smile as she says, "I would like to know the Peru story, though."

"It's mostly bullshit." Because I use the stories as a way of having her back without tearing her down; but just like club business, it's best if details never get out. So I change them, to make sure nothing I ever did for the government gets traced back to me or to the Riders. Peru wasn't even Peru. It was Venezuela.

"I like bullshit."

"I've noticed." I have to hold back a groan when she bites my finger in retaliation. Her teeth, my skin. Instantly I'm hard as a stone. "It's just the same old story. Petty arms dealer needs to be taken out, but he's careful and no one can get to him. But my bosses find out he has an arrangement where he flies out of his own city, buys out the floor of a hotel, and brings in some hired skin to fuck him. That hired skin usually fit my description."

"If I was going to pay, I'd make sure he looked like you, too," Lily says.

Shit. Grinning, I pull her under me, careful to keep my weight up off her chest. "You want to hear this story?"

She wriggles beneath me until the head of my cock lodges up against her pussy. Already so fucking wet.

Then she stills, and says, "Yes," and for a second I can't remember what the hell I was saying.

Peru. The bullshit version. Fuck me. I need to make it quick.

"So they send me in. Make all the arrangements, leave weapons in the hotel room. But what they didn't know is that he's a paranoid fuck, so he keeps a guard in the room while it's going on."

"Sounds like a plan gone to hell."

"It was. But I still have a job to finish. So when I'm sucking his dick, I get hold of the knife they've left on the back of the headboard, and rip him open from belly to chest. Then I throw it and hit the guard in the throat."

"No wonder half the brothers cringed." She winds her

long legs around me, because she doesn't mind that I'm so fucked up. "That's the bullshit version?"

"Yes."

"What's the real version?"

The real version is that the paranoid fuck moves to another hotel room and has three guards watching. So I fuck him, and as one of the guards escorts me out, I take his gun and finish the job.

"Nothing so fun," I tell her and push into the hot clasp of her pussy.

"Oh, God." Lily gasps as I begin pumping her full of my cock, her body arching, her nails scraping my back. "More, Jack."

I'll give her so much more. Everything I have. I'd give her my heart right out of my chest.

Except she already has it. Because that's what this fucking ache is. My heart's gone. Lily holds it right in her hands.

And I can't think of a better home for it.

FIVE

LILY

THE DEVIL'S HANGMEN GET ME ON MY WAY TO WORK. I don't see them yet, but I know it as soon as my tires blow. A strip of road spikes were laid across the asphalt, painted black, and I rolled right over them.

My heart jumps into my throat when rubber flies off the tires and the steering wheel jerks in my hands. This will be bad enough without rolling the truck.

I get the rig under control, ease to a stop, and grab my phone.

I didn't expect a goddamn ambush. Pretty much no one takes this road out to the airfield at fucking five o'clock in the morning and there's no goddamn curves, nowhere to hide. It's just a straight shot with a clear view either way. No one can sneak up on me—and my dad's big old truck could fuck up any bikers that tried to head me off. I thought that would be enough.

No answer on Jack's end. Shit. He left earlier than I did, after getting a message on one of his burner phones. We all carry extras around, numbers that can't be traced back to us. Just in case some shit goes down.

Shit's going down. But I see a train of headlights pulling off a side road, heading toward me, and I know it's too late to call for help. I'm not getting out of this. I can't run in this cast. No Rider lives nearby or can come quick enough. I've got a gun but if I go that route I'll end up dead faster.

Creek said I'd probably be shipped somewhere. That means I'll be alive.

So I just have to stay that way—and make sure Jack can follow the trail.

They're coming, I text him. *Five bikes, two vehicles. Vans, I think. Maybe SUVs.*

It's too fucking dark to be sure; I've only got their headlights to go by.

I'm off the airfield road. They blew my tires.

Must have known my schedule. My money's on Val, since he can't keep his fucking mouth shut.

The dickhole who walked away from the Riders after I tossed his ass onto a mat. He joined up with the Hangmen shortly after, and made quick friends with Croc and Sherlock by flapping his lips and giving info about the Riders.

Jack will probably figure all that out. I'm just texting on nerves now. They're closer.

I won't fight. Not until I have to. I'll keep the cell with me as long as I can.

On silent, no vibration. I'll shove it down into my cast and pray they'll only give it a cursory poke while searching for weapons. They'll look for a phone, but maybe they'll think the burner is the only one I have, and won't look hard for another.

I've got to put this one away soon. Their headlights are glaring through the back window. But there's one more message I need to send. Just in case I don't come back.

I love you, Jack.

JACK

I LOVE YOU, JACK.

The world goes gray. Everything fades around me, as if all that's bright and warm is sucked out right through my eyes. My knees hit the floor beside Lily's bed. Her scent fills my head but it's not her. Just the soap on my wet skin. The sheets.

Then everything turns fucking red.

Creek.

At two in the morning, the bastard sent a message saying the cargo they were picking up wasn't live. Escorting guns, not girls. But I went and looked for myself. Saw what I needed to see.

Lily had already left for work when I got back to the house. When her call came in, I was in the shower. Probably stroking my cock while she texted me.

I love you, Jack.

I never said it back. I never told her, as if saying the words was like writing in a ledger and making an accounting of how much I might lose. As if by never saying I loved her, that could never be taken away.

But I won't be the one who loses everything today.

I text Stone with one burner and call Creek with the other. He's riding point on the escort. Eight bikers and four men in a RV heading up Highway 97.

The rumble of his engine sounds through the headset in his helmet when he answers. "Creek."

"You picking up more cargo today?"

"You have the wrong number."

"Fuck if I do." I'm not sending a message to his goddamn burner and hoping he sees it before this job is done. "Where would they take Lily?"

A pause. "That's not our cargo and I haven't heard anything about a pickup. If she's being handed over, Daddy or God would give the location. If she's not, maybe the old kitchen. They won't take her home."

To the Hangmen's clubhouse. But they might use the Eighty-Eight's burned-out farm. Otherwise, either Red Eye or Sherlock's father would tell him where to take her.

"I'm sorry, man," he adds. "If I hear—"

I end the call. If he hasn't already heard, then he won't hear. This is Sherlock acting on his own. Because he's got something to prove.

My burner rings as I'm dragging on my jeans. Stone, the Riders' enforcer. I answer it. "You looking for Lily's phone?"

"I've got someone on it. You heading out to the airfield road?"

"Now."

"Gunner will meet you there. Widowmaker's calling the others, waking everyone up."

"I want a brother watching every road." I grab my holster, my kutte. "Lock down the whole fucking county. Bikes and vans or SUVs. Get the Coyotes on the horn, cover the roads farther south."

"We'll lock it down, call in every favor we got. We'll get her back."

Yes, we will. And then I'll fucking breathe again.

LILY

IT'S FUCKING VALENTINE AND SHERLOCK at the head of the pack, of course. I look for Creek, hoping to see him, but it takes me only a few seconds to realize that all the Hangmen surrounding my truck are younger ones.

That's bad fucking news. Older men can hurt me just as much as younger ones, but there's a reason our prez almost never allows Riders with fewer than five years under their kutte to sponsor their friends—get too many boys together, and nothing matters except measuring their dicks. I spent five years afraid that if I ever backed down, I'd lose my place. Boys together is like magnifying that fear into one seething and brainless testosterone-filled circle jerk, where each member never wants to look weak in front of the others.

When that happens, they never put the club first. But I've still got to try.

I have my window rolled down and my hands in plain sight on the steering wheel when Val and Sherlock come up to my door. Sherlock's wearing a brand-new "President" patch on his shoulder.

Quietly, I tell him, "I can say that you all stopped to help me change my tires. This doesn't have to end in a war between our clubs."

Sherlock scoffs, his mouth twisting up into a half grin. "No war ever started over a slut. Not when it's so easy to go pick up a new one." His greedy little eyes harden. "So get out of the fucking truck."

"I don't know," Valentine says. He leans in, hand braced on the window frame, his baby blues locked on my face. "I think you ought to give me ten minutes with her in the truck bed, first. For a…rematch. See how she likes being pinned on her back."

I won't fucking puke. I won't.

I'm just going to fucking kill them all.

"We've got no time, man," Sherlock tells him. "And no one touches her. The boss wants a look at her first. If he doesn't like her, then she's ours. So get the fuck *out*, bitch. We're on a goddamn schedule."

Stomach roiling, I open the door and step into the glare of headlights and a dozen stares.

"Pat her down, man," Sherlock says.

Every muscle stiffens as Val starts running his hands over me, tweaking my tits with his fingers, breathing heavy in my face. He finds the burner tucked into the back of my jeans and clucks his tongue. "Naughty girl likes to shove things down her pants."

"Fuck off."

"Oh, I will. Just gotta make sure there's nothing else down there first." His fingers push down the front of my jeans.

I stare ahead, jaw clenched. He doesn't shove his fingers into me like I expect. Instead he pulls his hand out of my pants without touching my pussy and moves down, sliding his hands over my thighs.

"She had a knife in her boot at the fight," Sherlock reminds him.

Valentine finds the knife. And the hope inside me sinks when he starts checking the cast. He slips his long fingers down between the brace and my skin, right into the phone.

He hesitates for an instant. Then keeps going, checking the hems of my jeans.

"She's clean," he says. His eyes are on mine as he gets to his feet.

He's still an asshole. Such a fucking asshole. But I could kiss him right now.

"Then get her into the fucking van," Sherlock says. "And let's roll."

JACK

THE HOOD OF HER TRUCK is still warm. I didn't pass a single fucking car riding out here. But they couldn't have gone long. Not more than a half hour. So they likely took a side road. That'll help them hide a little longer, but it'll also slow them down.

Gunner's searching through the truck cab, hoping to find her burner. Maybe she had time to snap a picture, get a license plate.

"Anything?"

He shakes his head, looks down the road. "You think they might have headed to the airfield—made her fly them out of here?"

"I called in. Her boss hasn't seen anyone but the regulars." I'll send one of the brothers there to look around, anyway.

"Stone got a ping from her phone yet?"

"No," I say and rub at my chest. He might not get a fix on her GPS. Out here in the middle of nowhere, there's a hundred fucking dead zones. And if she's on a side road, the chances of picking up a signal from her phone are even lower. "The prez and the veep are headed out to the Eighty-Eight's farm."

"You got eyes on the clubhouse?"

"Yeah." Two brothers waiting to see if anything other than a bike drives out to the Hangmen's home. I don't expect them to see anything. Not with the way Sherlock grabbed her and got out so damn fast. Like he's on a deadline. Which means I'm running out of fucking time.

My cell buzzes. Stone. My blood's pounding in my ears as I answer it. "You got something?"

"A hit on her phone's GPS. It's gone again, but she was on Black Butte Road."

I'm on my bike before he finishes telling me, firing up the engine. "You know which direction they're heading?"

"No. If I get another hit, I'll know."

I look to Gunner. Leaving the house, I only grabbed my holster and extra ammo. "What are you carrying?"

"Just the .45 I'm packing and some toys in the saddlebags. Two semi-autos, clips, a couple grenades."

Not much. But it'll be enough.

Just hold on, Lily. We're coming for you.

And we're going to mow the fuckers down.

LILY

THEY PUSH ME OUT OF the van and I stumble out into the pale morning sun, pain shooting through my ankle. Leaves crunch under my feet. An abandoned farm, it looks like. The house is weathered, the porch sagging and windows broken.

His gaze on the overgrown lane, Sherlock says to Val, "Get her inside until the boss arrives."

Val grabs my elbow, hauls me along. My ankle throbs with every step. A cable tie binds my wrists behind my back, the plastic cutting into my skin.

A screen door hangs on its hinges. Inside it smells like mold and mice. Quietly I tell him, "Blowback's coming for me, Val. I'll tell him you helped me, but you don't want to be here when he comes."

"You won't be here that long." He shoves me down into a corner of the room. "And I helped you as much as I can. I don't like you, Zoomie, but this shit isn't right."

"Shit like raping me in the back of a truck?"

He grimaces. "I was just going to try getting a few minutes to tell you—" His mouth snaps shut when the screen door creaks open. His voice raises. "Shut the fuck up, bitch. The only time you should be opening your mouth is if you're asking to suck on my cock."

From the doorway, a Hangman says, "They're coming up the lane. The prez wants us out there to greet him."

Leaving me alone…but there's nowhere to go. I can't fucking run. Just watch the two black sedans coming toward the house. The boss. Rolling up in an expensive town car, surrounded by muscle dressed in black suits. Jesus. No wonder Sherlock is bowing and scraping. Tall and tanned, with hair slicked back and wearing a bespoke suit, the asshole looks like he bleeds money.

Red Eye, I'm guessing.

My stomach crawls into my throat when his goons head into the house, ignoring me as they search the rooms. They're quiet, efficient. Not just meatheads with brass knuckles. That's training.

That's fucking trouble.

One of the goons searches me again. He doesn't grope or poke. And he finds my phone.

Shit. *Shit.*

That's my only link to Jack. I want to beg him not to take it, but the only sound that comes from my throat is a rough whimper. Fear's starting to ice up my skin in hair raising shivers. I clench my muscles, lock everything down as the goon heads out on the porch and hands off the phone to Red Eye. His jaw tightens as he glances at it.

Then he comes in. A fucking snake, smooth and oily. He crouches down in front of me, his gaze on my face. "So you're the one who took out Croc. You're just as stunning as they said."

Fuck off, I think. But I know a lot better than to say it. So I just stare back at him.

He looks down at my phone. "Who searched you before?"

I keep my mouth shut but in the next second I'm tasting sour bile when the goons bring Val into the house, the barrel of a gun pressed up against his throat. His frantic eyes meet mine and I hate him, fucking hate him, but he doesn't deserve what's about to come.

Sherlock hangs back by the door, looking suddenly uneasy. "Everything all right, boss?"

"We'll see." Red Eye taps the screen of my phone. "Your passcode?"

I don't care if he knows. There's nothing on there I need to hide. That's why we carry around burners. "Eleven thirty-two."

"Thank you," he says and begins poking around. "You know who this man is?"

"Valentine? Yeah. He's a fucking asshole." Not my friend. Not someone who would help me. "I beat him in the ring once and he couldn't handle it. That's probably why he's trying to sell me to you now."

"Revenge."

"I guess."

"Ah." He pauses, reading something on the screen. *"I'm off the airfield road. They blew my tires. Must have known my schedule. My money's on Val, since he can't keep his fucking mouth shut."'*

My chest feels like it's sinking in. "Like I said. He's just an asshole who sold me out."

"Yes." Red Eye draws in a long breath, as if he's so fucking weary. "But it's a problem when people can't keep their mouths shut. A problem with an easy solution—and a lesson for others. You need to teach your boys that lesson, Sherlock."

Fuck. I close my eyes when they start stinging. Such fucking bullshit. This asshole was going to teach them all a lesson whether they found the phone or not. To make sure they always knew the price of crossing him in any way.

They drag Val outside but I can still hear him pleading. Red Eye cocks his head and listens. He smiles faintly when a pistol cracks and Val goes quiet.

"There," he says. "Problem solved. And you, gorgeous girl, are going to be fine. We'll see you heal that ankle up, grow that hair out. You'll be well taken care of…as long as you keep winning."

"Winning what?" What the hell kind of competition do sex slaves enter? "The Rape Olympics?"

He grins. "The Cage. You just have to fight."

Or die. And hold on. Hold on until Jack finds me.

Red Eye waves one of the goons over. "You need to take this now, because you probably won't enjoy your mode of travel. No spitting."

A pill. To put me to sleep, most likely. So I can't see where we're going…or bring attention to myself as we're getting there.

I take the tablet, swallow it dry. I keep quiet as a goon comes back with duct tape and seals my mouth shut.

Red Eye smiles at me like I'm a good little girl. Just keep thinking that, asshole.

"Now," he says and stands with the phone in hand. "Let's say good-bye to your Jack."

JACK

I HIT BLACK BUTTE ROAD and don't know whether to go north or south. Gunner's just behind me. Two dozen other Riders are heading this way, riding toward Black Butte from all directions, using other side roads. No matter the route these fuckers take, a brother will come across them.

Reception's shit. I roll into the road, trying to get a bar or two. There's nothing out here but cows and barbed wire and trees.

The phone buzzes in my hand. Lily's picture pops up on my screen.

Hoarsely, I answer it. "Lily?"

"No." A male voice. Not Sherlock. "I'm sorry to inform you that Lily has been in an accident."

My chest fills with cold lead. "Let me speak to her."

"That's impossible, I'm sad to say. She's dead."

Bullshit. "Send a picture."

The laugh on the other end of the line blasts away my fear. Rage fills the hollows left, pounding like a burning heartbeat in my ears.

"Who are you, Jack? I can tell this isn't your first time

playing this game," he says.

A game? "Fuck games. Let's talk an exchange."

"Jack. I have everything you want. What could you possibly have left to give?"

"You let her go," I tell him. "And I don't tip off the feds about the Winnebago traveling north on Highway 97."

Silence answers me.

My heart's thumping through my chest. I don't want him to end the call. He's using Lily's phone. I need to keep him talking until Stone can see where she is.

I keep my voice level. "Not interested?"

"I'm suddenly interested in many things, Jack. But I'll pass on that deal. If this route is tainted, then that cargo will be lost, eventually. Better to keep the sure thing."

"You take her, I swear to you that you'll lose every-thing."

A smooth chuckle is followed by a sigh. "Her last words were that she loved you. Hold onto that, Jack. In an hour, she'll be out of your reach. There will be no use looking for her. So, for your sake, you should give up now."

"You don't *ever* want me to give up looking for her. Because that's when I'll come looking for you."

My burner vibrates. Stone. With a location for her phone.

"Good luck," the bastard responds. "And good-bye, Jack. I'm sorry we couldn't meet under different circum-stances."

We'll be meeting again. Real fucking soon.

I end the call and look to Gunner. "How far?"

"Ten miles," he says.

Almost ten minutes on these roads. Too damn long. "He said she'd be out of reach in an hour—I figure that's the airport in Bend. So they must be moving out soon."

And they have no fucking idea we're almost on them. I ride hard, looking ahead through every bend in the road for a sign of them.

We blow past her on a curve. Not a van or SUV. Two armored cars. California plates.

Those cars don't belong to the Hangmen. But they fit the voice on her phone.

I almost roll my bike on the one-eighty. I see the indecision on Gunner's face as I ride back past him but I don't have one fucking doubt. She isn't where her phone is. She's in those damn cars.

He's on my tail again a minute later. I catch sight of the vehicles and hang back. It's not going to do any damn good to ride in, guns blazing. Not against armored cars— and not with Lily in one. And we can't get on their ass. I got a look through the windows as we blew past, and I'm not mistaking the muscle sitting in the front seat of both vehicles. They can use their doors as shields. If we're too close, they only have to stop and start shooting. They'll pick us off easy on our bikes.

We just have to stay close enough not to lose her… and keep picking up numbers.

Widowmaker and Scarecrow come in off the reservoir

road, falling in behind Gunner. The prez and Thorne must have detoured away from the Eighty-Eight's old place when Stone picked up her signal the first time. They're riding toward the new location with four other brothers, but pull one-eighties as we shoot past. In five miles, we pick up ten brothers. By the time the armored cars turn off Black Butte Road, heading toward the airfield way, we've got nineteen following, our engines like the roar of a thundering horde.

And we're strong enough to ride in closer. I still can't see her. Just two in the front of each car. One in the back of the second car. That's not Lily. That's the fucker I'm going to kill.

Soon. Because this'll go down easy, or it'll go down real bloody. We can stay on their ass forever. We'll never stop; we'll just have more brothers joining in. As soon as we get off these back roads, that's going to attract a shit ton of attention.

The Riders can afford that attention. Red Eye can't. And he has to decide how much Lily's worth to him.

Not as much as she is to me. Because I'd never have ordered my drivers to stop. But the brake lights are flashing ahead of me, the cars slowing. I hold up my fist and the Riders slow, too.

The road's narrow. Just two lanes with a deep ditch on either side. We're in a straight stretch when the cars stop. I ease to a halt about twenty five yards behind.

There's a lot of scenarios where this goes to shit. In all

of them, someone does something stupid. Like shooting Lily and shoving her out the door before trying to run. Or four guards trying to take on almost twenty armed bikers.

Red Eye didn't strike me as stupid. So it means he's letting Lily go.

At the front car, the doors open. A guard shouts back, "You come and get her! Put your weapons away and walk forward with your hands on your head!"

I'll do that. After pulling off my kutte, I hand the vest and my harness to Gunner, then bend to remove the knife from my boot.

Ahead, the trunk of the second car pops open. The trunk. They stuffed her into the fucking *trunk*.

Slowly I straighten and tuck the knife into Gunner's saddlebag, where I pick out one of his toys, a grenade small enough to fit in my palm. I glance at him. "The guards on my signal."

He looks down at the grenade. "That your signal?"

I nod and tuck it into my palm. With fingers locked behind my head, I start forward.

I thought she'd be moving. Kicking the trunk lid open a little more. Even if she's tied, she could do that. But I can't even see her. The guards don't step away from their posts behind the doors of the first car, their guns trained on me with every step. My throat's a solid lump as I move in close enough to lift the trunk lid.

My heart stops for a long second. She's curled up, unmoving. Her eyes are closed and swollen as if she's been crying. They've taped her mouth. It looks like she's sleeping, then the light hits her eyes and her lashes flutter, slitting open.

My eyes burning, I reach in and rip off the tape, then cup her face. "Lily?" My voice is scraped raw. "I'm here. I've got you."

She lifts her head, blinking. "Jack?"

Disoriented. Drugged, maybe. I can't even drum up the rage now. There's just relief and the painful hitch in my chest. "Easy. Let me pull you out."

"These fuckers." She slurs the words. "Killed Val. He helped me."

"I've got something for that," I say, sliding my arms beneath her shoulders and knees, and scooping her out. The trunk lid's up, concealing us from the guards. I show her the grenade in my hand.

"That'll do." She gives me a sloppy grin. "I love it when you carry me."

"Then I'll carry you everywhere." I pull the pin, throw the grenade into the trunk, and slam the lid.

Holding her, I walk away. An armored car is designed to withstand attack from outside. It's just as good at containing explosions within—and that bastard Red Eye is sitting just one partition away from the trunk.

I count down and hit the ground with her when it goes. No hot blast, no fireball. Just the shriek of metal and shattering glass—then I drag her back against the shelter of the car while the brothers take out the last two guards.

"Boom," she says before her eyes close.
And I can finally breathe again.

SIX

LILY

Jack's still holding me when I wake up, but we're not huddled against the twisted wreckage of a car. Instead we're in my bed, and Jack's wearing his jeans and T-shirt, with his big body practically wrapped around mine.

Jesus, he looks bad. His eyelids are rimmed with red, like he hasn't slept in days. Or shaved in days. Or eaten much. He looks fucking *good*…but like he's ridden some rough damn road.

My throat thick, I touch his face. His eyes fly open

like he wasn't sleeping, but just waiting for me to wake. His dark gaze locks right on mine, brimming with so much emotion it seems to spill over and fill me up, tightening my chest.

"Lily fucking Burns," he says hoarsely. "I love you. I love your laugh, and the way you throw shit on the floor, and how you always fall asleep right at the end of a goddamn show so I have to tell you what happened. I love how fucking hard you fight, and how hard you fuck. And I love—"

I yank his mouth down to mine shut him up, because I'm about to start bawling, and maybe he loves that, too, but I can't right now. But he starts to fight me, fucking fight me, lifting his lips from mine to tell me what else he loves, and between kisses he lists them, adding my tits, and how I never take shit from the brothers, and how the world's so much fucking better since he started holding me.

God, it is. So much better. But I have to stop him, so I cover his mouth with my palm and bury my face in his throat, maybe crying a little but that'll pass. My breath hitches as I say, "I love you, too," and that seems to settle him.

He tips my face up, kissing me deep and long. Finally he draws back with a shuddering breath. "I can't ever lose you."

"You won't," I say. Because he would come for me. Fight for me. Just as I would for him. I smooth my fingers down his rough jaw. "How did it go down? I remember *Boom!* but not much else. Do the Riders need to worry about the cartel now?"

I'm not surprised when he shakes his head. That's what Jack does—make sure that shit doesn't blow back on us. "We scrubbed the site. The bodies are gone, the cars are gone. No one came by asking questions, and the Hangmen never knew we were coming that way. So they have no idea we followed the cars out."

"So it'll be like Red Eye vanished. No reason."

His mouth curves. "In a cartel, there's a thousand reasons he might vanish. And all of his higher ups will be wondering which of the others did it."

"They might think it was the Hangmen. A deal gone wrong."

"And that won't be our problem."

Maybe not a problem at all. "Did you go after them—after Sherlock?" When he shakes his head again, this time I *am* surprised. "Why?"

"We won't need to. With Red Eye gone, the cartel won't be using this pipeline, because they won't be sure whether they can trust it. The Devil's Hangmen will be out a lot of cash. And when the mother chapter takes an accounting of what went down here, Sherlock's going to be out, too. I doubt even his daddy will save him."

"So you don't care how he's gone, as long as he's gone."

He nods, his gaze searching my face. "Unless you want it—or to do it yourself."

Sure, I'd love to pound Sherlock's goddamn face in. But he's just a dumb, greedy fuck. He's not worth my time.

This man, however, is worth all my time. I tug at his shirt, then pull off mine—and I don't even want sex yet. Just to feel him against me like this, skin to skin. "They were going to put me in the Cage."

A frown creases his forehead. So he's surprised by that as I was. "To fight?"

"Yeah. So I guess there probably really are patch-holders disappearing from other MCs. So even though we don't need to connect that to the Devil's Hangmen, maybe it's still something worth looking at. Are Gunner and Stone still heading down to talk with the Butchers this weekend?" Jack nods. "And I'll be heading to Vegas the next."

"Hmm." I trace the mouth of the screaming demon inked on his left shoulder. "Want company?"

His grin is a sexy kick that gets my motor going. "Yes."

"Good. And I am all in, Jack. So maybe while we're there, we can go *all* the way in."

He stills against me. "You talking one of them chapels?"

Slowly I nod. I don't do shit by half measures. If Jack is mine, then he's going to be *mine*. "We can keep it quiet. No one needs to know our damn business. But you'll know and I'll know—"

"Yes," he breaks in roughly, then grabs my face, pins me down. "And don't you think of getting out of it."

"You think I'm going to back down? Fuck that. I said

I'm all in. Maybe we'll even get a goddamn dog."

A hard laugh shakes through him. "No dog deserves that."

Probably not. Grinning, I pull him down for a kiss. The best damn kiss I've ever had—until the next, when Jack groans and licks deeper into my mouth, tasting me, his hands like fire everywhere they touch. Hotter and hotter.

And together, we burn the fucking world down.

THE END

BEFORE
GUNNER

BONUS CONTENT

Before GUNNER
(Breaking It All)

Hello, book lovers! Kati here, with a quick explanation of the following content. Zach "Gunner" Cooper and Anna Wall's story, *Breaking It All*, became much longer than I anticipated. The plot I envisioned also underwent a fundamental change, so part of the way through writing the book, I decided to toss all of the scenes that originally opened the story—the chapter where Gunner and Anna meet, along with their earliest interactions.

Although their backstory was fun to write, and I refer to these events in *Breaking It All*, the chapters didn't add anything to the plot. So they had to go.

Readers asked me about them, however, so here they are. Happy reading!

—Kati

ONE

almost ten years ago

"Is now a good time to talk, Anna?" my doctor asks.

It's not, I want to tell her. I'm driving and shouldn't have even answered my cell. But I automatically accepted the call, and when I recognized Julia Wyndham's voice everything inside me turned to churning molten rock, as if the small lump I found three weeks ago had just erupted through my chest.

It's not a good time to talk about this. How could it ever be?

But I say, "Yes, of course," as if grief and terror don't

have a grip on my throat, and add, "Just let me pull over," as if I'm not about to puke all over my lap.

I knew this day might come. I'm only twenty-one but I survived leukemia when I was a kid, which means I'm at high risk for other cancers. So I've thought about this more times than most women my age ever have; I've pictured what I would do when I got the news. I hoped to be numb.

Instead I can barely see the road through my tears when I click on the blinker. This part of the highway is only two lanes, but the shoulder is wide enough to drive onto. Outside, the sun is bright and high and probably hot as hell, but my A/C is keeping me cold. Not cold enough.

I wanted to be numb. Eyes burning, I curl forward and brace my forehead against the steering wheel. "Okay. Hit me with it."

"It'll be a gentle blow," Julia says and I don't understand how she can sound so upbeat. By the tone of her voice, I can picture her smiling, her eyes bright, her gray hair in a tight roll at the base her neck. How can she smile? "The mass is benign."

Benign? My mind goes blank. I know what the word means, but…that *can't* be right. "It's what?"

"It's not cancerous, Anna. The biopsy showed it's a fibroadenoma, which is relatively common for women of your age group. Sometimes there's discomfort associated with the tumors but they're usually painless, just as yours is. Has that changed?"

I shake my head then realize she can't see me and choke out my answer. *Fibroadenoma.* Nothing to worry about. Except I haven't worried about anything else since I found it. Didn't worry about finals or my degree and I walked through my college graduation in a daze, because the only damn thing I could feel was panic and worry, thanks to a lump the size of a pea and with the weight of a boulder.

She begins to list options for treatment—and the first option is doing nothing, just letting the tumor stay put and monitoring it. So I jump ahead to the option I know I want.

"I need it gone."

"For your peace of mind, Anna, that might be your best choice. And, given the size and location of the tumor, you would be a good candidate for cryoablation."

Freezing the cells. Less invasive, less likely to scar, and the destroyed breast tissue would be gradually reabsorbed into my body. But I want it *gone.*

"I prefer a complete surgical excision," I tell her. "For my peace of mind."

"In that case, I'll refer you to a breast surgeon. You should receive a call from Dr. Gorin's office in the next few days."

"Okay," I say and *now* the numbness descends over me. After robotically answering her remaining questions, I snap my phone closed and toss it into the passenger seat.

Nothing to worry about. I should be dancing, laughing.

Instead I stare through the windshield at the road ahead. Pine Valley lies a few miles on. Bend, a little farther than that. If I keep going, eventually Portland, then Seattle.

Today I'm only going as far as Pine Valley, where I'm staying with my mom and dad in the house where I spent most of my childhood. In about a month, I'll be packing up and heading to med school.

Three weeks ago, that made a lot more sense than it does now.

From the moment I found the lump, I've been promising myself that I'll get through this, that I'll fight it, I'll survive it. I vowed the tumor wouldn't derail my future.

Now survival has been handed to me on a silver platter. But I think this stupid lump derailed my future, anyway—and right now I can't see myself taking the road I intended to.

To Pine Valley, sure. My parents expect me to stay home for a little while. I *want* to be home. My brother will be there for the next month, too, on leave from the Marines. Then Aaron will return to base in North Carolina and I'll be…

Doing something else. I don't know what.

Something.

But the first thing is: Get home and tell my parents everything is okay. I could call them. For this, though, face-to-face is better.

Then I'll figure out the rest.

I wait until a semi blows past me before pulling back

onto the highway. As soon as I hit the asphalt, my steering wheel drags heavily to the right.

A flat tire. Just as I'm starting down a metaphorical new road.

It must be a sign. The universe, telling me that this new path isn't going to be so easy to traverse.

Bring it on, universe.

I steer onto the shoulder again. And I was right—it's a freaking scorcher outside. Holy crap. Thank god for sunscreen. I can practically feel the UV rays bombarding every skin cell exposed by my pink tank top and white jean shorts. I don't burn easy, but I can't be too careful, so SPF is my middle name.

Okay, no, actually it's Marie. Anna Marie Wall. Childhood leukemia survivor. Anti-oxidant fanatic. New road taker.

Flat tire changer.

The right front wheel sits on a rubber pancake. Something must have punctured it when I pulled off the road.

I *knew* it wasn't a good time to take that call. Finding out the lump is benign almost proved me wrong, but this tire proves me right.

Man, I just love being right.

I grab an elastic band out of my purse and gather up my hair in a long ponytail before popping open the trunk. Dang, I really need to clean it out. I wrestle the spare out from beneath a pile of notebooks, an extra blanket and an assortment of random paint cans and craft supplies—

oooh, and my red Nerd Nation hoodie that went missing last winter! I love that one—and roll the spare over the rust-red cinder gravel covering the shoulder.

Time to tackle the flat. When I bought new tires this spring, the shop must have tightened the lug nuts with an impact wrench that had something to prove to the world. I'm straining against the tire iron, trying to crack the first nut loose as a car speeds by, followed by a motorcycle. I don't even have to look up to know it was a Harley. Mistaking the sound of that engine is impossible.

The rumbling roar of that engine changes to a low growl. Slowing down.

No, he's turning around.

Shit.

I look up. He's a hundred yards away and coming in fast. Is he wearing a kutte? There's a few motorcycle clubs in the area. God, if he is a patchholder, let him be a Steel Titan. My friend Jenny Erickson is the daughter of that club's president and most of the members know me. Even a Hellfire Rider wouldn't be so bad. My brother is friends with a few of those bikers and although I've heard some pretty crazy stories about the Riders, I've never heard of one hurting a woman. But if it's a member of the Eighty-Eight Henchmen, that could be bad. Really bad.

But I don't see a leather vest. Just a white T-shirt and tanned, heavily muscled arms. Eyes hidden by mirrored sunglasses, hair concealed under a half helmet. Jeans on long legs and feet covered in big black boots.

Lug wrench in hand, I reach into the passenger seat for my cell and keep a vigilant eye on the biker as he pulls onto the shoulder in front of my car. I'm pretty sure he wasn't able to see me when he rode by the first time—I was crouched out of sight beside the tire—which means he turned around without knowing if I was young or old, man or woman. So he's probably just seeing if I need help.

He cuts the engine and it's suddenly really freaking quiet. Though he couldn't see me before, I guess he's taking a long look now, though it's hard to tell with his eyes hidden behind those lenses.

I'm not wearing sunglasses and I'm not going to pretend that I'm anything but wary.

Wary and not at all threatening. I run every day so I'm in good shape, but I've got no illusions about being some kickass heroine. So if he intends to hurt me, I'm in trouble.

The biker must see that worry, because he doesn't get off his motorcycle yet, and when he speaks, his voice is a low, easy rumble. "You look like you can manage this by yourself."

"I can, thanks." As long as I can crack the lug nuts loose.

He nods but doesn't seem in a hurry to leave. "It's hot as hell out here. You want a little help so it goes faster?"

I do. But I don't want to end up dead in a ditch somewhere. "Can I text your plate number to my mom first?"

Oh my god, his grin. I could tell he had a nice jaw and a firm mouth, but until this second I was thinking of his looks in terms of "Could I describe him to the police?" But now I'm thinking that I want to make him grin again.

And again and again.

I want to see the rest of him, too.

"Go ahead," he says.

Send my mom his license plate. Right.

He doesn't move as I make a wide circle around his motorcycle and quickly send the message. *This guy is helping me change my tire. California plate.* I copy the number. Two faded camo packs are strapped tightly to the seat behind him. Not just a day ride. He's traveling. "What's your name?"

"Zachary Cooper." Amusement deepens his voice. "You want to see my driver's license?"

"No." I send his name, too, before adding that I'll be home soon. "If you're a roadside murderer you probably own a fake ID."

His grin widens. Oh, my heart. "You're the one with the tire iron."

"Not for long." I use the lug wrench to gesture at the flat. "I was having trouble loosening the nuts. If you can do that part, I can do the rest."

"All right." Long fingers unfasten the helmet's chin strap. His hair's dark brown, almost black, and cut military-short.

He's tall, too. Probably a little over six feet, but considering that I only hit five-three in my dreams, when he gets up off his bike I suddenly feel a lot smaller.

He leaves the helmet on his seat and hooks his sunglasses into the V of his T-shirt's neckline before facing me.

Holy shit.

Holy *shit*. I wouldn't need to describe him to the police. I could just say, "Look for the most beautiful man you've ever seen" and any cop would be drawn straight to his location, then fall in love with him, and he probably could get away with murder just because he'd smile.

He can't be real. Real people just don't look like him. Real people don't have eyes like that—so light blue that they're almost crystalline. And I thought his jaw and lips were nice? Jesus. Put together with the whole package of dark slashing eyebrows and high set cheekbones, they're just…just…

I don't even know. Indescribable.

And now that I think about it, that was pretty mean. Taking off his sunglasses like that. He should *prepare* people.

Those light blue eyes are locked on my face as he comes closer. I'm staring at him. My jaw might be hanging open, I'm not sure. My panties are probably falling off. I can't really tell because my brains have turned to jelly.

I bet this happens to him often. My voice sounds strange to my own ears when I ask, "Do you end up with a lot of bugs in your teeth?"

He grins again, and nope. No bugs. Just gorgeous, perfect white chompers. "You learn not to open your mouth while you ride."

"Oh, I know that." I've been around motorcycles my whole life. I don't ride them, but I know plenty of people who do, including my brother. "But what you've got going on there"—I indicate his face with a twirl of my finger—"almost knocked me over, so it seems you'd have extra trouble keeping the bugs away. Especially at night. Like, you don't even need a headlamp. You can just open your eyes and light up the world."

He's not even embarrassed. Just amused. His chuckle is low and deep and shivers right up my spine.

"Nights are rough," he agrees. "All those insects throwing themselves at me."

"I bet." Insects, women.

"Good thing about accidentally ingesting bugs is, they're packed full of protein."

Ew. "That's a good thing? That's the downside of being beautiful."

"I'm sure you're well acquainted with any downsides."

Did he just call me beautiful? Either that, or he's suggesting I know what it's like to eat bugs. So I'll go with beautiful.

I grin up at him. "You're my new favorite person."

"Well, if I want to hold that spot, I better get started."

He holds out his hand and I place the lug wrench in his callused palm. Thick veins trace tautly muscled forearms. Not just gorgeous, but strong. A sheen of perspiration glows over his tanned skin but the sweat isn't why his T-shirt clings to his chest the way it does. His broad shoulders and pectoral muscles are doing all the work there.

God, the way that shirt is hugging him, I bet it never wants to let go.

He crouches beside the flat and I back up to the car's rear passenger door—ostensibly to grab a water bottle from the six-pack in the back seat but really so I can get a good look at Zachary Cooper's whole package again.

I'm not a bit sorry for my blatant ogling. A) Because *not* looking seems like some kind of cardinal sin—I mean, if there is a God and He put that face on this earth, then surely He meant for us to appreciate it—and B) I'm never going to see Zachary Cooper again anyway.

Oh, and C) is the way his biceps flex when he fits the lug wrench onto the first nut and gives it a good tug.

I wish all my tires were flat.

But my mom taught me better than this. Just staring at someone? So rude.

I slide a water bottle onto the hood in front of him. "It's not cold, but the least I can do is offer a drink while I ogle you."

He smiles so easily, but he doesn't really look like someone who smiles a lot. He can't be much older than me—maybe twenty-three or twenty-four—but there's a rough edge to him that I recognize, because my brother has that edge, too. It lies in the calluses on his hands, the austere cut of his hair, and the chain around his neck.

Dog tags.

I crack open the cap of my own bottle. "Did you recently get out or are you on leave?"

He shoots me a sharp glance, as if he's surprised I picked up on that. "On leave."

"And passing through?" Maybe coming up from one of military bases in California.

"Visiting a friend."

"Not family?" That's usually the first place a guy goes on leave. Family, then to a bar, then to someone's bed.

"I did that yesterday." The response has a bite to it.

I don't need to know him well to read that tone and the tightening of his jaw. His family is a sore spot. So I won't touch it.

Anyway, his friend sounds more interesting. "Is she as pretty as you are?"

A huff of laughter shoots from between his teeth, clenched tight as he cracks the final nut loose. "*He* is all right."

I should have known. Gorgeous, funny, helpful? He's gay.

He's also a mind reader. Despite the glacial blue of his eyes, the glance he shoots me then isn't icy but hot and quick, a flickering blue flame, the kind of look a guy gives a girl just before he kisses her. But he doesn't kiss me. He just says, "No."

Not gay. Not that it matters one way or another. He's passing through and I'm not. Looking is all I'm going to get.

"Oh, hey—wait." I try to stop him when he reaches for the jack. "This is the part I'm supposed to do."

"Were you?" he asks like he doesn't remember agreeing to it and slides the jack under the car's frame. "I'm just trying to stay on your list of favorite people."

I snort. "If you want to do that, just look at my boobs and tell me they're not very pretty."

The jack's lever slips in his grip. That pale blue gaze is suddenly all over me—sliding down to my chest but it's my face he settles on. I try to smile but all the crap I swallowed down while I was waiting for my doctor to hand out my death sentence is rising up again.

Oh, shit. My throat thickens and burns; my eyes swim with tears. I sink onto the ground beside him but he doesn't move. Just watches me.

"Since you're my favorite person and I won't see you again, can I tell you something?" My voice is thick. "You can say no."

But he says, "Tell me."

"I found a lump about three weeks ago."

His gaze drops again when I cup my breast in my palm. He can't mistake what kind of lump I'm talking about.

A gruff note roughens his voice. "How old are you?"

"Twenty-one. But I was sick when I was a kid, and chances of it happening again are higher for me than most girls. So I had reason to think the worst." My breath shudders. "And I *did* think the worst. I mean, I was determined to fight it. Mastectomy, chemo, whatever it took. And I kept on a brave face with my mom and dad when I told them. But deep down I was convinced that I'd cheated death once and now it had caught up to me. So for three weeks I've been thinking of all the things I haven't done, haven't seen, and how I was never going to get a chance to."

He's utterly still. "Are you asking me to get a room somewhere?"

A watery laugh bursts out of me. "Oh, god. No. I mean, not this second. The way you look that would definitely be something for the bucket list, but the reason this tire is flat is because I pulled over to take a call from my doctor. And she told me the lump is just a fibroadenoma—a benign mass. So I didn't even cheat death this time. I just got a good scare. But I need to tell someone how terrified I was, and I'm not going to tell my family…" Jesus. I choke up again, thinking of it.

"Because you don't want to lay that on them," he finishes for me and I nod. "You're all right, though?"

"Yeah. I'm going to have the tumor removed and there will be some scarring. But what's scarring compared to dying? Nothing. My boobs just won't be as pretty as they are now."

His dark brows draw together over those pale, pale eyes. "And you want me to tell you they aren't perfect to begin with…so it doesn't seem like such a loss?"

God, that sounds stupid. "Is that stupid?"

He shakes his head. "Show me."

My breath rushes out. Like him, I'm crouching behind the car, so it's not as if I'll be flashing the world. Still, I should be feeling embarrassment or something other than this relief when I curl my fingers around the bottom of my tank and strip it off.

I'm not wearing a bra. I don't really need one. My body will never be anything near 'curvy.'

"It's this one," I tell him, cupping my left breast and pushing against the lump with my thumb, just beside my hardening nipple. My body thinks I'm playing but I've never been more serious. "There's not much tit here to start with, I know. When the surgery's done, it'll probably look like something took a bite out of it."

Quietly, he takes a long look, his fingers white-knuckling the jack lever. "I won't lie to you. They're pretty as hell." His gaze raises to mine with an intensity that makes me catch my breath. "But I bet they'll be beautiful when you're not scared. When you know you're healthy. That's when they'll be perfect. And any man who looks at them and doesn't see that isn't worth having."

Tears sting my eyes again. "Thank you."

He nods. "You just keep me in mind, sixty or seventy years from now. Whenever you start filling out that bucket list."

I can't stop my laugh. "I will."

Turning back to the jack, he starts pumping the lever. Though I'd love to drag him close and strip his shirt off, too, I drag my tank top over my head instead and watch the play of muscle in his arms. This won't take him too long.

So there's not much time left. Something in my chest pinches tight. I don't want him to go yet. I need to know more about him. "Were you overseas?"

"I was."

Right now, that probably means Afghanistan or Iraq. "Are you going back?"

"Most likely. After another training cycle."

"Do you ever worry?" God knows I worry about my brother during his deployments.

He reaches up for the bottle of water and watches me while he takes a swig. "You mean, do I get scared?"

"Yeah."

"Sometimes." He starts in on the lug nuts again, spinning the wrench until they come off. "But I train and prepare for every contingency I can. I trust that the men on my team will have my back. I stay frosty. I figure anything beyond that is out of my control. And if shit happens, I'll fight until I can't."

"Same here." When he glances at me, I explain, "Exercising, eating the right foods, and only indulging a little when I'm out with family or friends. Anything else is beyond my control."

"But you'll fight the shit that is? Even if you're scared?"

"Yes."

"All right, then." He pulls off the flat and rolls it to the side. "This scare isn't going to make you stop doing that healthy stuff, is it?"

"No."

"Good." The spare goes on and he starts tightening the lug nuts. "You'll need to take this into a shop, get them properly torqued."

I'll take it to Red Erickson, instead—my best friend's dad. He'll kick my ass if I pay money at Baxter's Auto in town, because it's owned by a Hellfire Rider. That won't mean anything to Zachary Cooper, though, so I just nod.

"I'm glad you stopped to help," I tell him.

"I am, too. You're like breathing fresh air after—" His jaw tightens before he sighs and shakes his head. "What I just came from."

His family. That sucks ass. Everyone should have a family as awesome as mine. My mom, my dad, Aaron. I don't ever need fresh air when I'm with them.

"I'll put that away," I tell him when he reaches for the flat. "My trunk is messy. I'd rather leave you with a good impression."

He grabs the tire anyway. "It'll take more than a mess to knock you from the top of my list."

Of new favorite people. God, that feels good. Smiling, I pop the trunk and open it with a flourish. "Behold the frightening disarray."

"I've seen messier," he says and makes a nest for the wheel in my extra blanket. "Stanford?"

Apparently he spotted my crimson hoodie. "Yes."

"So you're smart, too."

Too? Smart in addition to what? But I don't suppose it matters. He said that as if he actually admires smarts in a woman, then he looks at me like he admires me, too, but I'm thinking that I must be the stupidest idiot in the world because I'm about to let him ride away.

"Listen," I tell him and start digging through my trunk. Finding paper in a notebook is easy but I need a pen or a marker or an eyeliner. "I don't know how far you're going or if you're coming back this way, but I'll give you my number and—"

"Don't." His abrupt reply stops me cold.

I blink and step back, startled by the sudden change. Everything about him that had been nice and easygoing just turned hard and rough, as if I'd tripped across the edge in him I'd seen earlier. But I don't see anything in that sculpted profile to tell me what set him off. He's not looking at me. His eyes are closed, and he stands rigidly, one raised hand clenched on the edge of the trunk lid as if he's about to slam it.

But he doesn't. Instead the strong muscles of his throat work before he says, "No name, no number."

I nod, though it stings a little, because if he didn't want that info there are ways to get rid of it without snapping at me. Like tossing my number into the trash a mile down the road. I'd never know.

With that face, he's probably accustomed to getting numbers. And throwing them away.

God, and I hope he doesn't glance at me now, because I can feel the heat in my cheeks. He probably *does* get a ton of numbers. Maybe that's why he reacted like that. I mean, sure, someone tossing their digits at him is probably flattering, at first. Maybe after years of it, though, that kind of thing is just really fucking annoying.

Now I'm embarrassed—and pissed off, because I shouldn't be embarrassed. I didn't do anything wrong. But my face catches fire and I quickly move past him, heading for the jack. Going down on my heels, I wrestle the collapsed jack into its vinyl pouch and slide the lug wrench in beside it.

When I get to my feet, he's still standing behind my car, and I can feel his pale blue gaze on my face. Keeping my expression blank, I do my best not to look up at him when I toss the jack into the trunk.

There. All done.

I wipe my palms against the sides of my shorts to get rid of any extra sweat and dirt, then stick out my hand.

"I guess the no-number and no-name thing means I won't get a chance to thank you with a real drink," I say, as if that's all I intended to do after giving him my number, which makes me such a liar. But better a liar than a googly-eyed idiot. "So thanks for your help, and stay safe over there, and have a nice life after that."

His big hand closes over mine. Broad, callused palms; lean, strong fingers. I know I'll dream of them gliding over my skin later. I won't be able to help it. Zachary Cooper is probably going to feature in my every sexual fantasy for years.

Then a low, liquid burn fills me when, instead of shaking my hand, he gently pulls me closer.

My gaze flies up. Focused on my mouth, his eyes are so pale, so blue, like the glare of the winter sun through glacial ice. He's not dragging me. The pull on my hand is so subtle I could easily get away. He's letting me decide whether to come nearer.

Of course I will. I'm on a new road. I refuse to look back on today with regret, and I *would* regret not taking this step.

So I do.

God, he's tall. Or I'm short. I'm standing completely in his shadow, trying not to tremble when he lets go of my hand and cups my cheek in his palm, his heated gaze locked to mine.

His thumb slides over my bottom lip, a simple motion that stirs a torrent of desire inside me. "I'll take this as my thank you."

My mouth. Oh, yes.

Of course I can't stop what comes tumbling out of it. "My lips don't come off," I tell him, my heart pounding. "And even if you could take them, they won't travel well."

His laugh is a deep rumble and, sweet Jesus, his grin—

Is all over mine. He swooped in so fast the heat of his lips stuns me for an instant. Then my brain kicks in or departs altogether, because my astonishment melts into a kiss. There's too much teeth at first because I'm smiling and he's smiling, then his fingers push into my hair and I lift up on my toes, my hands braced against the iron wall of his chest.

His mouth softens then, and I want to stay here forever. Right here, with his lips barely parted over mine, his breath so warm, and his tongue just lightly tasting, not devouring but taking over my mouth in little sips that consume my senses faster than a deep kiss ever has.

But I want deeper now. This sweet kiss is tearing open a needy ache centered between my legs. I push closer and love the sound he makes low in his throat, a possessive growl that echoes in the tightening of his grip, as if he's not ready to let me go.

Then a horn bellows as a semi truck blasts past us on the highway, and he does let me go. His mouth lifts away from mine, and I'm too short to chase him up.

His hand slides from my hair to cradle my jaw in his palm. For a long moment we stare at each other, breath shuddering. His heart beats a rapid rhythm under my palm.

He's the first to move. His thumb traces the moist curve of my lower lip. His voice is hoarse. "You're wrong. That *will* travel well."

He's right. I'm going to carry the memory of that kiss with me for a long, long time.

But I don't understand him at all. "You don't make any sense," I tell him. "You don't want my number and the near-guaranteed hookup that comes with it, but you'll kiss the hell out of me before you go."

"I want your number," he says, but his tone tells me he's not asking for it. There's regret there, but unlike me, he apparently would rather have the regret than spend a night in my bed. "The problem is that I *will* come looking for you."

I don't see how that's a problem. Unless…

A sick knot starts to wind in my gut. "Do you have a wife? A girlfriend?"

The knot unwinds when he shakes his head. Good. I'd rather walk away thinking he's a decent guy, not a dickhead who kisses other women even though he's already taken.

Maybe he's a *really* decent guy, though. I ask, "Do you not do one-night stands?"

A smile curves his mouth but this time there's no amusement in it. Just something sad and weary. "I have. But I don't think any man could settle for just a night with you."

"Oh, they can," I reassure him. "There's a couple of guys at Stanford who could vouch for that. One night with me, then done."

There's some amusement in that smile now. "They sound like goddamn fools."

How in the world is he doing this? I'm being rejected but he's lifting me up instead of putting me down. Amazing.

"Okay, then." Though I'd rather continue touching

him, I force myself to step away, and keep my voice light. "Even though you've broken my heart, you're still my new favorite person."

"Good," he says, as if the opinion of someone he's walking away from might actually matter.

So this is it, then. The trunk's still open. I slam it and suddenly I'm feeling awkward again.

"But, really, thank you," I tell him for the millionth time.

He doesn't say anything. Just nods, his jaw hard, his gaze all over my face as if he's getting a good last look in.

Jesus, he needs to go. As soon as an idea gets into my head, I almost always follow it through to the bitter end. That kiss has given me too many ideas—about what I want to do to him, about what I want him to do to me—and I'm about to ask him to reconsider. Because his reasons for not wanting my number appear to boil down to "Gee, I like you so much I might want more than one night" and that's just stupid.

But I'm also pretty sure he's going to stick with his original answer and I'll only end up humiliating myself.

Then it's out of my hands. Slipping on his sunglasses, he hides those incredible eyes and starts toward his bike.

His gruff "Take care of yourself," comes a split second before the ring of my cell phone. My mom, I bet, calling in response to my earlier text. And if I don't answer, she'll probably call the police next.

"You, too," I say, as if there isn't a dull ache forming in

my chest.

I head for the passenger door, where the cell phone is lying on the seat beneath the open window. I was right. A call from home.

I answer it with a "Don't worry, I'm still alive," and watch Zachary Cooper swing his leg over his bike's seat. "He wasn't a serial killer. Or maybe he is, and just prefers to murder blondes, so I was spared."

He must have heard me. A smile touches his mouth. Good. If he's never going to see me again, that's how I want him to go. Smiling.

"That's great, pipsqueak." My brother answers instead of my mom, and the dull ache is overwhelmed by a happy rush. "Is Cooper still there?"

"He's just taking off," I say and my heart does a happy little dance. "How are you? And how the hell did you and dad get back from the airport so early?"

"I drove. Dad fell asleep and couldn't see how fast I was going. You need to tell Cooper to follow you home."

"What? Why?" To thank him? To beat him up?

On his motorcycle, Zachary Cooper frowns at me— and I realize I'm frowning, too, but only because my brother might be crazy. Which, honestly, is something I already knew. But to a stranger, it must look as if I've just gotten upsetting news.

"Because I gave him directions but following you will be easier," Aaron tells me. "Mom said you knew he was staying with us until next week."

I knew *someone* might be staying with us—one of the guys in Aaron's battalion. Someone he'd been deployed with and who was on leave at the same time. But that person wasn't named Zachary Cooper. "You called him Zed."

When I say "Zed," Zachary Cooper goes utterly still. I can't see his eyes through the mirrored lenses of his sunglasses, but I know he's staring at me.

"Yeah, because there were two Coopers in our platoon when we went through the Force Recon pipeline, and he was the one whose first name started with Z. So 'Zed' stuck."

Zed for Z? "What are you, Canadian marines?"

"Canada doesn't have a marine corps, Annie. Give the phone to Cooper."

Who is off his bike and coming this way. Who has been in combat with my brother. Who will be sleeping in the guest bedroom across the hall from me.

And who didn't want to know my name.

Holy shit, that's about to be blown right out of the water. I close my eyes and grip the phone tight. "Okay. But, remember, I didn't know who he was. So just to warn you—"

"Oh, Jesus help me," Aaron mutters before I even finish, because he knows me too well.

"—I flashed my boobs at your friend." Eyes wide, I stick the cell out at arm's length and try to ignore the groan coming through the phone's speaker. "My brother would like to talk with you."

His mouth flattens as he takes the phone. He answers with an abrupt, "Cooper."

I can't hear whatever my brother is telling him, so I just wait, with the sun beating down on my back and the cicadas buzzing in the trees.

With a short nod, he finally says, "I'll do that," and gives me the cell.

I flip it closed—probably hanging up on Aaron, but so what. I'll see him again in about twenty minutes and I'm far more interested in what Zachary/Zed has to say.

He leans back against the side of my car and hooks his thumbs into his pockets. Still watching me, and still at an advantage because he's wearing those sunglasses.

His deep voice is carefully even when he asks, "So you're Annie."

"Anna," I tell him. "Aaron's the only one who calls me Annie."

Mostly because I hate it.

Slowly he nods. "I pictured someone younger. Red dress. Curly red hair."

And that's exactly the reason why I don't like the name. It's also exactly the reason Aaron keeps using it. "I don't have a Daddy Warbucks."

There's his smile again. But it's guarded now. Maybe uncertain.

Because he kissed his friend's sister? Or because he really didn't want to see me again? Or because this is so damn awkward now?

I don't know. I'm not sure if I want to find out. What-ever happens, there's still a good chance this is all going to end with me humiliating myself.

With a heavy sigh, I ask, "So you know my name. Should I call you Zachary or Zed?"

"Zach's good." His voice is still low, still careful.

"Zach." I test it out and nod. "Okay. So you're following me home?"

In an easy movement, he pushes away from the car. "Yes."

"I hope your puny little bike can keep up." That draws another smile from him—a warmer one. Good. "And about, you know, what I told you about the lump and being terrified—"

"I'll keep my mouth shut."

"Thanks." I bite my bottom lip, wondering if I should say more. But what is there to say?

Nothing, I guess.

In my car, I wait until he's on his Harley and the engine is growling, then pull out onto the highway. This time, my tire isn't flat and the most beautiful man I've ever seen rides right behind me. Seems like a good start.

But this new road already feels pretty damn lonely.

TWO

"You can quit staring now," my mom says.

"I could," I agree. After she recruited me to peel potatoes for dinner, I set up my paring station on the kitchen counter overlooking the driveway—and overlooking Zach, who is outside checking out my brother's motorcycle, which has been in storage since the last time he was on leave. "But why would I?"

"Because he's our guest," she reminds me but trails off when she glances out the window. "And…because…"

"Because?"

"Oh, my."

"Uh-huh," is all I say. Because my brother is crouching beside his Harley and pointing out something in the engine, and to get a look at it, our guest leans over the bike, arms braced on the seat. Zach's T-shirt rides up just above his belt, exposing a tight oblique that could have made an anatomy instructor weep awestruck tears. His short sleeves hug sculpted triceps and can't contain the bulge of his biceps, so the soft cotton edges have rolled up and snuggled in at the base of his deltoid.

And then there's his face. It belongs in a magazine. In an underwear ad. Or just put him in a three-piece suit, turn that crystalline, heavy-lidded stare toward the camera, and let him sell a billion of whatever they're trying to sell.

Except…that's not right, either. I've never seen a fashion model capture the depth of expression in his face. That contagious grin. Those eyes, so serious and steady when he asked, *"You're all right, though?"* And so blistering hot when his thumb slid over my bottom lip. *"I'll take this as my thank you."*

I'd love to thank him again.

That doesn't seem likely, though. Not just because he already shot me down, but because shit got weird as soon as I realized he was my brother's friend—and that he *is* our guest. He's been painfully polite since arriving at my parents' house. I've been the same with him, because I have zero interest in making anyone feel too uncomfortable to stay.

All ogling aside. Ogling doesn't count, anyway. He

can't see me staring.

But I won't tease him. That doesn't mean I can't tease my mom, though.

"You know what we should do?" I say without tearing my gaze away from Zach's profile. "We should install hidden cameras in the guest room and sell the pictures."

"Anna." Tone sharp, my mom attempts a reprimand but the way her lips flatten after she says my name tells me how hard she's trying not to laugh.

Seriously, though. "We'd be so rich."

Her soft laugh breaks through and she shakes her head. "I'd rather keep my integrity."

"Boooo. No fun."

"Poor girl." Mom's reply doesn't hold a lick of pity. A second later, she draws in a sharp breath as my dad emerges from the garage and joins the little motorcycle admiration society Aaron and Zach have started. "Oh, dear Lord."

"What?"

"Your father." Abruptly she pulls at the ties of her apron and stalks across the kitchen toward the garage door. "His wagon is about to die."

His trusty old AMC Eagle, which has been on this Earth longer than I have been. Both Aaron and I learned to drive in the wagon. I can't imagine my dad in anything else.

"There's no hope for it?" I'm going to miss that car.

She shakes her head. "He said he hopes to stumble onto a vintage roadster to replace it."

With a startled laugh, I glance outside. My dad, speeding along in a roadster? He's like the racing tortoise: slow and steady. Also with a balding, shiny head—and more often than not, stuck in his cozy shell. "Really? Why?"

"Guess."

"Midlife crisis?" is my first hunch. But I should have known that would be too easy.

She shoots me a narrowed look. "Can you imagine your father suffering from insecurity?"

Which is usually the underlying reason for a midlife crisis. And, no—I really can't imagine it. My dad is on the quiet side and leans toward geeky, but he's like a rock. Unshakeable. And it would take more than bald spot and a few wrinkles to chip away at his optimistic nature.

No, he wouldn't want a roadster to recapture his youth or virility. Instead he's probably imagining taking my mom out on weekend adventures—just like he used to do with our entire family when Aaron and I were growing up. He was always loading us up into the wagon and heading out to some new location.

A roadster would just be a zippier way of getting there. "It's just for fun, isn't it?"

My dad is simple that way.

Mom clicks her tongue, which means I hit the nail on the head. "I told him he'd be forced to buy a more sensible vehicle for the winters, anyway, but that didn't change his mind. He says he wants to feel the wind in his hair while he has some left." While I'm laughing, she gives a significant look toward the driveway, where my dad is lovingly running his hand over the Harley's black leather seat. "Now I believe he's about to stumble onto a motorcycle. But if I'm going to be riding with him…I'd rather have the sexy little roadster."

With a wink, she heads out. Potato and knife in hand, I watch through the window as she emerges from the garage. My dad pretends to be absorbed by the motorcycle, not even glancing around when she appears, but I see the cheeky little smile he hides from her. He's going to play stubborn about the bike to rile her up. Of course my mom won't get riled—she never gets riled—but she'll poke him right back.

They're so cute together that it's sick. They're just perfect for each other, though they're complete opposites. My dad, short and awkward and always a bit disheveled; my mom, tall and reserved and effortlessly elegant.

And here I am getting all weepy, watching them.

Shit. It's so stupid. I'm not even cutting onions. It's just…I'm so lucky to have them. She didn't give birth to me. I was just fortunate enough to be adopted. So now I'm the only girl that tears up over potatoes, watching my dad tease my mom and seeing the moment Aaron realizes what's going on, seeing his quick grin, and the way he jumps in, too—probably telling my dad that he should *definitely* go buy a bike and take Mom for a ride on it.

My mom narrows her eyes at my brother. God, he's going to get it.

I'd love to hear it, but this window doesn't open, so I settle for watching. I can read their faces well enough to guess who's scoring the most points.

Zach's watching them, too, and his posture wipes away my grin.

He's standing apart from them, on the opposite side of Aaron's bike. His thumbs are hooked in his jeans pockets, his boots planted at shoulder width. A casual stance, at first glance, but there's something in the way he watches their byplay that looks…wary.

Not afraid. But as if, instead of watching a family toss a little shit at each other, he's watching a time bomb and is preparing himself for the moment the clock hits zero.

It won't. There's no bomb, because we don't like to hurt each other. Because we always know where we stand and try to not to pull each other's triggers. So if something *does* hurt, we know it wasn't on purpose.

An outsider wouldn't know that dynamic is in play here. But an outsider who is close to his own family might guess.

Looking at Zach, I doubt that's the case, and his wariness opens an aching little hole in my chest.

I've grown up with an amazing family. I don't think Zachary Cooper has.

When his posture suddenly seems to ease, I glance at my parents. My mom is laughing, and my dad's hands are lifted in surrender.

I knew she'd win. Now I can go back to ogling our

guest.

I grab another potato and almost cut off the tip of my thumb instead of the peel, because at that moment Zach turns to look at the house, at *me*, as if aware of exactly where I've been standing all this time, and when his pale gaze locks with mine, I forget what my hands are doing until a slice of pain penetrates the heat racing through my skin.

Sweet Jesus, those eyes. He *really* needs to start warning people.

WHEN I RETURN TO THE kitchen, my mom is finishing up the potatoes. She's already thrown away the one I bled over and cleaned the gore off the counter.

She gives my bandaged thumb a significant glance. "You did that just to get out of peeling these, didn't you?"

"No," I tell her. "I did it to get out of washing dishes later."

"Clever girl," she says, and we both look outside at the sound of a motorcycle pulling into the driveway.

Not Aaron's or Zach's. Their bikes are still sitting in front of the garage. This is someone else, a big dude with dark hair and wearing a Hellfire Riders kutte.

My breath catches a little when I recognize Saxon Gray. Holy shit. With wide eyes, I watch Aaron head over to greet the man, doing one of those fist bumps that guys do when shaking hands threatens their masculinity or something, so they say hello with a baby punch.

I didn't realize Aaron knew Saxon. Well, I kind of knew, because they're about the same age so they must have run into each other through junior high and high school. But I didn't realize they knew each other well enough to grin at each other and bump fists.

There's surprise on Aaron's face along with his grin. Although I can't hear him, I know exactly what he's asking Saxon.

"When did you get out?"

Of prison. Where Saxon was supposed to be serving ten years. But it's only been five.

God. Does Jenny know? She hasn't said anything about it. Maybe she wouldn't, though. She's my best friend, but she's always been a little tight-mouthed about Saxon Gray. Or maybe she hasn't heard the news yet. Like me, she was away at college until a few days ago—and now she's out at her dad's ranch, where she wouldn't hear all the gossip from town.

I don't even know what to think. But I know I need to call her. Though I'm not sure what to say. Her dad is prez of the Steel Titans MC and they aren't friends with the Hellfire Riders. So I'm not sure if telling her that Saxon's back in town would just complicate things.

Teasing my mom is a little easier. "It looks like Aaron's falling in with a bad crowd."

Her chuckle is just a soft breath of air. She probably knows Saxon a lot better than I do—she was counselor when he went through high school. Not that she'd ever share anything she learned about him then. Confidentiality and all that.

Maybe she would consider him—and the Hellfire Riders—a bad crowd. I don't know. It's all fucked up, because Saxon killed the president of another rival MC, the Eighty-Eight Henchmen…but he killed that man to save Jenny from being raped.

So instead of being afraid, I kind of want to hug him, instead.

Zach obviously wouldn't. He looked wary before but now he appears openly hostile. His jaw is set, his expression remote. When Aaron turns to introduce him, Zach responds with an abrupt nod.

But he doesn't know Saxon. That look can't be about the other man specifically.

Maybe the kutte, then? Or maybe he just doesn't like motorcycle clubs in general. I don't know.

God, I *want* to know. Zach's outside is incredible to look at but I want to see deeper. I want to see past his beauty. I want to know why his lips have flattened into a thin line and why the corded muscles in his arms have tensed. I want to know why those blue eyes seem icy instead of warm—and when Saxon continues talking and Aaron turns, as if to ask Zach's opinion, why he blinks so quickly, as if taken aback.

This time Zach's nod is slow instead of abrupt. His forehead creases as he gives Saxon another look over, as if he'd made up his mind about the other man but is suddenly rethinking that conclusion.

I want to know what the conclusion was. But not just that. I want to know *everything* about Zachary Cooper.

And I can't remember ever wanting to know so much about a man before. Probably because, in my experience, the more I know the more disappointing they are.

I don't think Zach will be. Or I just really hope he won't be.

Not that it matters. I mean, he didn't want to know anything about *me*. Not even my name.

I need to keep reminding myself of that. It's not my nature to give up easily. But this guy is a guest. And he's only going to be here a week, then he'll be gone forever. This isn't his hometown and few people ever move *to* Pine Valley. Usually they're trying to get out. Especially if they're young.

So, really. For my heart's sake, I should stop wanting to know so damn much.

"How's Jenny?" my mom asks—a question that seems out of the blue, but with Saxon here, not really. When I saw him, my first thought was of Jenny, too.

"Good." And much more certain of her path than I am. "Heading to Oregon State in the fall. She's going for her masters in business."

My mom frowns. "Business?"

"She decided against medical school. She plans to open a brewery, instead. She's all gung-ho about it."

Mom blinks a few times, digesting this info. Finally

she says, "Well. Good for her."

"Yeah," I agree with all the things she left unsaid, because she didn't need to say them. We both know Jenny is smart and ambitious and she'll probably do a brilliant job.

"And you?" she asks, and although her tone is light the weight of the world seems to rest on the question.

My heart squeezes tight—as tight as she held me earlier when I quietly told her the tumor was benign. She didn't say anything, just hugged me so hard and so close. Now my chest feels compressed again and suddenly I'm short of breath. I don't need to be. I know she'll support any decision I make.

But, God. This is a huge one.

"I don't know," I say, which is kind of true and kind of not. I don't know exactly what I'll be doing. But I know what I *won't* be doing. "I think…I think I'm going to withdraw from the medical program."

I feel her gaze on my face but I keep staring outside. Everything I want is out there. Somewhere. I just need to find it.

"Mmm-hmm," is all she says. Waiting for the rest.

But she probably already knows it. Sometimes I think she knows me better than I know myself. And maybe hearing her say it first would make this all easier.

So I tell her, "Guess."

She doesn't hesitate. "You intend to grab life by the balls."

Yes. Relief rushes through me in a tension-dissolving wave. I don't know how she does it. I haven't even put my intentions in words yet. But that's exactly what I want to do.

And I'm sure she knows why. "I just…when I first felt that lump—"

"I know, honey."

Throat thick, I nod. Of course she does. And I don't want to pursue that now. I don't want to start bawling.

I want to look ahead to this new road. "I'll get a job this summer. Something that's easy to leave. I'll work as a waitress or a cashier or flipping burgers. I don't care. I'll stay here at home so I can save up, and when I have enough, I'll go somewhere."

"Travelling?"

"Yes."

"Hmm." Her expression is thoughtful as she opens a cabinet and reaches for a stack of plates. Time to set the table. I head for the silverware drawer. "I wonder what your father and I will do with all of the money we've put aside to help you through med school. You could probably take several long trips with it."

I suck in a breath. I hadn't been angling for that. Not even a bit. "Mom—"

"It's still an education," she interrupts my protest. "And will probably end up being a much cheaper one."

A response won't come. My throat is tied in a fat, burning knot.

She pats my shoulder and says mildly, "And your father and I have become used to an empty house. It will be well worth the money to get rid of you again."

My laugh bursts through the knot in my throat. I tackle her with a hug and blubber into her shoulder—and that's really not the way I want Zach to see me, but of course that's what happens.

I hear heavy boots coming in from the garage and my brother says, "See? This is what I warned Zed about. One minute you're minding your own business, and the next minute my mom's got you in a therapy session. She'll have you crying before you leave, Zed. Just wait."

"Oh, Aaron, that's so cute," Mom says as she passes him, carrying plates to the dining room. "But making my children cry isn't therapy. It's my pleasure."

"I'm glad you had your fun with Anna instead of me, then."

Despite the teasing, I feel Aaron's gaze on my face, making sure I'm all right. And I am.

I wipe my cheeks and start grabbing silverware. "They were tears of happiness. Mom just told me I've always been her favorite kid."

"Oh, yeah?" Casually, he opens the fridge and pulls out a beer, then tosses a second bottle to Zach. Popping the cap, Aaron leans back against the counter. "Does Mom know her favorite kid flashed her tits at Zed?"

"Anna!" Mom's shocked response comes from the dining room.

Aaron grins and tips his beer at me. "Not the favorite now, are you?"

"I was thanking him for changing my tire!" I call to my mom and glance at Zach, praying he's not embarrassed by this.

If he is, I can't tell. Instead he's taking a swig of his beer, his gaze straight and steady down the length of the bottle…and if I follow the direction of that gaze, it's aimed at my lips. As if he's recalling how I really thanked him—with a kiss that melted my skin.

My skin feels like it's melting now. Just from a look.

Damn it. I should have given him a blow job to remember, instead.

Mom returns to the kitchen, apparently determined to forget about me flashing anyone, because she doesn't mention it. Instead she changes the subject to, "What did Saxon have to say?"

"He was checking up on Anna," Aaron says, surprising me. "A few of the Riders saw Zed follow her through town so he was making sure she was all right."

"That was kind of him," Mom says, but her gentle frown says she isn't really sure what to think of that.

I know what to think of it. Saxon hoped Jenny might be here, visiting me.

Aaron meets my eyes and the waggle of his blond eyebrows says he's thinking the same thing. "And we'll be riding out with him on Saturday, Mom, so if you have anything planned for us that day, better put it off for

Sunday."

"There's nothing planned," she says.

I'm nosier. "Where are you going?"

Zach answers me. "He told us that one of those fundamentalist groups plans to picket a soldier's funeral up in Eugene," he says, and you can tell he's definitely not from around here because it's actually *over* in Eugene. "The Hellfire Riders and a few other clubs will be forming a line to push the group back, so we're joining them."

"The Riders do things like that?" I know the Steel Titans do because I've heard Jenny's dad talking about it. But I was under the impression that the Riders were mostly interested in drinking and fucking and revving their engines in the middle of town at two in the morning.

Of course, maybe that's because almost everything I know about the Hellfire Riders is filtered through the Titans.

"It surprised me, too," Zach says and his smile has a bitter, self-mocking edge to it.

What prompted that look? "You've heard of them before?"

That would be even more surprising. As far as I know, the Riders are just a local MC. They aren't a big club with different chapters in different states.

He shakes his head. "Not the Riders. It's just not in my experience."

"What's your experience?" I slide the question in casually, as if I'm not dying to know.

With another shake of his head, he just as casually slides away from the question. "Are you coming with us?"

If that means spending a day with him? God, yes. I'd love to go.

But I can't.

Not that I get a chance to answer. Aaron chokes a little and says, "Not a chance in hell, Zed."

"Why? You worried about her safety? I've got enough room behind me if you can't ride well enough to pack double."

Zach says it so smoothly that it takes a second for me to realize that he just poked fun at my brother. Almost like I would. And it hits me all at once that these guys have known each other at least two years, the length of a Force Recon loop. Maybe longer.

Along with that understanding comes a strange little pain. Not *quite* like the feeling I've lost something. It's more like the realization that the percentage of overlap in the Venn diagram of mine and Aaron's lives will keep decreasing from this point onward, because our personal circles will grow…and they won't always include each other.

Of course I've known Aaron has been away and living a different life. Just like I've been away at college. Those friendships were always *there*, though, not here. And when we came home, it was just us again.

Not anymore. Aaron's got himself a brother. Maybe not related by blood, but still a brother.

Blood never mattered much in this family, anyway.

"Think about *after*, man." Aaron shoots a glance at my mom's back to make sure she isn't looking before jerking his hips back and forth and putting on an exaggerated leer. "You think that'll happen for either of us with my sister around?"

That strange little pain suddenly swells into something bigger. God. That's never hurt before. Aaron has said basically the same thing a hundred times since high school: Having a sister around is an automatic cock block. That gets no argument from me. I'd say the same about having a brother around.

But apparently the plan for Saturday is to hook up with whatever chicks they find. That shouldn't matter. Zach is essentially a stranger to me. A stranger who didn't want to know my name.

I wonder if he'll ask the girl he screws on Saturday what *her* name is.

God, and he's looking at me, his gaze searching my face. Wondering if that bothers me?

To give him an answer, I put on a smile. Of course I do. I'll flash my boobs without thinking much of it. I'll offer my number and an invite to my bed without feeling any shame.

But show my *hurt* to someone who isn't family? To someone who isn't Jenny? Fuck that all the way to hell.

"Calm your tits, Aaron." I deserve a freaking Oscar for how completely unaffected my voice sounds. "Jenny and I already have plans for Saturday, since it's the first time we can go out drinking together—"

Aaron coughs out a "Bullshit!" behind his fist. At the stove, Mom shakes her head. Either because she didn't know what Jenny and I used to get up to—or because she *did* know, and she's amazed that Aaron seems to think this is news to her.

Probably the second.

I narrow my eyes at him and finish, "It's the first time we can do it *legally*. So I'm hardly going to throw her over to hang out at a smelly biker bar with you."

"Maybe it won't smell too bad," Zach says, bringing my attention right back to him.

I stare at him in confusion. *It won't smell too bad.* Is he trying to say I should come with them on Saturday? Does he *want* me to come? Or is he just being polite because my brother sounds like a dick and Zach doesn't realize that my brother sounds like a dick all the time and that never bothers me, because I know Aaron doesn't mean anything by it. There's real security in knowing how much someone cares for you.

There's no security with Zach. I don't know what he means by that comment.

But I think I know. I remember how he lifted me up, making me feel smart and pretty even as he told me he didn't want to spend the night with me.

Zachary Cooper is *nice*.

That's a serious problem. Because if he were a jerk, it

would be so easy to ignore him, no matter how beautiful he is. But he's nice and I can't stop myself from liking him. And I'm afraid I won't stop at *liking*.

THREE

ON SATURDAY NIGHT, I HAVE NO INTENTION OF GOING home early—or sober—but that's what happens. Jenny's just as disappointed as I am. Unlike me, though, she's blaming herself for it.

"Sorry," she says again. We're in her truck and about five minutes from my house. This is her fourth 'Sorry' since we've left, but I'm glad to hear that, this time, there's more frustration in her voice than apology. None of this is her fault. "I really thought the Corral would be okay."

"It *was* okay. We got a few hours in." And only a few drinks, but we danced so much my makeup sweated off.

"Who could have guessed those assholes would show up?"

Because members of the Eighty-Eight don't usually show their faces at that bar—or anywhere else in Pine Valley. At least not while wearing their club's colors. The town is Hellfire Riders' and Steel Titans' territory.

More Hellfire Riders' than Steel Titans', in truth. If the town is a big circle, the Hellfire Riders call most of that circle theirs. Only a small slice of the east side is looked over by the Titans, along with everything from that slice to the county line.

The Corral sits in that slice of town, which is why Jenny felt safe enough to go there. The place isn't one of the Steel Titans' usual hangouts but it's in her dad's territory.

Her green eyes narrow a little as the headlights of a passing car catch her full in the face. "I can't believe they had the balls."

"*I* can't believe this town doesn't have more bars. I mean, it's got more than enough churches. What's the point of being forgiven if there's nowhere to sin?"

A smile touches her mouth before disappearing into a sigh. I don't need to guess what's putting the worry on her face. She's deciding whether to tell her dad about the two members of the Eighty-Eight who stepped through the Corral doors wearing their kuttes. She's worried because it means those supremacist assholes are poking at the Titans, and if they poke hard enough they might start a war between the clubs. She's worried because it can't be coincidence those guys showed up when the Hellfire Riders were out of town.

Which means the Eighty-Eight is scared of the Riders, but they're not so threatened by her dad's club.

But I bite my lip and don't say any of that. It's one thing to know the Titans aren't as strong as they once were. It's another thing to speak it aloud.

Even if Jenny must know it, too.

My stomach clenches into a knot as she turns onto my street. This is partially why I didn't want to come home early. From two blocks away, I can see a motorcycle in the driveway. But just one.

So it looks like our guest found somewhere else to stay for the night.

No big deal. In another few days, Zach will be gone every night. This is the same.

And if I tell myself that enough, it might actually feel true.

Pulling up to the curb, Jenny purses her lips and slides me a look. "Is this why you said we should call it a night instead of heading up to Bend?"

"Is what why?"

Eyebrows arched, she gestures toward the motorcycle. "Because *he's* here."

"Aaron?" Sure, I'm glad he's here on leave. But I wouldn't blow off Jenny just because he's home tonight. He'll be around for a month.

She rolls her eyes. "That's not Aaron's bike."

I look again. It's black and has silver handlebars. Zach's looks the same to me, so I suppose it could be his, but why would he be here without my brother? "How can you tell?"

"To start? Your brother's bike has a soft tail frame with apehangers. This one doesn't."

"Huh," I say as if that's only mildly interesting, as if my heart isn't suddenly pounding. Because I'm sure my parents are home, but the first floor windows are dark, which means they've gone to bed.

The light in the guest room is on, though.

Jenny's still giving me that look.

"I didn't know. I swear!" I raise my hands to ward off her narrowed stare. "But since I'm here, wish me luck. And pray my mom and dad don't hear anything."

"Oh, my God." She covers her face with her hands. "*You* are why this town has so many churches."

"I try." I grin and hop out of the truck.

"Tell me how it goes," she says. "And if he's really that pretty all over."

I'd bet anything he is. "I'll take pictures."

"Only of him, I hope."

"Nope." I palm my tits, give them a little heft beneath my shirt. "You're gonna get shots of these babies."

"You've already sent me pics of those."

Shit. I have. "Yeah, well—" I've got nothing. Not a single comeback. I flip her the bird, instead.

She shoots a middle finger right back. God, I love her.

The sister I never had.

Just before I close the truck door, her "Hey!" stops me. Her face is suddenly serious.

"Let me know how it goes on Monday," she says.

My appointment with the breast surgeon. I nod and swing the door shut before hightailing it up to the porch. She waits at the curb until I'm inside.

I don't bother with any lights. Partially because I don't need them, partially because I don't want to wake my parents. Not for the reason I led Jenny to believe— although if things with Zach started heading that way, I wouldn't put on the brakes. But mostly I just want a little time alone with him.

Out on the road, when he was changing my tire, we got on so quick and so well. It was so easy to talk to him and we never really got that back. He's nice here at the house—unfailingly polite—but I haven't had a second with him when my brother wasn't around. Which makes sense. Zach's visiting with Aaron, not me. Still, I'd like to have him to myself again. Even for just a few minutes. To see if it's still just as easy between us.

But maybe it'll just be awkward again.

I don't make much noise going up the carpeted stairs. The hallway is dark, except for a single yellow strip of light beneath the guest room door. My heart pounds double-time.

Maybe I should let him be. Sure, he's here instead of out screwing some nameless girl he met at a bar, but that doesn't mean he wants me to monopolize his time. Maybe he came home early because he thought I *wouldn't* be here. After all, that was the plan before the Eighty-Eight messed it up.

I knock before I can talk myself out of it. A couple of greetings ready themselves at the tip of my tongue.

Each greeting takes a suicide dive into a pool of stunned silence when he opens the door.

Because he opens the door wearing only a pair of gray sweatpants—hanging low on his hips—and a paperback in his hand. I recognize the book. A futuristic mystery, it had been crammed into one of the overstuffed shelves in the family room. He must have grabbed it before coming upstairs.

So he was reading. Probably in bed. Inside the room, the only light comes from the lamp on the nightstand and it's so easy to imagine him reclined back against the pillows, the yellow glow washing over his rippling stomach, his hard pectorals bare of everything except a dusting of coarse hair, his chin darkened by a day's growth of beard.

And a book in his hand.

I didn't think he could be more attractive. I really didn't. But, holy shit. He was *reading*. All he needs is a pair of glasses and he'd be Superman.

"Anna," he says and I force my gaze up, because my attention had gotten stuck on the index finger he inserted between the pages to mark his spot.

Lucky book.

"Hi," I finally say, but it sounds more like a croak than a word, so I add a stupid little wave. "I saw your light."

He nods and his gaze slides from my head to my pink-painted toenails. God, why didn't I stop by the bathroom to freshen up? All the dancing left my hair a crazy mess and my mascara smudged into shadows around my eyes.

But it's too late now. There's no way to go but forward. "You're home early," I say. "You didn't get lucky?"

That crystalline gaze snaps back to mine. "I could have," he drawls. "But I left because being there was ruining your brother's chances."

My eyebrows shoot up. He might be right. I know a lot of girls in town think my brother is hot but I'm not sure how many would look at him with Zach in the same bar.

But still.

A grimace pulls his mouth tight. "I sounded less like a dick when I said that to him."

I have to laugh. At least he admits it. "You probably did."

Expression abashed, he shakes his head. "Then let me start over. I didn't feel like being there, so I bailed and tossed a few friendly insults at Stone on my way out."

Stone. Aaron's nickname from high school football, when they called him Stone Wall. I guess the name must have stuck, even in the Marines.

"Don't sweat it." I wave his worry off. "I suppose the past couple of days you've heard plenty of things that would sound dickish if they were directed at anyone outside my family."

The corners of his eyes crinkle with his smile. "I'm becoming used to it."

Getting more comfortable around us. His being here still surprises me, though. "So you came back alone?"

His expression hardens, freezing that smile. When he moves out of the doorway—as if to show me the empty bed behind him—I realize how that sounded.

In a rush, I amend, "No, I mean, obviously you don't have company. But you came back without Aaron? Were my parents still up?"

Some of his tension eases. "Yes."

"*Awk*-ward."

"Yes." Now the humor returns. "On the porch, it took me almost a full minute to decide whether to knock or just walk in."

Because no one around here keeps their front door locked, unless they've gone to bed. "What did you do?"

"Walked in. And they were right there in the living room."

I laugh, picturing it. No way did my parents let him go without comment. "What did they say?"

"Your mom told your dad, 'So *this* is what it's like to have a responsible child. One who comes home at a reasonable hour.'" His grin flashes when I snort. "Then your dad offered to adopt me."

"They probably really would."

"I'd probably let them." Shoulder braced against the doorframe, he looks down at me. "They're pretty great."

I know. "I got lucky."

"You did," he agrees.

"So your parents wouldn't have reacted the same way if I showed up at their door?"

I almost regret being so nosy when his smile dims. He doesn't even answer, just steps back from the door and farther into the room.

Smoothly, he says, "Your mom says you're the one who painted this wall."

I'm sorry he changed the subject, but I'm not passing up this excuse to get into his room.

"I did," I tell him, walking in and turning to study the mural—an antique-style world map, with major land-marks drawn in an exaggerated hand. It's not bad, consid-ering that I painted it in a week. But it's not good, either. "Our cousin Aspen stayed with us last summer. My mom thought this was appropriately educational for a preteen, but still fun."

He moves closer to it. Oh, Lord help me. Considering how gorgeous his front is, can't he at least have an unim-pressive back? But, no. Instead he possesses a swimmer's broad shoulders and tight waist. Muscles move smoothly under acres of tanned skin when he presses his finger to a spot on the map.

My spot. Where Pine Valley would be, I painted a simple message—

"'Anna was here,'" he reads, then looks back at me. "Your signature?"

"Kind of. I write it on a lot of things." And have since I was a kid. "It's a coping-with-fear-of-recurring-cancer mechanism my mom taught me. It reminds me that I'm here and I can't be erased so easily."

Although, the truth is, I don't do it solely as a coping mechanism anymore. Not consciously, anyway. Instead I've internalized it so well that "Anna was here" really *has* become my signature.

His crystalline gaze holds mine for a long beat. Then he nods and looks to the map again. "Have you decided where you're going first?"

Because the topic of my upcoming travels has been raised several times in the past few days—with everyone in my family chiming in with their opinion of where I should go first. Zach hasn't offered his opinion, though.

"Where would you go?"

Immediately he points to the far eastern side of China. "Somewhere here."

That's…not specific. "Why there?"

"Because it's as far as someone could get from home without coming back around again."

Someone? Or him? Maybe Zach doesn't care where he is, as long as he's not home. But I'm not going to ask about his family again, not if it pushes him away like it did before. Instead I wait.

He's silent for a long second, then he shrugs those

ridiculously broad shoulders. "Maybe the Great Wall," he finally says. "Hiking along it would really be something."

Yes, it would. "That's on my list of things to do."

So is Zach. He's right at the top of my every to-do list. And I shouldn't say what I'm about to say. I really shouldn't. But I just don't know when to quit.

And I really, *really* want to write 'Anna was here' right across that magnificent chest.

"So, I was thinking…it's Saturday night and still kind of early," I tell him and my heart is pounding so hard, I can feel the pulse beating in my neck. "What do you think about heading out for a drink or a bite to eat?"

His body stiffens, every muscle snapping into sharp relief. His gaze shoots to mine, and I can't read his expression, I don't know him well enough yet, but I could swear that's *longing* I see in his pale blue stare.

Please, God, please—let it be longing.

And his silence is killing me. But I'm already throwing myself at his feet, so I've got nothing to lose when I add, "Or maybe we could do something else now and have breakfast together, instead."

His eyes close. His hands are clenched so tight, his long fingers between the pages are warping the book's spine.

"Anna." My name seems scraped from his chest, like he has to forcibly drag out the word and every one that follows. "I don't think that's a good idea."

Oh. Okay. Well.

I need to get the hell out of here, then. "All right," I say and head for the door, all at once feeling cold and tired and so damn disappointed. "I'm sure you'll have a better time with the book, anyway. It's a good one. The congressman killed the first victim but his aide tried to throw the detective off his boss's scent by using the same MO to kill other women."

A sharp breath sounds behind me. I don't hear him coming, don't realize he's after me until I'm at my bedroom door and his palm hits the wall beside me just as I'm reaching for the knob. His hand closes over it before mine does, preventing my escape.

Heart thundering, I spin around, my back against the door. Oh, God. He's so tall and gorgeous and his eyes glitter like diamonds in the dim hallway. And he's so big, his body so taut as he looms over me, I should be scared.

But I'm so turned on. Turned on and holding my breath as his head lowers. Not to kiss me.

Instead he gets into my face, his nose almost touching mine, his eyes narrowed. "That was mean, Anna Wall."

It was. But spoiling the end of the book must not have truly upset him, because he's grinning.

He continues, "Your brother was right about you. He said you were a terror. I thought you were sweet."

Not even close. "People always think that. It's my face."

His gaze drops to my lips. "It was something else that made me think so. But you *do* have a sweet pixie look going on—with those big, golden-brown eyes and that cute pointed chin."

"They're a lie," I tell him.

"I guess so." His thumb slips along my jaw, then he freezes when I shudder beneath his touch. Abruptly he steps back, leaving me feeling cold all over again. "There's no doubt I'd love having breakfast with you, Anna. And I wish…"

He wishes…? I really want to know the rest of that. "What?"

His jaw tightens and he gives his head a hard shake. "Nothing. The thing is, you're Stone's sister, and I'm his friend—and your parents' guest. So it's best to keep things simple between us."

Screwing each other's brains out seems pretty simple, too. Life at its most basic. But I'm guessing that's not what Zach's suggesting.

"You mean, 'let's just be friends' simple?"

He nods solemnly but some conflicting emotion flickers in his eyes again. If that emotion resembles *longing*, however, he beats the feeling back, and determination rings like steel through his voice when he says again, "You're his sister. I'm his friend. Simple."

It doesn't feel simple. But maybe he's right. And it *is* probably for the best. He's only here a few days more. If I like him this much now, and sleep with him, God knows how I'll feel about him by the end.

And after he leaves, it's not like I'm going to see him again.

That thought hurts more than it should. But I refuse to let Zach see the pain. Instead I shrug and smile.

"All right," I agree lightly. "We'll keep it simple."

"Good," he says, then seems to take an extraordinarily long time before he tears his gaze from mine and heads back to his room.

My shoulders slump as soon as his door closes. Simple. Sure. I can do that until he leaves. And then— even though I *never* seem to know when to quit—I'll quit thinking about him. I'll just forget him.

That will be simple. I've only known Zachary Cooper a couple of days.

So forgetting him shouldn't take too long.

***

*Almost ten years later, their real story begins…and it definitely doesn't stay simple. You can pick up **GUNNER** (the discreet cover) or "Breaking It All" with the original cover in print or as an ebook. Visit **katiwilde.com** for links and info!*

*Anna also mentions a cousin, Aspen — who is the heroine of **GOING NOWHERE FAST**, a stand- alone enemies-to-lovers romance. Available in ebook!*

GOING NOWHERE FAST

The brakes are off in this sizzling-hot new adult romance from the author of the Hellfire Riders MC Romance series…

One promise.
Two hearts.
Three rules.
Four weeks to break them all.

When Aspen Phillips' best friend invites her on a month-long road trip, she has serious mixed feelings. Sharing their tight quarters will be Bramwell Gage, overprotective brother and all-around jerk. Bram may be ridiculously sexy, but he's made no effort to hide how he feels about Aspen—that she's trash who's no good for his sister. But Aspen is determined to get along with the uptight millionaire—and to keep her promise, concealing a secret about his sister that Bram can never know.

But after a scorching kiss reveals that Bram's feelings toward her run much hotter than she believed, Aspen's emotions swerve into a complete 180. Suddenly the girl who has nothing has everything—but only as long as the truth about his sister remains hidden. Because when all the secrets and promises unravel, she risks losing it all…

AVAILABLE ONLY IN EBOOK!

ABOUT KATI

Kati Wilde is a tight-lipped, loose-hipped woman of indeterminate age and low breeding. She writes romantic fiction to assuage her darker urge to write Transformers erotica. You can reach Kati at kati@katiwilde.com or any of the Club authors (Ella Goode, Ruby Dixon, and Kati Wilde) at 1theclub1@gmail.com.

www.katiwilde.com

Facebook: www.facebook.com/authorkatiwilde
Instagram: www.instagram.com/authorkatiwilde
Twitter: www.twitter.com/katiwilde

www.katiwilde.com/newsletter

CONTENT WARNINGS

All of the Hellfire Riders stories include swearing, violence, explicit sexual content including references to group sex, sex in public and voyeurism (some main characters only watch while others participate), references to alcohol and drug use, sex trafficking, illegal cage fighting, and murder (mostly only bad guys, but there are exceptions.) There are no cliffhangers and no cheating.

For this particular book:

- as a child, the hero was molested by his father

- threats of sexual assault toward the heroine

- murders and assassinations

- public cunnilingus

- the bad guys kidnap the heroine with the intention of selling her to an illegal cage fight; she's forcibly drugged so that she'll stay quiet

www.ingramcontent.com/pod-product-compliance
Lightning Source LLC
Chambersburg PA
CBHW032112110726
47902CB00003B/553